PIRATE'S CARESS

"Let me up," Tori cried. She tried to sit up, but realized that not only was his arm around her, but her hair was caught firmly beneath his shoulder.

Serad chuckled in her ear. "It would seem that you are bound to me in more ways than one." He captured her lips in a deep, thrilling kiss.

"Don't!" Tori exclaimed.

"Don't what, Tori?" He braced himself on his elbows to rise above her. "I want you, Tori. I've waited as long as I can."

"Serad . . ." His kisses grew more passionate as he gathered her in his arms, cradled her to his chest, and strode into his bedchamber.

She meant to deny him, but she could not do it. In a last effort to stop him, she put one hand on his chest to hold him away from her. But when she lifted her eyes to his and gazed into the smoldering depths of his gray-eyed gaze, an answering response to his need was born within her. She was on fire. She wanted him.

"Serad, I . . ."

"Tori." Her name was a groan as he pulled her close to him . . .

Books by Bobbi Smith

DREAM WARRIOR

PIRATE'S PROMISE

TEXAS SPLENDOR

CAPTURE MY HEART

DESERT HEART*

Published by Zebra Books

*coming soon

CAPTURE
MY HEART

BOBBI SMITH

ZEBRA BOOKS
Kensington Publishing Corp.
www.kensingtonbooks.com

This book is dedicated to the memory of Doretha Smith (my mom), Roberta Grossman (Zebra Books), Nancy Ludington Donaldson (Louisville News), and Bob Denholm (Reader's Haven, Elgin, Ill.) who all died from cancer during the last eighteen months.

Dear Readers,
Please, if you haven't had a check-up lately, get one, and ladies, don't forget to do regular breast exams and get a baseline mammogram by age 40. There are people out there who love you and who will miss you terribly if anything happens to you. Take care of yourselves—for yourself and for them.
Love,
Bobbi

This book is also for Jacki Schneider, Gerri Hirst, Jeannine Hassel, and Mary Jane Palmer for their friendship through the years.

For my friends Brad Watkins, of Simon and Schuster, and Walter Knop, Rich Meeker, and John Nelson, of National Book.

And for the real Gerald Ratcliff, a true gentleman who bears no resemblance whatsoever to the character of the same name in this book. Thanks for everything, Gerald!

Chapter One

Spring, 1789

"Avery, you must do it! You must go back to your father and get more money!" twenty-five-year-old Vivienne Wakefield demanded of her husband, Lord Avery Wakefield. A tall, beautiful woman with black hair and icy blue eyes that reflected a shrewd intelligence, she stood now in the center of their sumptuously decorated parlor, her hands on her hips, glaring at the weakling she'd married some six years before.

Avery Wakefield stiffened at his wife's tone. He was a smoothly handsome, dark-haired, dark-eyed, twenty-eight-year-old man whose pale complexion testified to days spent sleeping and nights spent in endless debauchery, gambling compulsively and indulging his every other craving. Annoyed by her challenge, he drew himself up to his full six feet and turned from where he stood looking out the window to face her. He meant to put her in her place. He was, after all, the one with the money in this marriage. She certainly hadn't brought any great dowry with her. Once he faced her, though, and saw the very real fury in

7

her expression, he backed down . . . just as he always did.

"Well, Avery? When are you going to speak with him?" she demanded, pressing her point now that she knew she had the upper hand.

"You know, my darling, if you had ever learned to temper your spending, we might not have found ourselves back in such a difficult situation again so soon."

"My spending!"

"I told you what Father said the last time I went to him out of pocket. He threatened to cut me off without a farthing."

"Your father would never do that."

"Maybe not, but I hesitate to try my luck with him again quite so soon."

"I'm afraid you have no choice in the matter, Avery. We need money, and we need it now."

"I know that, but . . ."

"I understand why you don't want to push him, but we have leverage with him now that we've never had before," she told him cunningly. She had thought long and hard about how to get more money out of her clutch-fisted father-in-law, Edward Wakefield, the Duke of Huntington, and she was confident that she now had come up with the answer.

Avery cast his wife a doubtful glance, not following her line of thinking at all. "And just what kind of leverage do you think we have now?"

"Why, Alexander, of course," Vivienne told him smugly. When they'd eloped she'd believed as the future duchess she'd be living a life devoted completely to pleasure. It had been a very rude awakening for her to discover that since her father-in-law had completely disapproved of their marriage he had tightened his pursestrings accordingly. Only the birth of their son,

Alexander, seven years ago had eased the tension. Pleased with being presented with a grandson, the duke had relaxed his miserly ways to some degree, but the increase in funds still had not been enough to provide them with the lifestyle she craved. The duke had since taken Alexander to live with him, and the two had become almost inseparable. Vivienne was certain that the boy was the old man's one vulnerable spot.

"Alexander?" Avery wondered what their bothersome young son had to do with anything. He hadn't even spoken to the child in weeks, and, frankly, didn't care if he never saw him again. From the day he was born, he'd been nothing but trouble for them, and they'd both been secretly delighted when the duke had taken the boy to Huntington House to raise himself.

She nodded. "There's no one in the world he loves more and that makes him our bargaining point. If your father refuses to give you what is rightfully yours, threaten to take the boy back."

Avery's expression turned calculating, then smugly approving. "I always knew our precious son would prove useful for something." If Alexander could help put his family fortune at their disposal, then Avery might become fond of the child!

"It's just a simple matter of handling the situation right, that's all," Vivienne was saying, explaining what she wanted him to do. "We'll try a simple approach first, but if he doesn't agree, I want you to do exactly what I tell you. He'll come around fast enough then."

The tall, imposing, gray-haired man and the sturdily built, dark-haired boy stood atop the steep cliff that overlooked the sea. Their attention was focused on the huge sailing ship that was slowly disappearing into the sunset.

"Someday, Grandfather, I'm going to be the captain of a big ship just like that one!" seven-year-old Alexander Wakefield boasted with all the innocent confidence and bravado of one his age. His gray eyes were shining and his cheeks were flushed with the excitement of his dreams of adventure on the high seas.

"If it's what you really want to do, Alexander, then I'm sure you'll do it," Lord Edward Wakefield, Duke of Huntington, answered. His heart swelled with pride as he stared down at the child who meant so very much to him. A warmth he revealed to few others stole across his dignified countenance, and he no longer appeared the stern, forbidding duke. Rather, the tender smile and gentle love glowing in his eyes bespoke of the doting grandfather he really was.

The boy beamed at his words. "I'll do it, all right. You'll see. I'll be the best ship's captain there ever was!"

"I'm certain you will be," Edward assured him, seeing the intelligence and eagerness in the boy's features and knowing he'd been right in his assessment of him. His own son, Avery, Alexander's father, had proven such a bitter disappointment to him and to his beloved, now-deceased wife, Rebecca, that he'd almost lost hope for the future. Avery had been born with a selfish, cruel streak. From the earliest days of his childhood he'd taken great pleasure in tormenting those less fortunate than himself; and as he'd progressed to adulthood, he'd turned to hedonistic pleasures and degrading behavior that had sullied the Wakefield name and honor. Only Alexander's birth had given Edward encouragement; and that was why, when Avery and Vivienne had shown no inkling of interest in the babe, he had personally stepped in and taken Alexander into his home to raise and educate. It had been a decision he'd never regretted. The boy was a joy to his weary soul.

"Where do you think they're going, Grandfather?" Alexander asked, looking back out to sea to follow the faint image of the ship as it slipped beyond the horizon. "Someplace exciting?"

"I'm sure of it," Edward replied. Then, wanting to spin a tale of great adventure for the boy, he continued. "They're probably going to sail every one of the Seven Seas, and—"

"Do you think they'll run into any pirates?" Alexander interrupted, his eyes widening as he let his vivid imagination run free. He'd heard tales of the evil corsairs and had even seen an artist's drawing of the lawless demons who pillaged any vessel unfortunate enough to cross their path. The thought that the ship he'd just watched leave England might actually fall prey to the bloodthirsty, ocean-going bandits filled him with a mixture of excitement and fear.

"You can never know," Edward said in an ominous, low tone. "No one is ever really safe from them when they're sailing the Atlantic. The Barbary pirates are everywhere."

"Those are the ones from Africa, aren't they? The ones we saw the picture of in that book?"

"You're right, and they're a savage bunch." Edward recalled the fearsome picture. The barbarous North African corsairs depicted there had worn only loose-fitting trousers cut off at the knees and brightly colored turbans. Pistols were tucked in their waistbands. They carried their knives in their teeth and clenched wickedly curved scimitars in their fists as they swung aboard the ship they were attacking.

"Well, they'll never get me," Alexander returned with a wide, undaunted smile. "When I'm captain, I'll have the best ship with the best crew on the whole ocean. We'll fight them off and take their ship instead!"

Edward could almost imagine his grandson fighting

off a pirate attack. He smiled back at him. "And just what are you going to call this magnificent, unconquerable ship you're going to captain?"

The boy looked pensive for a moment, then remembering the pirate's glittering sword and how it had struck fear in his heart, he answered, "The *Scimitar!*"

"Why the *Scimitar?*"

"Because it'll scare everybody."

"You're right about that. You've chosen well," Edward pronounced.

"Will you help me paint the name on my ship?"

The duke was surprised by his request, and he began to explain that there were men at the shipyards who do such work.

"Not on the big ship I'm going to have, Grandfather!" Alexander laughed with childish delight. "I'm talking about painting it on the toy ship you gave me. Do you think we could paint the name on it?" He considered the replica the best present he'd ever received, his most prized possession, and he all but slept with it every night.

Edward laughed, too. "Decide what color you'd like, and we'll do it just as soon as I get back."

"Do you have to go?" Alexander implored as they turned away from the sea and started back toward the house in the growing darkness. He adored his grandfather and missed him dreadfully when he traveled.

"I'm afraid so. My other estates demand my attention, too. When you're older, I'll take you with me so you can see how vast our holdings are. Someday, Alexander, they will all be yours."

"I wish I could go with you now," Alexander pouted as he slipped his hand into Edward's, and the old man marveled at just how small he really was.

"Next year, when you turn eight, I'll take you along."

"Promise?"

"You have my word on it."

Their eyes met, and Alexander nodded solemnly, knowing his grandfather's word was law. If he said it would happen, it would.

They were following the path on through the gardens heading for the mansion's side entrance when they saw Catherine, Edward's nineteen-year-old daughter and Alexander's aunt, come hurrying outside toward them.

"Hello, Aunt Catherine!" Alexander called out. "Are you coming out to walk with us?"

"No, sweetheart, I have to talk to your grandfather for a minute," she said quickly, tousling his hair fondly.

It was obvious to Edward that she was upset about something, so he bid Alexander to go to his room and wash up for dinner.

"And use the side door," Catherine quickly directed, drawing a curious look from her father. She was greatly relieved when the boy did so without question.

"What is it?" Edward asked the minute Alexander was out of earshot. His gaze was serious as it rested on his lovely, fair-haired daughter. She looked so much like her mother, his Rebecca, with her pale-blond hair and aquamarine eyes that it sometimes pained him and filled him with a terrible longing for the past.

"It's Avery," she finally blurted out. "He's here."

"Avery?" Edward's expression first reflected surprise, then became guarded. "What does he want this time? Did he say?" he asked harshly. He knew his decadent son only showed up when he needed something, and he had a pretty good idea just what it was he was after. Unbeknownst to Avery, Edward had certain of his contacts in London keeping an eye on him. He knew of most of his son's depraved activities,

13

and they filled him with fury. Avery had no honor, and that was a shortcoming the duke could not overlook.

"I don't know. He didn't say much to me. We only exchanged the usual mindless pleasantries."

"Did he ask to see the boy?"

"No. He just wants to talk to you."

"Did he bring Vivienne with him?" Edward inquired, already sure of her reply, but needing to ask anyway.

"No. He came alone."

At that news, the duke's expression grew black. "I suppose I should thank heaven for that much, but wouldn't you think a mother would want to see her only child once in a while? It's been months since she's come for a visit . . ."

Catherine touched her father's arm in sympathy. "I know. It makes no sense to me, either. Alexander's such a wonderful boy. He's so full of life. So bright and so much fun. I couldn't love him more if he was my own. I don't understand how two such people could have given birth to him."

"Neither do I. Sometimes I wish he was yours." Edward patted her hand affectionately. "Then he would never have had to suffer their neglect."

"I may not be his mother, but between the two of us, he knows he's loved. Alexander's a good boy. He'll be fine, Father. You'll see."

"I hope you're right. Why don't you go upstairs and stay with him while I meet with Avery? Keep him up there if you can. There's no sense in upsetting him by letting him find out his father's here and doesn't care about seeing him."

"All right. You'll call us when you're through?"

He nodded. "And then we'll dine."

Catherine stood on tiptoes to press a soft kiss on his weathered cheek and then hurried away to see her nephew. Edward watched her until she had gone inside and then girded himself for the upcoming confrontation. It was never pleasant to visit with Avery, and he doubted seriously that today's encounter would be any different.

After his sister left him, Avery poured himself a healthy tumbler of whiskey and settled into the massive leather wing chair behind his father's desk in the study. Sitting back, he casually braced his booted feet on the desktop. Fancying himself already the duke, Avery silently toasted himself as he surveyed his domain, studying the expensive paintings that hung on the dark, highly polished paneled walls and the endless volumes of priceless leather-bound books in the floor-to-ceiling bookshelves that lined one wall of the study. Mentally calculating the value of just the contents of the room, he smiled, gloating over the bounty the future held for him. One day, it really would all be his.

Avery was so deeply immersed in thoughts of his own grandeur that he failed to hear his father enter the room. Only the sound of Edward's greeting brought him back to full awareness.

"Avery . . ." Edward was startled to find his son taking such liberties in his study. As always, Avery's good looks impressed him. There was no denying he had grown into a handsome man, and Edward knew he could be devilishly charming when it suited his purpose, but Edward also knew the truth about him, and he mourned the man he could have been. Try as he might, he had never found the answer as to why his son had turned out so badly, and, painful as it was, he knew he never would.

"Hello, Father," Avery replied with cool correctness, showing no embarrassment at being found sitting so brazenly at Edward's desk. He leisurely dropped his feet back to the floor, set his tumbler of whiskey on the desktop, then slowly stood up to acknowledge his presence.

"To what do I owe the honor of your presence? Dare I hope that you've missed us?" His words were a bit taunting.

"Of course I missed you, and Catherine and Alexander, too. Is the boy around, by the way? I'd half expected him to come in with you."

"He's upstairs getting ready for dinner. Would you care to join us and stay the night?"

"Unfortunately, I have important business in London that requires me to return this very evening," Avery lied as he circled the desk to stand before it, allowing his father to take the chair that was rightfully his.

"I see," the duke replied. "Shall I call Alexander down so you can have at least a short visit?"

"I'm afraid there's not even time for that. I came because I need to talk to you."

"Oh?" Edward watched his son from beneath hooded eyes.

"Yes," he went on eagerly, "I'm sure you know by now that I'm making every effort to change in the ways you suggested the last time we talked." He paused, hoping to hear an affirmative answer from his father.

The duke did not respond right away, but just pinned him with an emotionless gaze. His thoughts were centered on trying to understand how he and his beloved, gentle-spirited Rebecca could have produced such an accomplished liar. "Go on."

"Well, I have. In fact, I was meeting with some associates just a few days ago discussing various business ventures, and they offered me an excellent opportunity. All I need is enough money to make an initial investment, and they guarantee me that the return will be tremendous. I should be able to pay you back the principal in a matter of just a few years, and then Vivienne and I would be completely independent—" Avery explained smoothly, trying to convince his father to give him the funds he needed to "invest." It did not bother him that every word out of his mouth was a lie. All that was important was his goal—getting the money. Period.

"You'd be independent *now* if you managed your income correctly," Edward pointed out with maddening logic, interrupting him.

"But this is different. This is the chance I've been waiting for to prove to you that I really *have* changed my ways. I promise you that I'll . . ."

"Promises! Eternal promises! That's all you ever give me. In all these years, I have yet to see you deliver anything of substance!"

"But—" Avery started to protest.

"Enough!" Edward cut him off. "I've heard enough! The only way you're going to get any more money out of me is to prove to me that you can make something of yourself. You have the ability. You have the intelligence. Use it!"

"That's exactly what I'm trying to do right now," Avery answered tightly.

"I'm not giving you any more handouts. If you can show me over the next twelve months that you are capable of handling your financial situation with maturity and common sense, we'll talk again. Until then, consider this conversation over."

Avery couldn't believe that his father was turning him down when the story he and Vivienne had concocted to get the money out of him sounded so good. A sense of panic gripped him. Their gambling debts were huge and long overdue. They had to pay up. So great was his fury in the face of his father's refusal that his control shattered. Instead of casually leading into Vivienne's plan concerning Alexander, he erupted without thinking. "Why, you pompous old fool!" he shouted. "You sit in your mansion counting your fortune while Vivienne and I are living a nearly destitute existence!"

Avery's ugly words only reinforced what Edward had known all along. He went completely still, his features hardening into a mask of stone. "You are hardly destitute," he ground out. "What you need is backbone! Try earning your way for once in your life, Avery. Take responsibility for yourself and your family. It might make a man out of you!"

"Perhaps you're right." Avery immediately cooled, realizing he was getting himself nowhere. Drawing upon Vivienne's plan to bring his father around, he went on. "Maybe it *is* time I provided for my family. Maybe it *is* time for me to make a stable home for Alexander so Vivienne and I can raise him ourselves—far away from here."

Edward knew a threat when he heard one, and he bristled. "Alexander stays with me."

"He's *our* son," Avery countered, pleased that he'd gotten just the reaction Vivienne had said he would. "He belongs with his parents."

"It's a shame you didn't think of that a few years ago when you were neglecting him so badly."

"Things have changed. As you said, to prove my maturity to you I should take full responsibility for my family. We want him back now."

"You try to take the boy away from me, and I'll send for my lawyer the same day! When I'm done with you, my only son will be dead. Do you understand me?!" he thundered, unable to bear the thought of Alexander living with Avery and Vivienne.

Avery had seen his father angry on many occasions,

but never before had he witnessed a cold, deadly rage like this. Nor had the full strength of his forceful personality ever been directed at him this way before. It cowed him, and he backed down. "I'm sure something can be worked out . . ."

"The only thing that can be worked out is for you to take your leave! Get out of my sight! If you ever come back here again with such outrageous demands, you'll find my threat to strike you from my will was not an idle one. Do you understand me?!"

"Yes, I understand." Avery turned and headed for the door. As he reached it and put his hand on the knob, his father spoke again.

"And Avery, do not try to see the child as you leave. Just go."

Avery said nothing, but quit the room and shut the door tightly behind him. He was relieved to find that the hall was empty, and he leaned back weakly against the closed portal to think. As he stood there, his expression altered from fear to devious determination. Vivienne had been right all along. Alexander was his father's weak spot, and since negotiation didn't work, it would take a more direct action to convince the duke of the error of his tight-fisted ways. Pushing away from the door, Avery straightened his jacket and started from the house. He had much to plan and very little time to do it.

Chapter Two

Edward stood beside the bed, gazing down at Alexander as he lay curled on his side, sound asleep, his toy boat clutched tightly in his hand. The regular cadence of the child's breathing sounded so peaceful that he smiled. The more troubled and ugly the world became, the more the innocence of children shone like a beacon of goodness in the pitch darkness of night.

Edward sighed heavily as he watched the boy sleep, and he marveled again at his beauty—the full, dark sweep of his lashes against soft, rosy cheeks and the cap of tousled ebony curls that framed his childish features. He tried to imagine what he was going to look like when he came of age. Physically, Alexander was definitely a Wakefield, from the color of his hair and eyes to his promise of height, but any other resemblance to his father ended there. As a child, Avery had never shown any of the intelligent inquisitiveness Alexander did, nor had he ever displayed any act of kindness. Avery had always been self-centered and vain, thinking of his own pleasures first and unable to take any kind of constructive criticism. In contrast, Alexander was outgoing and gentle, with a strong sense of goodness. The boy had a real zest for life and learning, and Edward wanted to make sure he stayed that way.

Edward was annoyed to find his corrupt son slipping into his thoughts. He didn't want to dwell on Avery. He and Rebecca had done their very best by him, only to be rewarded by his displaying one failure of character after another. Edward decided then and there that he would no longer be a party to supporting his moral bankruptcy. Avery had grown into a scoundrel of the first order, and he saw little hope that he would ever change. From now on, Edward was going to concentrate only on making Alexander's childhood a happy, carefree one, and he would go to any lengths to achieve that goal. He would raise his grandson to take his place as the duke. He would entrust the duchy to the boy, for he knew Alexander would cherish the title as much as he did.

Warmed by the thought, Edward turned away from the bed to adjust the lamp on the dresser. He did not turn it down completely, but left it burning at a low, golden glow so that it provided just enough light to calm the boy should he awaken during the night and be frightened. After a last glance at his grandson to make sure he was still sleeping peacefully, he quietly left the room and closed the door behind him.

Avery was angry as he made the ride to London, and he covered the distance quickly. He was glad to find that Vivienne was still at their townhouse awaiting his return, for he was eager to seek her counsel about what course to take next. She had predicted his father's furious reaction, and he needed reassurance that he'd done the right thing.

Vivienne met him at the door. She searched his face for some clue to the outcome of his visit with his father

21

and saw all she needed to know in the disgusted look there.

"You were right about Alexander being his weakness, but you didn't take into consideration that he would be angry if we wanted to take the boy back."

"He was angry?"

"Livid," Avery confirmed as he strode into the dining room and helped himself to a tumbler of whiskey from the crystal decanter at the bar.

"What did he say?"

"He said if we ever threatened to take the boy away from him again, he was going to strike me from his will completely; and this time, dear wife, there was no doubt that he meant it."

"Damn! We have to do something. It's ridiculous that we are reduced to living this way. You're the future duke! Why must we grovel before him for every pound? We have to do something!"

"I agree with you, but what?"

Vivienne's eyes narrowed to pinpoints of savagery as she told him of her insidious plan. "We'll get rid of the boy. Your father wouldn't dare disown you if Alexander were gone. He'd have no other heir but you."

"Get rid of him? How?"

She elaborated on her scheme. "We'll arrange a kidnapping. That way we can not only rid ourselves of the brat, but we can also collect a tidy reward."

"You want to kill him!?"

Vivienne shrugged. "Frankly, I'd rather see your father dead, but there's no way we can manage that. He's too well protected. There's always someone near him. The boy, on the other hand, doesn't mean a thing to me. I don't care what happens to him, really. He's caused me nothing but trouble from the day he was conceived." She thought of how she'd had to curtail her traveling and other pleasures during the months of her confinement just so she could give birth to a baby she hadn't wanted. The concept of motherhood had been as foreign to her as fatherhood had been to Avery. The only natural instinct she possessed was survival! "What do you think?"

Avery pondered her suggestion and knew it was a good one. As much as his father despised him, Avery knew he wouldn't allow the duchy to fall into the hands of anyone else. With Alexander out of the way, there would be no competition for the title. It would be his. He was certain his father would never make the connection between him and his son's "disappearance." It seemed perfect.

"It's dangerous . . . outrageous even, but it will work," Avery agreed. "I believe you just might have outdone yourself this time."

"Thank you, darling."

"Now, what do you want me to do . . . ?"

She quickly laid out her plan in detail.

"It's settled then." Avery said once he understood exactly what she wanted.

"It's settled. How soon do you think you can you arrange it?"

"I'll make some very discreet inquiries around town tomorrow and hire the men. After that, it will just be a matter of picking the best time to set it into motion."

"We can't wait too much longer, dear. Remember that." Vivienne went to her husband and, wrapping her arms around his neck, pressed herself against him and gave him a deep kiss. She was pleased that he was eagerly going along with her plot, and she meant to reward him fully that night.

Ever her sensual slave, Avery responded immediately to her nearness. "Don't worry, my love. By this time next week, we'll have enough money to get us through, and then the rest will follow in good time."

"I've always wanted to be rich, Avery. Really rich . . ." She began to caress him.

All thoughts of the kidnapping fled Avery's mind as he gave himself over to her practiced touch.

Edward was sitting at his desk, his mood troubled. Though he wanted to believe that Avery's threat to take Alexander away was an idle one, the more he thought about it, the more it bothered him. He knew the kind of man his son was, and he didn't trust him one bit.

"Father?" Clad in her nightgown and demure wrapper, her golden hair brushed out and falling around her shoulders in a shimmering cascade, Catherine stood in the doorway of Edward's study, waiting for him to bid her to join him. He'd seemed distant during dinner, and she'd worried that something very ugly had transpired with Avery. She'd waited until she was sure Alex was abed before coming to see if he wanted to talk about it.

At the sound of Catherine's voice, Edward looked up to find her watching him from across the room, her expression tentative. "Yes, Catherine. What is it?"

"I was just wondering . . ." She moved into the room to stand before him. "We never did talk about Avery's visit this afternoon."

Edward grunted in agreement as he waved her into a chair. "No, we didn't, did we?"

She heard the slight edge of bitterness in his voice and knew then that something serious had taken place between them. "What happened?"

"Nothing unusual, really," he began. "I just informed your brother that he'd get no more money out of me unless he changed."

"I take it that bit of news didn't sit well with him?"

24

"He made a threat . . ."

"What kind of threat?" Catherine asked, her blue-green eyes widening at the thought of her brother being stupid enough to risk their father's ire.

"He was going to try to take Alexander from me."

"What?! But they never wanted him before . . ."

He held up a hand to slow her. "And they don't really want him now. I'm sure it was all just a ploy to force my hand, but I refused to take the bait."

"Thank heaven. I'd worry about Alex constantly if he was forced to go back and live with them."

"It will never happen. I'll see to it. I countered Avery's threat with a firm threat of my own. If he tries to take Alexander away, he'll pay the price."

Catherine smiled at her father, reassured. "Good. The boy belongs with us. He's happy here."

"And we're going to make sure he stays that way," Edward concluded. He felt a little better now that they'd talked, but an inkling of concern still haunted him. "One thing . . ."

"What?"

"Be extra watchful of Alexander!"

"You think Avery might try something?"

"I'm probably being overly cautious, but . . ."

"Surely they wouldn't . . ." she began, and then stopped. Knowing her brother and his wife as she did, she didn't put anything past them. She shivered at the thought.

"He'll be fine as long as you're with him," he reassured her. "I will only be away for three weeks or so at the very most."

"I'll make it a point to keep him close to the house, just in case."

At her words, he finally allowed himself to relax a bit. "You're a good daughter, Catherine. I hope young Ratcliff appreciates you." Edward's eyes were twinkling as he thought about her fiancé, Lord Gerald Ratcliff, the oldest son of the Earl of Woodley.

"Oh, he does, Father," she replied with a quick smile as she thought of the blond-haired, handsome man who was her betrothed. She'd fallen madly in love with him at their first meeting just a few short months before, and though he had a reputation as a bit of a rakehell, he'd come to return her feelings. He'd asked for her hand right away, pleading that he didn't want to give anyone else a chance to steal her from him, and now plans were already well underway for their fall wedding.

"Good." Edward pushed away from the desk and got to his feet. It had been a long day, and he was bone-weary. The prospect of rising at dawn did not appeal, but he knew he had to leave. His traveling plans were made. He came around the desk and accepted the soft kiss Catherine gave him.

"Good night, Father."

"Good night, my dear. Will I see you in the morning before I leave?"

"Of course. Alex and I both will be up to see you off," she promised, and with that they both retired for the night.

Catherine kept her word. The following morning she and Alex accompanied Edward out to where his entourage of outriders and crested carriages were waiting for him in front of Huntington House. Edward didn't quite understand the emotion he was feeling at that moment, but the same sense of unease that had plagued him the night before was still bothering him. He tried to dismiss it, telling himself he was just a foolish old man as he kissed and hugged his daughter good-bye and then turned to his grandson. But for some reason, it wouldn't be dismissed so easily.

"You'll behave yourself while I'm gone and do as your aunt Catherine says?" Edward asked Alexander in a man-to-man tone. He felt a driving need to scoop the boy up in his arms and hold him close to his heart, but he controlled himself.

"Yes, sir," Alex answered, standing at attention as he faced his grandfather. His lower lip was trembling a bit as he fought to contain the loneliness he was already anticipating in the face of his absence. He knew his grandfather did not like open displays of emotion, so he was determined not to disappoint him.

"Good boy. I'll see you when I get back." Edward patted him on the shoulder, then started down the walk toward his waiting carriage.

As brave as he'd been, Alex was still seven years old, and he couldn't bear to see Edward leave. His resolve not to hug him or cry were suddenly cast aside as he realized that his grandfather really was going. He charged after him, desperately needing a warm hug. "Grandfather! Grandfather! Wait!"

Catherine looked on with tears in her eyes as her father turned back to find the boy racing toward him. There was not the slightest hesitation as the duke bent to the child and took him in his arms. It was a deeply touching moment for all three.

"Grandfather, hurry back . . . I'm going to miss you," Alex was saying as he wrapped his little arms around his grandfather's strong neck and hung on for dear life.

"I will. I'm going to miss you, too," Edward admitted in a choked voice, furious with himself for the tears that were burning in his eyes. He hugged the boy, then set him back down on his feet. "As soon as I get back, we'll see about painting that name on your boat. How's that?"

Alex nodded eagerly. "Fine, sir." He threw his arms

around him one last time, gave him a hard, childish hug, then darted back to his aunt's side.

Edward stared at them for a moment, as if committing the loving sight of them to memory—his beautiful daughter and his handsome young grandson—then raised one hand in farewell and climbed into the carriage.

Catherine and Alex remained on the walk, watching until the duke's entourage had disappeared from view down the main drive. Only then did they go back inside. A strange sense of forboding shook Catherine, but she managed to convince herself that it was only because of her conversation with her father the night before. They were safe and very well protected at Huntington House. Nothing was going to happen. She was sure of it.

Thirty-one-year-old Lord Gerald Ratcliff watched out the window of his carriage as the driver turned down the tree-lined drive that led to Huntington House. It had been three weeks since Catherine had left London with her father, and he was looking forward to seeing her, and the duke, again . . . especially the duke.

A sly smile spread across Gerald's handsome, refined features as he thought of the financial benefits he was going to reap from his marriage to Catherine. True, he was heir to his father's earldom, but while his family did have the title, their money was just about gone. He was being forced by circumstances to seek out a match that would not only fill the coffers at Woodley, but also keep him in style.

It had been a pure stroke of luck that Catherine had been as innocent and naive as she was rich. With carefully chosen compliments and a few stolen kisses, he'd managed to make her fall in love with him practically overnight. He thought it quite a coup, for he was not the only young buck around who wanted to get his hands on her very considerable dowry.

As cutthroat and calculating as Gerald had been in snaring her, he was not completely displeased by the match. Unworldly though she was, Catherine was not an unattractive woman, and though he felt no wild passion for her, he knew she had all the qualifications to do well as his wife, the future Countess of Woodley. He smiled again as he realized that he would not suffer overmuch getting her with child. True, his current mistress was not overly enthusiastic about his taking Catherine as his wife, but he'd managed to convince her not to complain too much by buying her a very expensive bauble and promising more, much more, after the wedding—bought with Catherine's money, of course.

As the carriage took the final turn in the drive and Huntington House came into view, a frown suddenly creased his brow and a vile oath escaped his lips.

The banner declaring that the duke was in residence was not flying. The duke was not at Huntington House. Frustration gripped him. He'd made the trip all the way out from London, meaning to play the besotted fiancé to impress both father and daughter, and now it looked like a wasted effort. He couldn't very well make his beloved swoon with the ardor of his devotion if she was nowhere around. He gritted his teeth and resolved to find out from the servants exactly where they were so he could follow them.

Bo Kelly and Jack Landers were used to plying their devious trade in the city, so they were not particularly comfortable or at ease crouched as they were, waiting in the bushes at the rear of the Huntington House gardens. They had followed the directions to the estate their mysterious new boss had given them to the letter and so far had not encountered any problems, but now was when it got dangerous. They knew they had to be careful. They could be discovered at any time, and if they were, their chances to kidnap the boy and make a lot of easy money would be ruined.

It had sounded so simple, according to the gent that had hired them. All they had to do was nab the kid, get him back to London without being seen, and leave him tied up and blindfolded in a stateroom on board the *Dolphin*. Bo and Jack believed it would be simple, too. They just had to be quiet. No one could know they were there, and it had to stay that way. Surprise and secrecy were everything.

They heard a noise that sounded like a child's voice coming from up near the house, and they grew tense as they watched avidly for the youngster they were supposed to grab. At the sound of footsteps on the path leading to the reflecting pond a short distance from them, they looked up. Their gazes locked on the end of the garden walk where at any moment they were sure the boy would appear. Excitement surged through the two thugs. Soon, very soon, the reward would be theirs! Both men wanted to chortle their glee at how easy this was going to be . . .

Alex was thrilled. He'd been waiting all day for Aunt Catherine to accompany him to the reflecting pool, and now he was finally going to get to sail his boat! He scampered down to the water's edge and set the *Scimitar* out to sail while Catherine looked on from the safety of the grassy bank. Alex watched in delight as the small ship skimmed smoothly across the glassy surface of the pond.

The kidnappers had been ready. The location of the pond was perfect for what they'd hoped to do, for it was shielded from view of the house by a thick, high hedge. They believed this was the best chance they were ever going to get, and they moved cautiously closer to the pond, ever mindful that at any moment they might be discovered. They had meant to strike and strike fast, but just as Bo and Jack had been prepared to lunge through the bushes and get Alex, they'd caught sight of Catherine following right behind him.

Frustration gripped Bo and Jack, and they silently cursed the lovely young woman for interfering with their plan. The two men exchanged angry looks and then hunkered even farther down in the shrubbery to make certain she didn't notice them. Annoyed though they were, they would wait for another chance. The money was too good to botch this.

Catherine and Alex were having a lovely time together there at the pond. The afternoon was cool and the day perfect. They laughed and talked and just enjoyed being together. Alex thought that Catherine was the most wonderful lady in the world, and he wondered why his mother, a woman he thought of as cold and unapproachable, couldn't be more like her. He liked hearing Catherine laugh, and he loved her warm hugs and the sweet perfume that was just hers.

"Catherine?"

The sound of Gerald Ratcliff's call cut through the pleasant afternoon and ended for Alex what had been an idyllic time.

"Catherine?" Gerald emerged from the house and strode through the gardens, smiling happily. When he'd descended from his carriage, he'd expected to be informed by the servants that Catherine had traveled with her father to another one of their estates. His surprise at finding her there had been genuine, and he

31

was pleased that she was unchaperoned.

For a moment, Catherine couldn't believe that she was actually hearing her fiancé's voice. Then, when he called out the second time, it was all she could do not to let out a squeal of excitement. "Gerald? I'm here . . . By the pond . . ." She scrambled to her feet and quickly brushed all the grass and leaves from her voluminous skirts so that she would look her best for him.

Upon hearing Catherine call to him, Gerald immediately headed in her direction. He took great care to school his features into an expression worthy of a man madly in love. When he finally caught sight of her, he quickened his pace, and when they came together, he swept her into an ardent embrace.

"My darling, I've missed you . . ." he declared before kissing her.

Catherine was thrilled by his avid display of devotion, and she surrendered willingly to him. All thoughts of Alex standing nearby were wiped from her mind as Gerald's lips found hers.

Alex grimaced as he watched them and wished most fervently that his aunt would tell Ratcliff to let her go. He had only met the man a few times before, but from the very first he'd known that he didn't like him. Alex wasn't sure exactly what it was about Ratcliff that made him so repulsive, and it didn't really matter. He just remained where he was sitting at the pond's edge, waiting for them to finally break apart.

After a breathtaking moment in Gerald's arms, Catherine regained her senses. She quickly drew away from her beloved, coloring a bit in embarrassment over her lack of control. He had only to touch her and she melted in his embrace. "No, Gerald . . ." she told him in a hushed voice. "Alex is here with me."

Gerald glanced up to see the boy watching them, and he had to fight hard not to order the brat back into the house so they could have some privacy. "I'm sorry, darling, but I was so glad to see you again, I couldn't help myself."

Catherine's blush grew even deeper at his declaration. "I know, I missed you, too."

Pleased with her confession, he tilted her chin up with one finger and pressed another kiss on her lips. "I'm glad."

They stared into each other's eyes for a long moment. Catherine was dizzy with happiness. She thought him the most wonderful man in the world, and she was delighted that he'd made the trip out from London just to see her. Still, she knew she couldn't stand there in his arms forever. Especially since Alex was there with them.

"Shall we go inside and have some refreshments? I'm sure you must be tired after your long trip."

"It was a long ride, but worth every minute now that we're together," he told her smoothly as he slipped a possessive arm about her waist. "Let's go in and have a cool drink." He started to turn her toward the house, but she resisted a bit.

"Alex . . . Come on, dear. We're going in now."

"Do I have to? Can't I stay out here and play?" He hated having to go back inside, especially since Ratcliff was there. The farther away from him he stayed, the better.

Catherine was tempted to let him remain outside by himself, but her father's warning echoed in her mind. As much as she would have loved some time alone with Gerald, she couldn't risk her nephew's safety. "We can come back out again later. How's that?" She held out one hand to him invitingly.

Alex glared at Gerald, greatly resentful of his intrusion on their outing, but he did as he was told. He took his aunt's hand and accompanied her back up the

33

path without further complaint.

The three of them went indoors, looking to all the world like a happy group. Had he been told of the impression, Ratcliff would have laughed happily at the success of his acting ability. He despised children and their ways. They were a noisy, bothersome lot, and though he knew that someday he would have to sire offspring to carry on his title, he had no intention of ever devoting more than a passing glance to any son or daughter he might father until the child was old enough to make adult conversation.

Crouching in the bushes not far from the glistening pool, Bo and Jack were fuming.

"Damn! We was so close!"

"I'll say we was," Jack seethed. "Now what do we do? Leave?"

"No! We wait. You heard her say they'd be coming back out later, didn't you?"

"Yeah, but she coulda meant hours from now . . ."

Bo bristled at his complaining. "You got anything better to do?"

"Well . . . I . . ."

"You want the money, don't you?"

"Yeah."

"Then, shut up."

Chapter Three

It was almost dark as Alex sat on his bed in his spacious bedroom, holding his boat as he stared out the window. His expression was not a happy one as he watched the sun slip ever lower in the western sky. The day was nearly over and still his aunt Catherine had not come for him. Alex's bottom lip jutted out and his chin tilted in defiance of the hurt he was feeling but trying to deny. It had been bad enough that he'd been sent upstairs to eat dinner in his room all by himself, but he was *really* going to be angry if she broke her promise to take him back to the pond.

Unable to just sit and wait any longer, he jumped down from the bed and crossed the room to the door. He opened it and looked out, hoping to find his aunt on her way to get him, but the hall was deserted. There was no sign of her. Belowstairs he could hear the sounds of adult conversation interspersed with happy, easy laughter, and that intensified his hurt. Catherine's seeming betrayal played on Alex's already sensitive nature. He felt very alone. His grandfather was gone, and his aunt had completely forgotten him.

Alex closed the door. He glanced down at the toy ship he still held, and he made his decision. There was no reason to sit there and wait for her any longer. He wanted to go sail his boat, so he would. Leaving his room, he headed down the back stairway and went out of the house by way of the kitchen.

Downstairs, Catherine was walking Gerald to the front door to bid him good night. It was almost dusk, and since Catherine was unchaperoned, betrothed or not, it would never do for Gerald to spend the night at Huntington House. Convention dictated he stay at an inn. Luckily, there was one not too far away.

"You will never know how much I'm looking forward to our wedding," Gerald told her with a warm smile.

"Why is that?" she asked, gazing up at him, her aquamarine eyes mirroring the depth of her love for him.

"Because, my sweet, once we're married, I'll never have to leave you," he confided smoothly, slipping his arms around her waist and drawing her close.

Catherine's heart beat faster at his declaration, and she smiled up at him tremulously. "It won't be that much longer, Gerald, and then we'll be together always."

She sounded so hopelessly romantic that he had to fight the urge to smirk. He had won her and her fortune, and it hadn't even taken a serious effort on his part. *Sometimes,* he mused cheerfully, *life really could be good to you.*

"Yes, my darling Catherine, forever," Gerald vowed with convincing earnesty. He had no intention of letting his mask of devotion slip just yet. He didn't want to disillusion her. What she didn't know couldn't hurt her and certainly couldn't disrupt their wedding plans. "But for now, I really must go . . ."

They kissed good night then, a very chaste exchange, for they didn't want to give the servants anything to

36

gossip about.

"Will I see you in the morning?" he asked.

"I'll be waiting," she responded with all the enthusiasm of a woman in love.

Gerald took his leave of her, and Catherine watched until long after his carriage had disappeared down the drive before turning back to the house. Her heart was light and her whole being was glowing with happiness. Wrapping her arms about herself, she sighed. Gerald was so handsome . . . so thoughtful . . . so wonderful. She believed herself lucky to have him.

Catherine's expression turned dreamy as she lost herself in fantasies of their wedding day. The gown was already being made—a high-necked, long-sleeved confection of white satin, Belgian lace, and seed pearls, and on that wonderful day when she would wear it, she would also don her mother's veil and the Huntington diamonds. She would be beautiful, and she would make Gerald proud to be her husband. She would become Lady Ratcliff that day, and eventually, she would be the Countess of Woodley. Catherine was determined to do everything in her power to please Gerald. She loved him, and she was sure theirs would be a marriage made in heaven.

Catherine was about to go into the parlor when she suddenly remembered her pledge to take Alex back to the pond. Knowing how much her nephew loved to sail his boat, she was sure he was still upstairs anxiously waiting for her. The stars in her eyes faded as a twinge of guilt assailed her for having forgotten him. She tried to justify her lapse by admitting to herself that she'd been overwhelmed by Gerald's presence, but she still knew she had better go to Alex quickly and make amends.

As Catherine started upstairs, she realized that Gerald had done one thing that had troubled her.

Adore Alex as she did, she'd expected to have him eat with them in the dining room. Gerald, however, had been adamant in insisting that the boy eat upstairs in his room. He'd claimed it would be more romantic for them to be alone, and while she knew he'd been right, she'd still hated to send Alex off by himself. Catherine made up her mind to make it all up to him now, and she hurried the rest of the way up the curving staircase to begin.

"Alex, I'm sorry I'm so late, but . . ." Catherine was saying as she knocked once lightly on his bedroom door and then let herself in without waiting for a response. She came to a dead stop just inside the door, though, when she found the room was empty. A quick look around told her that he was gone and so was his beloved boat. "No!" The word was a gasp as a haunting premonition jarred her. Without another thought, she pivoted and raced from the room.

"Hello, Lady Catherine. Can I help you with something?" Bessie, the cook, a plump, good-natured older woman, asked. It was unusual for Lady Catherine to come to the kitchen this late in the day.

"Yes, I was looking for Alex. I had thought he'd be in his room, but he's gone. Have you seen him?"

"Yes, my lady. He went out in the garden not too very long ago."

"Thank you," Catherine replied, then hurried after him glad to hear that he'd only left the house a short time before.

Bo and Jack couldn't believe their stroke of luck as they inched through the shrubbery ever closer to the place where the boy was playing. They were getting another chance! He had come out to the pond, and it looked like this time he'd come alone! They paused within striking distance just to make sure the woman hadn't followed . . .

Catherine wasn't sure exactly why, but she felt compelled to run. As soon as she left the kitchen, she gathered up her skirts and rushed down the path toward the pond . . .

Alex was so busy concentrating on the *Scimitar* as it sailed the vast sea of the reflecting pool and on the adventure its crew was experiencing in his daydreams that he took no notice of how rapidly darkness was falling or of the unusual rustling in the bushes nearby. He was having too much fun. *There were pirates out there and they were about to board and* . . .

"Alexander Wakefield! I thought I told you to wait for me!" Though her relief at finding him playing happily at the pond's edge was immense, Catherine couldn't help but scold him for coming outside alone.

Shocked by her cross tone, Alex looked up at her a bit startled. "Aunt Catherine . . ."

"Yes, *Aunt Catherine,*" she repeated, her hands on her hips in emphasis of her annoyance. "I told you we would come down here together."

Alex's expression turned mutinous. "I waited for you for a long time and then it started to get dark . . ."

In spite of the defiant look on his face, Catherine heard the pain in his voice, and she immediately softened. There was no danger. He was fine. She would relax and enjoy the rest of the evening with him. "I know you did, sweetheart," she began apologetically, "and I'm sorry I was so late, but Lord Ratcliff and I had a lot to talk about."

"I just wanted to sail my boat some more before it got dark, so I came out by myself. I didn't think you'd mind," Alex told her honestly, glancing out to where the *Scimitar* sat becalmed near the center of the pool.

For a moment there in the half-shadows of the

39

fading twilight, Catherine could have sworn she caught a glimpse of what Alex was going to look like as a man, and she couldn't help but smile. Charmer that he was with those dark curls and wonderful gray eyes, she was sure the stubbornness in the line of his jaw would harden as he matured, not soften. He was going to grow into one extraordinarily good-looking man, and she knew many a maiden was going to swoon over him. She hoped the woman who finally captured his heart loved him as much as she loved Gerald.

"I don't blame you one bit for getting tired of sitting there. I was very late. But next time, please do wait for me. I was worried about you, you know."

"Why?" he asked simply. "Grandfather lets me come down here all the time by myself."

"Well, I . . ." She didn't get the chance to say any more, for at that very moment Bo and Jack came charging at them from their hiding place in the bushes.

The two men had been ready to jump on Alex and spirit him away without so much as a peep, when all of a sudden Catherine had come running up out of nowhere. They were nearly frantic at her appearance, but they were not about to stop this time. The man who'd hired them had insisted they do the job in a hurry, so they dared not let this opportunity pass. What did it matter if they gave him one extra person? All that was important was delivering the kid and then getting their pay. Their boss could do whatever he wanted with the girl, and if *he* didn't want her, they would be able to find someone on the docks to take her off their hands for a price.

With the element of surprise was on their side, they came raging out of their hiding place. Bo went for Alex, grabbing him and jerking him tightly against him. Pinning him against his broad, hard chest, he stuffed a filthy rag in the boy's mouth to shut him up and then pulled a big, burlap sack over his head and tied a rope quickly around his hips, binding his arms down at his sides. Alex had tried his best to fight, but he was no competition for a grown man. He'd managed only one small squeal as he kicked and tried to twist away, and soon he was completely overpowered.

Catherine saw Jack coming at her and she screamed for help, hoping that the servants would hear her. Then, fearing for Alex's life, she turned on Bo. She wanted to stall them as long as she could so help could come, so she launched herself at Bo, ready to do anything she could to force him to release the boy.

Her actions caught Jack completely by surprise. He'd thought she was going to run from him like a typical female, not turn tigress and attack his partner, jumping on his back and clawing at his face.

"Jack, damnit, man! Get the wench off me!" Bo yelled as he tried to control the squirming boy and knock Catherine off him.

Jack grabbed her by the waist and yanked her away from Bo. Then, with full force, he threw her violently down on the ground.

"You swine!" she swore, trying to get back up to continue her assault.

Jack closed on her as she struggled to get to her feet, her skirts tangling about her legs hobbling her. He snared her arms as she swung out at him. "I'd shut up if I valued my fair skin, your ladyship," he sneered in her ear, his hot, nasty breath vile to her senses.

Catherine continued to bite and kick at him, but Jack subdued her easily now, twisting her arms behind her in a vicious hold and then gagging her in the same manner he had the boy. Luckily, they had brought along another burlap sack, and he pulled that over her head just as Bo had done with Alex. After securing it, he slung her over his shoulder.

Catherine was terrified. She kicked at her assailant with all her might, trying desperately to dislodge herself from his hold, but he would have none of it. He hit her sharply, a single blow to the side of her head, and effectively silenced her struggles.

"If you want the boy to stay alive, stay still!" the unknown man's voice threatened in a tone that showed no mercy.

Catherine did as she was told, hoping that someone at the house had heard them and was coming after them. It would have sickened her if she'd known that no one had seen or heard a thing. The full, lush hedge had blocked the view and the noise from the house. It would be hours before the note Bo left behind with the ransom demands would be discovered and the toy boat found abandoned, floating in the pond. By the time a search for them was implemented, they would be well on their way to London.

Avery made his way in a hired carriage toward the docks for his late-night rendezvous with Bo and Jack. The waterfront dive where he'd chosen to meet them was a favorite of sailors just into the port, and he'd chosen it specifically, for he knew he ran little risk of being recognized there. As the conveyance drew to a stop before the tavern, Avery bid the driver to wait for him with a promise to pay extra for his time, then disappeared into the smoke-filled hovel.

"There he is!" Bo shouted to Jack above the din as he caught sight of Avery coming through the door. "C'mon, let's get him and get this over with!"

The two men moved off to meet the man who'd hired them.

"Evenin', guvnor," Bo greeted Avery boldly as they approached him. "We been waitin' for you."

42

"I'll bet you have," Avery answered, looking down his nose at the ruffians. It troubled him that he had to associate with lowlifes, but a man did what he had to do in order to accomplish his goals. Besides, Avery consoled himself, they didn't know who he was and they never would. "It's done?" he asked.

"It's done," Jack answered, taking another big swallow from his tankard of ale. They had been drinking steadily for the last hour, fearful of what the man's reaction would be to the news that they had taken the woman.

"I want to see him to make sure," Avery announced. He wasn't about to pay them until he was certain everything was in order. "You didn't have any trouble, did you?"

Bo and Jack exchanged a quick, uneasy glance. Avery felt an immediate sinking in the pit of his stomach.

"What happened? What went wrong?"

"Nothin' really happened," Bo began to explain. "It's just we got one more than you're payin' for."

Avery went completely still. He was glad for all the noise and ruckus that was going on around them. No one would notice his sudden look of distress. "What do you mean?"

"I mean, we had to take a woman same time as we took the boy," Bo blurted out.

"A woman?" Avery was stunned. Who had they taken? The answer came instantly. It could only be Catherine. "For God's sake, why?"

"There was no way to avoid it. She came up just as we was takin' him. There was nothin' else we could do, but take her, too," Jack defended.

"That was stupid!"

Bo bristled at his insult. "Would you rather we have killed her?"

Avery quickly assessed the situation, wishing desperately that Vivienne was there with him to help him make a decision. It came to him, though, that the decision had already been made for him. "No. Let's go. I want to see them."

Bo and Jack set their near-empty mugs on a nearby table and led the way outside.

Nothing was said as they made their way down the docks. The night air was heavy with the stench of dead fish and rot. Despite the lateness of the hour, there were still many people moving about. Prostitutes of all ages plied their trade with open enthusiasm, meeting with great success among the newly arrived sailors. Avery was glad when they finally reached the *Dolphin*.

The ship was captained by one Joseph Black, a thin, cold-eyed man Avery knew to be completely without conscience or morals. Money was Black's one and only love in life, and he would do anything and go anywhere for the right price. Before finalizing his plans with Bo and Jack, Avery had made certain that a cabin could be made available on Black's ship for a "less than willing" passenger if enough money was involved. It was to the *Dolphin*, under the cover of darkness a few hours earlier, that the two kidnappers had delivered Alex and Catherine, still bound as they had been when they'd been spirited away from Huntington House. No one on the ship had paid them the slightest bit of attention.

"Did you have any problems boarding?" Avery asked as they paused for a moment before going aboard the ship.

"No. It went just like you said it would."

"And no one saw you?"

The two kidnappers shrugged. "If they did, they didn't care."

"Good." Avery mentally rubbed his hands together.

Soon it would all be over. His father would pay the ransom, and then he and Vivienne would have enough money to tide them over until the title became his.

They said no more as they mounted the gangplank. The crewman on watch gave them a cursory lookover and then, recognizing Bo and Jack, let them pass. They went belowdecks to the small airless cabin that was serving as Alex and Catherine's prison. Bo had the key and he unlocked the door and shoved it open.

Avery stared in satisfaction at the sight of his son and sister blindfolded, gagged, and bound hand and foot lying on the two narrow bunks.

"What d'ya think, guvnor? We brought 'em here just like you said."

Avery hesitated to speak for fear Alex and Catherine could hear him. He nodded his approval to the two, then backed out of the room and closed the door.

"The key, please." He held out his hand.

"And I'll take the money," Bo countered.

"You left the note?"

"Right there by the pond where they could find it." The exchange was made.

"It was nice doin' business with you, gent," Bo and Jack said in unison as they went back out on deck. They were grinning from ear to ear over their good fortune. They might not have gotten the young woman for their own as they'd hoped, but the money they'd just received made that small sacrifice worth their while. "You ever need anything else done, you just let us know."

Avery waved them off, eager to be out of their disgusting company, and then went to seek out Captain Black.

"Ah, Mr. Smith," Black said sarcastically as he admitted Avery to his cabin. He knew the name was a fake, but he didn't care. The color of his money was all he cared about. "I think we have something that needs to be discussed."

"Indeed we do," Avery said, taking a seat in the chair the captain indicated. Avery had decided right away not to have Alex killed. He knew of a man who lived off the coast of France who had a taste for the unusual and could afford to indulge himself. Having met him some years ago, he'd contacted him about taking the boy off his hands, and he'd been pleased when the man had offered him a huge sum for the lad. They were to meet in five days. Avery wondered now if he'd be interested in having his sister, too.

"As you know, our original deal was only for the boy. The woman was not part of our agreement."

"I want to take her along as well when we sail. I'm sure I can work something out when I go to finalize the deal on the boy." Amoral as he was, he felt no guilt at all in getting rid of his sister, too. She meant nothing to him. She never had and never would. Only Vivienne was important in his life.

"It can be arranged, but you understand the charge will be double now?"

"Of course, I would have expected no less, and there will be a bonus for you if things go smoothly."

"I'm sure having her on board will be no problem, Mr. Smith."

"Good. When are you planning to set sail?"

"We must leave port in two days if we're to make your rendezvous point on time."

"Fine. I'll be here in plenty of time to sail with you."

"Good. Until then, I'll take good care of my 'guests.' No harm will come to them. We wouldn't want to sell damaged goods." The idea of a bonus appealed to him. He would protect the two without fail.

Avery gladly paid Black the outrageous sum he

demanded for Catherine's passage. Then, his business dealings set, he returned home. He hoped Vivienne would approve of the arrangements he'd made. He wondered as he made his way toward their townhouse whether news had come yet concerning Alex and Catherine's disappearance.

Chapter Four

Gerald was scowling blackly as he paced the parlor of Huntington House just before dawn the following morning. Late last night the servants had notified him at the inn of Catherine and Alex's kidnapping and he'd raced to the estate to take charge until Avery could arrive from London or the duke returned. By the time he'd gotten to the house, the servants had already searched the grounds for clues, but he'd insisted they go over everything one more time just to be sure. To his despair, the results had been the same. They'd found nothing. Whoever had taken them had known what they were doing.

Now, as Gerald waited for the family to arrive, his thoughts were focused on his own well-being, and he was furious. His whole future had been planned around the marriage to Catherine, and he wondered what he was going to do now. Taking care of himself was, and always had been, his utmost concern.

Vivienne and Avery sat silently in their carriage as they made their way toward Huntington House. Playing the part of concerned parents, they'd left

London as soon as they received word of Alex's disappearance.

Vivienne's expression was calm as she stared out the window into the darkness of the night. When Avery had first told her of the complication, she'd been angry. But then, after she'd had time to think about it, she'd changed her mind. She'd come to realize that with Catherine out of the way things would be much, much easier. She was one less person they had to deal with or worry about, and, ultimately, that much more money in their pockets—in more ways than one.

"We're here," Avery spoke up, breaking the silence as their vehicle made the final turn in the road.

"Thank heavens. The ride out here is always so dull."

"Ah, but this time, my love, the results will be worth it," Avery offered.

"Indeed they will," she agreed, smiling slyly at him. "Indeed they will."

When the carriage halted at the front entrance, Avery descended and then helped Vivienne down. There was a slight chill in the predawn air, so she pulled her light wrap a little more tightly around her shoulders, then leaned weakly against her husband as they mounted the few steps to the door. She wanted to give the impression that she was distraught over the loss of her son, but inwardly, she was wondering with perverse pleasure just what the servants would think if they knew she was the one who'd planned the whole thing.

Dalton, Huntington's most trusted servant, met them at the door. He was looking tired and strained over the night's events. "Good evening, my lord, my lady. Lord Ratcliff is awaiting you in the parlor."

"Thank you, Dalton," Avery replied. He took Vivienne's wrap and handed it to Dalton, then escorted her in to meet with his sister's fiancé. He greeted the other man as he met them at the parlor door.

"I'm glad you finally made it," Gerald said, relieved by their presence, then turned to Avery's strikingly beautiful wife. "Hello, Vivienne."

"I'm so glad you could be here with us tonight, Gerald. This is such a trauma. Our poor Alex—kidnapped!" She managed to sound quite desperate. "And our dear Catherine taken, too. I can hardly believe it."

"Neither can I," Gerald said slowly. "I can't imagine why anyone would want to cause them any harm."

"It's a tragedy," Avery added. "What's been done so far?"

Gerald quickly told him about the searches and the messages sent to both him and to the duke.

"Good, good. We can only hope my father will know what to do next."

"He will," Vivienne spoke up confidently. "I just wonder, though, how soon he'll be arriving."

"He's at Ellington," Gerald offered.

"Then it will be hours, maybe even as late as the afternoon before he returns," she said.

"Perhaps we should all try to get some rest?" Avery suggested. "It's been a long night for all of us, and the day promises to be even more arduous. Were you staying here at Huntington House, Gerald?"

"No. I came for a visit only to find your father had gone. I took a room at the inn."

"Well, there's no need for you to go back there now that we're here. I'll have Dalton prepare a room for you."

"Thank you, Avery."

"Darling? Are you ready to retire?" Avery inquired of his wife.

"I think I'll have a cup of tea first. I'm tired, but I'm so upset I don't know if I could fall asleep right away.

Will you join me?"

"No. I'm going on up. Gerald, I'll see you in a few hours."

"Of course, and thank you, Avery."

Avery nodded and left them alone in the parlor. After instructing Dalton to make up a room for Ratcliff, he went to his own bedroom. He was feeling immensely pleased with himself as he stretched out on his bed, and by the time Vivienne joined him over an hour later, he was sound asleep.

It was well past noon when the duke's entourage pulled up before Huntington House. The minute his carriage stopped, Edward climbed out. The ride had been an exhausting one, but he didn't bother waiting for help in getting down. There was no time . . . no time at all.

"Your Grace," Dalton greeted him as he held the front door. The entire household staff had kept a constant vigil, watching for the duke's return ever since they'd sent word to him, and Dalton knew all would be relieved now that he had returned.

Edward's anger was so great that he didn't respond to the man's welcome. He didn't trust himself to speak. Since learning that Catherine and Alexander were missing and that a ransom demand had been made for their safe return, he'd been furious. He knew exactly who had taken them and why, and he had come home to settle this matter once and for all.

Dalton was startled when Edward walked past him without speaking, but the expression on the duke's face told the servant all he needed to know. Still, he knew he had to get his attention. "Your Grace . . ." He spoke up again, this time in a more urgent tone.

His words finally penetrated the red haze of

Edward's outrage. "Yes? What is it?" he demanded curtly, not wanting to be distracted.

"Lord Avery is here, Your Grace," he blurted out, "along with his wife, Lady Vivienne, and Lord Gerald Ratcliff. They've been here through the night and are waiting for you now in the parlor."

Edward's gray eyes blazed with fiery inner fury. "Let them wait. There's something I have to see about first. Come into my study."

"Yes, Your Grace," Dalton answered quickly. He'd always considered himself rather stout of heart, but the duke's expression was so terrible that he had to fight down the urge to quake in fear. He was glad the anger was not directed at himself, and he wanted to keep it that way. He hastened to do as he was told, closing the door behind them once they were in the sanctuary of the duke's study.

"Where's the ransom note?" Edward asked as he moved to stand behind his desk.

"Right here." Dalton picked up the missive and handed it to him.

Edward took the letter, unfolded it, and quickly read the message.

"If you want the boy and the woman back, leave £200,000 in a valise at the side of the road near Bulwer Crossing at midnight Friday. If you try any tricks, you will never see them alive again."

Hard put to control his raging temper, Edward crumpled the obscene demand in his fist. Heat flushed through him, followed by a deadly coldness of the soul. He forced all emotion from him, and when he looked up at his servant again, his expression was calm and befitting one of his regal station.

"Send Avery and his wife in to see me. Tell Ratcliff that I'll speak with him last."

"Yes, Your Grace." He hurried out of the room to get them.

Avery was feeling quite confident as he lounged beside Vivienne on the sofa in the parlor. Everything was going according to plan. It was just a matter of time.

"Your father's back, but he's just left us sitting here. Do you suppose there's something else wrong that we don't know about?" she asked her husband worriedly, a double meaning to her words.

"No, my darling, I'm sure he's just taking a moment to pull himself together before we speak." Avery always underestimated his father and overestimated his own abilities. He looked up as Dalton appeared in the doorway.

"Lord Avery, Lady Vivienne, His Grace will see you now."

"Thank heaven," Vivienne snapped impatiently. "This is a matter of life and death and he's kept us waiting forever."

"Yes, thank heaven," Avery added, affecting a look he was sure would convince his father that he was grievously worried about his son and his sister.

"Lord Ratcliff, the duke said he would speak with you later."

"Thank you, Dalton." Gerald said, settling in to wait.

The servant held himself erect as he ushered Avery and Vivienne from the room and into the duke's presence. He then discreetly withdrew from the study.

Edward was a silhouette as he stood behind his desk, his back to the room, staring out the floor-to-ceiling casement window. He heard Avery and Vivienne enter, but did not immediately alter his stance. He stood stiffly, waiting. He wanted them to worry. He wanted them to wonder at his mood. When he finally did turn to face them and saw the worried looks upon their faces, the fire of his anger flamed to even greater heights. It took all of his considerable willpower not to physically attack them.

"Father, I . . ." Avery hoped to take control of the conversation and tell him how worried he and Vivienne were about Alex and Catherine. But his father was not about to allow him any such opportunity.

"Be still," Edward dictated in a flat voice.

"But . . ."

Edward noticed the sudden flicker of confusion on their faces and he was glad. They would be feeling more than just confusion when he got done with them. "I have tolerated much from you through the years, Avery, but this time you have pushed me too far," he ground out savagely.

Avery straightened a bit as he met his father's icy regard. "I don't know what you're talking about. Vivienne and I are devastated by this! Alex is our son. We love him and we . . ."

"You seem to have forgotten that I know you, Avery. I know you better than any other person on the face of this earth. I suspected all along that you would try something despicable, but I never thought you would stoop this low. My only consolation is that you've failed, and failed miserably."

"What are you saying? You think I . . . That we . . . ?" Avery and Vivienne both assumed looks of righteous indignation.

"I'm saying that you're responsible for this. I know what you've done! If you value your wretched existence, you'll have Alexander and Catherine back here before dark today. Do you understand me?"

"You're wrong! We know nothing about—" He tried

to proclaim his innocence, but his father would have none of it.

"Don't insult my intelligence for a moment longer with your denials," he cut him off, casting a scathing look at Vivienne, too. "Now, get out of my sight! The both of you!"

Avery and Vivienne had both blanched before the power of his fury. Avery wanted to continue to plead his innocence, but he thought better of pressing his point right then. He and Vivienne rose together.

"Father, you're wrong about this," Avery said solemnly, and then left the room with his wife.

Only after he heard them leave the house did Edward allow himself to get off his feet. He sat at his desk and stared blindly across the room, exhaustion and frustration beating at him. Now it was only a matter of waiting. He prayed with all his heart and soul that it would be over in the next few hours, that he would soon hear the gentle laughter of Catherine and Alexander once again ringing through the house. Edward ran a shaking hand over his face, then called out to Dalton.

"Yes, Your Grace?"

"I want you to send one of your most reliable men to follow my son. I want to know where he goes and who he sees. Do you understand me?"

Dalton was puzzled by the request, but answered in the affirmative. "Right away, Your Grace."

Edward nodded wearily. "Now, show Lord Ratcliff in."

As he waited for the young man to join him, he wondered miserably how much he should tell him about what was going on. In the end, he decided to say as little as possible and just keep praying that Catherine and Alexander showed up soon.

*　　　*　　　*

"I told you something was wrong!" Vivienne snarled as she sat down across from her husband in their carriage.

"I just don't understand how he found out . . . how he knew . . ."

"You fool, he doesn't know *anything!* He was bluffing you. Don't you think that if he knew what happened, he would have them both back here by now?"

"You're right."

"You know I am. Thank God we got out of there without ruining everything. And now we're going to show that old man he's not as smart as he thinks he is." Vivienne said coldly, shaking from the power of the emotions roiled within her.

"How?"

"We're going back to London and we're going to start our own massive search for them. We'll let everyone know about it. We'll even hire our own investigators to look for them."

"I'm supposed to sail with the *Dolphin* tomorrow," he worried, thinking he'd be missed and people would become suspicious.

"Don't worry, you'll still be sailing with the *Dolphin*. Nothing's going to interrupt our plans. If anyone asks where you are, I'll tell them that you're out searching for Alex, too."

"You know my father won't give up easily."

"Neither will we."

They shared a determined look. They knew what they wanted, and they knew how to get it.

"What about the ransom? Do you think he'll pay it?"

"He'll pay it, because by Friday he's going to be a very desperate man. Can you make arrangements for it to be picked up and delivered to me secretly?"

"I'll take care of it before I sail."

"Good." Vivienne smiled a diabolical smile as she thought of the pain they were going to cause the duke. "Maybe, when all this is over, in a month or two, it'll be time for us to consider your ascent to the title."

"What do you mean?" Avery's eyes met hers across the carriage, and he felt a very real fear when he saw the look of avarice on her face.

"I mean, it certainly would be a tragedy if the duke suffered some deadly accident so soon after losing his only daughter and grandson . . ."

"I thought we agreed that it was too dangerous to try anything like that," he hedged in cowardice. It was one thing to take the boy and Catherine, who were quite powerless; it was another thing altogether to deal with someone as influential as his father.

"I would have thought you'd be eager to be rid of him after the way he talked to you tonight," Vivienne prodded.

"Murder is not something to be taken lightly. Besides, we'll have plenty of money once we get the ransom and I receive payment for Alex and Catherine. We'll be able to live quite comfortably for a number of years, and then—"

"Comfortably?! You're content with living *comfortably?*" she demanded. "I want to be the Duchess of Huntington, Avery, and I won't wait forever!"

He backed down in the face of her tirade. "Let's take care of Alex and Catherine first, and then we'll worry about the rest."

"We're going to do it, Avery. We are." Her eyes were shining with a fanatical glow as she spoke the words. There would be no stopping her now.

"How long have we been here, Aunt Catherine?" Alex asked as he curled up next to her on the hard,

57

narrow bunk.

"About two days, Alex," she answered wearily, putting a protective arm about his small shoulders.

The small, stuffy, windowless cabin they were being held captive in had become a torture chamber of the unknown for them. It was dark and dreary save for the one lamp that burned low on the table beside the bed. They were both exhausted from the uncertainty of their ordeal. Frantic with worry over what the future held for them, they'd been unable to sleep much. Their clothes were wrinkled, and dark circles had formed beneath their eyes.

"What's taking so long? I thought you said that we were being held for ransom and that as soon as Grandfather paid them the money we'd be set free."

The questions he asked were the same ones that had been plaguing Catherine for the last day and a half. Surely her father knew they'd been taken by now and had paid the money. Why hadn't they been released yet?

"We'll be freed soon. You'll see," she told him with more confidence than she felt.

Her father's earlier warnings about Avery still haunted her, and she couldn't help but wonder if her brother really was connected with this, though she'd had no indication that he was. The sailors who'd come and untied them and given them their meals had not spoken a word to them. She felt cut off from all communication. It frightened her, and her fears were growing with every passing minute.

She had considered trying to escape, but the one time she'd managed a look out the door when the sailor brought them some food, she'd caught a glimpse of an armed guard in the passageway. They were trapped, and she knew they were just going to have to wait and hope rescue came soon.

"Grandfather won't let anything happen to us," Alex agreed, nestling closer. "He loves us too much."

"Indeed he does, little one. He's probably on his way to get us right now." She hugged the child close as she offered up a silent prayer for their salvation.

"What do you mean you lost Avery?" Edward bellowed as he faced James, the man Dalton had sent to follow his son.

"I'm sorry, Your Grace, but he's disappeared," James apologized. "I stayed with him for the first day and a half without a problem, but then he suddenly just disappeared."

The duke was almost beyond control. The first day had been terrible enough. Each minute had seemed an hour as he'd waited for Avery to bring Catherine and Alexander home. When the night had come and gone and they had not returned, Edward was furious. He'd added extra men to the search and had made preparations with his banker to get the money for the ransom together. He didn't for one minute think that someone other than Avery was responsible, yet he knew he couldn't take any chances with the lives of Catherine and Alexander. He would pay the money and get them back, but eventually there would be hell to pay.

"I want every inch of the city searched. I want a constant watch placed on their house. I want to know every move that woman makes until my son returns. Don't worry about the cost. Just do it."

"Yes, Your Grace." Relieved that his reprimand hadn't been any worse, James raced to carry out his orders.

*   *   *

Voices in the companionway just outside the cabin door jarred Catherine and Alex out of their rest. They quickly sat up on the bunk, watching the door and waiting to see if anyone was going to come in. When a key played in the lock and the door swung open they expected it to be one of the sailors bringing them something to eat. Both were shocked when Avery stepped into the room.

"Father!" Alex couldn't believe it was his father standing there and he almost vaulted from the bunk in his eagerness to embrace him. At last they were being rescued, and not by his grandfather, but by his father!

Catherine, however, had a sickening feeling that she knew what Avery's appearance meant. She straightened, cautious not to betray her hope that he had indeed come to save them. Her caution was rewarded, for he gave the eager little boy a ferocious look that stopped him in his tracks.

"Just stay right where you are, Alex!" Avery ordered abruptly.

"But Father, haven't you come to get us?"

An evil smile spread across his face as he stared down at his son. "What a tiresome child you are," he said, then he looked up at his sister, completely dismissing the boy from his thoughts. "Catherine, it's good to see that you're looking well."

"What do you want, Avery? If you haven't come to take us home, then why are you here?" As she spoke the words, though, she had her answer, for she felt the ship begin to move, pulling slowly away from the dock. "Avery! Where are we going?"

He gave an arrogant chuckle as he saw the terror on her lovely features. "I've made some special arrangements to help line my pockets, dear sister. It's *such* a pity that you got caught up in all this, but . . ." He gave a casual lift of his shoulders.

Unable to stand any more, Catherine flew off the bunk and tried to attack her brother. He subdued her easily, snaring her wrists and holding her immobile.

"Ah, ah, my sweet one, you must take care lest you bruise," he scolded. "Those who will be buying you wouldn't like it if the merchandise is marred in any way."

"I can't believe this! What have you done?!"

Now it was Alex's turn to attack. He hadn't been able to help his aunt before, but he would now. His father's callous rejection of him had destroyed any vestige of caring that had been left in his tender young heart. With the determination of a man full grown he ran to him and began to pummel him with his little fists.

"Let her go! You let her go!"

Avery released her with a bitter laugh, at the same time, backhanding Alex as hard as he could. "You little . . ."

"If you ever touch him again, Avery, I'll find a way to kill you myself," she threatened, hugging Alex to her.

"You'll never have the chance," he scoffed turning away. 'We're leaving England, and you'll never be back."

"But Father surely will—"

"You'll never see him again, Catherine." He saw her gaze flicker to the door and easily read her thoughts. "Forget it, my dear. There's a guard right outside. Besides, we're heading out of port right now, and I can't guarantee your safety should you try to leave this cabin. There are many men on board who are of unsavory character . . . if you know what I mean."

"Why you . . ."

"Save your breath, for your curses have no effect on me. In another day or so, you're both going to begin another life far away from here. Until then, I don't want to hear that you've given anyone on this ship any

61

trouble. If you do, you'll pay the price. Do I make myself clear?"

Catherine gathered Alex to her. "Perfectly. Leave us, Avery. As far as I'm concerned I have no brother and Alex has no father."

Avery turned and left the cabin, feeling victorious and omnipotent. He could do whatever he wanted and there was no one who could stop him!

Chapter Five

The time had almost come. It was Friday, late in the afternoon. Edward stared down at the once-crumpled note that had been smoothed out so he could read it again, one last time. He was tempted, oh so tempted, to send his people to capture the men who were to claim the ransom money, but he feared so greatly for Catherine and Alexander's safety that he didn't. He hoped and prayed that he wouldn't live to regret his decision.

"Dalton?" He slowly raised his bloodshot, troubled gaze to his most trusted servant. He had had little rest since the kidnapping and his face showed his fatigue.

"Yes, Your Grace?" he responded correctly. He had never seen the duke in such a state before, and he wanted to do all he could to help him.

"Shortly before midnight you will make the ride. I want my daughter and grandson back, and this seems to be my only hope."

Dalton nodded in understanding. The investigators the duke had hired had turned up nothing in their four intensive days of searching since the kidnapping. Every lead, every clue, had come to nothing. It was almost as if Lady Catherine and Lord Alexander had disappeared off the face of the earth. Lord Avery's strange absence still rendered him suspect, but they could find no connection between him and the kidnapping. As awful as it was, Dalton knew that at this point in time, there was nothing left for His Grace to do except pay the ransom.

"Shall I ride with him?" Gerald offered. He had been at Edward's side through most of the ordeal and wanted to be of help now, if he could.

"No," Edward answered quickly. "It would be too risky. The kidnappers are expecting one of my household, and I don't want to make them angry. It will be best if you to stay with me. Dalton will go alone when the time comes."

"Yes, Your Grace," the servant answered nervously. The responsibility was a big one, but he was honored to be trusted to do it. "As you say."

"Plan on leaving at quarter past eleven. That should give you plenty of time to make the ride to Bulwer Crossing and leave the money."

The three men agreed and then fell silent. They knew the balance of the day was going to pass very slowly as they waited for the coming of the midnight hour and, ultimately, for the return of Catherine and Alexander.

Wearing only a bright-red turban and a pair of loose pants cut short, Muhammed Ibn Abbas, fiercest of all the Barbary pirates, was the picture of power as he stood on the deck of his ship staring out across the Atlantic, his brawny arms folded across his darkly tanned, heavily muscled chest. He was an evil, black-hearted man, who commanded complete and utter obedience from his men. Corsairs that they were, his crew understood and respected brute strength, so they gave him their unfailing loyalty. Muhammed knew they dared do no less, for he dealt with any hint of betrayal with swift and harsh punishment.

Muhammed thoroughly enjoyed his life as a pirate, although he was finding this voyage very frustrating. They had sailed from their home port of Algiers several weeks before, yet to date they had taken no ship or bounty. His men were growing restless, and so was he. In a daring move, he had ordered his ship out into the Atlantic, and they sailed now off the coast of France, searching hungrily for prey.

"Muhammed *Reis* . . ." Selim, his second-in-command and most trusted friend, greeted his captain as he joined him. "Don't you think we've come far enough north?"

"Nonsense, my friend, you worry too much. There is a valuable prize somewhere nearby, I can feel it," Muhammed boasted.

Selim, however, wasn't so confident. "It's been days now, and we've seen nothing worth taking. How can you be so certain?"

The ship's captain turned a deadly gaze on his companion. "Do you doubt me after all these years?"

He had seen that look before and knew it was time to back down. "Never have I doubted you, and I do not now."

"Good. Then we are agreed. We will continue to hunt these waters until we have taken a prize worthy of us."

Selim nodded in agreement as he let his gaze sweep across the horizon. Somewhere out there was a ship holding riches, and he knew Muhammed would find it.

"Captain Black!" the sailor shouted. "Ship off the port bow!"

Black was not overly concerned. They were traveling

in one of the most trafficked sea lanes on their way to the rendezvous point Mr. Smith had designated, so it was not unusual to sight another vessel. "What flag is he flying?"

"French, sir," the man replied after lifting his telescope to check.

"Carry on, but keep a sharp eye just in case," the captain directed.

"Aye, sir."

Belowdecks on the *Dolphin*, Avery sat in his cabin savoring the moment. He glanced at his pocket watch and his expression turned to a very satisfied one. Within hours, they would reach the island. At approximately the same time the sale was completed tonight and Alex and Catherine were forever taken off his hands, the ransom would be delivered to England. It was definitely going to be a glorious night.

"Captain, it looks like the vessel's deliberately closing on us," the lookout informed Captain Black as he watched the oncoming ship draw ever closer. There was a touch of nervousness in his voice.

"Let's have a look," Black said. Taking the telescope from the mate standing nearby, he trained his experienced gaze on the ship that was fast gaining on them.

Until this moment, Black had always considered himself a man of the sea. He knew he was a more than competent captain, but what he saw when he leveled the scope at the nearing ship sent a shaft of terror through his soul. The deck of the ship was swarming with pirates. As they came even closer, he could make out that some were carrying pistols, others scimitars.

They looked as hideously vicious as their reputation proclaimed, and Black knew real fear. His first instinct was to order full sail, but he knew it was already too late. The corsairs would be upon them within the hour. There was nowhere to run and certainly nowhere to hide.

"Captain Black? Shouldn't we try to make a run for it or at least man the guns?" Warson, Black's first officer, asked.

The *Dolphin* was equipped with three guns, but the captain knew they were no match for the firepower of the pirate ship.

"No. If we resist and try to fight them, we'll be slaughtered."

"But Captain . . ."

"Enough!" He turned a burning gaze on Warson. "I've heard tales of what these pirates do to anyone who fights back." Black turned away to look at the pirate ship that was pulling ever closer to them even as they spoke. Even at full sail, there could be no avoiding their fate. "Tell the crew I want no fighting. When they board, we will offer no resistance. Understood?"

"Aye, Captain. What about the passengers?"

"I'll take care of them. See to the ship, Mr. Warson." With that, Black left him, going below to seek out Mr. Smith and warn him of the coming trouble.

The knock at his cabin door surprised Avery. He hoped one of the crew was coming to tell him that they had reached the rendezvous point early. He was eagerly anticipating the completion of his upcoming business transaction. It was going to feel very good having that large a sum of money in his hands.

"Yes? What is it?" Avery asked as he threw the door wide. It surprised him to find the captain standing there, but he wasn't concerned. He just assumed the man had come to discuss the last of the business details with him. "Captain Black . . . do come in."

"There's no time for pleasantries, Mr. Smith," Black replied.

Avery finally noticed the man's taut expression, and he frowned. "What's wrong?"

"We're about to be boarded," he answered tersely.

"Then we've arrived . . ."

"We're not going to 'arrive', sir."

"What?" Avery demanded incredulously.

"We are about to be overtaken by pirates."

"You must do something, Captain Black! You can't let this happen!"

"I'm afraid there's nothing I can do."

"Fight them off!"

"I will not endanger the lives of my crew by resisting a superior force. I know what kind of men these are. They show no mercy. They understand only complete victory. I suggest you prepare yourself and your 'guests' for the inevitable," he suggested.

"What do you mean?" Avery panicked.

"I mean we will probably be taken to North Africa in chains. There is a possibility that we could be ransomed back to England within a year or so." He paused to let his words take effect. "Now, if you will excuse me. I have other duties I must attend to."

"Captain, I insist that you do something! For God's sake, man, fight them! I paid you for safe passage!" Avery was frantic, and he reached out and grabbed the captain by the arm to stop him from leaving.

Black turned on him, his face mirroring pure fury as he threw off his restraining hold. "Don't ever touch me again, Smith. Do you think I like losing my boat and my crew? This is the only way to save our lives. We'll be sold into slavery, but eventually, if we have any luck at all, we'll be returned."

"Oh, my God . . ." Avery was physically quaking.

"Get control of yourself." Black gave him a disgusted look as he saw how shaken he was, then stalked off.

As Avery watched him go, he couldn't stop shaking. They were about to be taken by pirates, and then God knew what was going to happen to him! He had to save himself! He had to do something! But what? His mind was racing, but he could think of no way to escape. His gaze darted about the stateroom searching for some place to hide, and then he saw it . . . As he moved to conceal himself from the cutthroats who were about to seize the ship, it never crossed his mind to worry about his sister or son. He only cared about himself, as he always had.

In their cabin, Catherine and Alex sat waiting for what they believed was the end. They had felt the forward motion of the ship stop and had assumed that they had reached the place where Avery was going to carry out his dastardly plan. Catherine sat on the edge of the bunk, cradling Alex on her lap. She thought of Gerald, and a deep, abiding sadness filled her as she realized she would probably never see him again. Alex was all she had now, and she clung to him, fearful of a future that would separate them.

Catherine had had to explain what was about to happen to her nephew. The confrontation with Avery had made it necessary for her to tell him what she believed to be the truth. Alex had been brave in his response to her explanation, but she knew it was only because he was still much too young to understand what was really about to happen to them.

"Aunt Catherine?" Alex said her name softly as he nestled against her breast.

"Yes, darling?" she answered softly, pressing a gentle kiss to the top of his head. Her heart was aching at the thought of his being taken from her and subjected to a kind of treatment she couldn't even begin to imagine. He was an innocent and she loved him so. Catherine realized then what she'd really known all along. She would sacrifice her own life, if necessary, to keep the boy safe from harm.

"Will we see my father again?"

"I imagine so. Why?" His question puzzled her.

"I was just hoping we wouldn't have to. I know he likes to hurt you and make you sad, and I don't want us to see him any more."

She was amazed by his defense of her, and it only deepened the love she felt for him. "He hurts everyone, Alex. He's a cruel man. Will you promise me something?" She lightened her tone a little to try to ease the seriousness of the moment.

"What?" He lifted his head to gaze up at her with adoring eyes.

"When you grow up to be a fine, strong man, I want you to remember what an ugly person your father was and make sure not to be anything like him."

"I don't understand. He's not ugly . . ." Alex's expression turned troubled.

"Not on the outside, sweetheart, but inside, where it really counts. We all have the choice to be either good or bad. Some people, like your father, choose to be bad. It's important, then, that we learn not to make the same choices they did. Do you understand now?"

Alex nodded with all the solemnity possible for a seven-year-old faced with a grave problem. "I promise."

"Good." Catherine held him to her heart. "I know you're going to be a wonderful man. You know, your grandfather can hardly wait for you to get old enough to help him with all the estates."

"I'm going to do it, too," he answered happily.

"Grandfather and I will have a good time taking care of everything. You'll see. When I grow up, I'm going to be as good a duke as he is."

"I'm sure you will." She encouraged his daydreams, knowing how soon they would all be tragically destroyed.

"But Aunt Catherine . . ."

He sounded suddenly so unhappy that she wondered what was bothering him. "What, darling?" She kept a protective arm around him, loving the feel of his soft warm body snuggled against her.

"I just wish I'd had time to get my boat . . ." he sighed.

Catherine choked back a cry of misery at his loss. She bit her lip to keep her tears from falling. "Well, I'm sure it will be right there waiting for you when we get home."

Alex thought for a moment. "You're right." He mustered a smile for her. "Grandfather will take care of it for me . . . Aunt Catherine, do you think Grandfather's all right. I'm worried about him."

"I'm sure he's fine, and if I know him, he's busy looking for us right now. He loves us and he won't stop searching until he finds us."

"I sure hope he finds us soon. I miss him."

"I miss him, too," she replied, heavy at heart.

They were sitting there, clasped in each other's arms when they heard the first shot.

"What was that?" Alex asked, pulling away from her, his eyes big and round with worry.

"It was a gunshot . . ."

"A gunshot? Why would anyone be shooting at us?"

"I don't know. I . . ." All the color drained from Catherine's face as she heard the thunder of footsteps resounding on the deck overhead, more shots being fired, and the muted screams of men being murdered

71

up on deck. She'd heard enough tales to know what that meant. *Pirates! They were under attack by pirates!*

Muhammed loved the first moments of an attack when the boats came together, the grappling hooks were thrown, and they swung aboard to claim the other ship as their own. He enjoyed seeing the looks of terror on the faces of the sailors they were about to enslave, and he particularly enjoyed wresting control of the vessel from its captain. It gave him a feeling of great power to know they could strike such fear in the hearts of men. It was good to know that stories of their viciousness had spread around the world far and wide. Sometimes the rumors were enough to bring full capitulation without a struggle. This, however, was not one of those times.

As Muhammed and Selim led the way onto the deck of the *Dolphin*, pistols and scimitars in hand, a few foolish sailors under Black's command disobeyed his order to submit without a fight. They drew their own pistols and fired at the mob of oncoming corsairs, killing two of Muhammed's men before they themselves were cut down, decapitated by swift, terrible blows from the scimitars of the pirate captain and his second-in-command. The rest of the crew of the *Dolphin* trembled in uncertainty, not knowing if they would live or die at the hands of the gruesome invaders.

Muhammed ordered his men to seize the ship. With Selim in the lead, some of the men swarmed over the deck and down the companionways to search out the hold and the cabins for valuables. Others under Muhammed's watchful gaze took charge of captured sailors, chaining them and then stripping them of all personal goods. Any items they could take from the crew from shoes to weapons were important to the

72

pirates, for it was the only booty they would personally be allowed to keep at this time. All the other riches on board had to be carefully tallied and then a substantial percent offered in tribute to the dey of Algiers when they returned home. Only after the ruler had been paid would the pirate crew receive any further reward for their bloodthirsty efforts.

While Muhammed commanded on deck, Selim was growing furious belowdecks. It had angered and surprised him to find that there was no rich cargo in the hold. He dreaded bringing the news to Muhammed and was wondering about it when he discovered the locked door to Catherine and Alex's stateroom. He shot an evil smile at his men and then broke down the door in one smooth, violent move.

Catherine screamed. She hadn't meant to, but the sight of the pirate, his scimitar still glistening with the blood of the slain sailor, terrorized her. She and Alex hung on to each other for dear life.

"Ah . . . what have we here?" Selim joked with his men. "We were worried that there was no treasure on board, but perhaps we were looking for the wrong *kind* of treasure, eh, men?"

A hearty murmur of agreement came from the corsairs who crowded behind him trying to get a look at the woman.

Alex could hardly believe what was happening. He'd read so much about pirates and now here he was, face-to-face with the men he'd alternately admired and feared. He wasn't sure how to react until they spoke of their intentions.

"I think Muhammed *Reis* will be glad when he sees this one. Seize her and bring her up on deck!"

As one of the men moved to grab Catherine, Alex erupted, throwing himself from her arms to stand before the pirates without fear. "No! You can't have her."

"Hush, Alex . . ." Catherine pleaded, trying to shut him up before he got himself killed.

"Well, well, and what is this now? A little rooster with more courage than the entire crew?" Selim chuckled, gazing down at the small boy who would dare defy them. It would have been simple to kill him, but he was a man who admired bravery. This one would grow to be a fine man someday—if he lived that long. "Bring them both. We will give them to Muhammed *Reis.*"

One of the pirates snatched Alex up and, carrying him easily under his arm, he hauled the kicking, yelling boy away. Catherine followed after them, trembling in terror as she was herded up the companionway and onto the deck. When they emerged outside, she saw the carnage that had been wreaked there and felt a surge of nausea. Her gaze swept anxiously over the deck searching for some sign of Avery, but he was nowhere around. She was wondering where he was when she was brought to stand with Alex before Muhammed.

Having seen the two headless bodies littering the deck, Alex was even more scared now, but he refused to show his fear to the pirates. He stood stiffly at Catherine's side, his gaze level and unwavering as he stared up at the pirate captain.

"She and the boy were the only prizes on board, Muhammed *Reis,*" Selim told him.

"Ah, but she's a prize of great worth," the pirate captain agreed, his gaze traveling over Catherine's pale hair and slender, enticing curves with insulting familiarity. He gave Alex only a cursory glance. "Why have you bothered with the boy?"

"He's a brave little fellow. He would defend the woman, and I found his fearlessness amusing," Selim explained.

Muhammed then turned his piercing gaze on the boy with more interest. He studied him for a moment, then directed, "Take them both to my cabin. I think this is one prize the dey needn't know about."

Selim knew a moment of worry at his ploy. It was not wise to withhold anything from the dey, and trepidation filled him at the thought of defying the ruler. Malik el Mansour hadn't gotten to be the dey of Algiers by allowing his men to slight him in tribute. He was a proud and very powerful master who had spies everywhere. Still, Selim knew better than to counter any order given by Muhammed in front of his crew. He rushed to do his captain's bidding, delivering the woman and child to the privacy of his cabin. Later, when they were alone, he would question his wisdom in keeping her for his own. Beautiful though she was, she wasn't worth his life, and Malik would surely see Muhammed dead if he dared try to cheat him of his treasure.

As some of Selim's men continued to scour the *Dolphin* for additional wealth, they broke into Avery's cabin and began tearing the room apart. Inside the trunk where he'd hidden himself, Avery sniveled with fear. His hands were shaking and he was drenched in a cold sweat. He could hear the barbarians rummaging through everything, and he prayed desperately to be spared the end he was sure to come. When the lid to the trunk was thrown open and his cowardly hiding place revealed, he heard them laughing and knew true terror.

"Don't kill me!" he cried, trying to get to his feet.

"He begs for mercy, and we have not even threatened him yet," one of the pirates sneered.

"Perhaps we should see what he is trying to hide . . ."

Cruel, hard hands dragged him from the trunk and stripped him of his jewelry and clothes, leaving him standing before them barefoot and clad only in his trousers.

"Please don't hurt me. Please don't . . ." Tears of

humiliation poured down his cheeks as he sobbed and begged for his life. Groveling before them, he pleaded for mercy.

After a few minutes, one of the corsairs grew bored with his begging and silenced him with a single, murderous blow from his sword. The others stared dispassionately at the mutilated body of the dead Englishman, then turned and left the cabin. They felt no remorse over the murder. The man had been less than a woman and had deserved to die.

Chapter Six

Catherine and Alex were taken to Muhammed's spartanly furnished cabin and locked inside. Judging pirates by the stories he and his grandfather had read, Alex had thought the raiders of the high seas exciting, but after seeing the death and destruction they'd wreaked on board the *Dolphin*, he knew now that they were very dangerous, deadly men.

"Aunt Catherine, what do you think they're going to do to us?" He gazed up at her trustingly. In his heart, he believed that as long as they were together, they would be all right.

Catherine had a very good idea what fate had in store for her. A chill frissoned down her spine as she thought of the look the pirate had given her before sending them here to his cabin. She longed for Gerald to save her, but knew it was foolish to even consider it, just as it was foolish to even think that Avery might come to their aid. She had no one but herself to rely on now. It was up to her to make sure they survived and returned home safely.

"I don't know, Alex," she lied stoutheartedly. "I've heard that sometimes captives are ransomed back to their relatives in England. So once Father finds out where we are, he'll send the money for us."

Alex looked up at her, his expression nothing short of courageous. "We're really kind of lucky that the pirates took us, aren't we, Aunt Catherine?"

His statement surprised her. "What do you mean?"

"At least this way, we'll get back home to Grandfather."

Alex was so innocent in the ways of the world that Catherine couldn't stop the impulse to kneel down, gather him close, and give him a big hug and kiss. "You're absolutely right, and this way it looks like we'll get to stay together, too."

"Good. I want to stay with you. I don't ever want us to be apart."

"I want to stay with you, too, and I'll do everything I can to make sure we do," Catherine promised with all her heart.

Once the *Dolphin* was completely under their control, Muhammed left a skeleton crew on board to sail her, and then returned with Selim to his own ship. He was looking forward to having the woman captive all to himself, but Selim's private warning gave him pause.

"You know I would never question your judgment in any matter, Muhammed *Reis,* but I must speak out this time to caution you."

"What is it?" he demanded, his thoughts centered on the beautiful woman waiting in his cabin.

"The woman—"

"What about her?"

"I know you want her for your own, but have you considered what might happen if you do take her?" Selim remained quiet for a moment to let the full impact of his words sink in. "You know how powerful

78

Malik is. And you know he has men everywhere, watching. Wouldn't it be more prudent to wait until after we have seen him and shared what we have with him to claim her as yours?"

Muhammed looked thoughtful. Selim's words, while not welcome, were not unwise. Malik was truly a formidable foe. He'd known that for all the years he'd been trying to defeat him and take his place as dey of Algiers. The man's power was widespread and his supporters many. If just one person told Malik that he was withholding a captured prize from him, he could be killed on the spot. "Perhaps you are right. I will not take the woman now, though I am sorely tempted to have her. If Malik does not ask about her when we pay our tribute, I will know she is mine to do with as I please."

"As always you have shown what a shrewd man you are. I'm sure that one day your dream of ruling Algiers will be realized."

Muhammed smiled at Selim. "Come, let's go below. Let's make sure she is worth the risk of deceiving Malik. I would not test his good humor over a valueless female."

The two men went down the companionway to his cabin and entered to find Catherine and Alex standing by the porthole watching the activities on the *Dolphin*. At the sound of the door opening, Catherine and Alex both turned, startled, to face their captors.

"What is your name, woman?" Muhammed demanded as he studied her. She was dirty and unkempt now, but he knew once she was washed, perfumed, and dressed appropriately, she would be a glorious enhancement to any man's harem. There was no doubt in his mind that she was a valuable prize. He wanted her, and he would do whatever he had to to keep her.

"I am Catherine Wakefield, daughter of the Duke of

Huntington, and this is Alexander Wakefield, grandson of the duke," she replied with dignity. "If it's money you're after, I'm sure my father will pay handsomely to have us back."

The pirate grunted his satisfaction with the news. Now he knew for sure that he wouldn't part with her. First, he would have his fill of her, and then, he would sell her back to her English family for an outrageous amount. The arrangement pleased him very much. All he had to do was get her past Malik. He said a silent prayer to Allah that he might find success in this endeavor.

"Selim, take her and the boy to the forward cabin and lock them there. You will be responsible for them until we reach port."

Catherine had been bracing herself for the worst, and she almost collapsed in relief when he gave the order for them to be taken away together. She said nothing as they walked from his cabin, although she was certain her expression must have reflected her feelings.

Muhammed laughed silently to himself as Selim ushered them from the cabin. "Do not think I do not desire you, my pretty one. The day will come very soon, when you will be mine . . ."

Malik el Mansour, the brave and fearless thirty-year-old dey of Algiers, listened attentively to the tale of betrayal his man, Faid, brought him. His golden eyes narrowed thoughtfully as he considered his informant's story of how his long-time rival, Muhammed Ibn Abbas, who had just arrived in port and was about to pay his tribute, was trying to withhold a lovely woman captive and her child from him. Rumor had it that the woman was of exquisite beauty and poise, fit to grace any man's bed and that she had very rich relatives who would pay much money to get her and the boy back. Malik knew the female had to be exceptional for Muhammed to take such a chance in holding her back from him. He smiled cynically to himself as he thought of the pleasure he was going to take in embarrassing and humbling the other man.

"What would you have me do, Malik *Dey?*" Faid asked, ready even to commit murder for his leader.

"Nothing," he answered slowly. "Maintain your silence. I will deal with Muhammed myself."

"Yes, Your Majesty." Faid bowed and left the small audience chamber.

Alone now, Malik stood and paced the room. He was a tall, black-haired, black-bearded man, broad of shoulder and chest, whose physical strength and wisdom were legendary. He was no ordinary man. It had taken a very capable, very strong leader to accomplish what he'd accomplished so far in his seven years of ruling Algiers. He was admired by many and hated by a few. Those few enemies were a savage group.

The Barbary State of Algiers was a treacherous, dangerous place to live, especially for its ruler. Authority there was gained through intrigue and power, and there were always those just waiting for the opportunity to bring the current ruler down. So it was with Muhammed and Malik. Muhammed had been trying to wrest Malik's power from him ever since he'd become the dey. He had failed in his every attempt due to Malik's caution and his legion of faithful followers. Muhammed's setbacks had not discouraged him, though. He'd become even more determined to keep trying.

As Malik considered the situation now, he knew it would be best if he let the other man humiliate himself.

He found he was actually looking forward to Muhammed's audience. Pleased with his decision, he went off to his private chambers to dress. It would not do to look less than his most imposing when facing his rival.

It was a little over an hour later when Malik was finally ready for the meeting. He was a man of simple tastes, not given to gaudy dress, and the simplicity of the style of clothes he favored only served to emphasize his aura of manliness and power. He wore a white turban and a simple yet elegant white djellaba over loose-fitting pantaloons. At his waist, a gold belt cinched the tunic-like robe, and his scabbard held his scimitar with its golden, bejeweled hilt. He looked every inch the supreme leader as he awaited the pirate's arrival at the palace in the most impressive of his audience chambers.

"Malik *Dey,* Muhammed Ibn Abbas is here," Faid announced soberly a few minutes later.

"Bring him to me."

Within moments, the arrogant pirate entered the room and bowed low to him.

"Greetings, Malik *Dey.* I have come to offer my tribute," Muhammed told him, feeling quite confident that this audience would soon be over and the young woman he'd left locked up on his ship would be his. He had auctioned off the *Dolphin* and its contents for a goodly sum as soon as they'd reached port, and he was now prepared to offer Malik a full twelve percent of the money gained from the sale along with a number of the crew for his share of their booty.

"What have you brought me this time, Muhammed? Vast riches from another successful journey?" Malik asked benignly. He was careful to keep his expression reflecting only mild curiosity.

"Of course. Have you ever known me to be less than successful on any of my voyages?" he boasted. Then, turning, he called out, "Selim! Come and bring our gifts to our dey!"

Selim ushered in ten of the *Dolphin*'s crew chained together at the ankles, along with a huge wooden chest holding the money from the auction.

"It is with my greatest pleasure that I offer these gifts to you," Muhammed said magnanimously.

Malik rose and inspected the prizes the pirate had bestowed upon him. "I thank you for your tribute, Muhammed," he said evenly, then paused before adding, "But what of the woman and the child?" He watched with interest as the pirate *reis* blanched, then struggled to mask his surprise at his knowledge.

"I had saved the best for last, of course," Muhammed replied quickly. He glanced at Selim as he ordered tersely, "Have the woman and the child brought here immediately."

"As you wish."

Though Catherine had known the reprieve they'd been given was a temporary one, she'd weathered the storm of uncertainty during the voyage with relative calm. She'd passed the endless hours of travel playing games with Alex and trying to keep him entertained. But when they'd made port at Algiers, her fears had soared once again. The future she'd dreaded had arrived. There could be no ignoring it any longer.

When Selim came for them so unexpectedly, Catherine managed to maintain a stoic, dignified air in spite of her terror.

"Here," Selim said sharply, tossing a length of white cotton cloth to her. "Cover your hair and the lower half of your face."

She did as she was told without comment, keeping Alex close by her side. She was not about to let him be

83

taken from her without a fight.

"Let's go," the pirate directed, opening the cabin door for them and standing back to let them pass.

"Where are you taking us?"

"You will see soon enough, woman. Follow me." He headed up the companionway and across the deck to the ladder which led down to the small rowboat. They descended to the skiff, and he quickly and efficiently started to row them toward shore.

As they crossed the bay, Catherine stared at the whitewashed jumble of buildings that made up this foreign city, and she grew more and more nervous. "Has word been sent to my father that we're here?"

Selim gave her a cold look to silence her. "That is none of your concern, woman."

Catherine said no more. She caught sight of the *Dolphin* anchored there in the bay, too. Its decks were deserted except for a few pirates who'd been left on board as guards, and Catherine found herself wondering what had happened to Avery. As quickly as the thought came, she dismissed it. The man she'd once claimed as a brother no longer held any part of her affections. He was lower than the pirates who held Alex and her captive, and she was determined never to think of him again. The niggling worry that he might be ransomed back first troubled her, though. She wondered what would happen if he made it back to England before they did, and, what he would tell their father about them. The thought was almost as frightening as the uncertainty of the future she was facing right now.

Selim docked the small boat with expert ease and then hustled them through the crowded streets of Algiers. The streets were narrow and stifling, filled with men and women searching out the best bargains from the peddlers whose shops opened onto the thoroughfares. Camels and donkeys added to the smell and congestion, and more than once they'd all had to dodge a fast-moving animal or risk being run down. Catherine and Alex followed the corsair closely, ever mindful not to fall too far behind.

Selim wasted no time looking around the city. There was only one thing on his mind, and that was delivering the woman and child to the palace as quickly as possible. He was curious about how the ruler had found out about them, but then shrugged off his interest. Malik was the dey. He knew everything that went on. Hurrying on along, Selim glanced back to make sure the woman and boy were staying with him. It wouldn't do to lose them now.

The dey's palace stood on a low rise near the center of town. A magnificent whitewashed, thick-walled stone structure, it glistened brilliantly in the afternoon sun. Catherine and Alex were both impressed by the majestic sight of it. After they passed through the arched entranceway in the high, protective outer wall, they crossed a lush courtyard and finally entered the main building. They stared in wonder at the opulence of the palace. The cool shadows of the marble-floored entry hall contrasted sharply with the blinding sunlight and oppressive heat in the streets. Arched windows with crisscrossed iron grating admitted only a minimum of light while allowing whatever cool breeze there might be to pass through. Beautiful, ornately designed tapestries adorned the walls, and a variety of tropical flowering plants filled the room with rich color. They were a bit startled when a man emerged soundlessly from the shadows to speak to Selim.

"The dey is waiting for you," he said simply; and, at Selim's nod of acknowledgment, he moved off motioning for them to follow.

Catherine wondered who this "dey" was and why

they had been brought here. She didn't want to let her hopes get the best of her, but deep down inside she was hoping that their relationship to the Duke of Huntington had merited them special attention and a quicker return home.

"Where are we?" Alex whispered as he tugged nervously at her sleeve.

"I'm not sure, sweetheart, but I have a feeling we're going to find out real soon." She tried to sound confident and relaxed, but as she took his small hand in hers, she couldn't help but grip it a little too tightly.

"This way," the pirate ordered brusquely. They did as they were told and were led to the entryway of a larger room. They waited outside until they heard the man who had greeted them announce their presence to someone as yet unseen within. When they went into the chamber, Catherine was taken aback by the sight of the person sitting on a plush sofa at the front of the room. Arrayed all in white, he looked a splendid specimen of a man, and had she been less troubled, she would have thought him handsome, with his strong physique, dark hair, and golden eyes. As it was, she was too frightened to notice. She remained silent and wary as she listened to the dialogue between the pirate captain and this other man, who was obviously the dey.

"This is the woman and child, Your Majesty," Muhammed said graciously. "If you would like them, they are yours." It took all of his willpower not to say anything more, and he gritted his teeth in silence as he waited for Malik's reply.

Malik stared at the woman and the child with open interest. He studied Alex first and thought him a handsome, healthy-looking youth despite his dirty appearance. His gaze slid next to the woman, who his informer had told him was a prize of great value. The gown she wore was filthy and wrinkled. The length of clean, white cloth she was wearing as a haik hid all but her eyes. And oh, what eyes they were, the color of the Mediterranean on a sunny day—a deep, fathomless, blue-green. He wondered at the color of her hair and tried to picture the true shade.

"Remove the haik," he commanded, gesturing toward her.

Catherine was puzzled for a moment at the meaning of the word, but then realized he wanted her to take off the headcovering the pirate had insisted she wear. She did as he ordered.

Malik was a man of the world. He had dearly loved his first wife, Lila, the mother of his two children, who had died giving birth to his youngest child, his daughter, Talitha. Since her death, he had had many women, but never had any single female left him feeling as he felt now when this captive discarded the haik and revealed to him the glorious tumble of her molten-gold hair. It seemed he had suffered a physical blow to the chest, so difficult was it for him to breathe.

Malik's gaze was riveted on her. Even as unwashed and unkempt as she was, he thought the woman beautiful. He felt a heated tightening in his loins, and suddenly the thought of the miserable Muhammed touching her was unthinkable. Malik made his decision quickly. She would be his.

Glancing at Alex once more, Malik saw the resemblance between woman and child and wondered briefly about the husband she must have left behind. A sting of jealousy darted through him. Disliking the emotion, he denied it, pushing it away. A husband of the Christian faith meant less than nothing. He was the dey, and he wanted her. That was all that was important. His wishes were of primary concern. Many existed just to please him, and this female would be added to their number. Of the boy, he was not so sure.

What did he need the child for?

"You have done well indeed, Muhammed. I will take the woman as my due," he nodded toward Catherine and Alex.

"As you will, Malik *Dey*." Muhammed bowed low, gnashing his teeth in fury and frustration as he did so.

Catherine had suffered through the degrading kidnapping arranged by her brother, then this pirate's capture, and now the arrogant lout's insolent stare without balking, but when they started talking about her as if she were deaf and dumb, a trinket to be owned and traded by them at their will, she grew outraged. Her anger, fueled by her worry over Alex's safety, forced her to the breaking point. She wouldn't tolerate it any longer, no matter what it cost her, for, after all, what would her own life be worth if she lost Alex?

"And what of *my will?*" Catherine demanded, stepping forward in a fury, her eyes darkening to deep green as the storm of her temper erupted.

For a moment, Malik was struck speechless by this outburst from a mere female. "Your will?" he repeated with a sardonic lift of an eyebrow.

"I would think that I should have some say in what happens to me. I am not a horse to be traded or a piece of meat to be sold at the market. I am Catherine Wakefield, daughter of the Duke of Huntington, and this is Alexander Wakefield, his grandson! I will not stand for us to be treated this way."

Malik gazed at her for another moment, then threw back his head and gave a hearty laugh. He had never been so challenged by so magnificent a woman before, and he found himself intrigued by her spirit. She was going to be a handful to tame, but them, he'd always enjoyed a challenge. "By Allah, Muhammed, I fear I may have the last regret over what is done."

"Would you like to change your mind, Your

Majesty?" the corsair asked hopefully.

Catherine's breath caught in her throat, and she had to clasp her trembling hands together so neither man would know of her inner turmoil as she waited to hear their decision.

"No," Malik answered firmly. "She will remain."

Again, Muhammed had been thwarted. "You want the boy, as well?"

Malik saw the way Catherine kept the child protectively at her side and sensed her motherly worry for her son's safety might have been the cause of her outburst. "Yes," he answered. "The child will stay." Ever perceptive, he noticed the momentary look of joy that passed over her perfect features, and he was pleased to find that his intuition had been right again.

"Then I will take my leave of you." Muhammed retreated from the room with Selim at his heels, hating Malik more passionately in that moment than he ever had before. He had wanted the Englishwoman for his own, and he vowed someday, somehow, to make the dey suffer for taking her from him.

Malik was pleased with the way things had turned out, but when he faced Catherine once more, his expression was stern.

"I will not tolerate another outburst from you, Catherine Wakefield. Remember that," he spoke coldly, without feeling, wanting to let her know from the start that he was her master.

Catherine stayed quiet now that she was assured that Alex would be with her. She felt a little victorious having won that much.

"I see you do know how to control your tongue," he taunted, testing her. "That is good. It is an important trait in a woman." He clapped his hands twice and a servant appeared in the doorway. "Take the woman to the harem and see that she is taken care of."

Catherine paled. She had heard whispered stories about harems before . . . about how Arab men kept their women locked up there and only let them out when they needed. She went cold inside and would have cried out for Gerald if she hadn't had such a determined grip on herself. Again, she reminded herself that her own personal safety meant nothing. Alex was the innocent and his protection was foremost on her mind. She was just about to risk Malik's displeasure and ask him about the boy, when the servant spoke up.

"Yes, Malik *Dey*. And the child?"

"Take him to the boys' quarters."

"Yes, Your Majesty." He directed Catherine and Alex from the room.

Malik watched as Catherine walked away, and he couldn't help but admire the proud way she carried herself. She was certainly a woman worthy of his affections. As he watched the gentle sway of her hips in fascination, he reminded himself that Faid should be handsomely rewarded for the information he'd brought him about her.

Chapter Seven

Edward sat on the edge of his bed in his London townhouse staring morosely down at the toy boat he held carefully on his lap. He had kept the *Scimitar* with him ever since Alexander's disappearance, for he was unable to part with this one last, cherished reminder of his grandson.

Edward had always considered himself a man of sharp intellect and steady nerve, but the four endless, miserable weeks that had passed since the ransom had been paid without the return of Catherine and Alexander had rendered him overwrought. His frustration and his misery were complete. There was nothing left for him to do; nowhere left for him to search; no one left to question. He felt completely and utterly helpless. He could do absolutely nothing to help his beautiful daughter and his precious grandson. Holding the toy boat close, he got up and strode to the window to look out at the rain-drenched street below.

Though Gerald had been a tremendous help to Edward during this time, even he had begun to lose heart as the weeks had passed and there had been no word of Catherine and Alex. Edward realized that the young man's hope of ever seeing his fiancée again was fading, and it saddened him. The younger man's visits had become less and less frequent as the news had become bleaker. Until something turned up, there was little left for either of them to say.

Edward ran a weary hand over his bloodshot eyes. Even though he understood young Ratcliff's situation, he was determined himself not to let his own faith in their ultimate return die. Still, the pain of not knowing was taking its toll. He had given up eating, having absolutely no taste for food, and had begun to indulge himself with potent Irish whiskey. The powerful liquor gave him the strength he needed to face each new and empty day, but it had done little to ease the ache in his pain-filled heart. His weight had dropped and his eyes bore a haunted look that only Catherine's and Alexander's presence could banish.

Edward turned away from the window, frowning. He had received a desperate note from Vivienne early in the day requesting an urgent meeting with him, and he was waiting now for her to arrive. A part of him held out a slim hope that she might have some news, but the logical side of him cautioned against getting too encouraged. If his own highly skilled men hadn't been able to find out anything about the kidnapping, why did he think hers might have?

Edward had firmly believed that Avery and Vivienne were responsible for the whole ordeal, but when his son had unexpectedly disappeared leaving his wife behind, a seed of doubt had been planted. Over the last few weeks, Edward had wondered if he could have been mistaken. He'd had his investigators check to make sure that it wasn't a contrived disappearance to gain his favor, but their report had convinced him that his son might indeed have been a victim of foul play. Was it possible that Avery hadn't set up the kidnapping and ransom demand? Was it possible that he had gone to Catherine and Alexander's rescue, and the same terrible fate had befallen him? Avery in the guise of hero didn't seem realistic, but until Edward could prove positively one way or the other, he wasn't sure just what to think. A knock at the bedroom door interrupted his troubled thoughts.

"Yes? What is it?"

"Your Grace, Lady Vivienne has arrived and is waiting for you in the front sitting room," Dalton informed him as he entered.

"Tell her I'll be right down," Edward responded and he delayed a moment longer to muster enough control to speak with the woman who had borne Alexander. He placed the *Scimitar* carefully on the table beside the bed and went directly to the sitting room to greet her.

Vivienne was waiting anxiously for her audience with the duke. She had been planning this encounter ever since she'd become convinced that Avery would not return. Vivienne didn't know what had gone awry with her husband's carefully laid plans, but she did know something awful must have happened to him. Her sources had told her that he'd boarded the ship and that it had sailed on schedule. Beyond that there was no information. She could only speculate about what had happened once they were at sea, but she believed firmly that Avery would have returned by now if he could have. He loved her madly. Only some unspeakable fate could have kept him from her.

The thought of Avery's demise annoyed Vivienne. Without him, all the plans she'd made to ensure their ascent to the title were pointless. Without Avery, her entire life's goal was forfeit. She could never become the duchess. Still, as she mourned her lost position in society, the ransom money soothed her, and if she could convince the duke that she was in dire financial straits without her husband and needed his support in her widowhood, things might work out quite well. The duke just might feel sorry for her and come across with some extra funds to help her through these troubled times. She was, after all, still his daughter-in-law, and Avery's unexplained absence provided her with the proof she needed to convince him that she had not been involved in the kidnappings. Vivienne heard footsteps and glanced up as Edward came through the door.

"Hello, Vivienne," he greeted her with cool restraint.

"Your Grace, thank you so much for seeing me." Vivienne returned humbly. "I wasn't sure you would after our last encounter, but things have changed so drastically that I had to come to you." Tears glistened in Vivienne's beautiful eyes, and she looked every inch the helpless female. It had taken her nearly an hour of practice before her vanity mirror to perfect this expression, and she was rather proud of the results of her efforts. "You know that Avery is missing . . . that he disappeared the same week as Catherine and Alexander while he was out looking for them?"

Edward nodded slowly. "I was aware of this, yes."

"Well, since the day he vanished I've heard nothing from him . . . absolutely nothing. There's been no demand for money or any other kind of contact." Even in her distress, Vivienne looked radiantly lovely.

"Then you bring no news of any of them?"

"Not a word," she told him, adding just the right touch of desperation to her voice. "The last place Avery was searching for them was on the docks. I had the men we'd hired earlier check out the area thoroughly, but every lead they followed up turned out to be a dead end."

"I understand," he replied. "My own investigations told the same story."

Vivienne affected innocent distress. She and Avery had both known that the duke would stop at nothing to find Catherine and the boy. She was glad now that they'd taken such great care in covering their own trail of deception. "You were investigating?" she asked, stricken. "Then you really did believe . . . Oh, I'd better go. I'm sorry for having bothered you . . . I'll manage somehow . . ."

"Vivienne . . ." Edward said her name more gently. His doubts about her involvement were growing ever stronger. "Wait. Tell me why you've come."

She had been starting for the door when he'd spoken, and she hesitated in her exit to make it look as if she'd really planned to leave. She glanced strategically back over her shoulder at him, letting her tear-stained face tell him just how great was the agony she was suffering. "I know what you must think of us . . . of me . . . but you're wrong, Your Grace," she said. "We didn't kidnap Catherine and Alexander. I swear to you, we didn't do it!" *We didn't, some hired men did,* she told herself.

Edward sighed, thoroughly convinced at last by the depth of her heartrending emotion. "I believe you, Vivienne, and I apologize for my cruelty that day. I was an angry, desperate man." He let his gaze rest upon her. He'd never cared for her, had resented Avery's marriage to her, but he could certainly understand her misery. He was not a hard-hearted man; he was a gentleman of honor. He couldn't allow Vivienne to suffer.

"I'm alone in the world now, Your Grace," she told him, her heart pounding. This was the true test of her thespian skills. Would he believe her?

Edward realized sadly that this woman was the closest thing to family he had left except for a few, very distant cousins with whom he had little or no regular contact. He would have to stand beside her in spite of their past differences. "You're not alone, Vivienne. You're my daughter-in-law. I'll take care of everything."

Vivienne was hard put to keep the excitement she was feeling from showing on her face. It had worked! He was going to take care of her! Maybe, just maybe, it had been worth losing Avery to gain the duke's favor.

Catherine sat on a stone bench beside the fountain at the center of the lush, flowering garden watching the water as Almira, the heavyset servant woman who'd been assigned to take care of her needs when she'd come to the harem three days before, brushed out her hair. Had it not been for her fairness, Catherine might have passed for one of the other Arabic women in the women's quarters. She was barefoot and wearing a loose-fitting, turquoise satin brocade underdress with a drape of gold-and-red striped satin over it. She looked completely serene as she stared at the splashing, crystalline waters, but inwardly she was caught up in an emotional turmoil. When she'd first arrived there, her gown and underthings had been taken from her. In their stead, she'd been given the traditional garments of the Barbary women to wear, but she did not like them. The flowing garments that were wrapped around her seemed foreign and left her feeling vulnerable. She'd demanded her dress back, but Almira had refused, telling her that the gown had been ruined and could not be repaired. Catherine hadn't believed her, but there had been little she could do about it, for she was being held a virtual prisoner in the harem.

Restrictions had been put upon her movements and she was confined there, just as Malik's other women were. Catherine supposed that if she had to consider herself still a captive she was glad to be a captive in a gilded cage, for the harem itself was most pleasant. The rooms were large, airy, and spacious, the accommodations luxurious. The gardens were magnificent and there were fountains and reflecting pools in abundance. Since her arrival, she had been pampered and spoiled, bathed and perfumed.

Catherine almost enjoyed herself during the last few days, except for the haunting knowledge of the dey's unseen presence and power hovering over her. She had no idea what her future held. Had the Algerian ruler already sent word to her father? Would the ransom be paid soon so they could go home or did he have another fate in store for them . . . for her? Worst of all, she still worried that her brother might be ransomed back by Muhammed before them. She prayed desperately that the duke received word about them quickly and that they would be returned home as soon as possible. She missed Huntington House, her father, and most of all Gerald . . . her love.

The very first day there, she'd considered escape, but logic and practicality had asserted itself. With Alex living in an area separate from hers and the palace so vast that she had no idea where his room was located, it would have been folly to try. Not to mention the fact that there were guards everywhere, and even if she did manage to get them out, she would still have been an Englishwoman alone in Algiers with a small child. Painfully, she'd admitted to herself that she was going to have to wait for her father to pay the ransom. There was no other way.

Malik had sent permission for her to have a one-hour visit with Alex each day, and she was grateful for that. The fact that the dey allowed them time together eased her worries a little and made him seem less threatening. For his part, Alex seemed to be adapting rather well to his new surroundings, though he did ask her every day if she'd heard from his grandfather yet. As stifling as their existence now was, it was far better than the fate Avery had had planned for them.

"You are very beautiful," the servant woman remarked, interrupting her thoughts as she gave Catherine's shining cascade of curls another stroke with the brush.

"Thank you, Almira," she returned without enthusiasm. She was so upset that she not feel pretty at all.

Almira heard the subtle misery in her tone. "You are very fortunate, you know," she chided softly.

"I hardly think so," Catherine replied a bit sarcastically. "If I were fortunate, I'd still be in England."

"Oh, but you are!" Almira insisted, ignoring her reference to her home. "The others . . ." She jerked her head toward the courtyard area where Malik's three wives and several pretty concubines had gathered. "They all envy you, you know . . . and so do I."

"Envy me? Whatever for?"

"Malik has requested that you join him for his evening meal tonight," she said knowingly, her eyes aglow at the thought.

"They have nothing to envy," Catherine dismissed. "Haven't you told them that I love another and only want to leave here?"

Almira lifted her shoulders in an expressive gesture. "I told them, but they don't believe me. They think you are a liar."

Catherine was shocked, and she cast a quick glance

toward the group of women only to find their eyes upon her and their expressions less than friendly. She sighed. "I'm no threat to them. Why do they dislike me so?"

"Jealousy is a way of life here. They all want to be Malik's favorite, but since Lila died, he hasn't shown any one particular woman special attention."

"Who was Lila?" Catherine couldn't help but ask, her curiosity aroused.

"She was his first wife, and the one woman it is said he truly loved. She bore him his two children, Hasim, the oldest, a son, and Talitha, a little girl. It was a great tragedy when she died giving birth to Talitha three years ago." Almira paused, her eyes misting with tears as she remembered the gentle but spirited Lila. She then added with venom, spitting out the words, "The others didn't think so. They all wanted to take her place and were glad she was dead."

"How horrible!"

"We must be careful. Especially if he begins to show preference to you . . ."

"You don't have to worry about that. I'm not interested. The others are welcome to him."

Almira hid a smile as she listened to Catherine's words. She had been in Malik's household for many years now, and she had watched him from afar all that time. She firmly believed that the woman hadn't been born who could resist him. But then again, the dey had never had a woman like Catherine in his harem before.

"Come, we'd better go back to your rooms now and finish getting you ready. He will be sending for you soon," she encouraged.

As they left the gardens, Catherine was torn between looking forward to seeing Malik that night so she could find out if her father had been contacted and dread over what he might be expecting from her. She wanted Gerald, and no one else. She could hardly wait until this nightmare was over and they could be married.

"Here . . . wear this tonight," Almira held up a flowing, white silken garment when they returned to her bedchamber.

"I would prefer something less revealing," she said primly.

"You will look lovely in this."

"I'll wear what I have on."

"That will not please Malik since it is a day habit." Almira refused to give in to her wishes. "You will wear this. It is for evening," Almira carefully laid the white satin aside, then divested Catherine of the turquoise garment.

Catherine said no more, for she knew her only recourse would be to go to him without clothing at all, and that certainly wouldn't do! Fighting down an urge to flee, she allowed Almira to help her into the white costume and then adjust a delicate, gold-link belt about her slender waist. The servant then brought her several gold bracelets and necklaces to wear, added a touch more perfume, and slipped dainty sandals upon her feet. Finally, she stood back to admire her handiwork.

"You are truly beautiful. Malik will be pleased," she announced, noting how the Barbary dress fit her to perfection, clinging ever so lightly to her slim body as she moved, and how the gold jewelry brought out the vibrant color of her hair.

"I'm sure that's most important," Catherine said with sarcasm that was lost on the other woman.

A servant arrived to let it be known that Malik was ready for her, and Almira led Catherine from the harem under the resentful gazes of the other women. They traveled through the palace to the dey's private suite of rooms. "Go in. He is waiting for you."

Catherine was nervous . . . very nervous, but she was resolved to maintain every semblance of control. It had been obvious the day Malik had taken her from Muhammed that he would tolerate no defiance from her, but at the same time, she wasn't about to be completely submissive. She appreciated the fact that she and Alex were being treated fairly, but they were still being held against their will. Giving a stubborn lift of her chin, she took a deep breath to steady her frayed nerves and stepped into Malik's quarters.

"Welcome, Catherine. Please come in," he greeted her from where he sat reclining on cushions in the center of the room. There was a magnificent banquet spread before him on a low marble table that was placed just high enough to serve them from where they would be sitting on the floor.

Catherine thanked Malik and kept her gaze focused on him as she reminded herself that she had to face him without fear. Her sandal-clad feet made barely a whisper of noise as she crossed the highly polished white marble floor toward the dey. She was glad now for all her experience at court, for she could draw upon that discipline to see her through the next few hours.

Malik had been anticipating her arrival. He'd dressed this evening for what was to be a romantic tryst in the privacy of his own quarters, donning fully cut pantaloons, much in the Turkish style, a pair of soft desert boots, and a long, brightly colored vest that hung open leaving his hard-muscled chest and arms bare. Around his neck he wore a heavy gold chain with an amulet on it. He was sitting easily now, leaning slightly to the side on a cushion, one leg drawn casually up, a forearm resting across his knee. Despite his relaxed dress and pose, he still looked a man of power. His aura

101

of command was as much a part of him as the color of his hair and eyes.

As Malik watched Catherine cross the room toward him, his appetite to have her raged. The silken gown she wore seemed to gently caress her sweetly curved body, and he thought surely that he was dreaming. He'd had reports from the harem that she was lovely, but he found her far more gorgeous than he'd ever imagined she would be.

"Join me in my humble abode," he spoke in a deep, mellow voice as he gestured grandly about the room.

Catherine was so tense about this meeting that she paid scant attention to her surroundings. She gave not even a glance at the simply decorated yet very impressive room, concentrating instead on maintaining her self-control and not revealing her fears. Later, she would notice the arched windows that opened onto a terrace overlooking the garden below and the walls decorated in a very masculine design of mosaic tiles and hung with exquisitely patterned tapestries. For now, all that mattered was meeting Malik with dignity and poise intact.

"You look very beautiful tonight," he complimented her as he rose agilely to his feet and extended his hand to her. "Please, sit down."

"Thank you, Malik Dey." Realizing that there was no way to avoid his touch, Catherine put her hand in his to allow him to assist her in sitting down. That simple contact was so electric, that had she been a lesser woman, she would have jerked her hand away. Stunned, she looked up at him expecting to find that he was feeling the same thing. But to her amazement, he seemed undisturbed. Giving herself a mental shake, she steeled herself once again as she settled down on the pillows, and she was tremendously relieved when he released her hand.

"My name is Malik. You may use it without the formalities."

"Malik . . ."

He nodded his approval, liking the sound of his name on her lips. One day soon, he hoped to hear her call his name as he made love to her . . . Annoyed with himself, he jerked his thoughts back away from dangerous territory.

"I have ordered many different foods tonight for your pleasure. I hope you enjoy the meal," Malik told her with a warm smile, his eyes catching and holding hers in an intimate gaze.

She found herself staring into his eyes and thinking they were the most unusual color she'd ever seen. When they'd first met, they seemed amber, but now, they were a dark, dark gold. His graciousness and unthreatening presence were making her a little less nervous, but Catherine still felt she had to be cautious. She returned his smile, but without the warmth of his. "I appreciate your thoughtfulness in this, but I really would like to speak to you about several other things before we eat."

Her request took him aback. He had planned an evening of sensual enjoyment and she wanted to talk? What could they possibly have to talk about? She was a woman. "Such as?" he inquired, hiding his shock and amusement.

"Well, first, I'd like to know if you've sent a message to my father yet. Alex and I are quite anxious to return to England, and I know my father will send the ransom money just as soon as he receives word," she told him in a very businesslike manner.

Malik had realized from the start that Catherine was a very different kind of woman. No woman since Lila had dared to ask him his plans, and this display of spirit in Catherine piqued his already growing interest in her even more. While he was not a man who liked to lie, he did believe in doing things the most expedient way possible. Telling himself that the end was ultimately worth the means, he replied smoothly, "Word has already been sent."

"Good. Do you think it will be very long until we're freed?" she pressed, relieved to know that her father would soon find out they were alive and well.

"It is difficult to say exactly," he hedged. Her reference to being "freed" stung his conscience, but he denied the guilt. She was not his prisoner. She was now one of his women. Hadn't he seen that she was treated well? Hadn't he seen her every reasonable wish met? He wanted this Catherine as he had not wanted a female since Lila, and he was going to have her. As he sat there facing her now, he noticed how the thin fabric of the white garment caressed the fullness of her bosom just as he wanted to and how her glorious mane fell softly about her shoulders enticing him to run his hands through the golden strands. Forcing his thoughts back to her question, he went on. "Sometimes it can take several months, at least. Now, shall we eat?"

"Malik . . ." she began again, wondering why his gaze suddenly seemed so brooding, "There is something else. I was wondering if . . ."

"Yes?" He was growing a bit exasperated now.

"If it would be possible for me to have my gown back?"

"You find our style of clothing uncomfortable?" He deflected her question with a question of his own as his gaze slid over her, tracing her lithe body beneath the Algerian garment. "It is very practical for our climate, you know. Sometimes it can become very hot here." His words sounded innocuous enough, but his thoughts were far from innocent, for he was again envisioning how she would look stripped of her clothing, lying on the comfort of his wide, soft bed.

"I do not intend to stay here long enough to find out, so I really would prefer to have my own dress back to wear."

"I'm afraid that's not possible," Malik answered, rejecting the idea of seeing her in those confining European styles again. "The dress was ruined, so it was burned."

She bit her lip. It had been her only gown, her one connection to home, and now it was gone forever.

Malik saw the flicker of unhappiness in her eyes and felt a pang of guilt. Again, the guilt troubled him. He wondered why he should care that she was unhappy. She was, after all, only a woman . . . "Here, try some of the roast lamb," he said, offering her some of the succulent meat.

Knowing there was nothing left to say, she partook of the food. It was delicious, and as course after course was brought before them, she found herself actually enjoying the tempting fare.

As the hours passed, and Catherine and Malik shared food and drink, he managed to put her at ease and she slowly became less wary of him. To her surprise, she found him an interesting, well-educated man. Their conversation was intelligent and challenging and covered a myriad of topics. He continually intrigued her with his views. By the end of the meal, she had formed a certain respect and even a bit of liking for the man.

While Catherine's opinion of Malik was changing, his of her was being reinforced. The fact that she was a woman who voiced opinions based on education, common sense, and intelligence enthralled him. On some of the subjects they discussed, he thought her brighter than some of his advisers in the *divan*. This discovery about her pleased him. Now he not only desired her, he had come to respect her. She was a woman with a mind of her own. A woman worth winning. Yet, he realized she wanted nothing more than to leave him and go home. He wondered with some irritation what manner of man her husband was.

"Your home is very beautiful," she remarked some time later when the last of the dishes had been cleared away by the servants.

"Its magnificence pales next to you," he told her gallantly, his tone suggesting that he really meant it.

Catherine felt an unwelcome blush stain her cheeks. "You're too kind."

"You are the first to think so," he said, giving a meaningful chuckle. "There are many who would disagree with you."

"I would have thought you would be well liked by your people. You seem a fair man."

"Every man has enemies. It is important never to trust anyone too fully. That is the best way to stay alive and in power."

She glanced up, seeing then for the first time the chess set on the desk. "You play chess?" The idea fascinated her as yet another facet of his personality was revealed to her.

"Yes."

"So do I . . . a little," she answered.

Malik was astounded by the news that she knew the game and even more astounded to find himself inviting her to play. He'd always regarded chess strictly as a man's game.

An hour later, he'd been proven wrong. Catherine's strategy had been brilliant, and he'd been soundly defeated. No one had ever beaten him before. He frowned. "You're very good." It was a hard admission on his part, but one that added to the respect he was already feeling for her.

"So are you," she answered. It had been a challenging game, and she'd been forced to play to the best of her ability.

"We'll play again soon."

"I'd enjoy that, but I really think I should return to my rooms now." She stood up.

Malik rose from the table, too. His expression was thoughtful as he escorted her to the doorway and then called out for a servant to guide her back to the harem. He'd wanted nothing more than to make love to Catherine, yet here he was allowing her to go back to the harem untouched. He thought himself a madman and questioned his own sanity, for he had never before in his life denied himself a desirable woman.

It was then that Malik realized how much his feelings for Catherine had changed during the course of the evening. She was unlike any woman he'd ever known, and while he desired her strongly, he wanted her to come to him willingly. Tonight, pleasant as it had been, he would still have had to use force to make love to her. Malik knew it would take some time, but he fully intended to have her without coercion.

As they stood in the doorway saying good night, Malik lifted one hand to gently touch her cheek. It was the first physical contact they'd had since he'd held her hand earlier, and the same potent electricity charged through them both. He'd felt it before, but had kept his reaction to her hidden. He did so again now, even as he watched her eyes widen in shock at the ripples of awareness that flowed through her at his touch. He smiled.

"Good night, Catherine."

With that, he turned Catherine over to the servant who was waiting and disappeared back inside his chamber. She suddenly felt quite bereft without him, and as she made her way through the palace, her thoughts were completely centered on Malik and the puzzle he presented her. He'd been a perfect gentleman all night, and she'd actually found that she liked him. Confused, she returned to her bedchamber and sought rest.

Chapter Eight

Malik summoned Catherine to join him many more times during the next several weeks. Each evening was filled with a sumptuous feast, stimulating conversation, and ended with a game of chess. They were well matched in strategies, and Malik found her brave attacks on the chessboard hard to defend against. In all, each won as many as they lost, and they were both pleased with the outcome.

With each visit, Malik's desire for her grew. Any innocent touch they shared sent his passions soaring. He'd managed to control himself so far, but she had become like a fire in his blood. He knew he couldn't wait much longer to have her. An image of Catherine seemed to dance constantly in his mind, taunting him, teasing him, arousing him at the most inopportune times and leaving him useless for other endeavors.

Malik convinced himself that if he could make love to her just once, the hold she had on him would lessen. The trouble was, in the times they'd been together, she hadn't given any sign that she wanted him. She spoke mainly of impersonal things. She seemed more than content with the way things stood between them, and it was driving him to distraction.

Malik realized, as he thought about it now, that despite their hours of conversation, he really knew very little about Catherine. He suddenly grew annoyed with himself. His primary rule for taking up any challenge was to know his adversary thoroughly, and he had failed in that this time. He'd been so beguiled that he had cast his rules to the wind, concentrating only on his passion. He made up his mind, then and there, to find out everything he could about her before they met again that night. Malik knew where to start, too. Her son, Alex, would be able to help him if he handled it right.

With all the confidence befitting a man of his station, Malik left the audience chamber where he'd been sitting and made his way toward the boys' quarters in the palace. There was no way he was going to lose in his battle to win Catherine.

Catherine was sitting in her bedroom when Almira came seeking her out.

"Catherine, Malik has sent word that he wants you to join him again this evening," Almira related, thrilled by the news. She had no use for the other women in the harem and was glad they were being ignored.

At Almira's announcement, Catherine's mood darkened and she didn't respond right away.

"Is something wrong?" the servant asked, seeing how strained she looked. "Are you ill?"

For a moment, Catherine almost lied and said yes so she wouldn't have to go to him, but amazingly, what was troubling her so deeply and what also stopped her from lying was the fact that she was actually looking forward to seeing Malik again. During the time they'd been apart, she'd found herself thinking about him a dozen times and remembering little things he'd said or done during their times together. It was very difficult for her to admit that she had come to care about him in the few weeks she'd known him. She sighed. "No. I'm not sick."

"Then let's go to the baths. We must begin now if we want you to be perfect for Malik. You should be feeling very honored that he wants you again tonight."

Her eagerness to go frightened her. But then, there were many things frightening her lately. Last night, for example, when Malik hadn't sent for her, she'd spent the time alone in her rooms trying to think only of Gerald and the kisses they'd shared the day she'd been kidnapped. She'd managed just fine until she'd fallen asleep, and then instead of her fiancé's face dominating her dreams, Malik had been there. He had intruded on her tender memories and flashed her his triumphant smile as he took her hand in a simple gesture that excited her even in her slumber. She wondered what was happening to her. It was Gerald she loved, not Malik.

"Maybe Malik will take you for his fourth wife . . ." Almira was saying as they left the room.

Her words jarred Catherine to the depths of her soul, and she denied them a little too vehemently—to herself and to Almira, "I have no desire to become his wife! I am in love with another man! Gerald is the only one I'll ever want or need . . ."

"But your Gerald is not here, and Malik is. Surely, this Englishman is not as brave or as handsome—" Almira asked.

"I love Gerald," Catherine insisted, interrupting her. She didn't want to hear her sing Malik's praises. She knew how wonderful he was—how kind, gentle, intelligent . . . Aggravated, she cut him out of her thoughts.

The servant fell silent as she realized how very little

111

love had to do with anything. She pondered the evening ahead as they made their way to the baths. Earlier, when she had told Catherine that Malik wanted her tonight, she had seen the spark of interest that had shone in the young woman's eyes. Almira wondered how much longer Catherine could deny the truth of her desire to herself.

Hasim Ibn Malik, the darkly handsome, eleven-year-old son of Malik and his deceased wife, Lila, was busy playing in the gardens with his two friends, Mustapha and Uruj, when Alex came to join them. Hasim glanced up as he heard the younger boy's approach and then immediately looked away. His pride dictated that he act as though Alex's presence was of little consequence to him, but really Hasim greatly resented the youth. His father had never before taken a Christian captive into their home to live as one of them and this action puzzled him. When Uruj had told him that there was a rumor being spread that Alex's mother would soon become Malik's next wife, it all began to make sense and he grew jealous. He didn't want to share his father with anyone, and the thought that this little boy might suddenly become his brother bothered him greatly.

Alex saw the boys at play and approached them a little cautiously. He had met Hasim and the others and liked them, but they'd seemed to go out of their way to avoid him since he'd come to live in the palace. He probably wouldn't have sought them out now except that he was lonely. The only real company he'd had in the weeks since they'd arrived had been his short visits with Aunt Catherine. So, when he heard the boys playing and sounding like they were having fun, he wanted to join in. As Alex moved nearer, he was aware that they were completely ignoring him, and he didn't understand it since he'd never done anything to make them mad.

"Can I play, too?" Alex asked, his loneliness goading him bravely onward. It would be good to run and laugh again. The game they were playing seemed a lot like tag, and he had always been good at tag at home.

"You can't play. You're too young and too slow," Hasim told him bluntly, then turned his back on him in a dismissive gesture.

"No, I'm not! I'm almost eight, and I bet I can keep up with you!" he countered, ready to show them just how quickly he could run. "Watch!" Forgetting all of his troubles, Alex broke into a run for the sheer joy of it. It suddenly seemed as if eternity had passed since he'd sailed his boat and played in the garden at Huntington House. He charged back toward the three waiting boys, stopped right before them, and planted his hands on his hips. He was panting heavily, but he was smiling as he said, "See!"

"You're not fast at all," the pudgy Mustapha disparaged.

"Go back inside, little baby!" Uruj teased.

"I'm no baby! Let me play. Please?"

Though Hasim knew that Alex had been far quicker than they'd given him credit for, he could not back down and lose face in front of his friends. He shot him a disdainful look. "You're much too little to keep up with us."

"No, I'm not. I bet I can beat Mustapha in a race!" Alex challenged. He wanted only to join them, and he was resolved to do whatever was necessary to gain their acceptance. He honestly believed he would have a chance, for though Mustapha was a shade taller than he was, he was also a whole lot heavier.

"Mustapha? What do you say? Do you want to race

this baby? It should be an easy victory for you," Uruj asked tauntingly.

At being called a baby again, Alex's hands clenched into fists at his sides and his chin took on a stubborn set. The fierce determination that would become so much a part of him as a man manifested itself, and he swore silently that no matter what, he was going to win this race. He said nothing in his own defense, though, as he waited for Mustapha's answer.

"I'll race him," the older boy agreed. "How far do you think, Hasim?"

"To the stables and back," he pronounced. He turned to Alex. "You do know where the stables are, don't you?"

Alex nodded and pointed to the separate building on the far side of the court where the dey kept his three hundred horses. "There."

"Then go!" Hasim shouted.

Both boys were surprised at the unexpectedness of the start, and they took off running at top speed after an initial hesitation.

Hasim and Uruj were surprised when the shorter Alex managed to keep up with Mustapha all the way to the stables. They exchanged amazed looks when their friend's pace began to slow and Alex started to pull ahead. Hasim was impressed by the young boy's fleetness, but he didn't want to admit it out loud. He watched as the two runners came racing back toward them, and he couldn't help but notice that Mustapha was looking very red-faced and exhausted.

Mustapha was not about to lose to any seven-year-old. When the rock formation that had been chosen as the winning spot came into view and Alex was drawing ahead of him, he knew he had to act and act quickly. In a low, deceitful move, he stuck his foot out and deliberately tripped the younger boy, sending him sprawling in the dirt. Giving a hoot of delight, Mustapha raced on in triumph.

Alex never knew what happened. One moment he was running at full speed a step ahead of Mustapha and the next he was falling heavily, all the wind knocked out of him. He looked up miserably just as the older boy crossed the winning marker in victory.

Alex could hear the other boys' jeers and laughs, and fury fired through him as he strained to get his breath. Ignoring the pain in his chest and the tears in his eyes, he charged to his feet. He'd had all the tormenting he could stand. Without a thought to the fact that he was outnumbered three to one and that he was so much younger, he went after them all, his head down, his fists swinging wildly in anger.

"You cheated!" he cried, several of his untrained punches connecting with the winded Mustapha and retreating Uruj before Hasim managed to grab him and hold him still.

"You're not only a baby, you're stupid!" Mustapha continued to make sport of him. "You're still an infant, suckling at your mother's breast! Should we call her from the harem so she can tend her little boy?"

Hasim knew things were getting out of hand and he shot Mustapha a threatening look to silence him. But Alex wasn't about to stop now.

"She's not my mother, she's my Aunt Catherine!" He twisted free of Hasim's hold and turned angrily on him, knowing he was the leader of the little group. "But she's raised me to be honest and brave, which is something your mothers know nothing about! Your mothers raised a bunch of cheaters and liars!"

Hasim would never stand for any insult to be directed at his mother and he bristled visibly. "No one cheated, you tripped over your own two feet," he threw back at him, having missed Mustapha's dirty trick.

"I did not! You're just as bad as those two! You're all alike! You can't win without cheating!" Alex declared. Beyond control in his indignance, he swung out and hit Hasim as hard as he could. He caught the bigger boy off guard, surprising him with the force of his blow.

Hasim reacted instinctively and with equal violence, hitting him back with all his might. He knew Alex was much younger, but his words had stung, and now his physical attack was too much. He couldn't let him get away with it. Just as he hit back, though, Hasim looked up and caught sight of his father striding toward them with a thunderous look upon his face. A sudden, sickening wave of shame washed over him as he met that condemning glare. Humiliation followed in its wake, but he did not cower. He held himself erect and met his regard without trying to hide what he'd done.

Malik came up behind Alex and steadied him. "Easy, little one," he said in a soothing deep voice.

"Don't call me that!" Alex bristled as he tried to shrug off the dey's hand. "Let me go! I want to show them . . ."

"Show them what? That you don't know when to make a tactical retreat? The mark of a wise man is knowing when the odds are in his favor—and when they are not. I would say right now, you stand a good chance of losing any fight you may pick with my son. Perhaps in five or ten years you would like to challenge him again."

"I won't be here in five years!" he replied heatedly, using his forearm to wipe the blood that was flowing from the cut on his rapidly swelling lip.

"We shall see, Serad. We shall see. No man can know what his future holds," Malik said, a mysterious note to his statement.

"My name is Alex," he said stubbornly, his chin up, his hands still knotted into fists ready at his sides.

"From now on you will be called Serad."

"I don't want to be called anything but Alex."

"Serad means 'brave one,' Alex. It is truly a name that fits you." He paused to look at his son with pride. "Anyone who dares challenge Hasim must be brave. My son is a very good fighter."

"Serad?" Alex brightened as he repeated the name slowly, testing it on his tongue.

Malik nodded his approval. "It suits you."

While Alex pondered his new name, Malik turned his attention to his son, laying a loving hand upon his shoulder. "Hasim, I am much too proud of you to allow you and your friends to behave in this manner." He looked over at Mustapha, annoyance obvious in his gaze. "And, Mustapha, an honest man never needs to cheat. If you lost any challenge, let it be because the other man was truly better than you, as young Serad was just proving until you deliberately tripped him."

Mustapha had the grace to look guilty. "Yes, Malik Dey." He and Uruj quickly excused themselves and disappeared from the garden under Malik's censoring gaze. There would be no more playing today.

Once the boys had gone, Malik smiled down at Alex, now Serad. He met the boy's stormy gray gaze levelly. "Always remember, Serad, to gauge your enemy's strengths and weaknesses before the fight, not after."

Alex held himself stiffly erect as he listened to his words, and he nodded tightly in understanding. Though his lip was throbbing and he was angry and hurt, he wasn't about to let this man know the depth of his pain.

Malik, however, read his turbulent emotions. "Do not hate, either, Serad," he instructed. "Hatred is a wasted emotion. Those you hate do not care, and you carry that bitter burden alone. Concentrate, instead, on winning, no matter what the conflict or the prize.

The best form of revenge on your enemies is to prove yourself superior to them."

"Yes, sir," he replied with some difficulty through his puffy lips.

"Good boy. Now run along and see to your mouth. We'll speak again later. And Serad?"

Alex looked at him questioningly.

"Do not worry about the boys. They will give you no more trouble."

"I'll fight my own battles," he declared, not wanting the dey to protect him.

"I would have expected no less of you."

Their gazes locked, and suddenly Alex felt a bond with this man. He saw wisdom and faith and strength in his eyes and knew Malik was a man he could count on, a man like his grandfather. Alex gave him a small, painful smile that turned out to be more of a grimace, then turned and went back inside the palace.

As he walked, Alex kept repeating his new name Serad to himself. He decided with a sense of pride that he liked it very much.

Malik watched Serad walk away, and he nodded approvingly to himself. The boy was brave; any man would be proud to have him for his own. When the time came to take the beauteous Catherine as his wife, he would claim Serad, too. That decided, he turned his full attention to his son, who was still standing rigidly by his side.

"I assume there was a reason for your behavior, so I will not dwell on that. I do want you to know, Hasim, that the boy is no threat to you in any way." There was tenderness in his counsel, and he was pleased when he saw Hasim relax a bit.

"Yes, sir."

"Good boy. Now run along, but remember the little one is all alone here and needs friends. It would not displease me if you were to be kind to him."

Hasim understood much then, and while he still felt some resentment at Alex's intrusion into their lives, he knew he had to respect his father's wishes in the matter. "Is he going to be my brother?" he blurted out as he turned to go.

"It is a possibility, my son, and I would think not a bad choice, if one had to choose brothers. Serad certainly doesn't lack for boldness and daring."

Hasim nodded, his expression thoughtful as he considered how the little boy had taken on him and his friends without fear. As he ran off, he felt an inkling of respect for Alex growing within him.

Malik smiled to himself as he watched his son, and that smile broadened as his thoughts shifted to Catherine. He decided that coming here to see the children had been a very wise thing to do, indeed, and he was very sorry that he hadn't done it sooner. Now that he knew the truth about Catherine's relationship to the boy, everything made more sense to him. She was the boy's aunt, not his mother. Though she did profess to love another named Gerald, she had never called him her husband. It delighted Malik to think that she might still be a virgin. All along he had expected her to respond to him as a woman learned in the ways of men and love. The discovery that she most probably was an innocent explained everything.

Making his way to a bench near the center of the garden, Malik wondered briefly about Serad's parents, but then shrugged the concern off. It didn't really matter. The boy was here now, and he would be staying, just as his aunt would.

Thinking of Catherine again, Malik decided that tonight would be the night he would have her. He had dallied long enough. The recognition of her possible innocence, though, told him that he would have to plan carefully. She was in need of tutoring in the art of love, and he would be her teacher. The thought sent a rush of unbidden heat through him that surprised him in its intensity. He glanced up at the sky and knew by the position of the sun that already the day grew late. That pleased him, for it meant the hours until Catherine would be with him again were few. He stood and made his way indoors. There was much to be done, and very little time.

Catherine followed Almira to the privacy of the harem baths, where another servant, Raji, awaited them. Almira, along with Raji, helped her to undress and then handed her down into the sunken marble bathtub. Catherine still found it unsettling to be naked before others, and she quickly sank down into the welcoming, warm water, glad to be away from the servants' prying eyes.

With Almira looking approvingly on, Raji washed Catherine's hair with the greatest of care and then bathed the rest of her. Catherine had to fight down the urge to relax and enjoy the pampered treatment. She also had to fight down the rising excitement she was feeling over seeing Malik again. When Raji finished, she helped Catherine from the bath and toweled her dry.

The masseur was a eunuch named Khalil, and he was summoned to them next. On her first night in the harem, when Khalil had come to her, Catherine had balked, for she had never been touched so by a man before. But now after experiencing his skillful ways many times, she found herself looking forward to it. Khalil's manner was so gentle and respectful that, much as with Malik, she grew more at ease with him with every passing day.

Khalil greeted her pleasantly and then began to work

his magic on her body. With an expert touch, he massaged her silken limbs until every inch of her flesh came alive under his touch. Catherine had thought he was finished when he paused, but then he did something different this time, rubbing a deliciously scented oil into her bare skin. Her entire body tingled, and she felt marvelously relaxed when he finally left her.

It took a major effort for Catherine to force herself to remember why she was there. She told herself that she could not become enchanted with this lifestyle, that she had to get Alex back to England, and then, there was Gerald still waiting for her.

"You shall be pleased when you see what you are to wear for Malik tonight," Almira told her as she wrapped her in a large towel when Khalil had gone.

They returned to her bedroom, and there on the bed lay a shimmering length of gold-embroidered turquoise silk. There was no preventing the gasp of appreciation that escaped Catherine, and she quickly crossed the room to touch it.

"It's beautiful," she breathed as she caressed the fine fabric. "The color is exquisite . . ."

"It's the exact color of your eyes," Almira stated with confidence as she picked it up and held it to the light. "It's going to look lovely on you. But first, we must use the perfume . . ." The servant laid the silk aside and produced the small crystalline bottle that held the dey's favorite scent, a musky, heady mixture. After taking Catherine's towel from her she dabbed it generously at all of her strategic pulse points. "Now . . . the silk . . ."

Almira lifted the material once more and began to wrap Catherine in it with artful expertise. She finished by fastening the silk with a jeweled clasp on her left shoulder, leaving her right shoulder seductively bare.

The filmy fabric was a cool, intimate caress against

her body, and Catherine couldn't prevent the shiver that trembled through her. She stared down at herself in amazement, and an embarrassed flush stained her cheeks as she noticed that her nipples had hardened against the bodice of the wrapped gown. It was more revealing than any dress or negligee she'd ever seen, and she knew she shouldn't go to Malik this way.

"You must find something else for me to wear," she demanded. "I can't wear this."

"Why not?" the servant asked, confused because it looked so perfect on her.

"It's too . . ." Catherine paused, groping for a word. When she met with no success, she finally just blurted out, "I just can't wear it, that's all."

Almira's answer, while stated calmly, was unyielding. "Malik sent this to you with his express wish that you wear it tonight. You cannot refuse him."

"But—"

"You look wonderful," she cut her off. "You will win his heart."

"I don't want to win his heart!"

"You must have the jewelry . . ." Almira completely ignored her. She produced several gold bracelets encrusted with precious stones and slipped them onto her wrists. "Now, you only need sandals and you will be perfect." She retrieved a pair of gold sandals that went with the dress and helped her don them, then stepped back to admire her.

Catherine was a vision. Her hair was loose and tumbling around her shoulders in a halo of pale loveliness. The silken gown clung to her curves enticingly, hinting at the firm, high breasts and rounded hips beneath.

Almira smiled. "You are truly a gorgeous woman. Look at your reflection. You will see that I am right."

Catherine stepped before the mirror and couldn't

believe that the stunning woman she was staring at was herself. The woman in the reflection was a stranger ... a seductress ... a woman who appeared to know of men and their ways. Her heart beat a little faster as she realized that tonight's visit with Malik might prove to be far different from her other visits with him.

"It's time. We must take you to him now. He is waiting."

Chapter Nine

Wearing the white djellaba, loose-fitting pants, and gold belt that suited him so well, Malik paced his chambers in eager anticipation of the night to come. He strode to the arched window to stare out at the courtyard below as he waited for Catherine's arrival. As he gazed down at the reflecting pool and colorful profusion of flowering plants, Lila slipped into his thoughts. Malik thought of his wife with tender devotion. He remembered how much she had loved to sit in the courtyard by the pool, and he remembered, too, how much pain he had suffered when she'd died. He had sworn to never love again. He had taken three other women as wives to satisfy his needs, but had never really felt anything for any of them.

Now, this Englishwoman had come into his life, and suddenly Malik felt almost as if he'd been asleep and was now awakened. The pleasure of the coming evening stretched before him with tempting delight, and he could hardly wait for Catherine to join him. Tonight would be a night they would long remember.

"Malik Dey?" Ali, one of his servants, spoke from the doorway interrupting his musings.

He glanced toward the man.

"The woman is here," Ali informed him.

"Then send her to me and begin the serving of the meal."

Malik stepped away from the window and waited for Catherine to enter. He watched the doorway expectantly, hearing the soft sound of her footfalls as she drew nearer. And then she was there before him . . .

Malik stared with admiration at the absolute loveliness of her, and he knew he'd been right in his choice. The turquoise color matched her eyes perfectly. She was a priceless gem, a jewel beyond compare. Swathed in the deep, rich blue-green silk with one slender shoulder exposed, the shining glory of her tawny mane flowing about her in a golden cape, Catherine embodied everything a man could ever want. Malik longed to tangle his hands in those pale curls and press hot kisses to her lips, the sweet curve of her throat, and her bared shoulder.

"Hello, Catherine." He said her name softly, extending a hand toward her.

From the moment she'd stepped into the room, she'd once again been caught up in the power of Malik's presence. His dark good looks had the power to set her pulses racing.

"Good evening, Malik," Catherine greeted him breathlessly as she took a tentative step forward.

At her movement, the aquamarine gown offered him up a tempting display of her barely concealed charms beneath. The thrust of her sweet breasts, the trimness of her waist and the soft swell of her hips all urged him to action, but he controlled himself. The coming hours were going to be special for the both of them, and he would not rush it. He was determined that by the end of the evening, she was going to want him as much as he wanted her.

"The color is very becoming on you. You look most

125

lovely," Malik told her as she slipped her hand into his.

The touch of his hand on hers sent a shiver skittering up her spine. "Thank you," she replied, her eyes aglow as she stared up at him.

"Come . . ." He made a sweeping motion toward the dining area. "The servants will be bringing our meal shortly. Let's sit down . . ."

Malik led the way to the cushions, drawing Catherine down beside him. They sat close, his arm barely brushing against her, his thigh pressed to hers.

"I missed you, Catherine," he told her, leaning closer.

Catherine found his nearness mesmerizing. She almost blurted out that she'd missed him, too, but she managed that much control. The heat of his leg against her burned like a brand, and, innocent that she was, she had no idea what the coiling, aching tightness deep within her meant.

Malik hesitated, wanting to hear her say that she'd missed him, too, but when she didn't immediately respond, he asked, "Did you miss me?"

It seemed to Catherine that he had to be reading her thoughts, and high color stained her cheeks as she finally admitted, and then qualified that she had. "Yes . . . I missed our conversation and our chess games."

Malik was pleased with her answer. It was the first time she'd ever given any indication that she enjoyed their time together. He was hard put not to sweep her into his arms and kiss her right then and there. Instead, he restrained himself admirably, telling himself that there would be plenty of time later for love. Right now, his only goal was to please her.

The servants appeared and began to serve the meal, ending the intimacy of the moment, and Catherine was glad. She had seen something in his eyes that had set her heart racing, and she needed the reprieve. They spoke of inconsequential things as they dined on the perfectly roasted, savory lamb, drinks of mint tea and coffee, and desserts of honey-dipped pastries and Turkish sherbets, which were drinks of cooling, sweetened fruit juices.

Even though Catherine was still not accustomed to eating with her fingers, the feast was so marvelous that she consumed her fill. Malik noticed how much she was enjoying the meal, and it pleased him. He found he enjoyed making her happy. The sweet pastry he was eating was delicious, and he offered her a delicate morsel of it. She started to take it from him, but he refused to hand it to her.

"No . . . Like this," he said in a soft voice, holding the bite to her lips so she could nibble it directly from his fingers.

Catherine accidentally glanced up at him as she was taking the small bite with her teeth, and the look she saw in his eyes sent heat flushing through her. There was something so intimate in his regard that she dropped her gaze, only to find herself staring at his mouth and wondering suddenly what it would be like to kiss him. Feelings she hadn't known existed were stirring within her, unnerving her. Catherine tried to think of Gerald, but Malik's nearness was so potent on her senses that Gerald seemed only a distant, pale shadow of a man in her thoughts and her heart.

Malik had seen the dawning of sensual recognition in her gaze before she'd looked away, and he knew a great moment of triumph. Soon she would be his!

"Catherine . . ."

Her name was a caress, and her eyes flew up to his as he bent nearer. For a moment, she was absolutely, heart-stoppingly sure that he was going to kiss her, but instead, he gently reached out to brush away a small crumb at the corner of her mouth. An emotion terribly close to disappointment crashed through her, but when she regained her equilibrium she asked herself if she was losing her mind.

"Oh . . . thank you . . ." She suddenly felt very self-conscious and very foolish. Why would she even imagine he was going to kiss her when he'd been nothing but a gentleman during all their previous visits? Why would she even want him to? But even as she asked herself the last question, she couldn't ignore the truth of it. She had wanted him to kiss her. Nervously, she turned back to her dessert, finishing off her small glass of sherbet.

It was already growing dark when the last of the dishes were finally cleared away. At Malik's direction, the servants returned with low-burning lamps to bathe the chamber in a soft glow.

"Did you enjoy the food?" he asked solicitously.

"Everything was delicious."

"Good. I have something special planned for tonight."

"What?"

He turned to the servants and ordered, "It is time for the dancers. Send them in."

"Dancers?"

"I think you will like them. They're very good. Watch," Malik said as he leaned even closer to her and pointed toward the doorway.

A single musician came into the room then, and sitting down across the chamber from them, he began to play a lilting melody on his tambour. Catherine was finding the soft, gentle music of the small, stringed instrument quite pleasing, when suddenly he quickened his rhythm to an almost frenzied beat and two scantily clad female dancers spun into the room in a blaze of brilliant color and movement.

Catherine had never seen such costumes or dancing before. She watched in fascination as the women moved about the chamber in an exotic dance that required movements of body parts Catherine had never known moved before. Their costumes—what there was of them—were vibrant in color and of the sheerest cloth, but the women's movements were so quick and fluid that they afforded their audience only a teasing glimpse of their ample figures. Gold bangles draped from their wrists and ankles and added a tinkling cadence to their motions. Catherine watched them spellbound, and she was surprised when the music abruptly ended and the women dropped to the floor in supplication before Malik.

"Do you like my dancers?" Malik asked, already knowing the answer. He'd been watching Catherine through the entire melody and had seen her fascination.

"They're wonderful," she admitted, smiling brightly.

It was the first real smile she'd ever given him, and he felt his heart constrict. He knew then that he wanted to make her smile again and again. With a loud clap of his hands, he commanded, "More!"

The music started up and the dancers leapt to life to perform again for their master, the dey.

Malik knew he could hold himself in abeyance no longer. With a gentle hand, he reached out to brush one errant blond curl from Catherine's bared shoulder and then settle his hand there possessively.

Though Malik's earlier caress had set her senses reeling, Catherine had not visibly responded to it. This time, however, there could be no hiding the desire that was throbbing through her. She lifted her gaze to his and once again saw the smoldering look in his eyes that had so quickened her pulse earlier. Catherine told herself that she should go back to her rooms right then and there, but she could no more leave him than she could have stopped breathing. She wanted to know more of this man . . . much more.

"Tonight, Catherine, you will stay," Malik said simply as his thumb traced a fiery path along her collarbone. His body was aflame with the need to take her. He desperately wanted to lay her down right then and bury himself between her thighs. He wanted to give them both the pleasure he knew could be theirs, but he refrained, turning slowly back to watch the dancers in their sensual gyrations. "They're doing the dance of love, Catherine," Malik whispered huskily in her ear. "I requested it for you."

The beat of the music became more and more exciting, and the dancers became more and more erotic in their movements. Catherine wanted to look away from their sensual play, but she couldn't. She was caught up in the web of passion they were spinning around her and Malik. Thoughts of Alex's future and safety somehow vanished. She found she could only think of tonight . . . and of Malik.

Catherine turned to him, and in that moment, she was lost. She had thought Gerald attractive, but that was before she'd met Malik. Just the touch of his hand on her shoulder left her light-headed with delight. A last sane thought flitted through her mind urging her to flee, to free herself from the potency of his intoxicating nearness, but she couldn't. A tension was building within her—a tension that she could put no name to, but one that had to be eased, and eased only by Malik.

The music came to an end and the dancers and musician slipped away unnoticed. Catherine and Malik were alone in the softly lighted chamber, staring into each other's eyes, unaware of anything but each other.

Malik did not speak. He did not want to risk breaking the magic. He slowly lowered his head and sought her mouth with his. It was a soft, fleeting kiss, a gentle brush of his lips against hers, and it was meant to invite and encourage.

Catherine felt that single kiss to the depths of her very soul. She gasped at the feelings that were erupting within her. "I have to go . . ." she protested, but she did not move.

"I want you, Catherine. Stay with me . . ." His tone was warm and seductive.

When his mouth sought hers again, this time with flaming passion, Catherine knew she couldn't leave. A whimper escaped her as she felt herself being lowered onto the cushions, but she had no will to resist him. She wanted this! Oh, how she wanted this!

"You're beautiful, my golden one. More beautiful than any woman I've ever known," Malik told her as he trailed a line of hot kisses from her lips down to her throat and bared shoulder.

With deft fingers, Malik released the clasp on the gown, and his reward was great as the silk fell away, freeing her breasts to his hungry gaze and touch. His caress was slow and arousing as he cupped each creamy orb and pressed sensuous kisses upon that naked flesh.

Catherine had never before experienced anything so wildly exciting. Her breath caught in her throat at the first touch of his lips upon her breasts, and she found herself saying his name. "Malik . . ."

It was what he'd waited all these weeks for . . . to hear her say his name in the throes of her passion, and he rose up over her to kiss her once more.

Catherine's pleasure had been so intense from his bolder caresses that it was almost a relief to kiss him. She wrapped her arms about him, drawing her near, sighing in welcome as he moved over her. The weight of his body upon hers somehow seemed very right. Her fingers twined in the crisp, thickness of the black hair at the nape of his neck as she met his kiss with equal fervor. Distantly, Almira's haunting words that no woman could resist Malik echoed in her mind, but it didn't seem to matter right now. All that mattered was holding Malik close and kissing him and knowing him . . .

Malik was enraptured. Her response was everything he'd hoped it would be. He continued to kiss her as he slipped the turquoise silk completely from her body, giving him unrestricted freedom to love her.

Catherine was being swept up in a maelstrom of excitement as Malik's hands caressed every inch of her. His touch filled her with ecstasy, and instinctively she began to move against him, wanting him, needing him. When he drew back and moved slightly away from her, she was confused.

"Malik?" She opened her eyes to see him shedding his tunic and casting the garment aside. His chest was magnificent, broad and sculpted with hard muscle, and she knew a great desire to run her hands over the powerful expanse of flesh.

Half undressed, he paused to stare down at her. She looked the lioness as she lay there, all sleek and golden, and his heart thudded painfully in his chest. Catherine lifted her aquamarine gaze to his face and saw a tenderness there that touched her very heart. Without conscious thought, she reached for him and drew him down to her for a passionate kiss.

In that simple action, Malik knew complete and utter triumph. With practiced expertise, he began to kiss and caress her, wanting to bring her the most powerful bliss he could.

Catherine had never known such a sensual assault. Suddenly, her world narrowed to only the two of them. Nothing else existed or mattered except Malik. He was giving her such exquisite pleasure with his lips and hands that she couldn't think, let alone reason. At a great distance she heard him talking to her, and she had to force herself to listen to his words.

"Do you still want to go, Catherine?" Malik was asking in a hoarse rasp.

She realized he was giving her a chance to leave, but her body was clamoring for some secret release that only he seemed capable of giving her. She tried to kiss him again, wanting to silence his troubling question, but that wasn't good enough for Malik. He gripped her chin in a gentle but firm hold and forced her to look at him.

"Answer me, woman!" he demanded in a soft but fierce voice. "Do you still want to leave me?" It would have killed him to allow her to go, but he would have done it. He did not want to take anything from her that she wasn't freely giving.

Catherine was in the throes of passion. She had no choice. She wanted Malik . . . desperately. "No . . ."

Her answer was all he needed. With the most tender of caresses, Malik took her the rest of the way to the peak of excitement and gave her that blessed ecstasy. He felt her writhe beneath him as she attained the heights of her sensual glory. Holding her close, he shed his trousers and then moved between her thighs to claim her once and for all as his and his alone.

Malik was careful, and his care proved him right. She was an innocent, and he moved gently as he breached that proof. He felt her tense as he met with the initial resistance, but kissed her wantonly until thoughts of the momentary pain faded into the oblivion of fulfillment. They joined.

Malik had never known splendor so sweet. Once he'd entered her, he could no longer control the

133

rapturous delight that drove him. With an eager rhythm, he sought the depths of her womanhood until in a burst of shining splendor he reached his own pinnacle of desire. Clasping her to his chest, he relaxed on top of her.

Caught up in the wonder of the moment, Catherine held Malik close, and in a woman's instinctive way, she understood that he had just shared in the same glory she had. It gave her a feeling of power and satisfaction to know that she could please him. Contented, she rested in the afterglow of their lovemaking.

Soon, as the bliss of passion faded, reality intruded on Catherine's peace. She lay unmoving, her body still joined with Malik's, wondering in misery what she had done. She had given her most precious gift—her virginity—to Malik, a man she barely knew . . . a man who intended to use her and then claim a ransom for her.

For an instant, Catherine tried to hate him, but she was too honest for that. She had no one to blame but herself. He hadn't forced her or coerced her. He had even given her the choice of leaving. He had been fair, just as she knew him to be. He had also been devastatingly exciting, stirring feelings within her that she hadn't known herself capable of and making her want him to the point that nothing else mattered.

A single, burning tear slipped from the corner of her eye and traced a forlorn, damp pattern down the softness of her cheek. She had stayed with Malik willingly and had given him that which she had saved and treasured for Gerald and their wedding night. In her heart, she cried . . . for her loss of innocence and for the perfect future she had once thought was hers.

Gerald stood before a mirror in his London bedroom, straightening his cravat. He'd heard from his

134

cronies that there were many young misses in Town for the season and that more than one of them came with a large dowry—an enhancement to any chit, indeed. When he was finally satisfied with the perfection of his neckcloth, he donned his jacket with his valet's help and left his home heading for Almack's. He had every intention of discovering the wealthiest of the girls and making her his bride as quickly as possible. Some things could not wait. To Catherine, he gave barely a passing thought, other than to mourn the loss of what had been a rich, promising match.

Chapter Ten

"Malik . . ." Catherine said his name very seriously as they sat down to enjoy the evening meal together.

He was surprised by the solemnity of her tone and looked up at her questioningly. "What is it, Catherine? Is something wrong?"

"That's what I want to know," she returned a little tensely. "It's been four months. Has there been no word from my father at all?" She'd been meaning to broach the subject with Malik for some time now, but she kept holding out hope that news would come that their ransom had been paid. Now, though, she was growing desperate. Months had passed, and he'd told her nothing. Her concern centered on Alex, too, for he was changing. Under the influence here in the palace, the English part of him was fading away. She reminded him daily of his grandfather and his heritage, but more and more of his conversation was focused on Hasim and his other friends and what they were planning on doing in the future—Not on the life they'd left behind.

Malik studied her carefully. He had always known this moment was going to come, and he had been preparing himself for the confrontation he knew was inevitable. "There has been no word," he answered without lying.

"What about the other captives from our ship? Have they been ransomed back?" she asked. The worry that her brother had been returned home before them was still with her.

"Yes. Most of them were gone within the first two months."

"I don't understand . . . Surely if my father had heard about our situation, he would have contacted you immediately." Catherine was insistent. "Perhaps if you let me write the message, then I could tell him . . ."

"It is time for the truth between us, Catherine," Malik declared firmly. He wanted to end the charade, to tell her how he felt about her and to make her his wife. He wanted her to stay with him, to raise Alex as his son and to give her his world.

"The truth?" She went very still, almost afraid of what would come next. "What truth, Malik? Has something happened to my father in England? Has there been trouble at home?"

Malik stood and took several paces away from the table. His expression was somber as he turned to face her. "I know nothing of your father. I have had no contact with him."

"I don't understand," she said, frowning. "You sent the letter. You said . . ."

He held up a hand to silence her, ready to make a full confession of his deception. "I know what I said, Catherine. At that moment, I would have said anything to ease your fears and help you adjust to your life here."

"Adjust to my life here," Catherine repeated, stunned. "Malik, I don't have a life here. My life is in England."

Her words pained and annoyed him. She came to his bed. She responded wildly to his touch when they made love, and yet she continued to dream of England and the man who would be her husband! Did what they shared mean nothing to her? How could he touch her body and not touch her heart?

"I have no intention of sending you back to England, Catherine. I never did," Malik responded.

"What are you saying?" She went pale as she got to her feet and stood there staring at him. Her eyes narrowed, and her expression became accusing.

"I'm saying, Catherine, that there was no letter. I made no ransom demand of your father. I have wanted you for my own since the first moment I saw you with Muhammed, and I have no intention of letting either you or Alex go."

"You can't mean any of this!" Angry tears welled up in her eyes. She felt as if she'd been crushed.

"I mean every word."

"I thought you were a kind and fair man. But you're worse than Muhammed!" she hurled the insult at him. "At least if I'd stayed with him, I would have gotten to go home eventually!"

"Don't believe that for a minute," Malik struck back with the complete, ugly truth. Her accusation comparing him to that snake of a pirate had hurt. "Muhammed would have raped you without thought to your innocence and then shared you with others. Only when your beauty was gone and you could no longer bring him money, would he have sent you back to England."

Catherine glared at Malik. She was seeing a side of him now that she hadn't recognized before. He appeared now the autocratic ruler, a dictatorial and unyielding man who knew what he wanted and got it any way he could. Her heart hardened against him. "I'll never forgive you for this," she said in a hoarse, pained voice.

"Forgive me for what, Catherine?" Malik countered

hotly. "You'll never forgive me for saving you from that pig Muhammed? You'll never forgive me for satisfying your every want and need? For lavishing gifts upon you and treating you with respect?"

She knew he was right, but she couldn't back down. Not when her pain was so great and her hopes so devastated.

When she said nothing in response to his outburst, Malik went on. "I apologize for all my shortcomings."

She glowered at him defiantly. "You lied to me, Malik."

"I wanted you, Catherine, and I still do. I will not apologize for that." In one last effort to soothe her, he said, "I will give you whatever you want."

"The only thing I want from you is my freedom."

A muscle worked in his lean jaw as he fought to control his frustration. *Was there no winning this woman?* "You know full well that that is the one thing I cannot give you."

"Cannot or *will* not?" she challenged, heartsick.

"Whatever, Catherine. You are mine, and you will remain mine. Be my wife."

She turned cold inside at the realization that she would never be leaving, and her gaze reflected it. "I am betrothed to Lord Gerald Ratcliff. He is the only man I'll ever marry."

Her refusal annoyed him. "You obviously never responded to your English lord the way you do to me," Malik said with male arrogance.

"What do you mean?"

"Why else would you still have been a virgin when you came here?"

She gasped at his words. "I was untouched because Gerald was a man of honor," she countered, wanting to hurt him in any way she could. But even as she said it, in her heart she knew Malik was right. Gerald's touch and

139

kiss had never aroused the feelings in her that his did.

Malik gave a snort of derision at her answer. "No man of honor can make you feel what I make you feel," he declared, coming to her and pulling her into his arms. He thought her very exciting when she was angry, and he wanted her even now. His mouth claimed hers in a possessive exchange, and his tongue dueled with hers in an intimate caress. "Marry me, Catherine."

Had Catherine not been so angry and upset, she would have felt the fires of her desire for Malik stirring within her.

She broke free of his embrace. "I have no desire to become *one* of your wives. There will never be a marriage between us."

"Never say never, Catherine. It is a very long time."

"I'll wait as long as it takes, Malik," she told him stubbornly.

She looked so magnificent as she stood there before him, defying him at every turn that he was tempted to throw her down on the pillows and take her right then and there. Ultimately, he knew she would surrender to the passion they shared and couldn't deny, but he also knew she might come to hate him if he abused this moment. He would wait and bide his time. He was certain that eventually she would come around.

"Our dinner grows cold," he pointed out, deliberately refusing to carry on with the argument. "There is no reason to allow good food to go to ruin."

"I suddenly find that I have no appetite. If you will excuse me, I will return to my rooms."

"No, I do *not* excuse you," Malik replied. "I desire your company. If you do not want to eat, then you will sit with me while I dine."

Catherine gritted her teeth, but didn't reply. She dropped back down on the cushions and sat there quietly, resentfully, as he returned to his seat beside her. No torture could have been greater than to have to suffer his nearness right then. All she wanted to do was get away from him and this place, but she knew now that that was not to be. Unless . . .

As she sat there, a plan began to form in her mind. Escape! She had thought about it when they'd first arrived, but had been too afraid then. Now, she was no longer afraid. She had been in the palace long enough now to know her way around. Catherine knew it wouldn't be easy, but she didn't care. She would get Alex and they would go home now! There would be no more waiting.

"You may retire now, Catherine," Malik said some time later when he'd finished his meal. "If you want to, that is . . ."

His statement brought her thoughts back to the present. "Thank you. Good night." She rose with regal dignity.

"Good night, Catherine." Malik watched her go, and he wondered at her thoughts. He knew she was angry with him, but he believed that anger would fade. He had offered her his whole world. He was sure that, given some time, she would come to her senses.

Catherine could feel the heat of his regard on her as she walked away, and she was glad when she was finally out of sight. It was a great relief to her to return to her own chambers. She'd been worried that he might want to make love to her tonight, and it frightened her to think that all he would have had to do was touch her and she would have melted in his arms.

"You're back early tonight," Almira observed with surprise when Catherine returned to her rooms. She had come to care deeply for this young Englishwoman in the weeks they'd been together.

"Yes, I am," Catherine said without elaborating. She would have loved to have been able to share her problems with her and enlist her help, but she still felt she couldn't trust Almira completely. The servant was, after all, one of *them*.

"Are you feeling all right?"

"I'm tired. I think I'll just go on to bed," she lied. What she really wanted was for Almira to leave her alone so she could finalize the plans she'd made. She would not wait another day to make her escape. She was going to get Alex and they were going to leave this very night. Somewhere in Algiers there had to be someone who could help them. Surely, there had to be a church in the city where they could take refuge.

When she'd donned her nightclothes and Almira had gone from the room, Catherine sat on her bed in the darkness, waiting and thinking. It was essential that she and Alex get away now, for if Avery had already been returned home as Malik had seemed to indicate, there was no telling what lies he might have told their father. She had to get Alex back to England, and the sooner the better.

The moon rose late that night. Catherine waited until it had reached and passed its zenith before making her move. When she was sure all was quiet in the harem, she put on her most ordinary, dark-colored gown and a simple but comfortable pair of sandals. She then covered her hair with a haik and crept from her rooms, looking left and right as she darted from shadow to shadow. She took great care to avoid notice and moved in complete silence.

The tension within her built as she left the harem with its dozing guard and made her way across the deserted garden toward the boys' quarters. This was where she knew it would become very dangerous. She wasn't sure exactly which room was Alex's, so she

142

moved with even greater caution. There was one guard strolling through the area, but he seemed preoccupied with his thoughts. When someone called out to him from the other end of the hall and he went to see what they wanted, Catherine had the time she needed. She darted forth, peeking into each bedroom until she found her young nephew sleeping soundly in the chamber at the very end of the hall.

"Alex! Wake up!" she whispered as she knelt beside his bed in the darkness.

"What is it?" Alex asked groggily. "Aunt Catherine? What do you want? Why are you here?"

"Shhh . . ." She held a finger to her lips warning him to talk softly. "It's time for us to go home. We're going back to Huntington House."

"We are?" He sat upright in bed, rubbing the sleep out of his eyes. "Is Grandfather here? Did he finally come for us?"

"No, darling, I'm afraid he's not here, but we're going to go to him. Come. Get dressed."

"But . . ."

"Alex," she snapped, "don't question me! Just hurry!"

His Aunt Catherine had never hollered at him before and it shocked him into action. He jumped up and tugged on the pants, djellaba, and sandals that had become his normal dress in the last few months. He was darkly tanned now and could easily pass for an Arab boy, except for his gray eyes.

"All right. I'm ready."

"Good boy. Now, we have to be very careful and very quiet. No one knows we're going."

"Not even Malik?" He was surprised by this.

"Especially not Malik. Let's make a game of this, shall we? Let's see which one of us can make it all the way to the stables without making a sound. All right?"

"Sure," he replied, eager to try.

Catherine took his hand, and they moved soundlessly from the boys' quarters, staying in the darkness, skirting any place where there might be a guard. When they reached the doorway that led to the main gardens, Catherine felt victory was within her reach. They only had to cross this last open place and then they would be at the stables and near an exit from the palace grounds. Soon, they would be out of here and free of Malik's hold on them. Soon, they would really be on their way home.

Malik could not sleep. He lay upon his lonely bed, thinking of what had just passed between him and Catherine. He'd always known the moment of truth with her would be painful, and it had been. He had thought his offer of marriage would assuage any anger she was feeling, but it hadn't. Her reaction had surprised him. Of the women he knew, all would have been pleased and honored to know that he wanted them—but not Catherine. It was one of the few times in his life when he'd been wrong about an "adversary," and it bothered him. If he was to win, he was going to have to try a new strategy.

Rising, Malik called for a servant and issued the instructions he wanted followed first thing in the morning. Then, still feeling restless, he strode to his terrace that overlooked the gardens.

It was a warm, pleasant night. The moon hung low on the horizon, and a thousand stars twinkled overhead. Malik longed for Catherine. He regretted hurting her, but he honestly believed that one day she would come to think of Algiers as her home. He wanted her to be his wife. He realized now that it had been foolish to offer her marriage. She's been furious with him, and knowing how proud she was, there was no way she would ever have accepted right then.

Malik smiled to himself as he thought of his spirited English beauty. This was the first time since Lila that he'd cared deeply about a woman. In fact, lately, his memories of Lila had begun to fade as Catherine remained constantly in his thoughts. He'd believed in the beginning that once he'd made love to Catherine, his desire for her would lessen. It seemed now, however, that after having had her, he only wanted her more, and not just her body. He wanted all of her.

Love . . . The thought was profound as it struck him. He had married other women with no thought of love, but Catherine was different. She had touched his heart and his mind. But did he love her? Malik didn't need to ponder the thought long to have his answer. She had become as important to him as life itself. If he was to have any peace, he was going to convince her to stay with him and become his wife.

Malik remembered her remark about not being "one of his wives," but he had not visited with or taken any of the other women in his harem to his bed since Catherine had arrived. If it would help to win her, he would set her apart from the others, and he would never see any of them again.

Though Malik felt better having decided on that, it still did not ease the disquiet he was feeling over the way they had parted. Had he been less proud himself, he would have called for her to be brought back to him, but he could not do that. He would give her some time alone. Tomorrow would be soon enough to see her again. Tomorrow he would do everything he could to erase England from her thoughts forever and make her his.

As he turned to go back inside, out of the corner of his eye, he thought he caught sight of a movement in the garden below. He glanced down, peering into the darkness, waiting and watching. After a few moments when nothing else happened, he told himself he'd been imagining things. The nightbirds had never ceased their singing, and they always fell silent when there was anything unusual about. Retreating to his solitary bed, he lay down once again to seek the rest he so sorely needed. Sleep finally came, but his dreams were of an elusive Catherine, who was always near but never quite within his grasp.

Catherine and Alex huddled close together in the gloom of the garden. They had been just about to cross an open area when Malik had emerged on his terrace. Terror had seized Catherine and she had grabbed Alex and dragged him back into the protective shadows to hide. They'd waited, trembling and desperate, for long moments before she finally got up enough nerve to take another look in Malik's direction. They just couldn't get caught now! Not when they were almost free!

Catherine's relief had been immense when she'd seen Malik disappear back inside, but she wondered at the pang of emotion she felt in her heart. He had looked very troubled and lonely. The thought occurred to her that he might be sorry for what had passed between them and be missing her, but she immediately dismissed it as ridiculous. He had other wives, and if he was in need of female companionship, he had only to call on one of them to be satisfied. Certainly, they would be more than willing to please him.

Jerking her thoughts away from Malik, she tugged gently on Alex's hand to start them off again. When he resisted, she glanced down at him to find him gazing up at her with wide, terrified eyes.

"It's all right, Alex. Malik's gone now. Just be silent."

"But I like Malik," he whispered. "Why do we have to hide from him?"

"Do you want to see your grandfather again?"

He nodded.

"Then we have to leave here."

Catherine waited until she could see the acceptance in his eyes, then gave him a quick, reassuring hug and led him away. They slipped into the darkened stables and, though an occasional horse stirred at their unexpected presence, no great ruckus was raised. With utmost care, they traversed that last treacherous area and made it to the far stable entrance that exited to the streets of Algiers.

Catherine paused only long enough to cover all of her face but her eyes with the haik, then she unlocked and pushed open the door. She thought about taking a horse, but quickly decided against it. Having come here with just the clothes on her back, she was going to leave the same way. She wanted nothing from Malik but her freedom. She also knew that a woman and a child on horseback would be far more noticeable than just a woman and a child on foot, and the one thing she didn't want was to be noticed by anyone. They had to disappear into the city; it was their only hope of escape.

Catherine and Alex slipped from the stable, closing the door behind them. Keeping their heads down, they moved off into the labyrinth that was Algiers.

Chapter Eleven

The narrow streets were dark and scary at this time of night, and Catherine hurried Alex along until they were out of sight of the palace. Only then, when she was certain that they were safely away, did she stop to catch her breath. She was still so nervous that her hands were trembling and she was gasping for air.

"We did it, Alex!" she exclaimed in a hushed voice, giving him a quick hug. "We did it!"

"I was really good at being quiet."

"You were wonderful. If this had been a game, you would have won!"

He beamed at her praise. "I was worried in the garden when Malik came out. I thought he saw us."

"I did, too, but it appears he didn't."

"What are we going to do now, Aunt Catherine?" Alex asked simply.

"We're going to try to find a church. There should be someone there who can help us get home."

"What if we can't find one?" he worried, glancing around in the dark.

The thought had occurred to her, too, but she'd tried not to dwell on it. "We will," she answered with a confidence she wished was real. "It just may be

148

tomorrow morning before we do. Right now, we need to get as far away from the palace as we can. Then, once it's light, we'll start looking for the church."

"All right," Alex agreed, trusting Catherine completely. She had been his source of strength through all their trials, and he knew she would never let anything bad happen. As an afterthought, he added, "I love you, Aunt Catherine."

His words brought instant tears to her eyes, and she suddenly got down on her knees before him to hold him close. "I love you, too, Alex." A deep, heartfelt sigh wracked her. When she let him go, they both felt much better. "Come on now, we'd better keep moving. We want to go home to Huntington House. We don't want Malik to catch up with us and take us back to the palace."

Her attitude puzzled Alex because he liked the dey very much. As they walked on, he asked in a subdued voice, "I thought Malik was the one who was going to help us go home."

"I did, too, sweetheart, but I just found out tonight that he wants us to stay here forever."

"Oh." Alex turned thoughtful, considering the possibility. "It would be fun to stay here, but we'd better go back. Grandfather's waiting for us, and we've been gone too long already. I'll miss Hasim, though. He's nice. We have fun together now that we're friends."

"Well, maybe you can see him again someday."

"I hope so, but right now, I just want to be with Grandfather . . . and get my boat back. I sure hope he's kept the *Scimitar* safe for me."

"I'm sure he has."

They fell silent as they rushed on through the ancient, walled part of the city. They hurried under archways and past closed shops. After about an hour of walking, Alex seemed to grow weary.

149

"Are you all right?" Catherine asked as she felt him slowing down.

"I'm tired," he said slowly. "Can we rest for a while?"

In her desire to put as much distance between her and Malik as she could, she'd forgotten that her companion was only seven years old. She paused in their headlong flight to look around. Through one ornate archway, she spied a very private garden complete with a splashing fountain in the center. A wrought-iron gate barred the entrance, but when she tried it, she found it unlocked. After a quick glance around to make sure there was no one about, she led Alex in.

"We'll rest here until daylight."

He nodded, too tired to talk anymore.

They moved to a corner of the garden that was shrouded by an overgrowth of trees and then sat down together on the ground, leaning against the stone wall that hid the little oasis from street view. Alex climbed up on her lap, and they rested there wrapped in each other's arms. Alex was soon asleep. Catherine had been determined to stay awake and keep watch just in case someone should come upon them, but after about a half an hour, she couldn't keep her eyes open any longer. Fight as she might, her lack of sleep had taken its toll, and she fell into a deep slumber that left her blissfully unaware of her surroundings.

The cry went up in the palace early when the servants for the boys went to rouse them. They were shocked to find young Serad missing, and they set out to search the palace grounds, thinking he was just up early and out playing. By the time their fruitless search turned up nothing, Almira had ventured into the Catherine's chambers to find her gone. Frantic, she rushed from

150

the women's quarters to notify Malik.

Malik had not slept well that night. His dreams of Catherine had left him feeling as if he'd gotten no rest at all. When he heard his servant talking with someone in his outer chamber, he rose quickly and dressed.

"What is it?" Malik asked when he entered the room.

"It's . . ." his servant began, but Almira cut in to inform the dey.

"It's Catherine, Malik Dey. She's gone!"

"Gone? What are you talking about?"

"When I went to see to her morning needs, her chamber was empty. I checked the grounds, but found nothing. It's as if she's vanished without a trace."

Malik muttered a curse, then demanded, "What about the boy? What about Serad?"

Just as he spoke, Hasim appeared in the hallway. "Father, Serad is gone. He must have left sometime during the night."

The dey stood rigidly before them, his thoughts racing as he made a quick decision on what to do. He turned to his servant. "Call out my guard. I want every inch of the palace searched again. If they're not found in the next half an hour, we will search the city." The servant raced off with Hasim to do as he'd ordered.

"You don't think she took the boy and went into the city alone, do you?" Almira asked fearfully a moment later. It was not her place to speak up, but she cared about Catherine and didn't want to think that she might be in danger.

"I'm not sure what Catherine might do right now," Malik answered tersely. "Did she say anything last night or act strangely?"

"No, Malik Dey," the servant answered respectfully. "I was waiting for her when she returned. I commented on how unusual it was for her to come back to her chambers so early, but that was all that was said between us. She seemed tired, but fine. When I left her last night, she was resting."

He scowled, annoyed with himself for not having anticipated this. He'd been judging her actions by all the other women he'd known, and he realized even more forcefully now that this was Catherine. She was different. She was proud, obstinate, and possessed an intelligence and will as strong as any man's. He had finally met a woman who was his equal in every way. By escaping, she had done exactly what he would have done under the same circumstances. As of that moment, Malik vowed to himself to never underestimate her again.

"Go back to the harem and search there once again. Come to me immediately if you find anything."

"Yes, Malik Dey."

Malik left his chambers and headed for the stable. There he found one of his guards talking to a stablehand.

"Malik Dey, it seems someone left the door to the stable unbarred last night. Iqbal, here, swears that he locked it himself when he retired." He motioned to the stablehand.

He nodded, then ordered the hand to saddle his horse.

"We will be searching the city?" his guard asked.

"As soon as the others report back to me, we will ride. This woman is headstrong and foolish, and there is no telling what kind of danger she could have gotten into."

Malik knew that if their places had been exchanged and he was the one running away with a small child, he would head for sanctuary, and a sanctuary for Catherine would be a Christian church.

When his men reported to him that there was no trace of the woman and child in the palace, they prepared to ride out. At his direction, they split into groups to check each church in the area.

"Hasim, you will ride with me," Malik ordered.

"Yes, Father," the boy replied, glad to be considered old enough to be included.

"There will be a substantial reward for the one who brings her safely back," he told his men. "See that she is not harmed in any way. I will kill any man who mistreats her. If you search but have no luck, meet back here. Then, if none of us are successful, we will try something else."

"Yes, Malik Dey," they all replied.

Certain that he'd been understood, he mounted his favorite stallion, a big, majestic black named Mansour, meaning magnificent, which he truly was, and rode from the stable. Hasim and the guards followed, their expressions as fierce and determined as Malik's.

The sound of voices on a balcony above her finally roused Catherine. As she came awake, she blinked in confusion trying to remember where she was and what she was doing there. Reality dawned on her quickly, and she hurriedly nudged Alex from his sleep.

"Alex, wake up. We've slept far too long already, and there are people about," she urged.

The boy awoke instantly, his look of bewilderment changing quickly to understanding.

They hurried from the garden before they were discovered. Judging from the height of the sun, she estimated that the day was already several hours old. The fear that their absence had already been discovered at the palace haunted her, but she couldn't let that paralyze her. They had to find safety, and fast.

The streets that had been so abandoned in the night were now teeming with people. Merchants had already appeared to set up shop and begin hawking their wares. Since Catherine hadn't eaten dinner, hunger began to gnaw at her, but she ignored it. No matter how good the fresh vegetables and fruits looked on the vendors' displays, she had no money to pay for any and wouldn't ever consider stealing.

After traveling down what seemed like an endless number of streets, they finally reached a place that afforded them a good view of the city as it spread out below them to the port and the sea. In a distance, Catherine could see a cross on the top of a building.

"Alex, look!" She pointed toward it. "We're almost there!"

She altered their course to head in that direction. Her spirits were high for the first time in months. Her heart was singing. She honestly believed that they would soon be on their way home, and she would see her father and Gerald again. They raced on, eager to reach that safe haven.

It was only at the last minute as they came around a corner near the church that she noticed several of Malik's men talking with the priest. Catherine quickly backed up, pushing Alex behind her. Her heart was pounding in her breast both from the exertion of their run for freedom and the sudden terror that possessed her.

Think, Catherine! Think! she demanded silently of herself as she moved off slowly with Alex in the opposite direction. There had to be a way to get out of Algiers. There had to be!

"What's the matter?" Alex asked. "Why aren't we going to the church?"

She explained quickly, and Alex said no more as he stayed right with her.

Catherine knew their situation was treacherous. She couldn't go to a mosque. The religious there would be

154

supportive of Malik. She couldn't go to the Christian churches, for they were obviously being watched. The waterfront remained the only place left where she could seek help. She set her fragile and fading hopes on the distant chance that there might be a ship in port from England or another European country doing regular trade, and that the captain might help them. She headed down toward the waterfront, keeping Alex's hand tight in hers.

Malik and his men met near the palace entrance several hours later.

"Did you find anything? Any trace of them?" he demanded.

"Nothing, Malik Dey, but the priests all promised to keep watch and let us know if they have any contact with her," they informed him.

He scowled. He knew Catherine was out there in the city somewhere, and, whether she knew it or not, she was in grave danger. "Next we will search the waterfront."

After telling the men where to rendezvous with him after the search was done, they again rode forth.

"Do you think we'll find them, Father?" Hasim asked.

"I hope so. A woman cannot survive here long without protection. During daylight hours they should be all right, but when the night falls, it could become deadly for them."

"Then we'll have to hurry. I don't want anything to happen to Serad."

"You have become good friends, then?"

Hasim nodded. "You were right, Father. Now that I know him, I do like him. He's brave and smart for one so young."

Malik almost chuckled at his son's reference to youth, for Hasim was not exactly aged. "Let us hope they are both smart enough to stay out of trouble until we can find them."

"You don't sound very angry with them," the boy observed.

"I'm angry, but I am also worried."

"Then you have come to like them, too?"

"I do," he admitted to his son. "I intend for them to stay here with us."

"I'm glad."

They said no more as they guided their horses through the streets on the trek toward the waterfront.

Catherine drew Alex closer to her side as they entered the rough area near the docks. Algerian women of virtue would never frequent such a place, and she could feel the eyes of the men upon her as they moved along. Offering prayers that they would be saved, she glanced at each man they passed hoping to find a face that looked sympathetic, but all stared at her in suspicion.

Suddenly, out of nowhere, a heavy, rough hand grabbed Catherine by the upper arm from behind, and she was spun forcefully around to face the biggest, ugliest man she'd ever seen. The man was completely bald. His face was round and pie-shaped. His eyes were cold, hard, and black, and what few teeth he had were rotted and discolored.

"Let me go!" she demanded. "How dare you touch me!"

Alex had lost his grip on her hand, but was still clinging to her skirts.

"Ah, so you speak English, do you? I thought you might not be a native woman. No good woman would be brazen enough to come down here."

"I'm here looking for someone."

"Well, you just found him. My name's Grimes." He leered at her.

Desperate, Catherine decided to appeal to his sense of honor. "Mr. Grimes, we have come here because we need help. Will you help us?" She deliberately glanced down at Alex so the horrible-looking man would pay attention to the fact that she had a child with her. "We must get away from Algiers. We need to get back to London."

"Supposing I have a way to get you back, what's in it for me?" he asked cagily, almost drooling as he stared at her. Though he could only see her eyes, he could tell even beneath the voluminous folds of the North African dress that she was a shapely wench.

"I'm sure there would be a great reward in it for you if you could get us on a ship bound for England. We must return home." She was watching his expression, and when she saw no softening in his regard, she feared that he was just toying with her and that he had absolutely no intention of helping them.

"And just who's going to pay this money?"

"My father. He's the Duke of Huntington."

"And my father is the Prince," he guffawed. Keeping a tight hold on her, he started to drag her along with him. "Come on. Let's go have us a drink and talk about this some more."

"What are you doing? Get your hands off of me! Where are you taking me? I don't want to have a drink," Catherine resisted, digging in her heels while keeping a hand on Alex.

"Sure you do. It'll help you relax. Then we can talk some more and figure out exactly what we need to do to get you out of here," he urged, licking his lips hungrily as he stared at her wide, frightened eyes above the concealing haik.

"I'm not going anywhere with you," Catherine told him. "Release me, now!"

Her attitude infuriated the man. He gripped her by the shoulder, intending to force her to go along, but he accidentally grabbed her by her headcovering and stripped it from her. The glory of her golden hair was revealed to him. His gaze went over her with avid interest before he started to drag her along again in earnest. "You're coming with me. Let's go . . ." The ache in his loins was growing by the second. She was beautiful . . . and blonde.

"I said no!" Catherine started to fight him in earnest. "We're not going anywhere with you!"

"Oh, yes you are!" He slapped her so hard that her head rocked back.

Alex charged at the man, but he easily brushed the boy off as if he were nothing more than a pesky insect.

"No!" Catherine cried, thinking her nephew hurt and suddenly fearing for her life. She tried to pull free to go to Alex, but the man would not release her. Instead, he kept pulling her along against her will, forcing her away from the boy.

"Shut up!" he snarled, drawing back to hit her again, this time with his fist, but the sound of thundering horses hooves interrupted him. He looked up to see Mansour running down on him at full speed. On the horse's back he caught sight of a fierce-looking warrior brandishing a scimitar. Indescribable terror jolted through Grimes, and with a scream, he shoved Catherine away from him and made a break to run. It was too late, though. With lethal effectiveness, the scimitar's curved blade sliced through the air, putting an end to his miserable life.

Catherine had fallen heavily into the dirt, and she and Alex looked on in horrified fascination as Malik felled the evil man.

"Malik!" Never in her wildest dreams had Catherine imagined she would be glad to see him again, but she was. She longed to throw herself into his arms and know the haven of his embrace.

Those who had gathered to watch Grimes and Catherine scattered to the four winds in fright and horror at the bloodshed.

Malik reined in his mount and maneuvered back to Catherine's side. She had gotten to her feet by the time he reached her, and Malik leaned over to grasp her by the waist and haul her up on his saddle in front of him.

"Serad, mount up with Hasim," Malik ordered, his features a stony mask. He was so tense he couldn't decide whether to beat Catherine or hold her close to his heart. The feel of her slender, quaking form clinging to him nearly drove him out of his mind. He had feared he would never see her again. He had thought her lost to him forever. He offered up silent thanks for her safe return.

"Yes, Malik," Alex answered as he scrambled to get up and then raced to his friend's side. Hasim helped him climb up behind him on his horse.

"Alex . . ." Catherine finally managed a word. She wanted to make sure he was all right.

"His name is Serad. You will use that name for him from now on," Malik ground out as he wheeled his stallion around and rode for the palace.

"His name is Alex. He's the future Duke of Huntington," she protested, tears glistening in her eyes as she realized the futility of her battle with Malik. It was over. She had lost. They would never be leaving Algiers. There was a bitterness in her heart as she faced the finality of it, but at the same time, she found that being safe in Malik's arms was a heavenly sensation. It confused her tremendously.

159

"His name is Serad!" Malik thundered. "He will be raised here along with Hasim to become as one of us. I will not hear of him being schooled in your English ways any longer. You will not speak to him of your home, your heritage, or your family. You will not talk about the past. As far as you are both concerned, the past began the day you arrived at the palace."

"But . . ."

"If I find that you have disobeyed me in this, I will separate the two of you, and you will never see the boy again. Do you understand me?"

The terrible look he gave her convinced her that he was serious—deadly serious—and she trembled before the force of him. "Yes," she managed in a strained voice.

"And, as the boy is called Serad now, you, too, will be known by another name. No longer will you be called the English Catherine. I give you the name of Rabi, and you will use it at all times. I do not ever want to hear the other names again." As if emphasizing his decree, he put his heels harder to his mount's sides and urged it to an even quicker pace.

Catherine accepted then and there that her future happiness depended on her ability to accept completely that which she was powerless to change. She only hoped she could do it. She knew it would not be easy.

Chapter Twelve

Spring, 1807
Eighteen years later in Boston . . .

> "Lady Wakefield—
> His Grace, the Duke of Huntington, has
> suffered a serious setback in his health. While his
> condition at this time is not critical, it is not
> known whether His Grace will make a complete
> recovery. I will keep you informed if there are any
> changes.
>
> *Sincerely,*
> *Sir Henry Townsend*
> *Solicitor-at-Law"*

Vivienne read the note again, still absorbing the
import of the message. When she looked up from the
missive, her expression was apprehensive. She'd
always known that eventually she would have to face
the duke's death, and it was not a pleasant thing.

Not that she personally cared about Edward. She
didn't. It was just that in the years since he'd had taken
her under his wing, he had provided her with a very
comfortable monthly allowance. While not extrava-
gant, when coupled with the ransom money she had

stashed away, Vivienne had never had to worry about her income again.

Now, though, it seemed to Vivienne that her security was threatened. She had no idea what provisions Edward had made for her in his will, and that worried her greatly. Certainly, as the widow of his only son, she was entitled to something, but it surely would not be much. Most likely after his death, her standard of living would depend on the good graces of the new Duke of Huntington, and the way things stood now, barring a miraculous return of Avery or Alexander from the dead, the title was due to pass to a distant cousin who neither knew nor cared about her. Her days of living on the Wakefield money might soon be coming to an end unless she took some action.

Vivienne's eyes narrowed thoughtfully as she reconsidered the wild idea she'd had not too long before concerning the young, handsome, dark-haired actor, David Markham. She'd seen him on stage in Boston and had not only appreciated his fine thespian skills, but his uncanny resemblance to Avery. Seeing him had given her a gem of an idea, and while she hadn't acted on it before, she knew now she would. It was a risk, a wildly outrageous plan, actually, but it was one she was willing to take. Certainly, she had nothing to lose in trying if Edward died.

Vivienne knew she was going to have to act quickly. She jotted off a note to a man she knew who did investigations, then summoned her servant. Giving instructions to the young girl to deliver the letter, she sat back to wait. With any luck, this wouldn't take too long at all.

David Markham was despondent. He sat by himself

in the bar near the docks, nursing his glass of whiskey. When he'd gotten up that morning, he hadn't believed that things could get any worse, but he'd been wrong. First, there had been the loss of his parents, killed in a tragic fire that had swept through their home six months before. Then, to add to David's misery, he'd discovered that his father had run up large debts against the family business, a small dry goods store. Creditors had descended on the estate like vultures before his parents were even cold in the ground, and when all had been said and done, David had been left penniless with some of his father's debts still left to pay. He'd managed for a time, giving the creditors a little bit each week out of the money he earned from his acting, but then yesterday had come the final killing blow. He'd been informed that the play he was performing in was closing suddenly, and he was out of work immediately.

David took a deep drink, suddenly wanting to drown his sorrows. The emotional strain of the last few months had taken their toll. He felt alone and desperate. The creditors would be expecting their payments, but he had nothing left to give them, only his few suits of clothing and a very few personal possessions that he kept in his room in the rundown boardinghouse where he stayed. At twenty-six, he almost felt as if his life were over.

When the bargirl appeared at his side, David did not send her away, but fell victim to her charms. After downing a few more of the drinks that she served him, he quickly took her up on her proposition. His steps were unsteady as he followed her upstairs to her room.

David didn't stay with her long. He returned to his room at the boardinghouse and slept soundly the rest of the night, thanks to the potent liquor. The next morning found him completely confused and bewildered when constables showed up at his room to arrest him for the girl's death. She had been found strangled in her room. His pleas of innocence fell on deaf ears, and he was dragged away and locked up in jail. Forsaken, terrified, and very hung over, he was left to rot in the jail cell.

David told himself he couldn't have done it, that he was not a violent man. But the proof against him was so overwhelming that after a few desperate days and sleepless nights, he almost convinced himself that he had, indeed, murdered the girl.

Alone and without hope, David sat in the spartanly furnished cell. He heard the sound of voices in the outer part of the jail, but paid little heed believing it could have nothing to do with him. He had no one to call upon as witness, for no one had seen him return to his room at the boardinghouse. He'd been alone from the moment he'd left her. He could mount no reasonable defense.

"Markham, you're free to go," the constable said grimly as he appeared before his cell and unlocked the barred door.

David was in complete shock. After all the accusations that had been leveled at him, he couldn't understand why they were finally releasing him.

"The lady you were protecting has come and told us the truth about where you were that night," the officer said with gruff resentment. He had thought they'd had the murder solved, but the lady's testimony had proven them wrong. "You're free to go."

He was totally dumbstruck. What lady? What was going on?

"She's waiting for you in her carriage outside."

David was still having trouble comprehending what

was going on. He frowned. "You finally believe me? I can go?"

The constable nodded.

David didn't take the time to question his good fortune. He didn't know who this mysterious woman was who'd rescued him, but he intended to find out right now and thank her for her help.

Vivienne was sitting in her carriage watching discreetly out the window. When she saw the young man emerge from the jail and head straight toward her carriage, she smiled. Soon her plan would be fully under way, and all because she'd been smart enough to utilize the right people. It had cost her a lot, but looking at Markham now, she knew it had been worth it.

"Please come in, Mr. Markham," Vivienne invited in a quiet voice as David approached the carriage.

Puzzled, not recognizing the soft, cultured English voice at all, he hesitated for a moment, then opened the carriage door.

"Join me."

Squinting against the darkness of the interior, David tried to get a good look at the woman who'd saved him. But she was sitting back in the shadows and he had only a vague impression of wealth and presence. "Thank you," he said, climbing in adroitly.

"You may close the door."

David did as he was told. He took a seat across from her, and there in the dimness of the interior he could see more clearly and knew that his first impression of her had been correct. She was a stunning woman, although some years older than himself. He also realized that he had never seen her before in his life. She was a complete stranger to him, and he had no idea why she had saved him from jail.

"Do I know you?" he asked, breaking the momentary silence.

"No," Vivienne answered slowly, enjoying the feeling of being a powerful predator about to take its prey, "but *I* know *you.*"

"I don't understand. How could you know me? And why would you come and get me out of jail? What did you tell them?"

She shrugged carelessly. "Merely that you passed the entire evening with me that night and could not possibly have been with the girl."

"But they had witnesses at the bar who saw me there, and I *was* there."

"I have witnesses who saw you with me."

He blinked at that statement, and then his gaze narrowed. She had to have some other motive for lying to get him released from jail. "What do you want?"

"I have an offer to make you, Mr. Markham," Vivienne said coolly.

"What kind of offer?"

"A business proposition, so to speak. I have an acting job available. I'm looking for a young man of your qualifications. Tall, handsome, dark hair and . . ." She leaned forward to get a better look at his eyes. She'd had no idea what color they were, and she was thrilled to find that they were gray, just as Alexander's had been. A wolfish smile curved her lovely mouth. "And gray eyes. You're perfect for the part, but then I knew that before."

"Wait. This is a little overwhelming." He didn't know who she was or what she really wanted. "You say you know who I am and that you came here to the jail to get me out because you need me to play a part for you?"

"I always sensed you were brilliant," Vivienne replied with a touch of snideness. "I need you to

166

become my missing son."

"Your son? Why?" he asked, really confused.

She gave a sinister laugh. "For money, of course. There's a fortune at stake here, and unless I can produce the heir, my son, Alexander, all will be lost."

"Where is your son?"

"He disappeared at sea some eighteen years ago, and his body was never found. We're still searching for him, but there's not much hope left now. The duke, however, is very old and he's sick. If he dies without an heir, the duchy will pass to a distant relative. I want the money and the power, and I can get it through you."

"You're related to a duke?" David was stunned.

She paused, then said with assurance, "Allow me to introduce myself. I am Lady Vivienne Wakefield. My father-in-law is Edward Wakefield, Duke of Huntington."

He went a little pale. Though he had been born and raised here in America, he knew all about English nobility and how the dukes were very rich, very important men. "You can't be serious?"

"Oh, I'm very serious," she returned. "I've seen you act on stage, Mr. Markham. I know you could manage it."

"What exactly would I have to do?" He was still hesitant, his moral upbringing deeply imbedded in his character.

"We would return together to establish your true identity. Your story would be that you were taken by pirates, sold into captivity as a child, and eventually went to sea. You ended up here in America, where, miraculously, the men I've had searching for you all these years found you, and we were reunited. It's a touching story, don't you think?"

"Yes, but it's illegal . . . isn't it?"

Vivienne gave him a piercing, deadly look. "Mr. Markham, I can suddenly change my testimony, admit that I was lying, and put you back in jail in about two minutes. Do I make myself clear?"

"Very."

"Good," she smiled. "It's very simple, really. You would be living in luxurious splendor, eat exotic foods every day, and have more money than you can spend for the rest of your life."

"There would be money?" he repeated, thinking of his father's debts.

"Yes, but I would control it," Vivienne informed him sharply. "You will claim the money, but it will be all mine. If we strike a bargain now, I promise you that you will never want for another material thing for as long as you live."

David had always been painfully honest and hardworking. He balked at what amounted to stealing the duke's fortune, but he knew if he refused her offer she would do exactly what she threatened, and then there would be no tomorrow for him. He would end up being hung for a crime he had not committed. It troubled him that this Lady Wakefield knew so much about him while he knew nothing about her, but he concluded it didn't really matter. The only possible choice he had was the one she was giving him. Maybe, David thought on a brighter note, if he were free, he might be able to find the person responsible for the girl's death and prove his own innocence. It was worth a try.

"What is it you want me to do?" he asked, ignoring the sting of his conscience.

"From this moment on, you will follow my direction in all things and never question me in anything I may ask you to do," Vivienne told him curtly.

David was silent for a moment, then answered tightly, "All right."

"Good." She tapped on the carriage roof twice and the vehicle lurched to a start.

"Where are we going?"

"To my home."

"But what about my things at the boardinghouse?"

"What do they matter? I want you to forget everything you knew before today. David Markham is dead. He's gone forever. You are now Alexander Wakefield, my son, and the future Duke of Huntington. You are about to get an intensive education concerning your new 'past.'"

David stared out the window, listening as her words bound him to her more tightly than ropes and chains ever could have.

The following two months passed in a blur of activity for David as Vivienne took over every aspect of his life. He was drilled incessantly on manners and protocol. He was lectured constantly on the Wakefield family history, and his relationship not only with his grandfather, but also with his aunt Catherine and Avery. She even described certain expressions that had been common to Alexander and had him practice before a mirror. Finally, by the sixth week, David began to act the part of the future duke with an accomplished, natural ease that satisfied Vivienne's perfectionist standards.

Vivienne then turned her tutoring to other areas that would be necessary if he were to pass for Alexander. She had David memorize the floor plan of Huntington House so it would be familiar to him when he returned, and she reminded him over and over again of

Alexander's love for the sea. She took him to a tailor and had an entire wardrobe made up for him. No expense was spared, and David almost would have enjoyed it, if his conscience hadn't bothered him. They were on their way now for the final fitting at the tailor's.

"Once more, Alexander, what was your favorite toy?" Vivienne quizzed. She had stopped calling him David that first night, for she'd wanted him to become accustomed to the name Alex. She was pleased that he now answered her without hesitation.

David looked thoughtful. For some unknown reason, he could not remember this. "A gun?" he asked rather than answered, and he was rewarded with a verbal barrage from his "mother."

"I have you told you a hundred times that your favorite toy as a child was a *model boat*. Your grandfather gave it to you and you practically slept with the thing! I'm sure it will come up at some time, so be prepared for it."

David looked shame-faced. "I'm sorry. It just seems so unimportant."

"It may to you and me, but we're not the ones we need to convince, now, are we?" she asked sarcastically as she glared at him across the carriage. Everything was going well, but she didn't want one little mistake to ruin things for them. "We have to be careful. Our stories need to match flawlessly. You have to be believable. If you're not . . ." She let the sentence hang.

David could almost feel the bite of the hangman's noose around his neck, and he gave her a determined look. "I will be. You chose me because I am a good actor. There will be no doubt in anyone's mind that I am Alexander Wakefield."

Satisfied with his response, she said, "I sent the letter to England three weeks ago informing the duke of your miraculous return from the dead. I'm sure Edward will want to verify everything before he accepts you as really being Alexander, so I imagine I will be hearing from him or his representative some time in the next week or so."

"And you've arranged everything so no one knows about me or my real background?" David worried that some of his old acquaintances might reveal his true identity. Had he known Vivienne better, he wouldn't have concerned himself.

"I've handled it. Our story is perfect, and there are witnesses in place to testify to it all under oath, if need be." Vivienne smiled again, silently congratulating herself on her brilliant tactics in paying off or eliminating anyone who might possibly interfere with her plans. In her usual devious way, she had covered every possible angle. All she needed now was for Edward to believe David's performance. Her life would finally become then what she'd always imagined it would be.

At her words, David fell silent. He thought it a rather sad testimony to his existence that he, David Markham, could disappear so completely and not one of his acquaintances even noticed; or, if they did notice, cared enough to ask questions. It left him feeling even more isolated than he already felt.

The carriage drew to a stop before the tailor's establishment, and David climbed out to help Vivienne in her descent. A few moments later, Vivienne was seated in the outer room waiting for him to emerge in one of his new suits. When David appeared, it was all she could do to control her surprise over how much he truly resembled Avery. He was wearing a gray dress coat, cut-away in style, a burgundy-colored vest, a white shirt and matching cravat, and tight, perfectly fitting gray breeches. If Edward were to judge on physical appearance alone, Vivienne was certain there would be no doubt in his mind about the authenticity of his claim.

"What do you think?" David asked her as he approached.

"I think you look wonderful, Alexander," she answered. "I'm proud to have you as my son." Her next words were for his ears only. "Now, we have only one more trial left to face before our goal is met."

"Grandfather?" he asked.

"Yes. Your grandfather."

"I can't stand this confounded waiting," the now seventy-two-year-old Edward complained to Dalton as he sat in a wing chair in his bedroom, watching out the window that afforded him a view of the front drive. There was a blanket across his lap to ward off any chill, and on the bedside table nearby was a bottle of the elixir his physician had prescribed for him to take three times a day to bolster his failing health and spirit. Both Edward and Dalton knew, though, that the news of Alexander being found had done more for him than any medicine could hope to do. He had been weary of life, but now had a reason to go on. "For nearly twenty years I have anticipated this moment, and now, these last few hours seem to be longer than all the rest . . ."

"I understand completely, Your Grace," the aged Dalton sympathized as he remained close by his side. He had suffered through the painful loss of Lady Catherine and young Alexander just as the duke had, and he, too, was eagerly anticipating the boy's return this day. It was heartbreaking that Lady Catherine wouldn't be returning with him, but they'd both read

Townsend's explanation as to what had happened to her.

"I just can't help but wonder, though . . ." Edward glanced over at his servant, and Dalton could see the grain of doubt flickering in his eyes.

"How Lady Vivienne managed to find him after all this time when you couldn't?" he finished for him.

"Exactly," the duke replied heavily. "I never stopped hoping, but . . ."

"I'm sure everything's going to be fine, Your Grace. Sir Townsend did send a man to investigate, did he not?"

Edward nodded. "And everything Vivienne claimed in her letter appears to be true."

He thought of the report Henry had received that confirmed it all. It had detailed how Vivienne had never stopped searching for Alexander, how her reason for moving to America was to be close to her own investigators who had information concerning her son's whereabouts there. It went on to say how her men had finally located the future duke and seen mother and son reunited. It was a touching story of faithful, unending devotion. But Edward still harbored a niggling doubt about Vivienne's true motives. He had helped her through the years, since she was family and he'd been grateful that she'd never disgraced the Wakefield name, but he had never developed any warmth or affection for her, and he was positive the lack of deep feelings ran both ways.

"Then I should say that today is a day for rejoicing, Your Grace."

Lost in his depressing musings, the duke looked old, very old, but at Dalton's comment, he brightened again. Just the smile he smiled and the renewed twinkle in his eyes made him look and feel younger again.

Dalton had been his mainstay during all the troubling times since Catherine and Alexander had disappeared. Edward sometimes wondered how he would have gotten along without him.

"Indeed you're right, Dalton. If Townsend's men say it's so, then it must be true. He's a very thorough fellow and one I trust implicitly. We shall celebrate grandly when I see my grandson again." Tears, long denied, blurred his vision, and he quickly blinked them away. "Damnit, man, what is taking them so long!" he blustered to cover the deep emotions that were ravaging him as he turned his attention once more out the window so he could watch for Alexander's return.

The duke's carriage was racing from London toward Huntington House. Vivienne sat close beside Alexander while Henry Townsend sat on the seat opposite them. She was nervous, but she was revealing that apprehension only as excitement over her son's return to his childhood home, not as fear of David's being discovered as an impostor.

"This is so exciting, Alex," she said to him, giving him a very motherly smile. "I can't wait to see your grandfather's face when he sees you. He's going to be so happy . . ." Conjuring up just the right amount of tears for the occasion, she dabbed daintily at the corner of her eye with a lace handkerchief.

David was playing his role to perfection. He looked nervous, uncomfortable, and excited all at the same time. "Do you think he'll really believe it's me?" he asked, glancing back and forth between the solicitor and Vivienne. "It's been so many years, and things have changed so much. I've changed so much . . ."

"Don't you worry," she reassured him, patting his

hand. "Your grandfather will recognize you immediately. You look very much like your father . . ."

"You certainly do, Lord Alexander. I don't think you have to worry on that account. I doubt His Grace will have any trouble seeing the family resemblance in you," Henry reassured the young man.

"Good. I am looking forward to seeing him again so much. It's been a long time."

"I am terribly sorry about your husband and Lady Catherine, Lady Vivienne," Townsend offered his sympathy.

"Thank you, Sir Henry. It hasn't been easy for either the duke or myself, but now that Alexander's back, everything will be just fine."

"It certainly should be," he reassured her. He'd heard the story from them about how Avery must have been searching the docks after the kidnapping and been caught by the same unknown thugs who'd taken the boy and Catherine. All Alexander could remember was that they'd all been locked up together in a windowless cabin on board a ship. The vessel had sailed from London, but he'd had no idea what the final destination had been. The young man's memory had been vague on a few things, but Townsend had been impressed with his tale all the same. He had been, after all, only seven years old at the time, and it was a pure wonder that he'd turned up now. The most tragic part of the whole affair was that no one had ever been able to find out exactly what had happened to Lady Catherine and Lord Avery. According to Alexander, they were separated when the pirates captured the ship, and he never saw or heard from either his father or his aunt again.

Sad as that discovery had been, though, Townsend still knew that the duke was going to be thrilled to have his grandson back. He also knew that this just might be the thing that would help him regain the will to live. He'd been watching him slowly deteriorating over the last few years as he gave up that last thread of hope of ever seeing his family alive again. Now that was all changed, and he hoped His Grace's health would improve.

"Look, Alexander! There's Huntington House now!" Vivienne exclaimed, pointing out the carriage window toward the majestic mansion that had just come into view.

"Yes, Lord Alexander, you're finally home," Townsend added, pleased at this happy ending.

Chapter Thirteen

David turned in his seat to look out the carriage window, and his first view of Huntington House left him speechless. His carefully maintained façade of control almost cracked as he stared in astonishment at the palatial manse that looked big enough to house most of Boston. Of the finest brick and stone, surrounded by perfectly manicured emerald lawns and flowering gardens, Huntington House rose in stately splendor to be silhouetted against the cloudless blue sky. Never in his wildest dreams had David ever expected the Wakefield family home to be this grand. He'd known from what Vivienne had told him that the duke was rich, but he'd never given any serious consideration as to *how* rich. It rendered him numb to think that if Vivienne's plan was successful, this would all be "his" one day.

"Does anything look familiar?" Vivienne prompted innocently, sounding as if she was trying to jog his memory.

"A little . . ." David said with a premeditated confusion that seemed real. "I remember the gardens mostly, I guess. I think I must have played outside a lot."

"You most certainly did," she approved. "Oh, I'm so glad you're back. You just can't know what this means to me," Vivienne sighed happily as she gazed at her "son" with tender adoration. She wasn't lying; without "Alex," her fortunes would soon have taken a turn for the worse.

Henry watched the exchange and felt happy that things seemed to have worked out so well. He wanted nothing more than his old friend's happiness, and he was sure Alexander's return would accomplish that.

David glanced at Vivienne nervously, and she gave him a triumphant smile.

"Are you nervous, Alex?" she asked.

He nodded. "Very."

"Don't be. You're home. Everything's going to be all right now."

The carriage drew to a stop at the front door, and they descended and started up the stairs. Dalton appeared at the door to meet them.

"Welcome home, Lady Vivienne. Good afternoon, Sir Townsend," the elderly servant greeted them, and then his full gaze fell upon "Alex." For a moment, he stared at the young man, studying his features and his gray eyes. Then, as if finally, truly believing, he smiled in spite of himself. "This must be Lord Alexander. Welcome home. We've missed you." It was a heartfelt greeting, and as close to a show of emotion as the family would ever get from Dalton.

"Hello. You must be Dalton?" David returned with a warm smile of his own, recalling the lectures Vivienne had given him on the oldest and most influential of the duke's servants at the Huntington Estate.

"Indeed, sir."

"It's good to be back."

"Where is the duke, Dalton?" Vivienne interrupted.

"He's in his study awaiting you, your ladyship."

"Thank you. Come, Alex, let's take you to your grandfather now. I'm sure he's eager to see you again. Sir Henry, you will join us, won't you?" she asked when she noticed that he was hanging back a bit.

"I'll be in directly, Lady Vivienne. I thought perhaps His Grace would like some time with you in private."

Vivienne granted him a beatific smile. "Why thank you, Sir Henry. That is most thoughtful of you."

With Dalton in the lead, Vivienne and David started down the wide hall to the duke's study. David had to struggle to keep from gaping at his surroundings. Vivienne's descriptions of the riches of Huntington House had been glowing, but he'd still underestimated in his own mind. From the Aubusson carpets on the floor to the crystal chandeliers to the portraits of past dukes on the walls, the entire manor bespoke of elegance, wealth, and tradition. He understood fully why Vivienne longed to claim Huntington House and the fortune for her own.

David's conscience reared its head, whispering in the back of his mind that he was not a Wakefield nor would he ever be a Wakefield, but he turned away from the critical thought. He focused on the encounter to come, knowing this was going to be the true test. He had to convince the duke that he was Alexander. Everything Vivienne had ever taught him raced through his mind—the family history, the expressions and mannerisms that were Alexander's as a child, the duke's unfailing love for the boy. David felt confident yet cautious as they walked on. Ahead of him, he saw Dalton pause and then knock on a door, and he knew the time had come. He drew a deep breath and prepared to face the future Vivienne had set for him.

Edward had seen the carriage pull up to the front

entrance, and he was hard put to control the emotions that raged through him. He alternated between excitement and fear. The old man kept his gaze riveted on his study door, knowing that at any moment the boy he'd thought he'd never see again was going to come through it.

Edward was certain his reunion with Alexander was going to be the happiest moment of his life . . . unless the young man turned out not to be his grandson. In agitation, Edward scowled blackly over having had such doubts. Townsend had indicated Vivienne possessed written proof, yet there remained a flicker of uncertainty in his mind. Edward decided then and there that he would base his decision on his feelings. He would know instinctively whether the boy was Alexander or not. He was sure of it.

There was the sound of footsteps in the hallway, and Edward's hands began to tremble. He clutched at the blanket that lay over his lap to steady them. Soon . . . very soon now.

Dalton's knock came at the door. "Your Grace, Lady Vivienne and Lord Alexander have arrived."

"Please show them in, Dalton," he called out, his eyes glued on the portal.

Dalton pushed the door wide and held it open for Vivienne and David to enter the room.

"Vivienne . . ." Edward greeted her as she approached him. He noted that although she was as attractive as ever, she was also still as cold. Despite the smile on her lips and her congenial expression, he could recognize the coldbloodedness in her nature.

Vivienne hadn't seen her father-in-law for several years now, and she was shocked by how ill he looked. He certainly didn't appear to be long for this world, and that made her even more pleased with her plan.

She did not let her reaction to the state of his health show in her carefully schooled expression. Instead, she went to Edward's side and pressed a kiss to his weathered cheek.

"It's good to see you, Your Grace," she told him. Then, straightening, she said with feeling, "I'm glad I bring you good news today. The men I hired finally managed to locate Alexander. It's still even hard for me to believe. Our Alexander is back . . . my only lasting connection to Avery. Alexander, come and see your grandfather again. It's been far too long."

The duke's shrewd, blue-eyed gaze swung to the tall young man standing just slightly behind her and nailed him with a penetrating look. Edward's breath caught in his throat for he knew this was exactly the way Alexander should have looked as a grown man—the dark hair and gray eyes. Yet, even as he acknowledged that his physical resemblance to Avery was uncanny, a hint of doubt remained that would not allow the old man to accept him without question.

"It's good to see you, my boy," Edward spoke slowly, giving him a slight smile.

"Grandfather . . ." David responded with warmth and affection showing in his eyes.

David started to kneel beside his chair, but Edward waved him away and struggled to stand. Dalton came to his aid, and only then did Edward get to his feet, standing eye-to-eye with David. David accepted his serious regard without flinching. It had been nearly nineteen years since the duke had last seen his grandson, and David had expected that there would be such close scrutiny. He was as prepared as he would ever be for this encounter. Vivienne had warned him that the old man might not believe him immediately, so he stood silently before him, returning his gaze and

181

waiting for his reaction.

Vivienne maintained a controlled manner as she, too, waited for Edward's response. She'd hoped he would accept him right away, but it didn't surprise her when he didn't. The future of the duchy was at stake, and it was obvious now that he was going to take his time in coming to his conclusion.

"It's good to have you back," Edward said, opening his arms to embrace the young man and breaking the tenseness of the moment.

David went to him and was enfolded in his warm embrace. He felt the frailty of the old man and suddenly knew a deep sense of shame. The duke looked nothing like the ogre Vivienne had painted him to be, and David felt real guilt over the deception. He realized with finality that unless the duke rejected him, he would be trapped in the guise of Alexander Wakefield, the future Duke of Huntington, for the rest of his life. For a moment, he was torn; then, with a fierce effort, he pushed his sense of honor from him. David Markham was dead, or *would* be dead if he tried to exist again. He *was* Alexander Wakefield now, and according to Vivienne there wasn't anyone who could prove differently.

"I've missed you, Grandfather," David said with deep emotion as he imagined himself reunited with his own dead parents.

"You were so small when you left . . . barely eight," Edward spoke softly as he released him and then slowly levered himself back down in his own chair.

"I know. I don't remember much about that time, but I do remember you . . ." As he said it, he almost wished that he did.

"Sit down and tell me everything that happened. I especially want to hear about Catherine . . . and your father," he requested.

David launched into the story Vivienne had so painstakingly invented. He was vague where she'd told him to be vague and detailed where she'd insisted upon details. It was some time later when he finished.

"You were set upon by pirates . . ." Edward remarked thoughtfully, finding no fault with his story, but still feeling vaguely uncomfortable in offering complete acceptance right away. The good Lord knew he wanted this boy to be Alexander, but that element of doubt hovered relentlessly in the back of his mind. "You used to think pirates were exciting."

"I don't anymore," David answered firmly.

"I don't doubt it," the duke replied with a smile. "Dalton? Are the refreshments ready?"

"Yes, Your Grace. If you'd care to come into the dining room, Sir Townsend is waiting for you there."

The servant went to help the duke, but David offered first.

"Dalton, would you mind if I helped him?"

Their eyes met in understanding, and Dalton relented graciously.

Edward gave Alexander an appreciative look as he leaned on the young man's strong arm to walk the short distance into the dining room.

They passed the next several hours in conversation, and the longer they were together, the more impressed Edward became. Later, when he grew weary, the duke excused himself to go up to his room for to rest for a while before dinner.

"Your Grace . . ." Dalton began a little hesitantly once they were in the privacy of his chambers. "You seem less than certain that this young man is our Alexander. Is there something troubling you? I was most convinced myself."

"There's nothing that I can pinpoint exactly, Dalton. I suppose I'm more puzzled than anything," he confided as the servant helped him into bed. "When I brought up the subject of pirates, which he was once so keen on, Alexander didn't react strongly at all, and then there's the matter of the boat . . ."

"His toy boat, Your Grace?" Dalton knew exactly what he meant. Alexander and the boat had been inseparable until the day he'd disappeared.

"Yes. He hasn't asked about it at all," the duke said, frowning. "Maybe he was just too young to remember . . ."

When Dalton went back downstairs, the others were still in the dining room.

"Would you like me to show you to your rooms?" he offered. "Sir Townsend, you will be staying the night, won't you?"

"Yes, thank you, Dalton."

The servant took them upstairs and directed each to their own bedroom. He showed David to his room last.

"Here you are, Lord Alexander," he said as he opened the door to the same room he'd had as a child.

David stepped inside and found it much like Vivienne had described it. It seemed just from looking around that the duke had not disturbed a thing in all the years the real Alex was gone. He cast Dalton a sidelong glance. "He didn't change anything . . ."

"Not a thing," he confirmed. "I'll leave you now. If there's anything you need, just use the bellpull. Dinner will be served at half past seven."

"Thank you, Dalton."

When the old man had gone, David stood alone in the middle of the bedroom of the man whose identity he'd stolen. He felt the interloper, a stranger in a foreign land. He moved around touching the massive walnut wardrobe and the sturdy four-poster bed.

On impulse, needing a breath of fresh air, David left the room. He moved through the house quietly, not wanting to draw attention to himself. Studying Vivienne's drawings of the house had helped him tremendously, and he made his way easily through the massive mansion gazing at the portraits on the walls and glancing out the windows to familiarize himself with the gardens and lawns. Remembering that Vivienne had told him the real Alexander liked to go to the reflecting pond at the back of the garden, he let himself out of the house and wandered along a brick path that skirted the building. Within minutes he found himself at the edge of the flower garden, and he moved on down the walkway, through a high hedge to the very back where he found the pond just as she had told him he would.

David sat down on the mossy bank to stare out across the small pond. He could well imagine how special this place had been to the little seven-year-old boy who had played here every day. He found himself sympathizing with the missing, and very probably dead, real Alexander. David thought it tremendously sad that the boy had been stolen from his loving grandfather, and he made a silent promise to try to be the very best Alexander Wakefield he could be.

As David was sitting there alone, lost in his thoughts, the sound of voices came to him from the other side of the hedge.

"Did you see him, Mattie? Did you see how very handsome he is?" a breathless feminine voice with an Irish lilt was asking of her unseen companion.

"Oh, I saw him, all right, Miss Tess," the woman

named Mattie answered, but she sounded a bit disapproving.

"Didn't you think he was grand?" Tess sighed.

"He's as good-looking as his father was," the one named Mattie disparaged.

"That's bad?" Her question was surprised.

"You're too young to remember. You weren't here when Lord Avery was. We can only hope that 'like father like son' doesn't hold true for another generation."

"I don't understand."

"His Grace is a good, fine man," Mattie lectured Tess, "but his son, Avery, was nothing like him. He was a scoundrel. It was a shame. He put the duke through hell."

David was amazed at what he was hearing and said nothing, not wanting to reveal his presence.

"What did he do?"

"Rumor had it that he gambled and the like. Of course, we were never really sure, and though Dalton knew all the particulars, he wasn't one to talk. Just know that he was not a good man, and the duke is well rid of him."

"And you think Lord Alexander is like him?"

"We'll have to wait and see, Tess, but I wouldn't be looking at him as if he were the Savior returned, if I were you. Remember your place, girl." Their voices faded out as the two women moved away, completely unaware that he'd overheard them.

David had at first found their conversation amusing, but he was stunned by what he'd heard concerning his "father." It was a shock to him that Avery had been a wastrel. Vivienne had never so much as hinted at any flaws in her beloved husband. It certainly explained a lot about the way she manipulated and used people.

She'd probably learned from her husband, or they might have been two of a kind from the start. The realization left him feeling even worse. Getting to his feet, he went back inside to get ready for dinner. As he entered the house, he wondered idly which one of the servants was Tess.

Several days passed in calm activities. Vivienne seemed completely satisfied with the way things were going. David knew he and the duke were getting along well enough, but he'd noticed that in all their conversations the old nobleman had yet to refer to him by name. When he spoke to him he always used the terms "my boy" or "son," never "Alexander." It was the one clue David had that he had not been completely accepted yet.

It became a pleasant habit for David to walk out to the pond late every afternoon. He was there lingering on the bank the third day after his arrival when he looked up just as the duke came slowly down the walk past the hedge.

"I had a feeling I might find you here. Dalton told me you come out every day," Edward said, observing him closely.

"I like it here. It's so peaceful and serene . . ."

"This was where you were taken from. Do you remember any of it?" His gaze did not waver from his face. He was tired of the uncertainty. Dalton seemed positive that this was Alex. Vivienne and Townsend seemed sure it was him. Why did he still doubt?

"Not really. I just remember being afraid and . . ." David looked thoughtful as if wracking his memory for details of a trauma long past. He glanced up at Edward then and saw the small toy boat he held in his hand.

"My boat! You saved it!" He was immensely relieved that Vivienne had warned him over and over about the boat, and he moved forward to take it as the duke held it out to him.

"You remembered . . ." Edward breathed in relief, then tested further for the one last bit of proof he needed. He watched as the young man cradled the boat like a treasure. "Do you still want to paint the name on it? We'd planned to do that together when I got back from my trip all those years ago."

David had no idea what Alexander had wanted to name his boat and obviously neither had Vivienne. Covering his sudden fear well, he thought quickly and replied, "I still want to paint a name on it, but I want to call it the *Homecoming* now, Grandfather. Nothing else matters except that I'm back and we're together."

There was no need for David to hide his true feelings behind his actor's mask. He was truly beginning to care for this man. The duke was honest and forthright and a gentleman through and through. He was all the things that David was not. Their gazes met and locked.

Edward looked up at him, knowing he had to make his decision now. He wanted him to be Alexander. It wasn't as if the boy hadn't remembered the boat. He had. That alone should have been enough, would have been enough for any other man, but it bothered him that this young man seemed to have no recollection of calling the boat the *Scimitar* when it had been so very important to the both of them at the time. Wanting to believe, Edward finally cast that last nagging misgiving aside. He looked like Alexander would have looked. Some of his expressions and mannerisms were just the same as they had been as a child. Just because he couldn't remember the name he'd made up almost nineteen years ago for a toy boat didn't prove him an impostor.

The duke took a step closer and rested a trembling, aged hand on David's broad shoulder. "You're right, Alexander. Nothing else matters except that we're together again . . ."

David knew in that moment that he'd been accepted as the true grandson. He knew he should have felt like celebrating. Instead, he he only felt miserable.

The only redeeming thought David had as he bent down and set the boat to sail on the mirror-smooth waters of the pond was that he would do everything he could to make the duke happy during the time he had left. He would become a duke Edward would be proud of. He owed him that.

Chapter Fourteen

"Alexander . . ." Edward's voice rang out from where he sat in the parlor. He'd been meaning to have this discussion with his grandson for several weeks, and now that rumors were starting to come to him concerning the young man's successes among the ladies, he knew he could put it off no longer.

"Yes, Grandfather?" David appeared in the parlor doorway looking quite the man-about-town. He had been on his way out for an evening of cards and drinking with the new friends he'd made in London.

"I need to speak with you for a moment."

"Of course. I was just off to the club, but it can wait. What is it?" He moved comfortably into the duke's presence and settled in the wing chair opposite him. They had become close during the past weeks and David really enjoyed his company.

"I have something very important I must relate to you," Edward began, hedging a bit.

David sensed his nervousness and was puzzled by it. "Is something wrong?"

"Oh, no, nothing's wrong."

David waited expectantly.

"I have heard that you are cutting quite a wide

swath through the young women," Edward mentioned.

David grinned. "There are many beautiful women in London, Grandfather, and I think they're quite impressed with my title." One of the benefits of becoming Alexander Wakefield, he'd discovered, was a sudden, marvelous success with females. Obviously, they found his future prospects quite impressive.

"With you, too, my boy, and that's what brings me to our present conversation . . ."

David looked at him expectantly.

"Years ago, when you were but a babe, my good friend, Alfred Lawrence, the Marquess of Ravensley, and I privately drew up a marriage contract between you and his granddaughter, Victoria Lynn." He paused.

There was silence for a minute as David digested this news. "Are you saying the contract is still in force?"

"Most definitely. You, my dear grandson, are engaged."

David blinked in surprise. *He was going to be married and he'd never seen the girl?*

"The marquess's fortunes nearly match ours. The arrangement will be a coup for both of your families."

"But I've never met her . . ." he protested, stunned.

"You will."

"Is she here in London?"

"No, she's living in India with her parents. Alfred and I spoke shortly after you returned, and he signified his willingness to agree to the marriage. Victoria has been informed of your return."

"I see . . ."

Edward could well imagine the panic gripping his young grandson, and he chuckled sympathetically. "Don't worry, Alexander. It will all work out. Alfred and I think the public announcement of your engagement should come soon, but there's no need for the two of you to rush into marriage. You can take your time and get to know each other, see if you're compatible."

David looked bewildered. Suddenly he found himself engaged to a woman he'd never seen or heard of in his life. Marriage was important to him. His parents had loved each other dearly, and he'd hoped for the same for himself. He hadn't wanted to marry just for wealth and position, but it appeared now, though, that the decision had been taken out of his hands. He knew he had no choice but to accept it.

"There's no need to worry about the girl," he assured him. "Alfred gave me this small portrait of Victoria, and she's quite a lovely young lady. I think you'll be pleased." He handed him the miniature and watched as he studied it.

"You're right, Grandfather. She is quite attractive," David agreed, staring down at the raven-haired, green-eyed beauty.

"Then it is settled," Edward pronounced, not giving his grandson any chance to discuss the matter any further. "I'm just surprised your mother didn't remember when the plans were set. Of course, it was shortly before you were kidnapped, so she probably forgot it in all the heartache that followed."

"What about Victoria? How does she feel about this?"

"I don't think you have to worry about any arguments coming from her, Alexander. You're the best catch in England. There isn't a woman who would turn down the opportunity to be your bride. She'll be thrilled."

"Yes, sir."

"Very good. I'll send word to Alfred today to draw up the final contracts. He can notify his son in India of the official announcement of betrothal after that. It might be a good thing to include a picture of yourself in the letter he sends. Do you have one?"

"No, sir."

"Then we'll plan on getting one made right away. Once all this is done, it will just be a matter of time before your future bride is on her way back to England to meet you. Congratulations, Alexander. I'm sure you won't regret your decision," Edward told him happily. His heart was light as he considered how perfect his plans were. The future that had once seemed so bleak, was now full of promise. Life was good.

"Thank you, sir. Have you spoken to my mother about this yet?"

"No. I thought a man-to-man discussion was warranted first."

"I'll tell her later this evening when I see her."

Just outside the study door in the hall, one of the maids had escaped Dalton's eagle eye and had been hovering near enough to listen in on the conversation. Within minutes of the duke's announcement, she rushed back to the kitchen area to spread the word of Alexander's engagement. All of the household staff was ready to celebrate at the news except one—the young chambermaid, Tess.

At eighteen, Tess was a beauty of an Irish lass, with fair skin, burnished hair, and shining hazel eyes that usually lit up with an inner glow that mirrored her basic good nature. Finding out just now from the others that Lord Alexander was to marry was like a knife in her heart, and for the first time in her young life, Tess knew bitter pain.

Tess had fallen in love with Alexander the moment she'd laid eyes on him the day of his homecoming; and in the way of all innocent young girls, she'd dreamed that one day he would notice her. He had on several occasions greeted and smiled at her, and that alone had given her hope. The duke had never paid any attention to her when she was around, but Lord Alex had actually spoken to her!

Now, facing the reality that she would never attract Alexander's eye or know his kiss, Tess was devastated. She slipped away from the work area as soon as she could manage it so no one else would know of her distress. It was going to be difficult enough for her to handle her feelings without bearing the ridicule and scorn of the older servants, too. Mattie, in particular, knew she thought Lord Alex handsome, and Tess was sure she would look upon her desire for a member of the Wakefield family as pure folly. Logically, Tess knew her love for him was hopeless, but then, there could be no dictating the ways of the heart. As she hid near the back of the gardens, out of sight of the house, her tears fell in silent testimony to the love she believed she would never know.

It was in the early morning hours that David returned from his night of gaming. He saw that the light was on in Vivienne's bedroom, and he knocked softly on her door as he made his way upstairs to bed. She was still fully dressed when she opened the door to him.

"Come in, my son. I understand you have news to tell me?" she greeted him with a wide, avaricious smile.

"You've spoken with Grandfather?"

"Earlier this evening, yes, and I couldn't be more pleased with this turn of events. A marriage between the Lawrences and the Wakefields will set this town on its ear!" The thought of all that money and prestige thrilled her. "I can't tell you just how pleased I am with you, Alexander. The money from this marriage will be more than I ever dreamed. You're doing very well. Keep it up."

"I don't have much choice, do I?"

"No," she stated flatly, her eyes mirroring her murderous intent should he falter. "You don't, *son.*"

David was thoroughly disgusted as he left her. He went to his room and began to undress, telling himself to concentrate on the good parts of the arrangement. Though he tried, he still felt uneasy about marrying this girl. As he untied his cravat and tossed it aside, he picked up the small portrait once again. She was a beautiful young woman, and she had every reason to believe that she would be marrying Alexander Wakefield. The depth of his guilt grew.

Lady Victoria Lynn Lawrence was a tall, willowy, ebony-haired young woman with expressive green eyes and a quick smile. Wearing a sedate, pale-green daygown that highlighted her coloring and brought out the sparkle in her eyes, she strolled on the deck of *La Mouette* enjoying a bit of fresh air and sunshine with her traveling companion, the gray-haired opinionated Miss Edith Jones.

The indomitable Miss Jones, ever concerned about the state of her delicate complexion, had her umbrella up to protect her from the harshness of the late-morning sun, as she had each day since their departure from India. The voyage had been long and tiring, but now that they had passed the equator and the temperatures were moderating, they knew it wouldn't last too much longer. Every day was bringing them closer and closer to England, and their excitement about returning to their native land was growing.

"It won't be long now, Miss Victoria," Miss Jones said with confidence as they paused by the railing to gaze out across the blue waters.

"I know, Jonesey. Isn't it wonderful?!" Victoria said

with a bright smile, her emerald eyes alive with pure pleasure as she imagined what the future held for her.

"It most certainly is," she agreed wholeheartedly. There was no one alive who would appreciate returning to England more than she. "I must confess to you now that, even as devoted as I am to you and your parents, I almost refused their offer to accompany you to India. England has been and always will be my home, and it was a trauma for me to leave her."

"It seems like a long time since we sailed from London . . ."

"It *was* a long time ago, my dear. It was three very long years ago," Miss Jones pointed out; then she smiled to soften the sharpness of her words. "You changed a lot while we were away, you know."

"I've grown up," Victoria said with pride. When they had sailed from England she'd been a young miss, just shy of sixteen. She was returning now, a young woman in full bloom. Victoria was thrilled to think that she could now partake of all the activities that had been forbidden her before they'd gone—the balls and the parties and the dancing. She could hardly wait until they made landfall. It would be good to see her grandfather, the Marquess of Ravensley, again. She adored him and had missed him greatly.

"And you'd better remember that, too. This isn't going to be India, you know. There will be no more riding astride, no more shooting, and no more wild hunting adventures," her companion dictated. "You're about to become the future Duchess of Huntington. You'll have to behave like royalty."

Victoria pulled a face, then broke into delighted laughter. She was innocently unaware of the members of the crew who turned to look at her. She was so lovely and her laughter so light and gay that she was a balm to their travel-weary souls.

"You're right, of course, Jonesey, but it *was* fun while it lasted. Especially tiger hunting!"

"Well, maybe someday after you're married you can go back, but for now, I think you'd be best served if you pretended that you'd never done such things."

"Do you think Grandfather might object?"

"As far as your grandfather is concerned, I'm quite sure he believes you can do no wrong. What I'm thinking is, your new fiancé might not want to know that his wife can probably ride better than he can and shoot straighter, too."

In a moment of sweet camaraderie, Jonesey let her strict demeanor slip and shared an impish look with her.

"The ego of a man my dear, is a fragile thing. You must learn how to handle them."

"I have to know the man before I can handle him, and I know so little about Alexander. I wish I'd had the chance to meet him before the engagement was announced. What if . . .?"

"You don't have a thing to worry about where your new fiancé is concerned," Miss Jones said.

"You're sure about that?" Victoria asked, knowing she could count on Jonesey to tell her the absolute truth. The elderly woman always voiced her opinions, solicited or not, if she thought they might prove helpful to her in any way.

"I'm positive. Your grandfather loves you so much that I'm certain he would never have taken any chances with your future. He must think highly of young Wakefield or he wouldn't have kept to the contract. He could have broken it, you know, if he'd thought there might be a problem."

Victoria sighed. "You're right. I trust Grandfather . . . and Alexander is quite handsome . . ." She lifted the locket she wore on a gold chain around her neck

197

and opened it to stare down at the miniature portrait her fiancé had sent to her.

"He's *very* handsome," Jonesey emphasized, "and devilishly wealthy to boot. It's a wonderful match. Why, think about it. Do you know how many women would trade places with you in a second? One day, you'll be a duchess!"

Victoria laughed at the older woman's enthusiasm. "I most certainly will be, won't I? It rather boggles the mind, don't you think?"

"Not at all," Miss Jones answered, turning serious. "In spite of your best efforts to avoid it, you have been raised and educated to become a great lady, and you will be, my dear. I'm sure of it." She patted her hand with assurance.

They exchanged a fond look just as they heard one of the sailors call out to the captain that he'd spotted another ship on the horizon. Both women looked in the direction the crew member had indicated and were able to make out a vague expanse of white sail in the distance. They thought it quite exciting, for they hadn't seen another vessel for days, and they decided to stay up on deck and watch a little longer.

"Serad *Reis!* There! To the north!" the lookout's voice rang out across the deck of the *Scimitar*.

Serad abruptly broke off conversation with his second-in-command, Tariq, and swung around to see what it was the man had sighted. When he saw the French merchantman, he smiled, the white of his teeth flashing against the blackness of his beard. At twenty-seven, Serad had grown into a fine, handsome specimen of a man. He was tall, well over six feet, and powerfully built. His shoulders were wide and corded with thick muscle from the years of vigorous sailing.

His waist was trim, and his legs were long and straight. While at sea, he wore only a white turban and a pair of loose-fitting pants cut off at the knees for freedom of movement, and so he had tanned to a dark bronze. He looked the part of the fierce corsair that he was, and he reveled in the glory of his adventurous life aboard the *Scimitar*. There was nothing he enjoyed more than captaining his ship and claiming booty from a slow-moving merchantman.

"Let's intercept her, men! Run up the French flag, and ready the guns! As low as she's sitting in the water, she must be carrying a full cargo. There's no way she can outrun us." He would take this oncoming ship as his own, for he knew how pleased Malik would be when he returned to Algiers with another full load of fine tribute.

On board *La Mouette,* the captain and crew were growing suspicious as they noted the way the other ship, French flag or not, kept angling toward them.

"I don't like this, Jacques. I don't like this one bit," Capitaine Duval growled half under his breath as he kept an eye on the *Scimitar*. "I haven't been able to read her name yet, but I've got a feeling . . ."

"Shall I change course and see what she does?"

"Yes, steer hard aport. Let's see what happens . . ." Capitaine Duval lifted his telescope to scan the other vessel once more. He wasn't quite sure what he was hoping to find, but the safety of his own ship, crew, and passengers were paramount. He couldn't put them at risk. The odds were with him that this was just another merchant ship heading home, but there was always the chance that it wasn't, and he wanted to be prepared.

The crew watched and waited for an answering response from the coming ship, and when it altered its course to intercept with theirs, they knew they were in for trouble. Capitaine Duval kept his glass trained on the other, faster vessel, and when he saw the name *Scimitar* painted on its side, he knew real terror.

"Full sail! Jacques! It's the *Scimitar!* We're going to have to make a run for it! Get us out of here now!"

"Oui, mon capitaine!"

At the news that this was the infamous *Scimitar,* of the Barbary States closing on them, the crew of *La Mouette* was jarred into action. The pirate ship's reputation had preceded it, and the men of the merchantman grew afraid. They'd heard how wild Barbary pirates were, and they were certain of what their fate would be if they were caught. If they fought, they'd be killed, and if they surrendered, they'd be transported back to North Africa and sold into slavery. The horror of either situation was enough to drive them to extraordinary lengths to save their ship and themselves.

On board the *Scimitar,* Serad watched as the other ship made every effort to escape him.

"They've obviously heard of our reputation," Tariq observed as he stood at his *reis's* side.

"I wanted our fearsome reputation to make them so afraid that they'd surrender without a fight, not run and force a battle."

"Maybe they're carrying something of great value," his second-in-command suggested with a smile.

"Then why risk our firing on them and all being lost?" Serad countered. "The captain is a fool." He turned and called out to his men, "Fire now, a single shot across the port bow. Maybe a warning will be enough to stop them."

One of the *Scimitar's* twenty-four cannons let loose a round that skimmed through the air just ahead of the fleeing *La Mouette.*

*   *   *

Ignored in the midst of the chaotic activity, Victoria and Miss Jones watched all that was happening around them in fascination, not quite sure what it meant. Only when the other ship fired their gun did it finally dawn on them what was about to happen.

"My God, Jonesey, they must be pirates!" Victoria exclaimed as she strained to get a better look at the ship.

"We must go below, Miss Victoria. Right now!" the elderly woman insisted. In a quick motion, she lowered her umbrella and grabbed Victoria by the arm.

Capitaine Duval looked up just then to see them on the deck. "Ladies! Get belowdecks to your cabins and stay there until I come for you!"

Recognizing the command in his voice, Victoria gave up her quest to catch a glimpse of the pirates and acceded to Jonesey's pressure to go below to their connecting staterooms.

"What do you suppose the captain's going to do?" Victoria asked when they were finally locked safe inside her cabin. Her eyes were wide and questioning, and her heart was pounding from the excitement of it all.

"Captain Duval will fight them off, of course!" Miss Jones insisted, rapping her umbrella on the cabin floor to make her point. In her eyes, to do less would be cowardly, and no ship's captain would ever be a coward. They were brave and hardy souls.

Just as she finished speaking, though, they heard the boom of another round being fired. They hurried to the single porthole to look out.

"It's so close!" Victoria said, stunned to see that the approaching ship had greatly narrowed the gap between the two vessels. She could make out its multitude of cannons now, and she went cold inside. She would have liked to believe that Captain Duval would be able to resist, but to the best of her knowledge, the merchantman was carrying only four guns.

"The French ship refuses to yield, Serad *Reis!*" one of his men informed him.

"Aim for the riggings" came Serad's solemn order. He did not want to damage the vessel so severely that it couldn't make the voyage back to Algiers.

Several of the cannons roared to life once again, and the men of the *Scimitar* let out a loud cheer as the shot shredded the sails and tore out the main mast.

"Prepare to board!" Serad ordered.

On *La Mouette,* the men were frantic. Though no one had been killed when the sails and the mast destroyed, the ship itself was now dead in the water. The crew knew they were helpless to do more than wait for the inevitable.

Capitaine Duval, however, was furious. He turned to his men and directed, "Bring our guns to bear. We'll not go down to these cutthroats without a fight! Let's give them something to remember us by!"

Though they had only four small cannons, two on either side of the ship, the men were thrilled to have at least this one chance to wreak vengeance on their attackers. They were not experienced at battling at sea, but they tried their best nonetheless and managed to get off two shots at the pirates. One dropped uselessly in the ocean just short of the *Scimitar,* but the other scored a hit. Crashing into the ship above the waterline near the stern, the shot only caused some superficial damage.

Serad had not wanted to damage the other ship, but

he could not allow anyone to fire on his vessel without answering back. "Silence those guns before they cause us any real trouble and aim a shot at the helm!" he ordered in disgust.

Several of the *Scimitar*'s cannons flamed to life with a vengeance, raking *La Mouette*'s two guns with deadly fire, rendering them useless and taking out all of the ship's controls. Knowing the merchantman would be firing no more, the pirate ship boldly maneuvered in close alongside.

The pirate crew was ready with their grappling hooks, guns, and scimitars as the boats came together. As always, Serad led his men in the boarding. Throwing his hook with precision, he swung across to land lightly on his feet on the deck, his scimitar held tightly in hand and a loaded pistol stuck in the waistband of his pants. Looking equally savage, his crew followed him. They screamed at the top of their lungs at an ear-splitting pitch to strike terror in the hearts of those they were about to face in triumph.

Capitaine Duval stood on the deck of his ship. Hatred coursed through him as he watched the pirates boarding. Though his men had been willing to fight on, he'd given strict orders that not one hand was to be raised, not one weapon fired. Duval realized now that as outgunned as they were, it had been foolhardy to fire on their attackers. Several of his men had been killed during the exchange of volleys, and he wanted to risk no more carnage.

Duval stared with open enmity at the first corsair who had come aboard and who was walking straight toward him. The Frenchman's gaze darkened with controlled fury. He considered these North Africans little better than animals, naked to the waist as they were and carrying the fierce barbarian swords that could behead a man with one swing. The pirates looked

203

exactly as he'd heard they would, and he knew if he valued the lives of his passengers and crew that he would have to control his anger.

"You're the captain?" Serad asked as he approached Duval, Tariq staying close by his side.

"I'm Capitaine Duval."

"I am Serad, *reis* of the *Scimitar*. It was very foolish of you to try to fight me." He glanced around the deck at the strained faces of the French crew and at the damage his guns had caused. "Some of your crew is dead and your ship is now useless to the both of us."

"I would rather see it at the bottom of the ocean than in your hands," he declared tersely.

"If you're not careful, you may get your wish and visit the bottom of the ocean with her," Serad returned, his silver eyes glittering dangerously as he stared his adversary in the face. He saw the other man stiffen at his words, and he was pleased. After a moment of silent intimidation, Serad issued orders to some of his crew to go below and bring up everything they found of value so it could be loaded onto the *Scimitar*. That done, he remained on deck to supervise the chaining and transfer of the French crew to his ship.

Chapter Fifteen

Belowdecks, the excitement that had intrigued Victoria in the beginning had been replaced by pure, unadulterated fear. She and Miss Jones had heard the last round of shots being fired and the shouts of the pirates as they'd boarded. Huddled now on the bunk in Victoria's cabin, they waited, praying that Captain Duval and his men would be able to fight them off.

"I wish I had my pistol," Victoria whispered to her companion when they heard the sounds of men moving down the companionway.

"It might be the captain coming for us."

"It might not be, too. At least, if I had my pistol we'd have some protection."

"Your pistol would only stop one man, Victoria," Edith Jones cautioned, "and I'm afraid from the sound of things that that really wouldn't do us much good." She felt amazingly calm even in the face of their desperate situation.

When the heavy footsteps paused right outside their cabin door, they were both silenced. They held their breaths, their hands tightening as they clutched each other. Someone tried the doorknob, and when he found it was locked, he began to batter the closed portal relentlessly with his shoulder until finally the solid wood door gave way in a splintering crash.

Victoria and Miss Jones cringed as it flew open, and they stared in shock at their first good look at pirates. Big, burly, and nearly naked, the corsairs advanced into the room brandishing wicked-looking scimitars and striking terror in the souls of the two women.

"Look what we have here," Najib said with a leering smile.

"Serad *Reis* will be greatly pleased. The young one alone may make up for his disappointment over the damage to the boat . . ." Hassan agreed.

"Let's get them up on deck so he can see that all was not lost."

When the evil Najib made a grab for Victoria, Jonesey flew into action. With no thought to anything but protecting her young ward, she attacked.

Neither of the pirates had given the old woman more than a passing thought. They'd thought it would be a simple matter to haul the two of them up the companionway and deliver them to Serad. But they were wrong. When Jonesey clobbered Najib over the head with her umbrella, he was caught totally off guard.

"Get away from here, you filthy monster!!" Jonesey shouted, making a valiant effort. But once she lost the element of surprise, her challenge to their superiority was over.

Hassan quickly snatched her up and threw her, kicking and screaming, over his shoulder. She gave a squawk of surprise at being so manhandled, but she still managed to keep a tight hold on her precious umbrella.

When Victoria saw how rough they were being with Miss Jones, she lunged forward trying to go to her companion's aid. "Let her go!" she cried, but it was a pointless effort.

Najib had recovered from the old woman's unexpected attack, and he grabbed Victoria up and tossed her over his shoulder in the very same manner.

As the pirate carried her up the companionway and out on deck, Victoria struggled to lift her head and look around. She hoped to see someone who could come to her aid, but to her despair, the entire crew of *La Mouette* had been lined up against the rail and was under heavy guard by the pirates. Capitaine Duval had been separated from his crew and already transported to the other ship.

The realization that there would be no rescue hit Victoria hard. Her emotions threatened to run away with her, but she was determined not to break down in front of these men. She remembered how her father had often counseled her that a cool head always prevailed in difficult and dangerous situations, so she tried to be logical. Victoria told herself that they were not going to die. Had the pirates wanted to kill them, they surely would have done so by now. Obviously, from what little the two brutes had said, she assumed she and Jonesey were worth something to the pirate captain. She would concentrate on that theory and would not be cowed by these men. If they knew she feared them, they would exploit it. She was determined to stay in control.

Suddenly, without warning, the pirate who was carrying Victoria stopped and dumped her on her feet. Victoria had been unable to see where they were going, and she staggered for a moment before regaining her balance and turning around.

Serad and Tariq had been standing apart from the others, watching over the transfer of men and goods from the hostage ship to the *Scimitar*. Serad had his back to the deck, so he had not seen Hassan and Najib coming with the women. Tariq, however, had been watching them coming their way, and his smile widened as Victoria and Miss Jones were dropped unceremoniously to their feet before them.

The crew of the *Scimitar* all turned to see what their captain would do with the two women. It wasn't often that a female as pretty as the young one was captured, and they knew she was a prize any man would want to keep for himself. They were eager to see Serad *Reis's* reaction.

"What have we here?" Tariq asked, eyeing Victoria with open interest. A quick glance at Miss Jones had told him she was unimportant. "It looks like the men have found quite a prize on board, eh, Serad?"

Serad turned around then to speak with his friend, and Victoria saw her captor for the very first time. She was tall for a girl, but this Serad loomed over her, forcing her to tilt her head back to look up at him. He was darkly tanned, and he wore a white turban. His hair where it showed beneath the turban was black as night, as was the beard that framed his face and added a touch of fierceness to his already wild appearance. She could have called his features handsome in a strongly masculine way if she were romantically inclined, but right now, fear for her life kept all thoughts of anything besides survival from her. She continued her measure of the man who was her captor. His chest was broad and bare and covered with a sheen of perspiration from the heat of the day. His shoulders were wide and heavily muscled. He was an intimidating figure of a man, and Victoria swallowed nervously as she fought to keep in control of her weakening defenses.

"She's a pretty one, all right," Tariq was saying as he reached out to touch her cheek.

Jonesey had been watching both men with eagle eyes and the moment Tariq tried to lay a hand upon Victoria, she attacked. Moving forward to block his way and wielding her umbrella like a sword, the birdlike woman gave the big, muscle-bound pirate a painful rap on the arm as she knocked his hand away from her precious ward. "You so much as lay a hand on Miss Victoria and I'll . . ."

"Jonesey, don't!" Victoria grabbed her and pulled her back away from the pirate to protect her. Though she knew if they'd wanted to kill them they would have done it already, she also realized that there was no point in tempting fate or pushing their already doubtful luck.

Tariq's shocked expression was so comical that Serad threw back his head and roared with pure amusement. "So, they're English and not French, are they? And the little wren is really a hawk and not so defenseless after all. When will you remember never to underestimate your enemy, Tariq?"

His pride was hurt over being so humiliated, and he took a menacing step toward the elderly woman.

"Hold your temper," Serad told his friend easily, putting a staying hand on his shoulder. "She's an old woman."

Serad hadn't really had a chance to take a good look at the women yet, and he glanced at Victoria now as she stood protectively in front of Miss Jones. Amazement was the only word to describe his reaction to her, but he was careful to keep it from showing in his expression. She was the most beautiful female he'd ever seen. From her flowing ebony mane to the gentle but generous curves of her slender figure, he thought her stunning. As Serad stared at her, he realized with some surprise that had he been captaining the French ship, he, too, would have made a run for it rather than allow this lovely creature to be put in any danger.

"She needs protecting," Tariq was saying as he stared hungrily at Victoria. "She is worth all the treasure we've taken for a month."

"That she is, Tariq," Serad agreed, his gaze still resting upon her with no visible show of emotion.

Victoria refused to play the submissive female. She bravely lifted her gaze to meet Serad's. A shiver of apprehension ran down her spine as she saw the coldness in his gray eyes. His casual, dispassionate appraisal of her struck more fear in her heart than any open threats of violence could have. Victoria had never before come across a man so commanding in presence.

"Where shall I put them? Shall I have them taken below with the others, Serad *Reis?*" Tariq asked.

For the first time ever, Serad found himself concerned about a captive's condition. He didn't want either woman subjected to the heat and degradation the men of *La Mouette* were going to suffer on the trek back to North Africa. The trip would be more than uncomfortable for those in chains in the belly of his ship. "No. They will stay in my cabin."

"Your cabin?" Tariq was surprised. Never before had his captain taken a personal prize from any bounty.

"They're too valuable to leave down below," he offered in calm explanation, looking away from Victoria.

Victoria was angry. *He was going to keep them in his cabin, was he?* Fury sparked in her as the pirate went on to remark about their worth. She chose to deliberately misunderstand his purpose. With a determined lift of her chin, she spoke up with cool disdain. "You are obviously a man of good breeding and exceptional judgment, Captain Serad. It is *Captain,* isn't it?"

Surprise registered on Serad's face that she dared speak to him with such firm assurance. "Yes, I am Serad, *reis* of the *Scimitar.*"

Victoria gave a curt nod as if acknowledging his position of command. "Well, Captain Serad, I appreciate your thoughtfulness in allowing my companion, Miss Jones, and myself the use of your cabin for our private accommodations."

Jonesey, fully aware that the pirate captain had no such intention, tugged at Victoria's arm, but the younger woman ignored her subtle warning.

Serad was unable to believe that this mere slip of a woman was being so daringly outspoken. Except for his Aunt Rabi, Serad had had no dealings with English women. The women of the Barbary States were to be seen, occasionally and at the male's discretion, and definitely not heard, unless asked to speak. This was certainly a new experience for him, and one that tugged at vague and distant memories. Still, there was the matter of maintaining the respect and loyalty of his crew. No mere female could speak to him in this manner and get away with it.

"You will stay in my cabin, true, but know that your stay there will not be *private*," He said the last with emphasis, just to put her in her place.

Jonesey tightened her hold on Victoria. The younger woman still ignored her. There was too much at risk here to give in without a battle of some sort, even if it only was her wits.

"Sir, as captain, our safety is completely in your hands." Victoria kept her head held high as she countered. "You are totally responsible for us and our well-being."

"That's very true," Serad agreed with artificial mildness, wondering why she didn't realize that she was completely in his control and be pliant to his wishes.

Victoria knew he had the power of life and death over them, but she refused to let him think even for an instant that she would kowtow to him. "Good, then we understand one another," she responded with haughty bravado. "You see, I am Lady Victoria Lawrence. My

211

grandfather is the Marquess of Ravensley. He carries much influence with the King and he would not take kindly to any harm befalling me or Miss Jones." Her arrogance in the statement shocked even herself.

Tariq was staring at the Englishwomen in disbelief. No man spoke to Serad in that manner and tone and lived very long, yet this woman dared.

Serad knew without a doubt that this was the most outrageous female he'd ever met, but to give any credence to her demanding ways would be to lose face with his men. Without another word, Serad picked up his grappling hook that lay nearby and with a very accurate throw, sent it high into the *Scimitar's* riggings.

"What are you doing?" Victoria demanded, her eyes growing round.

"Well, Lady Victoria Lawrence, if your safety is truly in my hands as you say, then I should see to your well-being personally, shouldn't I?" He spoke softly, for her and her alone to hear. Then in one smooth move, he slipped a powerful arm about her waist and drew her tightly to his side.

"Let me go . . ." she resisted.

At her panicked look, Serad almost smiled. It pleased him to have cracked her sophisticated veneer. Known by his crew as a man of action, Serad reaffirmed that opinion when, without another word, he grasped the rope with a sure grip and swung them both across to the deck of the *Scimitar*.

The moment Serad lifted off, Victoria instinctively threw her arms around his neck and held on for dear life as they swooped through the air. Clasped to his naked chest, his arm securely wrapped around her waist keeping her safely against him, Victoria was very aware of his strength, and she was actually grateful for it. The wind whipped her skirts around them, and she was forced to bite back a shriek as they crossed over the small patch of open ocean below.

They landed with an amazing lightness on the pirate ship's deck, and Victoria was breathless from their flight. Serad didn't immediately release her after they gained the footing, and she was relieved, for her knees were quaking from the excitement of their flight. After a moment, though, she knew she had to move away from him. Victoria glanced up to find the pirate captain gazing down at her, a look of amusement in his silver regard. His finding humor at her expense stung her pride, and she pushed away from his support to glare up at him.

"Thank you for that 'safe' trip," Victoria said angrily.

Serad had expected her to be terrified, and her display of bravery earned respect from him. If at all possible, he thought her even more lovely now, standing as she was there before him with her hands on her hips. He was about to offer a retort when a feminine cry of outrage split the air.

"Unhand me, you barbarian!" Miss Jones's voice rang out.

Victoria and Serad both turned to find her being held in Tariq's arms as he crossed the deck of *La Mouette,* a look of complete and total indignation on her face. She tried several times to hit at Tariq with her umbrella, but he successfully managed to control her actions, leaving her even more frustrated.

"Don't hurt her!" Victoria exclaimed. She started to run to the edge of the deck to go to her aid, but Serad caught her by the arm and held her back. She turned on him, furious, her fear for Jonesey showing plainly on her face.

Serad read her concern. He nodded in Tariq's direction, and said, "Watch."

Tariq set the small woman, umbrella and all, down

upon a large crate and stepped back. "Now," he directed.

"What is he doing to her?" Victoria demanded, her gaze flying from Serad to her companion and back again.

Serad never had the chance to answer as the men on board the *Scimitar* tightened the ropes around the net that lay beneath the crate of merchandise from the French ship. Jonesey squawked in surprise as the net closed around her, and she and the crate were lifted off the deck and sent swinging across to the pirate ship.

"What do you think you're doing, hauling me around like nothing more than a piece of freight?" Miss Jones demanded, struggling to maintain her dignity while perched in such a precarious position. "Watch out, you ruffians! You have a lady on board here! You!" she shouted down to the pirate who was waiting for the crate to be lowered so he could guide it to its final resting place on the *Scimitar's* deck. "You take care! I don't want any nasty accidents now!"

Tariq watched the little old woman go, and his smile was relieved as he saw her safely landed on the opposite deck. Only then did he cross to the other ship himself. He'd had no intention of swinging over with that old woman in his arms. The young one, yes, the old one, never! He'd rather swim to Algiers! He'd felt the pain of her attack once, and he wasn't about to give her a second chance to inflict damage with that umbrella of hers.

When Serad's hold on Victoria's arm finally loosened, she broke away and ran forth to meet her companion. Had their situation not been so dreadful, Victoria would have laughed at Jonesey. She looked comical, seated as she was on a huge crate, her umbrella held threateningly in hand as she fended off the pirates who'd gathered around.

"Get back! Don't you touch me! I'll get down on my own . . ." she ordered in a loud voice as she swung her legs over the side and got down, unaided, with some difficulty. In a very dignified, ladylike gesture, she arranged her skirts, then patted her hair into some kind of order. She looked up just as Victoria got to her side.

"Are you all right?"

"Are *you?*"

"I'm fine, I expect," Victoria replied, really thinking about it for the first time.

"So am I, although I must say their methods of transportation are quite primitive, to say the least," she huffed as they stood together in the middle of the deck.

Capitaine Duval had been watching all this from where he was being held by a guard near on the far rail. He was livid over the loss of his vessel and his feelings of impotence over his lack of ability to protect the women were driving him to near madness. He eyed his guard with malice.

"See them to my cabin, then post a guard at the door," Serad was saying to Tariq as they walked toward the women, their backs to Duval.

When Duval heard his order, he went wild. Far better to be dead than to suffer the humiliation of losing his ship and being responsible for the women's horrible suffering. In a vicious move, he hit his unsuspecting guard and grabbed the knife out of his hand. He charged toward Serad and Tariq with murder on his mind.

Serad and Tariq had just joined the women when they heard Victoria gasp and saw both women's eyes widen in shocked terror. Tariq turned first to find Capitaine Duval running toward them, his eyes glazed, his hand upraised, clenching a big knife that was aimed at Serad's back. In a quick move, he attempted to shove his friend out of the way and take on the attacker alone, but he was not quite fast enough. Duval's knife sliced through the air and struck Serad in the upper arm before Tariq could stop him.

Neither Victoria nor Miss Jones could prevent the cries of horror that erupted from them. They clung together in fear as they watched the dangerous, hand-to-hand battle.

"Stay away from the women!" Duval shouted as he grappled with the pirate. He was trying to wrest free so he could continue his assault on the captain.

Tariq was more than his match. Though the fight took a few minutes, eventually his superior strength won out. He landed a punishing blow to the back of the Frenchman's neck that laid him low.

"He's dead!" Victoria and Miss Jones gasped as they stared at Duval's prostrate body.

"He's not dead," Tariq replied in disgust as he took the knife from the unconscious man's grip. "But it would be his due if he were."

"Thank you, my friend," Serad told Tariq as they shared a knowing look. It was not the first time someone had tried to murder him, and they both knew it would not be the last. "Take him below and chain him up. I don't want to see him on deck again until we make port."

"Aye, Serad *reis,*" two of his men answered in unison as they complied with his wishes.

Victoria and Miss Jones looked on helplessly as Duval was hauled away.

Serad saw the women's expressions and grew even more irritated. "My men are sworn to defend me as I am sworn to defend them." His voice was cold and condemning as he continued. "Duval was a fool to try anything."

Victoria stared at the man who was her captor, and the fear she harbored within her grew even more

216

potent, and so did her anger. "Duval was a man of honor who was trying to help us," she defended.

"How would getting himself killed help you?" he scoffed, disgusted with the whole ordeal. The man had cost him the prize of his ship and now he had almost lost his life over nothing. Serad found it difficult to believe that his real motive was to defend the women. This Lady Victoria was beautiful, but not worth certain death. He dismissed the idea as ludicrous and turned back to Tariq. "Take them below," he ordered. "There is still much that needs to be done, and we have wasted enough time already."

Victoria knew better than to say anything more. She held her silence as Tariq led them belowdecks to Serad's cabin and left them there.

Chapter Sixteen

Victoria and Miss Jones looked at each other as they stood in the middle of the cabin, then they glanced nervously at the closed door behind them. Without another word, Victoria hurried to try the knob, but to her dismay she found that it was, indeed, securely locked. She heard the sound of voices through the door and knew that Tariq had posted the guard as Serad had instructed. They were trapped. Her hands clenched into fists as her fear and frustration turned into anger.

"Damn!" she exploded.

"Miss Victoria," Jonesey scolded primly, "remember yourself. There is never any need for a lady to use such language."

"I don't feel very much like a lady right now!" Victoria countered with a harshness unusual for her.

"But you are one, and you must remember that at all times. You handled yourself quite brilliantly on deck, I thought."

The rare words of praise from the fastidious Miss Jones soothed her somewhat.

She felt some of the tension drain out of her. "I wasn't quite sure what to do, but I couldn't let them know I was afraid."

"Well, you were magnificent. I'm sure your father would have been very proud of you."

The thought of pleasing her father pacified her, but still did not erase the turbulent emotions that were raging with her. "I may have acted the lady, but it didn't really change anything, did it? Our ship's been taken and we're still being held against our will . . ."

"We could just as easily be dead," she said with certainty. "You and I both know how bloodthirsty men like these can be. So far, I think, we've done very well. Nothing untoward has happened to us."

"Yet," Victoria added with dark meaning, thinking of Serad's earlier words. The memory of his intention to share the cabin with them spurred her to take some kind of action. She didn't trust the man one bit. "We have got to get out of here, Jonesey!" She stared about the sparsely furnished cabin, taking in the wide bunk, the desk and chair, and the large sea chest against the wall.

"And just where would we go if we did manage to get free?" Jonesey pointed out with a logic that Victoria found maddening. "I, for one, do not plan to swim back to England."

"We can't just go along with them!"

"What else would you suggest?" the elderly lady went on. "As long as we're together, we'll be safe enough, and they've shown no interest in separating us. From what I've heard about these people, they will send us home once a ransom is paid for our release. Until then, we'll probably just be locked up safely someplace."

"But that could take months!"

"Indeed, it could. We just have to maintain our dignity and wait it out."

Victoria knew Jonesey was right, and it only made her angrier. She didn't want to be anywhere near that pirate captain. She wanted to get as far away from him as she could. Her gaze finally settled on his sea chest, and a desperate idea formed in her mind. "There has to be something we can do . . . Some way we can fight them . . ."

"Miss Victoria, I don't like it when you get that look on your face." Every time Victoria got that determined expression, chaos reigned.

The words were barely out of her mouth when the headstrong young woman sprang into action. She crossed the room to the captain's trunk and threw open the lid.

"Miss Victoria! What are you doing?!" she demanded in shock.

"I just can't accept this, Jonesey," she told her tightly as she began to sort through the pirate's personal belongings, tossing them haphazardly out of the sea chest in her quest to find something to help them escape.

The older woman glanced nervously toward the door. "But he might come in and catch you . . ."

"I don't care. I need a weapon!" Victoria continued to riffle through the contents of the chest. "There's got to be something in this cabin we can use to defend ourselves."

"You saw what happened to Duval when he threatened Serad with a knife."

"Duval must have been crazy to think he could do us any good by attacking Serad in front of all his men like that."

"Capitaine Duval is a gentleman." Jonesey sniffed.

"True, but he was almost a dead gentleman. If I can just find a gun, I could force the pirates to let us all go."

"And just how do you propose to do that with only one shot?"

"I'll think of something. Don't worry."

"I do worry, Miss Victoria. Have you forgotten how

220

you lost your seat and fell from your horse in the middle of the tiger hunt last year? As I recall, you would have been the tiger's dinner if it hadn't been for your father's timely arrival and excellent shooting ability."

Victoria had the grace to look embarrassed. "If I had managed to keep hold of my gun when I fell, I wouldn't have needed my father to save me. I would have shot the tiger myself."

"But you *didn't,* and you could very easily have been killed. And then what about the time when—"

"Don't say any more, Jonesey," she cut her off. "You're not going to stop me. I'm going to get us out of this one way or another."

There could be no doubt about her firm resolve, and Miss Jones looked on with increasing anxiety as she wondered what the girl would do next.

Victoria rummaged through to the bottom of the trunk, then slammed the lid in disgust. "Nothing but clothing . . ." All of which were now strewn about the cabin and the floor.

Not caring one whit about the mess she'd made, she headed for the desk next to check out all the drawers. Victoria carelessly tossed aside the charts and maps she found on the desktop and kept looking. When she discovered that one drawer was locked, she suddenly grew hopeful. *There had to be something important in there! There had to be!* She forced the lock on the drawer and found a pistol. She eagerly snatched it up, brandishing it with excitement.

"Put that back! You're going to get us both killed!"

"Let me see if it's loaded." Victoria ignored her, glad that her hunting abilities were proving helpful. "It is," she breathed. The gun in her hand renewed her fading inner strength. She knew how to use it, and she would if she had to. Not that she'd ever wanted to shoot anybody before, but if he forced her to, she would.

"Miss Victoria . . . don't . . ." Jonesey started to tell her to put the gun away when the door to the cabin suddenly opened.

Serad had intended to stay on deck with Tariq and finish supervising the transfer of the goods and men, but the wound to his arm was proving more troublesome than he'd first expected. It hurt like the devil, and, though he'd tied it off with a piece of cloth, he'd been unable to completely stifle the bleeding. He was coming below to his cabin now so he could doctor it correctly. He'd dismissed the guard and let himself in, only to find his entire cabin in disarray.

Shocked, he stood in the doorway, staring at the destruction before him. Fury rocked through him, and Serad moved threateningly into the room and slammed the door behind him.

"What's been going on in here? What do you think you're doing?" he thundered, his steely gaze fixed on Victoria and Victoria alone as she stood, straight and proud, behind his desk, her hands down at her sides. He knew the gun was in the locked drawer, and he wondered if she'd found it. He didn't dwell on that possibility too long, for he still thought of her as a spoiled English lady. Even if she had found the weapon, he doubted she knew which end of a gun was which.

Miss Jones cringed in the face of the pirate captain's outrage, but she moved forward to stand firmly in his path as he strode menacingly toward Victoria. There was little Jonesey could do to stop him, though, when he swept her aside with a single brush of his arm. She had no more effect on him than an annoying pest.

"Stay right there," Victoria ordered, lifting the pistol. "I'm a dead shot and I'll use it if I have to."

Serad was angry and his arm was hurting. He found

it hard to believe that the emerald-eyed, deadly determined woman standing on the other side of his desk holding his pistol pointed directly at his heart was the same inane, sophisticated beauty he'd dealt with up on deck. He would never have guessed that she'd had any knowledge of guns, and he derided himself for having underestimated her just as Tariq had earlier underestimated her companion.

"Just what do you plan to do with that?" Serad asked in a deceptively calm voice, stopping a few paces in front of the desk.

"I plan to make you let us and *La Mouette* go."

"With one bullet?" Serad's expression turned sardonic.

"One bullet is all it would take to kill you."

"But after I'm dead, then what?"

"Oh, I have no intention of shooting you unless you force me to."

"I'm certainly relieved to hear that," Serad mocked, deliberately trying to anger her. He wanted her to get so flustered that she made a mistake. He smiled widely at her, his white teeth flashing against the darkness of his beard.

"I'm glad you find this so amusing," Victoria returned with courage, although the coldness of his smile sent a shiver through her.

"It is hardly amusing. I take threats on my life very seriously."

"This isn't a threat, it's a promise," she responded firmly. "Now, I want you to turn around and walk toward that door. We're going to go up on deck and you're going to order your men to free everyone from our ship."

"Now why would I do that?"

"Because if you don't, I'll shoot you."

"You'll end up dead."

"And so will you."

They regarded each other in silence over the barrel of the gun, each gauging the strength of the other's purpose.

"After everyone's been freed, we'll board *La Mouette* again. You're going to go with us, though, just to make sure your crew doesn't fire on us again. When we near the English coast, you'll be set adrift in one of the longboats."

"A very ingenious plan." Serad didn't bother to tell her that *La Mouette* was a complete loss and that it would never sail again. It was something that really didn't even matter, for there was no way he was going to allow her to reach the deck holding a pistol on him. She was his captive, his slave. It was time she accepted the inevitable.

"You can start walking right now," she ordered, nodding in the direction of the door. "Jonesey, open it, and check outside. I don't want any unpleasant surprises."

Miss Jones had to give Victoria credit. So far, it looked as if her hastily conceived plan just might work. She hurried to open the door then peeked out into the corridor to find it deserted. "There's no one about."

"Good. Stay out of his reach. I don't want him using you for a shield. Now, let's go up on deck, Captain."

Serad almost told her that no self-respecting man would hide behind a woman, but he remained silent. Far better to let her worry about everything. It gave him a better chance to distract her.

Serad turned away from the desk, and his eyes narrowed to dangerous silver slits as he looked around the room and considered his options. There was little he could do with the desk between them, but once they moved toward the door and she came within range, he knew he might be able to surprise her and wrest the gun away. It would be a matter of timing and luck. This Lady Victoria might be a good shot, but she was only a woman. It was then, as he moved slowly toward the door, that his gaze fell upon one of his shirts she had thrown carelessly across the room while digging through his things. It had landed on the foot of the bunk near the door, and Serad knew then exactly how he was going to distract her. He just wished his arm wasn't aching so badly for he feared it might slow him down a little. When the time came, he had to move and move quickly.

As Serad approached the open portal, Victoria came out from behind the desk to follow. She knew the important thing was to keep the gun trained on him at all times. If she wavered for even an instant, he was certain to take advantage of her weakness, and if that happened, their lives were as good as over.

Serad kept his fury at having been duped by a female well in check as he prepared to disarm her. There would be time later to be angry about his own stupidity. Right now, the important thing was to get in control of the situation again.

Serad's move was lightning quick when he made it, and though Victoria had been expecting him to try something, he still caught her by surprise with his daring. Feinting to the left, Serad then darted to the right and snatched the shirt off the end of his bunk. In a fast motion, he swung it around, startling Victoria and knocking the pistol askew.

Victoria knew she had to fire before he came at her, and she squeezed off her one and only shot in frantic desperation. By then, though, it was too late. The round went wide and lodged itself in the paneled wall near the bed.

Serad was used to fighting men who were far stronger, far more cagey, and far more accustomed to

225

these deadly games than Victoria was. As the pistol went off, he dove at her, knocking her from her feet and sending them both crashing to the floor. The power of his attack jarred all the breath out of her, but still she fought on. She hung on to the gun for dear life, for it represented her one and only connection to freedom. Serad was just too strong for her, though. His big hands closed on her forearm with brutal force. Try as she might to hang on to the weapon, the pressure he was exerting on her wrist threatened to snap the delicate bones there. Finally, the pistol fell from her numb, nearly paralyzed fingers.

"I won't go with you! I won't!" Victoria cried, trying to pummel him with her fists.

Serad used the full weight of his body to pin her to the floor and then managed, finally, to grab both of her wrists and hold them still. But to his complete annoyance, just as he thought the battle won, he received a stinging, forceful blow on the head. Jonesey and her umbrella had returned to join the fracas.

"Unhand her now, you heathen! Let her go this instant!" Miss Jones was beyond caring about what happened to herself. Victoria had taken the risk to help them all and now it looked as if the pirate was going to force her to pay the price. "Harm me if you must, but release Miss Victoria!" she demanded as she continued to bludgeon Serad with her umbrella.

"Enough, woman!" Serad bellowed, letting one of Victoria's wrists go in order to grab the damned umbrella out of the old woman's hands.

Victoria saw the chance to inflict pain on her captor, and she took it. With all her might, she swung at him, but now he knew to expect the unexpected from her and he was prepared. He dodged her blow and trapped that arm again with the other. In disgust, he threw the umbrella across the room just as two of his men came charging in on them, fully armed.

"Serad *Reis!* We heard a shot and thought there might be trouble!" They weren't sure what to think when they found their fearless leader lying on top of the lovely English captive in the middle of the cabin floor with her elderly companion looking on.

"There was no trouble," Serad bit out as he got to his feet and dragged Victoria up, too. He held her tightly by her wrists and did not even consider releasing her as he faced his crewmen. "But I want these two separated from now on."

"No!" both women cried in unison.

Serad's mind was made up. Together they were treacherous; apart, they would be easier to control. "Take the old woman to the storeroom and lock her in there. See that she has what she needs for comfort, but make sure the door is barred."

"Yes, Serad *Reis.* Do you need anything else?"

"No. Go."

"I have to stay with Miss Victoria! It is my duty! You can't do this!" Jonesey argued vehemently as the two pirates led her away.

Serad shot Jonesey a black look and ignored her words as they took her from the cabin.

"I want my umbrella! Give me my umbrella back!" the old woman demanded as they closed the captain's cabin door behind them.

At the sound of the shutting door, Serad turned his full attention to Victoria. His wounded arm felt like it was on fire. His mood was anything but charitable as he still held her wrists in his powerful grip.

Victoria was afraid. She'd attacked him, and she lost. She couldn't even begin to imagine what kind of terrible punishment he would wreak upon her. Swallowing nervously, she prepared to face whatever was to come with as much serenity as possible. With what little pride she had left, she lifted her gaze to his and saw the fury that filled him. She trembled, but did not grovel or look away.

Serad stared down at Victoria, amazed that even now she did not cringe before him or beg for his mercy. Her continuing courage in the face of defeat surprised him. Had she been a man, he would have considered her a most worthy rival, but she was only a mere female. As such, she needed to be trained to her place, not honored for her defiance, and he intended to start doing that right now.

The strain of the continuing silence and Serad's unfathomable expression wore on Victoria's already frayed nerves. She wanted to scream, but she contained the urge. She waited, knowing her impatience to know her fate didn't concern him in the least.

Serad's gray eyes bored into hers, and Victoria felt as if he were looking into her very soul. The sensation was unsettling, and it frightened her. Her hair had come unbound in their struggle and it hung about her shoulders now in wild disarray. When Serad lifted one hand toward her, she shrank away from him thinking he was about to strike her. She was surprised when he gently brushed her hair back from the side of her face so he could see her more clearly. His touch was soft and unthreatening. She had not expected that of him.

Her initial reaction to his touch annoyed Serad. He had never made it a practice to hit women, and he wasn't about to start now. "I take no pleasure in hitting women," he stated with obvious distaste. "There are other, better ways to control them." He smiled slightly as he deliberately let his gaze run over her slender figure, hidden from him beneath her high-necked, long-sleeved daygown.

"You will never control me," Victoria denied as she fought hard to still the trembling that wracked her. She

228

wasn't quite sure what he meant by his "other, better ways," but she had a good idea.

Serad gave a laugh, then grew very serious. "So, even when conquered you do not admit defeat. Know this, Lady Victoria Lawrence, I already control you." He tightened his hold on her wrists to emphasize his point. "You are my captive, my slave. Until I choose to part with you, you will do my bidding when I tell you to. You will attend me and obey my every command."

"Never!" she hissed, using anger to cover her terror.

Serad's expression darkened at her continual denial of his supremacy over her. Irritated, he grasped her forearms and jerked her tightly to him. He wanted her to realize just how small and helpless she really was next to him. Unfortunately, the feel of her very feminine body against his hard, muscular one stirred fiery desires that were better served banked. "You are mine, woman, to do with as I will. Remember that." He gave her a bone-jarring shake, then pushed her away from him, even more irritated by the unexpected physical response he'd had to her nearness.

Inwardly, Victoria was quaking in terror, but she held her ground before him, waiting to see what he would do or say next. She remained standing and watched warily as he moved to settle heavily into the chair behind the desk.

Serad, his arm aching miserably, leaned back in the chair and rested his glowering gaze upon her. He was finding her challenging and maddening at the same time. He was used to docile females who were eager to please him. This one was nothing like that. In fact, as he considered it, she reminded him a bit of his aunt Rabi. The thought unsettled him for some reason, and he chose to ignore it.

Victoria was watching the pirate captain closely, trying to figure out what he was thinking. Serad's expression was thunderous, and she had no idea what he was planning. At first, she'd thought he would kill her instantly for her attack on him. He'd had the opportunity, yet he had not harmed her. Now, she didn't know what to expect. She waited there before him, her breathing strained and shallow in her fear, her hands clasped together to still their shaking. Her mind conjured up a thousand things he could do to her to make her pay for threatening him and they were all terrible.

When Serad finally addressed her, his voice was harsh and commanding. "Clean the cabin. I want it exactly the way it was when you were first brought here."

Chapter Seventeen

Clean the cabin? Victoria had been expecting the absolute worst and relief washed through her. She stared at him blankly for a minute, unable to believe she'd heard him right.

"Move, woman!" Serad barked. He was in no frame of mind to continue this struggle of wills with her. In his mind, he had won and that ended it.

The sharpness of his command compelled Victoria to move. Her feelings were a tumultuous mix of anger at being forced to do his bidding and ridiculous happiness at being let off so lightly. Picking up the mess she'd made in the search for the gun was hardly the punishment she'd imagined and her fears were eased a little. Though she had never cleaned up much of anything in her whole life, she hurried to do as she'd been told.

Moving hastily about the small stateroom, Victoria grabbed up all the clothing she'd thrown so haphazardly out of the trunk. Serad's brooding gaze was upon her as she worked, and it made her decidedly uncomfortable. When he finally looked away and busied himself with something else, her nervousness at being so constantly observed faded.

With her arms full of assorted discarded clothing, Victoria knelt beside the sea chest to begin putting everything away. She heard Serad opening a desk drawer but didn't look up. The less he noticed her the better as far as she was concerned. Only his loudly muttered vile oath shocked her into looking his way again. She glanced up to discover that he was trying to doctor his own injured arm.

As if he noticed her sudden interest, Serad directed, "Come here, woman."

"My name *is* Victoria," she said properly.

"Victoria . . ." he said it slowly. "You would have the name suit you, but remember who the victor is between us."

"It's not over yet."

"It *is* over," Serad dictated with finality. "From now on I will call you Tori, also. Now, come here, Tori, and tend to your master's wounds."

Tori bristled, but knew she had no choice but to obey. Laying his jumbled clothing aside, she rose and went to him. "What do you want me to do?"

"I can't see it very well, so cleanse the cut and bind it tightly, but be careful that you don't cause me too much pain," he told her, his eyes catching and holding hers.

For one heart-stopping moment, Tori stared into the depths of his now-stormy gray gaze and was held spellbound. The coldness and harshness was gone, and there was something reflected in his regard that caught her up and sent her senses spinning into confusion. The color of his eyes told her he was no naturally born North African, and she wondered where he had come from and why he'd become a pirate.

Tori frowned as she knelt next to him. She didn't want to think about him or wonder about him. He was her captor, nothing else. She directed her attention to the deep, ugly gash on the back of his arm, but even touching the warm, solid flesh of his arm disturbed her. To cover her bewilderment, she spoke up sarcastically, "It's just a pity Capitaine Duval didn't lower his aim and move it more to the left."

"So you would have preferred to see me and your wonderful Capitaine Duval both dead? That would leave you and your companion at the mercy of my men . . ." Serad was beginning to anticipate her biting remarks, and he was more than ready to counter them.

"Surely, they're not as—"

"As what?" he demanded. "Forgiving?"

He turned in the chair to face her with the truth, and Tori found herself once again very aware of the overpowering maleness of him. They were barely a breath apart as he spoke, telling her what her fate would have been without him.

"My men are controlled because I control them. They are pirates. Men accustomed to making their living by pillaging. They are used to being without a woman for months on end while they're at sea, but if the opportunity arose to have a taste of you, it would matter little to them that twenty men had gone before them or that there were twenty men left to come after. Even your precious defender, Miss Jones, would not be safe from their lust if it were given free rein."

Tori couldn't prevent a gasp at the horrible reality he was painting for her with his words.

"Now, unless you find that fate more appealing, I suggest you tend my arm and do a good job of it. I have no desire to die from an infected knife wound because you sought to finish with your doctoring what your precious capitaine wasn't able to with his blade."

Shocked by his graphic truths, Tori wasted no more time, but began to thoroughly wash the painful cut. After applying the medicine he gave her, she bound it with a clean, wide strip of cloth. She was relieved when she did not have to touch him any longer.

"There. It's done."

Serad had remained perfectly still while she'd worked, and at her declaration, he flexed his arm to test it. The pain was still there, but it had lessened somewhat. "Has the bleeding stopped?"

"Yes, but it could easily start again if you put any strain on it," she advised.

He nodded and stood up. Taking the now-empty pistol with him, he strode to the cabin door. He looked at her for a moment, then dictated that she finish her cleaning. With that, he left, pausing only long enough to lock her in again.

Tori stared at the closed door, and she wasn't sure whether she was more angry or frustrated. She had done what he'd told her to do, and yet there had been no word of thanks and no promises where Jonesey was concerned. Miserably, Tori wondered if she would ever see her friend again. Moving to the sea chest, she began to fold his personal things once more. For one vindictive moment, she considered ripping all his clothes to shreds, but she controlled the desire. Nothing good could be accomplished by antagonizing him further right now, and since she wanted to be reunited with Jonesey as soon as possible, she decided to do a good job of taking care of his things.

When all his clothing had been neatly folded and packed away, Tori went to the desk to straighten all the papers and charts she'd thrown about in her search for the gun. Curiosity got the best of her as she stared down at the once-locked drawer, and she wondered what else he kept there. She opened it and went through the contents to find a miniature portrait of a blond-haired woman.

For some reason, Tori was stunned by the discovery.

She wondered who the pretty woman was. Safely placing the portrait back where she found it, she finished her cleaning and retreated from the desk to think about her find and to wonder at the woman's connection to her captor.

Serad gingerly tested his arm again as he emerged up on deck. Finding that the bandage was still holding and that the bleeding had stopped, he went to join Tariq near the helm. Tariq saw him coming and smiled broadly at him.

"There was shooting in your cabin?" he asked, and he enjoyed his friend's look of discomfort.

"There was."

"And?" he probed, wanting to hear the truth and not just the talk among the men.

"As you underestimated the old woman, so I underestimated the young one. She's very proud, much like that Arabian mare I purchased several years ago."

"Is she going to prove as hard to tame?" Tariq joked. "As I recall, the mare gave you a very difficult time . . . and she was unarmed."

His taunts gained him a black glare. "The horse threw me only once. The woman will not try anything again."

"Oh?" His dark eyes lit up with interest. "How can you be so sure? She sounds bloodthirsty to me. I'd watch my back if I were you."

"That's what I have you for, my friend," Serad returned with an answering smile. "But there will really be no need. She had already accepted her fate. I'm confident she will cause us no more trouble."

"Be careful, Serad. Remember your own advice to me."

Serad knew Tariq was right, but he said nothing. He

did not want any of his men to know the resourcefulness of his captive. It was enough that he knew. He would handle her. She was his.

A sudden shout went up on the deck of the French ship. The crew of *La Mouette* had not yet been moved across to the *Scimitar,* and in a desperate attempt to escape the miserable future the pirates had planned for them, several of the men rioted against their guards. Shots were fired and knives flashed in the brilliance of the afternoon sun as the corsairs brought the captives under control. When all was said and done, three men from Capitaine Duval's crew had been felled. A resigned acceptance fell over the vanquished. To stifle any further attempts at escape, they were quickly herded on board the pirate ship and taken belowdecks to be chained in the positions where they would remain for the voyage back to Algiers.

It was many hours later when the last load of goods was transferred from *La Mouette* to the *Scimitar.* The order was given to cast off from the crippled ship, and Serad's men hastened to do so. Now that they had their bounty, they were eager to return home. The sails were quickly set and the pirate ship slowly moved away from the merchantman.

"We won't be so fleet on the trip home," Tariq commented as he considered the wealth of merchandise they'd just taken aboard.

"I'm pleased with our success, as Malik will be, but I regret losing the ship." He watched as they distanced themselves from the damaged boat.

They said no more until the range was right, and then Serad gave the order for his men to fire a full volley at the vessel. The boom of the cannons rocked the *Scimitar,* and the pirates looked on as their captain made good on his promise to send the French ship to the bottom. The vessel splintered and slowly sank beneath the surface. Only flotsam and jetsam remained to mark the grave of the once proud *La Mouette.*

Tori was tense as she waited for Serad's return. She had finished straightening the cabin over an hour before and now had nothing to do but think. Knowing she was trapped in the stateroom left her feeling quite helpless. Still, her indomitable spirit asserted itself. Just because Serad had overpowered her in physical ways didn't mean she had to surrender. She vowed to continue to battle him with the only weapon left to her—her intelligence.

The hours dragged by. Tori found herself listening for her captor's footsteps so she could be prepared to face him when he returned. When the *Scimitar's* cannons roared to life unexpectedly, she was shocked. Her heart leapt to her throat as she imagined that the pirates were firing at another ship that was coming to their rescue. She waited breathlessly for the sounds of further battle and victory for her imaginary heroes, but no one came. Time passed and nothing else happened. Tori grew depressed as she realized that there would be no rescue. Whatever reason the cannons had fired, it hadn't been for that.

The sound of the lock turning in the door startled Tori, and when the door opened she expected to see Serad there. To her surprise a man she'd never seen before came into the room carrying a tray of food.

"I am Mallah. Serad *Reis* told me to bring this to you," the pirate announced.

"He's not coming back?" she asked quickly, hopefully.

The crewman gave a disinterested lift of his shoulders in answer to her question. He had no idea what his captain's plans were.

237

Desperate for conversation and information, Tori asked him what the shooting was about.

This he knew the answer to, but he kept his reply curt to discourage her from asking anything else. "The merchantman was too damaged to sail, so we sank her." He said no more, just placed the tray on the desktop and left.

Tori heard the click of the lock again as she was once again entombed. She moved to the desk and took a few bites of the food, but her nerves were stretched so taut that the fare not only seemed tasteless to her, but her stomach rebelled.

The day had been long and fraught with danger, and as darkness proclaimed the coming of night, Tori realized just how exhausted she was from the fight. Serad's bunk looked more and more inviting as she stared at it from across the cabin, and she almost wished she could go to sleep and wake up to find that it was all a dream.

A sigh wracked her as she moved to the bed. The pirate had been gone for hours and it appeared he wouldn't be back any too soon. Tori knew she should rest now so she would be wide awake later when Serad returned. She touched the bed tentatively, and finding it soft and inviting, she lay down upon it.

But sleep did not immediately come to Tori. Serad's presence was all too real to her as she lay in his bed. Surrounded by his things, she couldn't put him completely from her mind. She remembered the power of command he exuded and the feel of his stong arm beneath her hands as she'd taken care of his wound. She thought of how he could have killed both Capitaine Duval and herself, but had not, and of how he'd touched her so gently that one time. As elusive sleep finally claimed her, the image of the fair woman in the picture drifted through her mind along

238

with a vision of her captor's gray eyes . . . and she wondered . . .

Serad and Tariq stayed on deck until the *Scimitar* was well under way, then they went below to celebrate their success. They shared the evening meal together as they usually did, and it was quite late before Serad made his way back to his cabin.

Earlier, Serad had ordered food brought to Tori, and he expected to find her well fed, awake, and waiting eagerly for him so she could do his bidding. He was looking forward to seeing just how submissive she had become.

Serad had been thinking about Tori for most of the evening and had come to the decision that he would keep her for himself rather than ransom her back. Malik had been after him for some time now to consider taking wives and starting a harem, and though Serad knew he wasn't interested in marriage yet, he certainly would enjoy keeping Tori as an odalisque. He wasn't certain she would prove amenable to the plan, but he knew that ultimately her wishes didn't really matter. She had been obeying him without question when he'd left her, and he expected that to continue.

When Serad reached the cabin door, he unlocked it and then pushed it wide, entering cautiously. He had not forgotten her resourcefulness. The interior of the stateroom was completely dark, and he moved slowly, ever alert for her possible attack. To Serad's surprise, there was no movement in the room, and for a moment, he almost feared she'd escaped. Only when he lighted the lamp did he discover his fear was unfounded. The plate of food he'd ordered for her was on the desk, looking mostly untouched, the cabin was spotless, and Tori was curled on her side on his bed, sound asleep.

Serad walked silently to the side of the bunk and stood there staring down at his captive. She had more courage and inner strength than many of the men he knew. Yet, in her sleep, this English vixen looked the lovely innocent.

Serad took advantage of the moment to study Tori. From the silky length of her shining, dark hair, completely loose now and spread seductively about her, to the crescent sweep of her long black lashes against her cheeks, she was flawless. She had a mouth that begged to be kissed and a body made to satisfy any man's dream of ecstasy. Serad found it hard to believe that this delicate sleeping beauty was the same quick-thinking, sharp-tongued female who'd caused him such aggravation earlier.

Serad smiled at the thought of how Tori challenged him at every turn. Except for his aunt, he'd never met a woman who'd dared defy a man. He wasn't sure whether he liked it or not, but it certainly kept him from becoming bored with her.

Serad continued to stare down at Tori, and an unfamiliar emotion stirred within the heart of him, a kind of protective possessiveness. He wondered at it, trying to understand what it meant, for if there was ever a female who didn't really need his protection it was this one.

Tori stirred. Her sleep had been plagued by restless dreams of the terror of Serad's attack. As if suddenly becoming aware that someone was watching her, she came awake. Her emerald eyes opened to find her nemesis standing over her. Serad had an amused expression on his face and looked exceedingly virile and handsome. A jolt of awareness of him as a man shot through Tori, troubling her. Suddenly embarrassed at her own thoughts and at being found in such a compromising position, she immediately sat upright and glared at him.

"You're back." She stated the obvious for she was furious with herself for having fallen into such a deep sleep. She'd wanted to be mentally sharp for him, not drowsy and weak.

"As I have every right to be," Serad responded casually, not making any effort to move away from the bedside. "This is my cabin."

"Then take it and give me one of my own."

"We will be sharing this cabin for the voyage to Algiers."

"I would prefer to share a cabin with Miss Jones." She rose from the bunk and moved across the room to escape his nearness.

"You should have thought about that earlier. I had intended to allow you to stay together."

"If I give you my word that I will not cause you any more trouble, will you bring her back to me?"

"You will not cause me any more trouble, regardless," Serad stated the truth, "for if you do, your companion will pay the price."

"I see." Tori watched as he sat down upon the bunk she'd just vacated. "Will your men be bringing another bed in for me to use?"

"Did you not find comfort in my bed already?" he asked with a slight smile.

"By myself, yes. But if I take the bed, where will you sleep?"

"I mean for us to share more than just the cabin . . ." His gaze was warm upon her.

"I am on my way to London to marry my betrothed." It was as close to pleading as she could come.

This news startled him, and for some unexpected reason, angered him, too. "You *were*. Now, you are my captive."

Her brave front faltered. He had already proven that

241

he could force her to do anything he wanted. She knew he could force her to do this, too. Tears filled her eyes, though she refused to let them fall.

Serad witnessed the battle that was being waged within her, and suddenly his conscience, long silent, interfered. He grabbed the top blanket off the bed and tossed it to her.

"Seek your own rest, woman, but know that this bed is soft and the floor is very hard, and I have no intention of giving up my rest." With that, he lay back and, folding his arms behind his head, closed his eyes. Without looking at her, he ordered her to put out the light.

For a moment, Tori could only stare at him in something akin to shock, then she hurried to blow out the lamp. Moving as far away from him as she could get, she spread the single cover on the floor near his sea chest and lay down to get whatever rest she could.

Serad was mystified by his own actions. The most beautiful woman he'd even seen was sleeping right there in his cabin within arm's reach, and he wasn't going to take her. He shook his head in disbelief. He could just imagine what Tariq and Hasim would say if they knew the truth. He tried to understand what there was about Tori that kept him from acting upon his baser instincts, but he could find no easy answer. It was a long time before he fell asleep.

Chapter Eighteen

Serad awoke at first light as was his custom. Swinging his long legs over the side of his bunk, he sat up to see Tori still sleeping on the cabin floor. He swore under his breath at her stubborn pride and stood up to cross the room to her. Without saying a word, he gently scooped her up in his arms to carry her back to the bed.

Tori let out a small murmur as he crossed the room holding her carefully to his chest. For all that she was a firebrand when she was awake, she was as gentle as a kitten asleep. He was amazed at how light she was, and how soft. It felt strangely right to be holding her this way, and as he gazed down at her, she instinctively nestled against him. He deeply regretted that he had only to carry her across the room.

Serad was glad when she did not stir as he settled her on the bunk. He tenderly covered her with his own blanket, then stood there watching over her for a minute to make sure she did not awake. When he was certain she was sound asleep, he went about his own business. After washing and changing into clean clothing, Serad took one last look at his captive, then left the cabin to tend to his duties. As he locked the door behind him, he almost regretted that it would be many hours before he'd get the chance to return.

Since Tariq had come on deck half an hour before, he'd been watching for Serad. When he saw his friend emerge from belowdecks looking quite satisfied and very well rested, he smiled broadly in complete approval of what he was sure had been an exciting night for his *reis*. He envied him the dark hours just passed. "Good morning, Serad. You're looking quite fit this morning. You slept well, I take it?"

"Very well, my friend," he returned with a confident grin that deliberately misled him. There was no way he would admit to Tariq or any other man that he had not shared his bed with Tori and sampled of her delights last night. He would answer noncommittally and allow them to draw their own conclusions.

Knowing Serad as well as he did and knowing how much he enjoyed beautiful women, Tariq did misinterpret his answer and self-satisfied expression. "Your success with women is well known among the men, and your legendary reputation only grows more so," he told him approvingly.

Inwardly, Serad grimaced, but outwardly he took the compliment as his due. "Tori is a stunning beauty. I have definitely decided to keep her for myself."

"You're not going to ransom her back?" He was stunned.

"No," he answered quickly, and then wondered at his response.

"She must be quite a woman for you to forfeit the fortune she would surely bring you in ransom."

"She is," Serad agreed.

"I am surprised that you have given your heart so quickly," Tariq commented.

"I did not say she had my heart," he corrected, troubled that his friend would think so. "But Tori is

244

very easy on the eyes, and she is more than agreeable in other ways."

"You have tamed this English woman much faster than you tamed your mare," he approved.

Serad smiled again, then boasted. "Perhaps this woman is smarter. She recognized her master more quickly than the horse did."

They shared a laugh over the comparison. But even as he did, Serad wondered if he had really mastered Tori at all or if she was just biding her time until she could try something outrageous again. He knew instinctively that no matter what he said before his men, he could never let his guard down around her. Oddly, Serad found the challenge of outwitting her very intriguing.

Tori had passed a terrible night trying to get comfortable on the hard floor. She'd had no intention of sharing the bed with Serad, though, and so had suffered her chosen fate in silence. It seemed to her that an eternity had passed before she'd finally fallen asleep.

The loud knocking at the door jarred her awake, and she suddenly became aware of where she was lying. Though she was still fully clothed, Tori was completely confused and embarrassed at being caught there in the middle of Serad's bed. Distraught, she clutched at the covers and yanked them all the way up to her chin just as the lock was turned and the door started to open. She watched in bewilderment as the same man who'd brought her dinner the night before came into the room carrying her breakfast.

Mallah entered and, upon seeing the woman still lying in Serad's bed looking very tired, he smiled to himself. His *reis's* reputation with women was well

245

known on board the ship, and he was certain she was exhausted from a night of wild lovemaking. Mallah knew he would make sure that this bit of gossip was added to the tales of Serad's prowess. Then, fearful of angering his *reis* by acting too boldly with this woman, he averted his gaze from Tori and went about tending to his business. He quickly placed the food upon the desk, then picked up the dishes of the uneaten cold food from the night before and left without a word.

Tori watched all this in complete befuddlement. *How had she gotten into Serad's bed?* The question hung ominously in her mind. She tried to remember moving there, but no memory came. That much gave her some relief, for at least she knew that she hadn't willingly climbed into bed with her captor. Still, the intimacy of lying where he had lain made her uncomfortable, and Tori threw off the covers and got up.

Her appetite had been nonexistent last night, but now she was hungry and the fare smelled wonderful. She moved to the desk to partake of the food, wondering what she was going to do with her time today.

Tori was still wondering the same thing nearly ten hours later. She had passed the entire day bored and restless. She'd managed to wash up a little bit, but still felt dirty after wearing the same gown for more than twenty-four hours. She longed for the opportunity to bathe fully and change into fresh clothes, but she'd had no opportunity to see Serad to ask him for her trunk of clothes from *La Mouette*. Mallah had been her only visitor throughout the entire day, and he had refused all her attempts at conversation, remaining cold and silent when he'd brought her her noonday meal. Tori only hoped that Serad would return soon so she could get cleaned up.

It was near dusk when Serad stood with Tariq near the helm. "If these winds stay as steady as they are, we might reach Algiers within ten days," he pointed out, pleased.

"I'm surprised that we're making such good headway, considering the load we're carrying."

"Maybe luck is just with us this trip," Serad mused, feeling good about their progress.

"Luck has certainly been with you," Tariq returned. "I don't know how you've managed to stay on deck and work all day. If I were *reis* of the *Scimitar* and the Englishwoman was waiting below for me, I would have found much that had to be done in my cabin today."

"And that is exactly why you are not *reis* of the *Scimitar.*" Serad grinned. "You know there's nothing more important in my life than my ship."

He knew of Serad's all-consuming love for the sea. Still, as pretty as the Englishwoman was, she had to run a close second.

Tori barged into Serad's thoughts again just as he denied her importance to him. She had been on his mind off and on all day long. There had even been several times when he'd been tempted to go back to his cabin just to look in on her, but he would never admit that to Tariq. Now, though, he knew it was time he returned to her.

"I'll be eating in my cabin tonight," he told Tariq, fully expecting the smile his friend shot him.

"Somehow I find I agree with your decision completely," Tariq said good-naturedly. "I'll see you in the morning."

Serad moved off to find Mallah and order two meals brought to his cabin. Then he headed belowdecks. Serad was perplexed. In all his romantic experience with women, there had never been one who could hold his attention for any length of time. Tori, however, was proving to be different. He'd tried all day to analyze it, but he could not figure out exactly what it was about her that kept him so intrigued. She was lovely, true, but that in itself didn't make her special. The other women he'd known had also been beautiful. Serad wondered if the attraction he felt for her would remain so exciting once he'd made love to her or if it would fade as quickly as his feelings for other women had.

Serad stopped to unlock his cabin door. He found Tori standing near the window gazing out to sea. Once again, he was struck by her beauty and grace. His gaze swept over her with a hungry intensity. He wondered how he'd managed to spend last night in the same room with her and not make her his in all ways. He wondered, too, if he could do it again tonight. When she glanced his way, Serad quickly masked his expression.

Tori was glad Serad had returned. He had monopolized her thoughts against her will almost all day. She'd told herself that he was not the overpowering man she was making him out to be in her mind, that she'd just been intimidated by him yesterday. But now, facing Serad again, Tori realized just how wrong she'd been. Serad was handsome and powerful and mesmerizing. As he stood there before her, he seemed to fill the entire cabin with his presence. He radiated an animal magnetism. Tori stared at the bronze width of his chest and had the wildest urge to run her hands over that hard, muscle-sculpted flesh.

Suddenly realizing the direction of her thoughts,

Tori jerked her gaze away from Serad. She told herself she was just responding to him this way because she was desperate for company. She had to remind herself that this man was her enemy, not her friend. Just because he'd given her that one reprieve last night did not mean that he would never try to force her to his bed. Serad was no cultured English gentleman. He was a Barbary pirate, and judging from the stories she'd heard about them, that made him one of the most savage, barbarous men sailing the seven seas.

Serad was unaware of her turbulent emotions as he closed the door and came farther into the room. "It's good that you are up and ready to see to my needs," he remarked smugly.

"You expected me to be in bed?"

"Now that I consider it, it is not a bad idea. I would not object if you wanted to greet me that way," he taunted, his eyes growing hot upon her.

She stiffened at his implication. "I prefer sleeping alone on the floor."

"You did not act that way this morning when I carried you in my arms and laid you in my bed."

"I was asleep," she defended.

"I find you're most amenable when you're asleep," Serad commented, thinking of how wonderful it had been to hold her.

"Then I will endeavor to stay awake," she retorted with a proud lift of her chin, her eyes flashing defiantly.

Serad closed the distance between them. His gaze darkened with the intensity of desire he suddenly felt for her. "Nights can prove to be very long when your body aches for the release of sleep, and your mind refuses to surrender," he said slowly and with a deeper, hidden meaning as he came to stand before her.

"My mind and body work together," Tori replied haughtily.

"We shall see" came his mysterious reply as he towered over her, forcing her to look up at him.

"Did you want something?" she asked innocently, wanting to change the topic. She could have groaned in mortification when Serad chuckled.

"There is much that I want, but all in due time," he answered with a confident smile as he moved away to sit at the desk. "I will be eating here with you tonight, so see to my arm now while we wait for Mallah to bring our food."

Tori found it easier to breathe once he'd distanced himself from her, but his command to tend his wound left her disquieted again. She didn't want to touch him, but there was no way to avoid it. Without a word, she followed him to the desk and retrieved the medical supplies from the drawer where she'd stored them earlier. Tori knelt beside him and unwrapped the bandage she'd applied the night before. The cut, while still raw and sore-looking, had not broken open again, and for that she was pleased.

"How does it look?" Serad asked, glancing down over his shoulder at her.

"A little better, but it would still be wise not to use your arm too much for the next day or two. It needs time to heal," she cautioned.

Serad only grunted in response to her advice. The *Scimitar* was his life and his love. There was no way he would neglect his duties on board his ship. He remained perfectly still as Tori began to cleanse the wound. The only outward sign he gave that he was suffering any pain was a slight tensing of his body as she applied an antiseptic. She was amazed at his strength of will, for the wound was deep and had to be

250

painful. When she was done, she bound it again with a clean bandage.

"That should keep until tomorrow," Tori said.

Serad tested his arm, found it flexible enough, then snared her wrist just as she would have moved away from him. "An obedient servant should be properly rewarded for a job well done." He slid his hand insinuatingly up her arm to draw her near as he stood.

His unexpected touch sent currents of awareness racing through Tori, startling her. Her eyes widened as she looked up at him.

Serad gazed down at her and was lost in the emerald pool of her eyes. With a gentle touch, he nudged her even closer.

The heat of his body so close to hers jarred Tori back to sensibility. Terrified of the feelings Serad was stirring within her, she stiffened. "I would like to choose my own reward."

Serad saw a brief flicker of emotion in her eyes that could only be identified as fear before she hid it behind a brave front, and the ardor that had begun to burn within him was thoroughly and effectively doused. His own reaction to her bewildered him. *He wanted her. Why should he care what she wanted or thought? Why should it matter that he struck fear in her heart instead of desire?* Confused, he retreated from his need to press her for more. "Do not ask for your freedom or your companion's return. Those are rewards I would not grant."

"Is Miss Jones all right?" she asked worriedly.

"She is as you are," he confirmed.

"Then for my reward I ask only for a bath and a fresh change of clothes," Tori then requested, that concern eased.

Serad found her request not unpleasing. The

thought of watching her bathe appealed to him, and though he knew it might prove to be the ultimate in torture for himself, he agreed. "You will get clean clothes, and we shall see what we can do about the bath."

"Thank you." For the first time ever, she smiled at him, and for some strange reason, he felt quite satisfied with himself.

Mallah arrived with the food and, after setting up a small table for them to use, he was sent off to bring the tub Serad used for bathing to the cabin. Alone again, they sat down to eat.

The intimacy of sharing a meal with Serad in his cabin made Tori very nervous. She watched him from beneath lowered lashes as he ate. It was absurd for her to be so mesmerized by him. She knew what he was. But still, she couldn't deny the fact that while he frightened her, he also fascinated her. She wanted to know more about him.

"Serad?" she ventured bravely.

He lifted a questioning gaze to hers. "Yes?"

"Why did you become a pirate?"

He didn't have to think long to answer that. "I've always loved the sea, and I always wanted to captain a ship. This was the legacy of my people so I, too, became a corsair for Algiers."

"But you're not a native North African. I mean, anyone can tell by your gray eyes that you're not."

"I was raised in Algiers. It is my home."

His tone stopped her from pushing any further on that issue. "Are you married?"

He gave her a curious look. "No. I have not taken any wives as yet."

"Wives?" she blurted out, stunned at his use of the plural.

"Wives," he repeated with unchallenged male authority. "In my culture a man may take as many wives as he can afford to keep. He can also have concubines and odalisques."

"Concubines and odalisques?" Tori had never heard those terms before.

"Female slaves kept in a man's harem for his personal pleasure."

"Do you have a harem?"

"I spend too much time at sea."

Tori found this news oddly pleasing. "If you aren't married, then who is the blond woman whose picture you keep in your desk?"

Her question surprised him for a moment, but then he realized that she must have seen his aunt's picture while she was putting things away.

"She is my Aunt Rabi."

"What of your parents?"

He was slightly uncomfortable with this question. Malik was really the only father he'd ever known and his aunt the only mother. He had no idea where his real parents were, nor did he care. "As far as I know, they're dead. I was raised by my aunt and Malik."

"Who's Malik?"

"He is the *dey* of Algiers, and Aunt Rabi is his."

It sounded so much like he was talking about an inanimate object that Tori couldn't stop herself from asking, "What do you mean she *is* Malik's?"

"Many years ago Malik claimed her as part of his tribute."

"Are you telling me that your aunt was taken captive the same way you've taken me?" She stared at him aghast.

"She is happy with Malik," he said defensively.

"Why wasn't she ransomed back?"

"He wanted to keep her." Serad thought it very simple and couldn't imagine why she'd asked.

"What about what she wanted?"

"Malik cares for her and has placed her above all others in his household, that should be enough."

"And you agree with that?"

"Of course, Malik is *dey*."

"Piracy really does run in your family . . ."

"It was my decision to go to sea, but then there was never really any choice. Even as a boy, I longed to captain my own ship and to name it the *Scimitar*." Vague and distant memories of a hand-crafted toy boat with the same name drifted through his mind. Giving himself a mental shake, Serad brought himself back to the present. He was doing exactly what he wanted to be doing right now, and nothing else mattered but that. As determined as he'd been to enjoy the evening with his lovely captive, though, Serad found his mood sobering.

"You must be very pleased that you have achieved your dream. It is a shame that your goal was to be a predator and steal what others have honestly earned."

"The strong and the fast survive." He shrugged, then added, "You would be wise to mind your tongue, Tori. I have stolen nothing from you yet."

"You have stolen my freedom."

"A woman is never free. She goes from her father's house to her husband's. She is bound from the day she is born to servitude of one kind or another."

"You're wrong."

"Am I? This man you are to marry. Did you choose him?" He knew immediately by her expression that he'd been right. "You see? A woman belongs to a man. Either daughter or wife, the woman is the man's to do with as he pleases. It is the way of life."

Tori was seething. "I am, and always have been, my

254

own person. I have never done anything that I did not want to do."

"Oh? So you care for this man of your father's choosing?"

"I love him," she blatantly lied, not about to give Serad an inch in any confrontation. "He's a wonderful man. Unlike men of your culture, he's kind and gentle and respectful of women," she said pointedly, letting him know by her tone that her betrothed was everything he was not. "I can't wait to return home and marry him."

Her singing of praises for her English fiancé irritated Serad. He was glad when Mallah returned with the tub and hot water right then, interrupting their conversation.

Chapter Nineteen

Tori looked on with barely concealed eagerness as Mallah and the men who had come with him set up the tub and then filled it with the hot water. The thought of a good soak was heavenly to her, and she couldn't wait to wash the grime from the past several days from her body.

Serad had been watching his crewmen as they went about setting up the bath. He glanced over at Tori, and seeing the happiness shining in her eyes, he felt pleased with himself over having granted her this small pleasure. When he looked back at Mallah and the others, he discovered that they'd finished their task and were now openly regarding his captive with avid interest. The thought of their eyes upon her in this intimate setting bothered him, and he ushered the men from the cabin.

"Your reward is set," Serad announced once they were gone.

"Thank you," Tori replied primly, hoping against hope that he was going to leave, too. "It's good to know that you're a man of your word."

"There was never any doubt of that. I keep every

promise I make and I take no vows I can't live up to," Serad told her firmly. His smoky gaze held hers for a moment, as if to add emphasis to his words, then swung back to her waiting bath.

The wooden tub filled with warm water looked very inviting, and Serad wondered what his English beauty would do if he chose to bathe with her. The idea intrigued him, but he dismissed it for now. There would be other baths in the days to come. It was far better to share a bath with a willing woman than a fighting she-devil. He would give Tori whatever time she needed to completely accept her fate. He wouldn't rush or force her. That wasn't his way.

Serad suddenly realized that he had to get out of the cabin. He turned to go, saying only that he would be back.

Tori was tremendously relieved when Serad left. For a little while, she'd been afraid that he'd meant to stay while she bathed, and she'd had no intention of undressing in front of him. With almost pagan delight, she unfastened her gown and slipped out of the soiled garment. Throwing her dirty clothing in a pile, she hastily stepped into the tub to take advantage of every second of her privacy.

There was no preventing the sigh of pleasure that escaped Tori as she sank down in the heated water. As she leaned her head back against the side of the tub, she closed her eyes and let the soothing water ease the ache of her worries. She sighed again and let her mind go blank. She needed the time to restore her inner peace.

Serad, meanwhile, made his way down to the bowels of the ship in search of Tori's trunk. It took him a while, but finally he located it among the bounty from *La Mouette*. He was definitely not familiar with the way

Englishwomen dressed, and he sorted through the huge chest in confusion. After searching through her mounds of clothes, he finally chose a daygown and some other personal things he imagined would be essential to her comfort.

As Serad made his way back to his cabin, a major battle waged within him. A part of him wanted Tori to be done with her bath and already dressed in her dirty clothes. The other side of him, the less civilized part, wanted her to still be in the tub.

When he reached the cabin door, Serad paused for a moment, then entered without preamble. Having been gone nearly half an hour, he'd honestly expected Tori to be finished. To his complete surprise, and pleasure, she was still in the tub. He stopped just inside the closed door to feast his eyes upon her. Her back was to him, and he relished the view of her slender, bare shoulder and the sleek fall of her wet hair. Heat rushed through his entire body, then settled with a pounding vengeance in his loins, leaving him aching to have her.

Tori had just finished washing her hair when she heard the cabin door open. She gasped in shock as she realized just how much time had passed and that Serad was back. She'd been enjoying herself so much that she'd forgotten she should hurry. Nervously scooting lower in the rapidly cooling water, she drew her knees up and then crossed her arms protectively over her breasts to shield herself from his eyes. "Serad, wait! You can't come back yet. I'm not done."

Serad was not about to be denied this moment. He smiled as he moved confidently forward. His gaze was riveted on the tantalizing curve of her shoulder, and he had an almost uncontrollable desire to press a kiss to that sensitive spot.

"This is my cabin, Tori. If I want to stay, I will," he

said in a soft but determined voice.

The sight of her enthralled Serad. He longed to take her in his arms and lift her, wet and dripping, from the water. He wanted to lay her upon his bed and make passionate love to her. He wanted to bury himself within her and keep her for his own. He fought for control. He was normally a man of action, a man who took whatever he wanted, and it required a superhuman effort on his part to restrain himself. With outward calm, Serad merely crossed the room to stand beside the tub so he could feast his eyes upon her.

Tori was aware of the burning intensity of her captor's regard. She knew this could very well be the moment of reckoning . . . the moment she'd feared from the first. With all the courage she could muster, she raised her eyes to meet his. She said with dignity. "I did not mean to sound as if I were trying to order you about, I merely needed a few more moments of privacy to get dressed. If you could just leave the clothes and step outside for a moment, I could . . ."

"But what if I said that I liked you this way?" he asked, leaning down to trace his fingertips along the sensual line of her collarbone and then lower . . . His gaze followed his hand and he didn't stop until he reached the barrier of her crossed arms.

Serad's touch was like an open flame on her skin, but somehow Tori managed not to jerk away from him and risk exposing even more of herself. She deliberately ignored his leading question as she asked in return, "I take it you're not going?"

"No," he answered, still smiling as he drew back to stand over her. "I think I'll stay and enjoy the view." He found it amazing that even though he had her cornered, she refused to surrender to his superior power. She was a beautiful, spirited woman.

Tori reasoned that she had absolutely nothing to lose by brazening it out with him. Serad seemed to respect bravery more than any other attribute, so she gave him a look of pure disdain as she politely requested that he hand her the towel.

Serad eyed the towel, then Tori, and finally did as she had asked. His reward was a glimpse of one pale, rounded breast as she reached out to take it from him. Hard put to keep the tight rein on his growing passion, Serad decided to move a safe distance away from her. Sitting behind his desk, he tried to relax and look casual while watching her attempt to rise. It was not an easy task.

Tori wrapped the cloth around her as she sat in the tub and then stood in one smooth motion. She thought she managed quite well considering the circumstances, but in truth, her action in wetting the towel only made her look all the more seductive. The damp material clung like a second skin to the sweet curves of her body.

From where he looked on, it took all of Serad's mighty willpower to remain in his seat. Tori appeared the goddess rising from the waters of the deep. She was a natural-born temptress, for none of her actions had been deliberately designed to entice him, yet no learned odalisque's play could have aroused him more.

It was this realization of her artless and guileless nature that ultimately stopped Serad from acting on his growing desire for her. He knew the last thing Tori wanted to do was to purposefully stir him to passion. She'd made it clear from the first that she wanted nothing to do with him. Yet, Serad found that he wanted her as he'd never wanted another woman in his life.

For a moment, he considered acting on his desire. He thought about taking her in spite of everything, but something his aunt had said to him in the distant past echoed through his being. *Above all else, you must be a man of honor.* Serad could hear her words as plainly as if she stood beside him, and he knew he could do no less than what Aunt Rabi expected of him.

"May I have my clothes?" Tori was asking as she stepped from the tub and walked proudly toward him, her hand out to take her garments from him.

Serad watched her as she crossed the cabin, her head up, proud and unafraid. She was a magnificent woman. A muscle worked in his jaw as he strugged with himself, and he suddenly knew that he had to get out of the cabin in a hurry.

"Here." Abruptly, Serad stood up and dropped her things on his desktop to avoid touching her hand. Without saying another thing, he rushed from the room, not trusting himself to look back.

Tori watched Serad go and couldn't believe her luck. He'd left her alone! Perhaps he wasn't the ogre she'd been making him out to be. Her spirits were high as she sorted through the few things he'd brought to her. She was pleased to find that along with her daygown and comb and brush, he'd also retrieved one of her nightgowns from the trunk. Tori donned the high-necked, long-sleeved cotton garment hastily for fear that he might return at any minute.

Once dressed, she managed to relax a little. Facing Serad nearly naked had almost unnerved her, but now, covered from neck to wrist to feet she felt as safe as she could. She moved about the room constantly anticipating his return. After a while, when he didn't come back, she gathered up her blanket from his bed and spread it on the floor again. She turned down the lamp to a low glow, then lay down for the night.

Up on deck, Serad stood alone. His hands grasped at

the rail so tightly that his knuckles turned white. He was lost in troubled thought. He wanted Tori and yet he was denying himself. It made no sense, but then it made complete sense. At that illogical conclusion, Serad swore under his breath.

"Serad? What are you doing up here?" It was Tariq's voice that sounded from out of the darkness, startling him.

"I just came up for a breath of fresh air before going to bed."

"It's hot in your cabin, eh?"

"Very," he answered, and then, needing to be away from his friend, he bid him good night and disappeared down the companionway.

Tariq watched him go and smiled as he thought of who was waiting for him below.

Serad returned to the cabin to find Tori already asleep on the floor. Knowing how completely miserable she had to be lying there, he was tempted to pick her up and put her in his bed. He stopped himself, though. So far, he'd kept himself under control, but there was no telling what he might do in a weak moment if she was actually in the same bed with him. Leaving her to her solitary rest, Serad blew out the lamp, shed his own clothes, and lay down. The night proved very long as he wondered just what he was going to do with her.

The British ship, the *Sea Maiden,* bound for London, came upon the wreckage of *La Mouette* and the one survivor clinging to the wreckage shortly after sunup. Every effort was made to rescue the wounded man from the sea, and when he was brought on board, many wondered if he would live through the day. By late afternoon, the sailor had recovered enough to talk, and he told the *Sea Maiden's* captain of the pirate attack. He told them the identity of the captives who'd been taken and of his own fruitless attempt to rebel against the corsairs. He explained how he'd been cut down and left for dead on deck just before the ship was sunk. At full sail, the British vessel rushed on to London bearing the news of the fate of the French ship.

When Tariq came on deck early the next morning, he was amazed to find Serad there.

"Your night was a short one. I'm surprised you're already at work," he observed, joining him at the rail where he stood gazing out across the endless blue-green waters.

Serad almost gave a sarcastic laugh at his statement. If anything, he felt as if the night had lasted forever. It had certainly seemed that way when he'd been trying fruitlessly to sleep. Every fiber of his being had been aware of Tori slumbering on the floor nearby. He'd never been so glad to see a sunrise in his life.

"My duties to the ship do not cease merely because I have other pleasures with which to occupy myself," he pointed out.

"You're a far better man than I am." Tariq grinned.

"That's generally known, I believe," Serad answered tongue-in-cheek, managing a smile at long last. He liked Tariq and was suddenly very glad for his distracting company. He was very tired of thinking only of the elusive woman who was at that very moment sleeping peacefully where he'd left her in his bed in the cabin below. Turning his gaze back out to sea, Serad asked his friend's opinion of the clouds on the horizon. "It looks to me like we may be heading into a storm later today," he observed.

Tariq agreed, spotting the building clouds for the

first time.

"Have the men begin to prepare the ship. We may be starting into it as early as noon."

As Tariq hurried off to spread the word, Serad sought out Mallah. He wasn't sure how long the bad weather would last, but the least he could do was offer Tori a chance to get some sunshine before the storm hit. After finding Mallah, he directed him to give Tori breakfast and then bring her up on deck. Then he, too, began readying the *Scimitar* to weather the coming blow.

Tori was already up when Mallah knocked at the cabin door with her breakfast. She'd awakened earlier to find herself, once again, alone in the middle of Serad's bed with no recollection of getting there. The softness of it had felt wonderful, but Tori had had no intention of being caught there again by Mallah. She'd quickly risen and donned her clean clothes. After brushing out her hair, which she was forced to leave loose around her shoulders, she took advantage of the time alone to wash out her dirty things in the now-cold bathwater. She laid them out around the room to dry, then busied herself with straightening the cabin once more.

Mallah was glad to find her already up and dressed when he arrived at the cabin. He placed the breakfast tray on the desk.

"Thank you." She was hungry and the food smelled good, so she sat down right away and began to eat.

Mallah silently went about taking the tub from the cabin along with the table and dishes from dinner last night. After making several trips carrying things out, he was satisfied that the room had been straightened to Serad *Reis's* expectations. He looked to Serad's

264

Englishwoman expectantly as she finished off her meal.

"Serad *Reis* said that when you finished eating you were to be allowed up on deck for a while," he told her.

Tori was thrilled at the chance to leave the confines of the cabin, and she quickly got up from the desk. "I'm ready."

"Serad *Reis* will be waiting for you."

Eager to be out in the sunshine again, Tori hurried past him and up the corridor toward the stairs that led to the deck. As she stepped out into the light, she took a deep breath of the fresh sea air. It seemed like forever since she'd felt the warmth of the sun beating down on her and a refreshing breeze stirring her hair. Turning her face to the sun's radiance, she closed her eyes and savored the moment.

"Miss Victoria!"

Jonesey's shout of excitement jarred Tori from her reverie, and she turned to see her friend trying to maintain her dignity as she hurried from the companionway.

"Jonesey!" Tori openly embraced the little woman as they came together. She didn't know why Serad had decided to allow them a visit, and she wasn't going to question it. She was just glad to see her friend.

"Thank God you're alive! You can't imagine how I've worried!" Jonesey proclaimed. She hugged her young ward to her, then, still holding her hands, she stood back to take a good look at her, her sharp-eyed gaze missing nothing.

"Well, thank God you're all right, too!" Tori returned. Though Jonesey looked tired and unkempt, still wearing the same gown she'd had on the day they were separated, she otherwise seemed to have suffered no mistreatment.

"I'm as fine as I can be given our circumstances. But,

265

Miss Victoria, how are you? I haven't been able to stop fretting about you since that night they dragged me away!"

Tori patted her hand reassuringly. "I'm fine . . ." At Jonesey's skeptical look, she emphasized, "Really, I am."

"But you've been all alone . . . and with Serad . . . Is he still keeping you in his cabin with him?" she asked, thinking of the unorthodox intimacy she was being subjected to.

"Yes."

"And he's treating you well?" Miss Jones's gaze grew troubled as she tried to read Tori's expression to find out if he'd harmed her in any way.

"Very well, considering."

"He hasn't pressed you in any way to . . .?"

"No!" she quickly denied.

"Thank heaven." Jonesey was visibly relieved. The night she'd been hauled out of Serad's cabin away from Tori, she'd feared desperately for her ward's innocence. Serad was a half-wild, fierce man, and she'd been haunted by the thought of Tori being left alone with him with no one to defend and protect her. Watching Tori's expression carefully now, Jonesey's fears were eased, for she could tell she was being truthful. She was glad to find out that the pirate captain had some sense of honor and was not a defiler of innocent women.

"What about you? Have you been all right? I've been worried, too." Feeling uncomfortable talking about Serad, Tori changed the subject. It was bad enough that she was in such close contact with him and that she was becoming so very aware of him as a man. She certainly didn't want to talk about it.

"I have not had an easy life, as you well know, but I must tell you I have suffered endlessly these last few days."

266

"Why? What happened?" Tori worried that the terrible things Serad had warned her about might have happened to her guardian. "Have the pirates hurt you in any way?"

"No, not physically, although I feel quite abused being locked up all by myself in a hot, dark, windowless storeroom. I have no means to wash and as you can tell, no clean clothing! Not allowing me the minimal standards of personal hygiene is barbaric!"

"I'll speak with Serad for you."

"I would appreciate that. It was kind of him to allow us to see each other. Do you suppose he's going to let us stay together."

"I don't know," Tori answered. "Mallah said he was here on deck, but I don't see him anywhere . . ."

Jonesey happened to glance up at the sails just then and saw Serad and another sailor climbing about in the riggings. She touched Tori's arm as she pointed heavenward. "He's here all right . . ."

Tori looked up, and her heart lurched wildly in her breast as she saw Serad moving about on the crossjack high off the deck. She couldn't believe the grace, power, and confidence of his actions as he and the other man worked on the riggings, but tempering her awe of his ability was the terror that at any moment he might fall. Tori watched in helpless fear as he continued to work.

The strength of the emotions that filled Tori as she held her breath waiting for Serad's descent bewildered her. She asked herself why she cared about him, but she could find no answer. He was a pirate, a man whose goal in life was to sail the high seas and raid unsuspecting ships. Yet Tori knew there was much more to him, and the conflict within her was growing, leaving her more perplexed than ever.

"I can't believe he takes risks like that," Tori

267

whispered in a strangled voice.

Jonesey heard her distraught tone and glanced at her sharply. "This is his ship, and I'm sure he knows every inch of it by heart."

"He did say that sailing was his life, that he'd loved ships and the sea since he was a small boy."

"It would appear that there's more to this man than I originally thought."

"I'm pleased and very reassured now that I know he's respected you," Miss Jones said. "I must tell you I feared for the worst when we were separated."

"So did I," she agreed. "After seeing what happened to Capitaine Duval, I wasn't sure what kind of punishment he would mete out to me. Luckily, he chose to be kind."

"He did?"

"I only had to clean up the mess I'd made in the cabin."

"He's a better man than I gave him credit for. I wonder how he became a pirate . . ."

Their conversation was interrupted as Serad came sliding down to the deck on one of the nearby ropes. He had seen them from above and now joined them.

"Thank you for allowing us to have this visit," Tori spoke up first.

"It was very kind of you," Miss Jones added.

"It will be your last for some time," he said sternly as his concern for the weather tempered his words.

"But . . ." Tori immediately assumed that he was punishing them again.

He explained quickly to silence her. "The weather will be changing soon, probably within a few hours. By dark we're going to be caught up in a bad storm. Enjoy the few hours of quiet you have for now. It's not going to last."

Both women were satisfied with his explanation.

When one of his men called to him, they watched him walk away. Tori's eyes followed him, and she couldn't deny that she was drawn to him in spite of herself. Miss Jones was studying him, too, and, though she would never have admitted it to Tori, she decided Serad was certainly one magnificent specimen of manhood.

Chapter Twenty

The storm struck with fury shortly after midday. The *Scimitar* was a worthy vessel and with Serad's sure hand at the helm, it rode the crashing waves with assuredness. High winds buffeted the craft, tearing at the riggings with violent force, but the crew had done their jobs well in lashing everything down and nothing was lost.

For endless hours, Serad, Tariq, and the *Scimitar's* seasoned crew fought the battle. Each man knew what was expected of him, and each did his duty without question. They were one against the elements in their fight to survive.

Serad's concentration was fierce as he piloted his ship, but several times during particularly dangerous moments, concern for Tori's safety was foremost on his mind. It bothered him that she could slip into his thoughts when he was trying to tend to this treacherous task, and he wondered how she had come to be so important to him that he would find himself worrying about her instead of his ship. The only consolation Serad could offer himself as he forced his full attention back to handling the *Scimitar* was that if he saved his beloved ship, he would also save Tori.

Belowdecks, Tori sat alone in Serad's cabin. She had sailed often in her life, but she'd never experienced a gale of this force or duration before. Moving to the small window, she watched helplessly as the sea raged around them, and she waited anxiously for the tempest to end.

The storm did not lessen with the progression of the day, if anything it seemed to grow in intensity. Tori wondered how Miss Jones was holding up and decided that, as stalwart as she was, she was probably doing fine. Darkness came, and she lit the one small lamp that was safe to use as she continued her vigil.

Tori hadn't paid much attention to the sounds of the ship before, but now that it was night, the creaks and groans of the *Scimitar* seemed magnified to her. She shivered as her thoughts ran away with her, and she imagined the pirate ship sinking with her locked in the cabin. On impulse, she went to the door and tried the knob. To her surprise, she found the portal unlocked, and she realized that Serad must have ordered Mallah to leave it that way after he'd brought her lunch earlier that afternoon. It eased her anxiety considerably.

Tori closed the door again and went to sit at the desk. As the winds howled about the ship, she found her thoughts centered on Serad. She wished he would return so she could be sure he was safe. Tori told herself that the only reason she cared about the state of Serad's health and safety was because if anything happened to him, she and Jonesey would fall into the hands of his crew. Even though she felt satisfied with that justification, she remained restless and apprehensive as the night slowly passed and he didn't return.

Dawn came, but the skies remained gray and threatening, lending little brightness to the new day. The sea was rough, but not nearly as turbulent as it had been throughout the night. The worst, it seemed, was over, though the wind was still strong out of the north and a steady rain was still falling.

"You should go get some rest," Tariq advised Serad as he joined him where he stood at the wheel.

"You're right," Serad replied. He was desperately in need of rest. The battle had seemed endless until now, but it was over. It was the new day, and the *Scimitar* was in one piece. They had made it through the night. They had won.

"Go on below. I'll take over for now."

"If the weather changes . . ." Serad glanced up at the leaden sky.

"I'll let you know, but you don't have to worry. It won't. It's about blown itself out."

Serad was bone-weary as he made his way below, but foremost in his thoughts now was Tori. He needed to make sure that she was safe. She had haunted his thoughts throughout the night. Several times during the course of the storm when things had turned particularly violent, he'd been very glad that he'd told Mallah to leave her cabin door unlocked for her. If the *Scimitar* had gotten into serious trouble, he hadn't wanted Tori trapped below.

Had Serad been less tired, he would have wondered at the unusual amount of concern he was feeling for this woman. True, he desired her, but he'd desired other women before. Tori, however, had a hold on him that defied explanation, and it only seemed to be growing more powerful with time. Right now, though, Serad didn't care about any of that. Right now, he only wanted to return to his cabin, make sure she was all right, and then get some sleep.

Serad entered his room quietly to find Tori fully dressed, sitting at the desk, her arms folded on the desktop, her head resting on her arms, sound asleep. He stood there just inside the door, his hand still on the

272

knob, just staring at her for a long minute, before he finally entered the room and locked the door behind him. With care, he moved to the desk to take her in his arms and carry her to his bed.

"You're back?" Tori murmured as she felt Serad's arms go around her. She had been wide awake all night and had only fallen asleep a few minutes before.

"It's over," he said softly in a husky voice. "You're safe now." He wasn't sure if he was reassuring himself or her.

"Good," she sighed, and when he lay her upon the bed, she curled on her side and was once again fast asleep.

Serad stood over her, debated for all of one fraction of a second whether to join her on the bed or not, then came to his decision. As exhausted as he was, there was no way he was going to sentence himself to sleep on the floor. He stripped out of his wet clothing, donned a dry pair of trousers after a moment's hesitation, and then stretched out beside Tori. Twenty-four hours before, he would have had trouble keeping his desire for her under control. Right now, sleep was the only thing on his mind.

Serad lay still, thinking of how right it felt to have Tori slumbering by his side, and then closed his eyes. Within minutes, he found the rest he sought.

Tori wasn't sure exactly what it was that woke her, but she slowly became aware that she was very hot and that something heavy seemed to be holding her down. She was lying on her side facing toward the cabin and she opened her eyes to look around, wondering how she could be so warm. As she did, the sight of a man's arm possessively wrapped around her waist came into focus. It was then that Tori realized that Serad's body

273

was pressed tightly to hers. Her back was flush against his broad chest, her hips were nestled with great familiarity against his.

Tori stiffened instinctively, and when she did, Serad's arm tensed around her. Though his hold on her was not at all painful, it was like a solid steel band pinning her to him. She tried to move away, but he held her still.

"Why do you need to get up?" Serad asked, his voice sleep-husky and soft as his hand splayed out across her ribs, stopping teasingly just below her breasts. He'd awakened the moment Tori had attempted to move, and though he had no idea how they'd come to be in such an intimate position, he had no objections to holding her this way.

"I told you before I wouldn't share your bed," Tori said sternly, pushing his hand away. If she hadn't been so nervous, she might have enjoyed being so close to him. As it was, she fought to remember how she'd gotten there. She had a faint recollection of Serad's return, but she'd been so tired at the time that she hadn't come fully awake. Now, however, she *was* awake, and she wondered desperately how long they'd lain together and how in the world she was going to escape from him.

"You just did," he pointed out with some humor.

"Against my will."

"You certainly didn't put up much of a fight," Serad reminded her, enjoying the feel of her soft curves pressed so tightly to him. "As a matter of fact, I don't remember your offering any resistance at all."

"I was tired then, but I'm not now. Let me up." She tried to sit up, but at her very first movement realized that not only was his arm around her, but her hair was caught firmly beneath his shoulder.

Serad chuckled in her ear. "It would seem that you

are bound to me in more ways than one."

His words sent a shiver of excitement through her. "Only because I am forced to be." Tori denied the feelings that his nearness were evoking within her. Drawing on the only defense left to her, she used her fiancé as a shield against Serad. "I love my fiancé."

"We are not speaking of love, Tori," he dismissed her claim as he sensuously moved his hand up over her ribs to her shoulder.

"I am. Love means everything to me," she insisted, wondering how her body could be responding to his touch when she knew who and what he was. "Please, let me go . . ." It was a frightened whisper, but was it her fear of Serad or of what he was making her feel?

"Let me see if I can help," Serad said, brushing the thick, silken cascade of her hair aside and leaning forward to kiss the nape of her neck.

"Don't!" Tori exclaimed, twisting to her back to escape him as an almost electrical current jolted through her at the touch of his lips.

Serad braced himself up on his elbows to rise above her. His movement freed her hair, but his expression was so intense as he looked down at her that Tori was held motionless.

Serad's gaze raked over her, taking in her flushed cheeks and sparkling eyes. He knew she was angry, but he didn't care. He'd heard her words about love, but they didn't matter. Right then, he could no longer resist his need for her. He had to kiss her. He wanted her . . . bending toward her slowly, his eyes locked with hers as he moved closer and closer . . .

Tori could manage only a strangled, "No . . ."

Then their lips met and it was too late. Serad's kiss was soft at first. Only after he felt her relax a little did he unleash the explosive passion that he'd kept under rigid control.

His mouth slanted over Tori's with a fiery possession that stunned her into acquiescence. Her breath caught in her throat at his powerful arousing dominance, and she felt as if her very soul was being stolen from her. She told herself that she should deny him, that she should conjure up the image of her fiancé and hang to that for strength, but somehow under the onslaught of Serad's rapturous embrace, no mental picture of Alexander Wakefield would come to her mind.

Tori's only previous experience with kissing had amounted to a few stolen kisses in a garden by a very young would-be suitor just before she'd learned of Alexander's return. That fumbling, rather sterile exchange had done nothing to prepare her for Serad's mature, demanding embrace. Serad was no untried youth. He was a man—a man who knew what he wanted and how to get it.

As his lips claimed hers again and again, Tori could feel her will dissolving. She knew she should fight, but his kisses held her mesmerized. She had never imagined anything could be so wonderful. Without conscious thought, Tori linked her arms around his neck to hold him to her. With that, Serad knew complete and utter triumph. He took her action as a signal of her surrender and as an invitation. He moved over her and fitted his body to hers.

The sensation of having Serad lying on top of her was unlike anything Tori had ever known. Heavy though he was, it was an erotic weight, a burden of desire. The very male heat of him seemed to burn her through her clothes, and deep within Tori, she felt a compelling need to get even closer to him. Instincts driving her, she began to move restlessly, her hips inadvertently rubbing against his, seeking that elusive something that would ease the ache he was creating inside her.

Serad had never known kisses so exciting. His masculine pride and confidence were soaring over having conquered Tori's resistance to him without force. When she began to move invitingly beneath him, it was all he could do to keep from tearing their clothing from their bodies and taking her without delay.

With eager hands, Serad began to loosen buttons at the bodice of her gown. He longed to caress the pale orbs that he'd only caught a glimpse of during her bath. His mouth left hers to trail heated kisses down her neck to her shoulder. Brushing aside the fabric of her gown, he continued to press hot, devouring kisses across the tops of her breasts, barred from him now only by the shift she wore. He stopped only when he came to the fine gold chain and locket that lay nestled between her breasts.

Tori had been nearly mindless with building pleasure and excitement as Serad had caressed her, but the moment he paused to touch the locket and chain, the reality of her situation came back with a shocking vengeance. Her hand came up automatically between them to grasp the chain and Alexander's picture safely hidden away in the locket.

"Tori?" Serad asked, sensing the sudden change in her. "What is it?"

"Let me up!" she demanded, pushing at him with all her might. She caught him so off guard that she managed to dislodge him just enough so she could slip from the bunk. "Leave me alone . . . I don't want you to touch me!" Her eyes were wild as she contemplated the terrible thing she'd almost done. Backing across the room, she kept one hand on the locket that was the badge of her conscience. She never looked away from her captor, for she feared that he would be coming after her.

Her sudden flight from his arms hit Serad painfully. He stared after her in confusion for a moment, then with a growing sense of anger and frustration. She had almost been his. He couldn't imagine what it was that had caused her to draw away from him at the very last minute.

As he struggled to bring his raging passions back under control, Serad finally noticed how Tori was holding on to the locket so tightly, and he knew the piece of jewelry had to mean something important to her. Getting up, he stalked across the cabin, looking very much the fierce, savage pirate.

"Stay away from me . . . I don't want you to . . ."

"Shut up, Tori," he commanded.

Tori did as he ordered, though her terror showed plainly on her lovely, strained features. She did not retreat any farther, however, but watched with great trepidation as he came ever closer. Tori felt vulnerable, weak and very, very, frightened. She knew she shouldn't give in to her fears, so she attempted to give him a look of utter defiance, but it did not work. She was too afraid—afraid of Serad as her pirate captor and afraid of the power of her own reaction to his touch.

Serad stopped before her, his gaze fixed upon what Tori thought was her bosom. She was shocked when he reached out and impatiently forced her hand open to take the locket from her grip. Flicking the catch to open it, he stared down at the miniature portrait she was keeping so safely cherished there. The moment he saw the likeness of her fiancé, he understood what had happened.

Serad silently cursed the man whose image was staring back at him from the center of the golden bauble. Tori obviously loved this man and was trying to save herself for him. Unable to express his anger any other way, Serad snarled as he tore the chain from around her neck with a savage yank.

Tori gave a little whimper of fear and pain as the fine chain snapped and her one connection to Alexander was severed. "What are you going to do to me?" she asked in a strangled whisper.

He lifted his icy, silver regard to her face. The fear he saw once again mirrored in her eyes chilled him even further. "Nothing." He stared at her for a minute longer, then turned away and left the cabin. This time, he locked the door behind him.

Tori stood unmoving as she watched Serad leave. When the door was finally shut and locked, the terror that had held her hostage left her. Her relief was so great that she almost slumped to the floor. Her knees felt so weak that she grabbed the back of the desk chair for support. She didn't know what was going to happen when he returned, but at least she was safe for now.

Serad made his way up on deck. Every fiber of his body was still aching from his denied desire for Tori. The afternoon sun was shining and the sea was relatively calm, but he paid it little attention as he walked directly to the rail.

Looking down at the locket once more, Serad stared again at the man Tori loved. It was then, as he studied him that Serad noticed how very much he and her fiancé resembled each other. The man who held Tori's heart also had dark hair and gray eyes. Knowing this didn't change how he felt, though, and in a moment of pure anger, fueled by an emotion he would not put a name to, Serad threw Tori's chain and locket into the depths of the blue-green sea. He watched with bitter pleasure as it disappeared from view and sank to the bottom.

*   *   *

Tess was miserable. She had thought she would be able to deal with her feelings for Lord Alexander, but as the weeks had passed since the announcement of his engagement to the, as yet unseen Lady Lawrence, her love for him had grown even stronger. He had been spending more time at Huntington House since becoming officially engaged, and so she had been running into him constantly. It had not been easy for her to deny her heart's desire.

Tess had taken to sneaking out of the house every night at dusk and sitting by the reflecting pool to dream about him. She knew that the pool was one of his favorite places on the grounds, and she held out hope that he would come there one night.

This evening was no exception. Tess had finished her duties early and had left the house to follow the shrub-lined path to the pond. Spreading the dark skirt of her servant's dress about her, she sat down on the mossy bank, then pulled her white cap from her head. With a sigh, she removed the pins from her hair and freed the heavy, burnished braid from its hated confinement at the back of her neck. Her fingers were practically flying as she unplaited the thick mane and then she shook her head to enjoy the sensuality of having her hair falling loose about her shoulders. It made her feel almost decadent to wear her hair down, for as a house servant she was commanded to style it sedately up at all times.

Unexpectedly, Tess heard the sound of footsteps approaching, and a combination of fear and excitement filled her. It might be Lord Alexander coming or someone else . . . someone who might report her to Dalton for being there. She sat still and held her breath as she waited.

David's brow was furrowed and his gray eyes dark

and stormy as he moved down the path toward the pond. It was only here in the seclusion of the gardens that he could let his real emotions show, and his expression now was bleak. He felt completely isolated. The day of reckoning was coming, and he was helpless to prevent it. He was Vivienne's pawn to do with as she pleased, and the feeling filled him with rage and disgust. He was going to be married to a woman of honor who thought him as forthright and honorable as she herself was. Having always considered himself a very good actor, David knew he could be authentic, but the dishonesty of the whole situation was wearing on him more and more every day.

David had never expected his conscience to cause him such trouble when he'd arrived here with Vivienne. But that had been before he'd come to love the duke and Dalton and all the others who seemed to have cared so much about the real Alex. Now, he felt dirty for having been a party to this cruel jest, yet he knew there was no way out without giving himself up to a sure death back in Boston—which Vivienne would see to personally if he did anything to upset her plans. So, David suffered in silence, longing for an escape, longing for a real friend, longing for the time when life had been far more simple and based on truth.

David stopped abruptly as he emerged at the reflecting pool. He had expected to spend some time here alone to sort out his thoughts and convince himself again of the necessity of continuing the charade. He had not expected to find anyone there. He was surprised to see that it was the maid, Tess, and that she was looking astoundingly pretty.

"Good evening, Tess," he greeted her, recovering quickly from his surprise.

Tess jumped to her feet at the sight of him. "Good evening, Lord Alexander."

"What brings you out here?" David asked.

"It was such a nice evening that I took a walk in the garden and ended up here," she explained, thinking it was mostly the truth. "I'll be going back in now, so I won't be bothering you. I won't intrude on your privacy . . ." she offered as she started to move past him, but he put out a hand to stay her. That simple touch of his hand on her arm sent her pulse racing. Her eyes met his questioningly.

"No, wait. There's really no need for you to go."

"But . . ."

"Stay, we'll talk."

"Talk?"

"I don't bite, Tess."

She couldn't help but give a little laugh. "I didn't think you did, Lord Alexander."

They shared a warm smile, then sat down together on the bank. David didn't know what there was about this girl, whether it was her blatant honesty, natural beauty, or her unwavering cheerfulness, but whatever it was, he enjoyed being with her, talking to her and listening to her.

"Are you worried about something, Lord Alexander?" Tess ventured, noticing the tense look on his face.

"No. Why?" he lied.

"I don't know. You just looked unhappy, that's all," she offered.

David turned their conversation away from himself, and they drifted through a long, easy, comfortable dialogue as they spoke of many things. It was over an hour later when Tess heard someone calling her name from the direction of the house. She was shocked to discover that they had spent so much time alone together. Dalton and the others would never approve.

"I have to go . . ." she insisted, quickly rising and heading for the path.

David stood up, too. "Tess . . ."

"Yes?" Tess turned to look back at him.

"I enjoyed our talk tonight," he told her earnestly, somehow feeling like a light was going out of his life because she was leaving.

"So did I, but if any of the other servants find out I've been talking to you like this . . . Well . . . it just isn't done, you see."

"I understand," he answered, giving her another warm smile that made her heart leap in her breast. "Good night, Tess."

"Good night, Lord Alexander," she replied, and then disappeared from view up the path.

David watched her go. "Sweet dreams," he said softly into the night.

Chapter Twenty-One

The storm had knocked the *Scimitar* off course, and it took the corsairs several extra days to reach their destination. Finally, though, the lighthouse on the western point of their home port of Algiers came into view, and a shout of excitement went up among the men.

Normally, when a ship had been raided and taken captive, the pirates would sail it into the harbor closely behind the *Scimitar,* flying its flag upside down. This time, however, they had no vessel as bounty, only the French ship's cargo. Still, the men were proud enough to want to let everyone know that they were not coming back empty-handed. Serad directed that they bring out the French flag they'd taken from *La Mouette* and fly it upside down on their own mast along with their flag. That way everyone in the city would know they'd had a triumphant voyage even though they had no ship to show for it.

In Algiers, word of Serad's imminent arrival, along with his success, spread quickly. At his palace, Malik heard the news with great gladness as did Hasim, who was with his father at the time.

"See that the palace guns are fired to welcome the

Scimitar home," Malik ordered in line with corsair tradition when he heard that Serad was flying a French flag to show that he'd met with victory.

"I'll do it right away, and then I'll go down to meet him," Hasim told his father. "It will be good to see my brother again after all these months." In the years since his father had taken Rabi to be his only woman, Hasim had come to look upon Serad as a true brother. The younger boy's determination and courage had won his respect and admiration.

"It certainly will," Malik responded, thinking of how pleased Rabi would be to know that her nephew had returned. "Tell Serad when you see him that I will be awaiting him in the main audience chamber."

Hasim left to do as his father had instructed and then hurried down to the waterfront to welcome Serad home. As he waited for the *Scimitar* to tie up, he let his thoughts drift over the years they'd spent together. Hasim had often wondered how he would have fared if their situations had been reversed. He was only now coming to realize just how hard it must have been for Serad at age seven to lose his home and family and be forced to begin a new life with them. Hasim was sure he wouldn't have adapted nearly as well as Serad had.

On board the *Scimitar,* Serad and Tariq stood at the rail watching Algiers come into view. They saw the palace of the *dey* first, for it was located high on a hill in the fortified, walled section of the city known as the Kasbah. The town itself spread out below the Kasbah all the way down to the water's edge, and its white buildings gleamed brilliantly in the afternoon sunlight. The domes of the mosques could be seen among the rooftops along with the few crosses that marked the Christian places of worship. They were home, and it felt good.

When the salute was sounded from Algiers, Serad smiled at Tariq. "Fire our guns in response. We'll return the honor."

The *Scimitar's* multitude of guns roared to life to acknowledge the city's welcome, and they continued on into port eager to be home again.

Tariq took charge of readying their bounty for the presentation that had to be made to Malik *Dey*. It was another corsair tradition that the captives and loot be paraded through the crowded streets of Algiers all the way up to the palace where the tribute would be paid. Tariq knew Serad always liked to go to Malik as soon as possible, so it was important that they be ready when the ship finally tied up at the dock.

Serad thought of Tori waiting below in his cabin and knew it was almost time to bring her up on deck. He considered going to her himself and then decided against it. He would send Mallah to get her and her companion, both.

Serad tried to turn his attention back to his business at hand, but now that Tori had entered his thoughts it was difficult to banish her. The time they'd spent together since the storm had been nerve-wracking. She had returned to her bed on the floor as he had sought the solace of his lonely bunk. The memory of how close they had come to intimacy was still hot within him, though, and it took only an occasional glance or word on her part to reheat his blood to the boiling point.

During the first several days after the bad weather, Tori had continued to tend to Serad's injured arm, but after suffering through her touch for three straight days, it had been all he could stand. In a fit of frustration, he'd told her it was healed and did not bother him anymore, just so she wouldn't put her hands on him again.

Serad knew Tori had no idea how her touch was affecting him. She seemed blissfully unaware that his endurance had been pushed to the breaking point. His entire being had cried out for him to take action on his desire for her, yet he'd denied himself again and again. His mood had grown very black and his temper surly, especially after he'd accidentally walked in on her during her bath that night.

Though Serad was relieved now that they'd finally reached port, but Tori would still be within arm's reach. As long as she was near he would want her, and he certainly had no intention of ransoming her back. Refusing to act on his desires pained him, but the guilt of forcing her to give herself to him would pain him, too. There seemed no solution.

"You sent for me, Serad *Reis?*" Mallah asked as he appeared at his side.

"It's time to bring the women on deck."

"Shall I bring them both together?"

"Yes. There will be no danger in that. Even if they tried to escape, there would be no place for them to go."

Mallah nodded and hurried off to take care of matters. He went to Serad's cabin first and unlocked the door to find Tori staring out the window, her back to him.

"It is time to go up on deck," Mallah announced.

"We've reached Algiers?" Tori asked solemnly as she turned to look at him. She'd always known this moment would come, but she had never been sure of what to expect when it did. What would happen now? Would she and Jonesey be kept separated or be reunited? Would she be locked up in a dark, dank prison somewhere until she could be ransomed back or would Serad lock her in his home and leave her there as his slave?

"Yes," he answered with his usual curtness. "We'll be leaving the ship soon, for we must take our tribute to Malik."

Suddenly, Tori wondered in horrified desperation if she and Jonesey were part of that tribute.

Tori wanted to rant and rave at him, to force him to tell her what was going to happen to her now that they were in port, but she knew it was usless. Mallah knew nothing. He only did as he was told. Her heart sank as she followed him from the room.

Mallah led her in a different direction from what she'd expected and her spirits were lightened a bit when they stopped long enough to release Jonesey from her confinement in the miserable little storage room. The indomitable woman emerged from her incarceration in a huff. She glared at Mallah, then embraced Tori with heartfelt affection.

"How are you, my dear child?" Jonesey asked, eyeing her critically in the dimly lighted hall.

"I'm all right. We've reached Algiers," she offered quickly.

"I had thought as much," she replied.

"Are you well?"

"As well as I can be," her companion said tightly. "It is not easy for a woman of my station to become accustomed to such degradation, but I've managed. Thank you. You didn't happen to bring my umbrella, did you?" She gave Tori a hopeful look.

"I didn't dare."

"I understand," Jonesey said with a sigh. She felt positively naked without her umbrella, but there wasn't much she could do about it.

"We must go," Mallah was brusque as he interrupted them and started off.

Jonesey gave him a scathing look as she shepherded Tori down the companionway. "Let's go then."

Mallah ignored the old woman as he led them up on deck.

The moment the *Scimitar's* gangplank had been lowered, Hasim hurried aboard. He caught sight of Serad on deck and rushed over to greet him.

"Serad! My brother! It's good you're back! We've missed you," Hasim told him as they embraced.

"It's good to be back. How are my aunt and Malik?"

"They're fine. Malik is waiting for you now in the audience chamber. I saw the flag. Did you have a successful voyage?" he inquired.

"Indeed, we did," Serad replied proudly. "We took the French ship and all her cargo."

"What about the vessel?"

"It was too damaged to sail."

"I see. I . . ." Hasim was about to say more when he happened to look up past Serad.

It was at that very moment that Tori emerged from below with Miss Jones and Mallah. Though she was dressed in the confining manner of European women, Hasim was so taken by her beauty that all he could do was stop and stare.

Serad noticed the abrupt change in his brother's expression and how he had gone suddenly quiet, and he glanced over his shoulder to find out what had distracted him. Serad scowled when he realized that Tori was the source of his distraction.

"She is beautiful. Is this part of your prize from the French ship?"

"Yes, she . . ." he started to answer, but the other man was not listening.

Hasim brushed past Serad in his eagerness to get a closer look at Tori.

Tori had seen Serad and the stranger talking when

she'd come out on deck, and she wondered at the relationship between them. The stranger was definitely a native of Algiers. His eyes were a dark chocolate brown, his hair black as a raven's wing, his skin a darker shade of bronze that her captor's, his features regular and not unattractive. He was wearing what she would come to recognize as the traditional Algerian male dress, the djellaba and loose-fitting trousers and headpiece.

When Tori heard the man comment on her beauty, she grew very nervous. And when he walked boldly toward her, she tensed and averted her gaze from his avid regard.

Hasim came to stand before her, lifting her chin with his hand to look her fully in the face. "How much do you want for her?" he exclaimed without pause, "I will buy her from you right now."

Tori wanted to do nothing more than flee, but she held her ground and met his gaze with her own defiant one.

Behind them, Jonesey tried to go to Tori's aid, but Mallah physically restrained her and hauled her away so she could not interfere.

"No, Hasim. This one is not for sale," Serad answered in terse tones.

Tori had never thought she would consider Serad her savior, but she could have thrown herself into his arms to express her gratitude at his curt refusal.

Hasim didn't give up. He released her chin to pick up a sable curl where it lay on her shoulder just above her breast. He rubbed the silken tresses between his fingers as he continued to negotiate, never taking his eyes from her face. "Name your price, my brother. Money does not matter when the pearl is of such luster."

"She is not for sale," Serad repeated, wondering why he was growing angry at the sight of Hasim's hands on

Tori. He understood why Hasim wanted to touch her hair for he'd longed to run his hands through its glossy, silken length for days. Still, understanding it didn't ease his aggravation.

Tori glanced nervously at Serad, and she was surprised when she saw how furious he looked. She had no idea what she could have done to incur his wrath.

Hasim was completely unaware of Serad's discomfort as he dropped his hand away from Tori's hair and looked back at him. "If you ever change your mind, you have only to let me know. She would add grace and loveliness to my harem."

The two men turned from her then and walked away as if she were no longer of any importance to either one of them. Tori was left standing there all alone in the middle of the deck feeling degraded and humiliated. It was then she realized just how lowly her status really was. She was Serad's slave. He could have sold her to the other man without a second thought if he'd wanted to, and there would have been absolutely nothing she could have done about it. She was his to do with as he pleased.

A tremor of horror shook her. She swallowed and tried to control the nervousness and uncertainty that filled her. She didn't know what the future held, but at least she knew for right now Serad intended to keep her for himself.

A trumpet and a drum sounded on the docks, and Tori was glad for the distraction as she let her attention be drawn away from thoughts of her own trauma. She watched in fascinated misery as the still-chained men of *La Mouette* were herded down the gangplank and assembled on the dock. Some of the *Scimitar's* crew came to stand behind them carrying trunks and cases of the bounty they'd stolen.

Tori was wondering what was happening when Mallah came back to her side with a very subdued Miss Jones.

"It's time to go to the palace," he said in way of explanation as he urged them both toward the gangplank.

Tori and Jonesey shared a worried look as Mallah directed them to the rear of the gathering. Tori looked around for Serad and finally saw him standing in front of the chained sailors with the other man he'd called Hasim. As the drum and trumpet continued to sound their rhythm, the procession began its slow trek through the narrow, winding streets to the entryway to the Kasbah and then on to the entrance of the dey's home.

Both Tori and Jonesey were aware that they were the center of attention as they made their way through the city. Afraid, they clasped hands and hung on to each other for dear life. Tori looked for Serad ahead of them again, but could not see him now, for he was deep in the crowd. She wondered why she felt so afraid without him nearby.

When they reached the palace, Hasim and Serad entered first and went straight to the audience chamber to meet with Malik. Serad never failed to be impressed by his adopted father. As he entered the room and saw him sitting on a plush sofa conferring with one of his advisers, he thought of how very little the man had changed through the years. Only the graying of his hair at his temples betrayed his age. Otherwise, he was still the same impressive, robust, vigorous man he'd been when Serad had first come to Algiers.

"Hello, Malik," Serad greeted him.

"Serad, my son! Welcome back! You've returned and you are well!" Malik rose to embrace Serad.

"Yes, I'm fine, thank you. How is my aunt?"

"She is fine. I'm sure she'll be expecting to see you

when we finish here."

"I will visit her without delay," he promised. He had missed her during his time away.

"So, how was your voyage?"

"Very successful," Serad told the older man with pride. Even after all this time he still took great pleasure in proving his worth to this man. A single word of praise from Malik was worth more to him than the bounty of ten ships. "We took a French ship, but the foolish captain tried to escape us and we were forced to fire. It was too badly damaged to bring back, but we did have time to empty the hold before we sank it."

"Once again you have proven that you are truly worthy of your name, Serad," Malik told him. The young man's successes and abilities never ceased to impress him. "Let us see what tribute you have brought me today."

Malik settled on his couch looking every bit the powerful ruler while Hasim and Serad moved to stand one on each side of him. The order was given and the French crew and Malik's share of the loot were brought into the chamber before him. Tori and Miss Jones were the last to enter. They stood at the very back of the room farthest away from the men where they couldn't hear what was being said.

"Father . . ." Hasim spoke up when he saw his father look their way. "Serad took two very special captives. I offered to buy the young one from him, but he wouldn't sell her. Do you suppose he's brought her to you as part of the tribute or do you think he has finally found a woman he wants to keep for himself?" Hasim knew his father hadn't taken any women in tribute payment since Rabi had come into his life, and he was deliberately teasing Serad now just to find out what his reaction would be.

"Well, Serad?" Malik glanced at him with open curiosity, a twinkle glowing in his golden eyes. "Which is it? Did this Frenchwoman catch your eye or is she mine to add to my harem?"

"She's not French, Malik. She's English, as is her companion." Serad was hard put to make his answer sound casual.

"You didn't answer my question."

"No," Serad admitted with a quick grin. Try as he might, he had never been able to get away with anything before this man. "I didn't."

Malik and Hasim both laughed at his attempt to avoid telling the truth.

"Then the two women are part of my tribute?" Malik threw out again watching his adopted son's expression as he spoke.

"I give you freely all the riches we have taken from the ship, but I claim the women for my own," Serad declared.

Malik nodded approvingly after seeing the flare of fire in his eyes. "So, a female has finally caught your attention."

"Yes."

"She's a pretty one," Hasim agreed.

The dey studied the young woman and her companion with interest before asking if he had considered ransom.

"I have not decided yet. Maybe in time I will send word, but for now I plan to keep her in my harem."

"I understand," Malik said, and he did. Memories of another time swept through his mind. He knew exactly what Serad was feeling.

"What is the older woman to her?"

"She is her companion," he explained.

"Then take them both and enjoy with my blessing. It is long past time that you began to think of having a family and children."

Serad wanted to argue that he didn't plan to marry the woman, but he knew it would be a pointless debate. Malik had already changed the subject and was speaking of something else. Serad gave Mallah a signal that the sailor interpreted correctly, and following the instructions he'd been given earlier, he quickly ushered Tori and Miss Jones from the audience chamber.

The two women were surprised at being so quickly and summarily dismissed, and they voiced their objections to Mallah.

"Don't we get the opportunity to speak with the dey? It's important we tell him who we are so he can arrange for us to be sent home. Where are you taking us now?"

"I am taking you to Serad's home. You will be staying there in his harem."

"In a harem?" Miss Jones was aghast.

"But . . ." Tori, too, tried to argue, but Mallah cut her off.

"There is nothing more to be said. That was my order from Serad."

Tori and Jonesey fell silent, knowing it was pointless to argue with this man. They had not paid much attention to their surroundings as they'd been led into the chamber, but now as Mallah took them through the palace on their way out, they were awed by the obvious wealth of the ruler of Algiers. Gold-inlaid mosaics adorned the tile walls. Fine tapestries hung in splendor in the wide, airy halls. The floors were of polished marble, and the doorknobs were of solid gold and silver. Every now and then they would catch a glimpse of the center gardens of the house, and they were overwhelmed by the lush foliage and splashing fountains there. Even in their fear and uncertainty there could be no denying that they both found it all quite beautiful.

Mallah led them from the palace to Serad's home a short distance away. Though not as palatial as the dey's residence, it was spacious and luxurious in its own right. Because the harem had not been occupied before, Serad had sent orders to his servants before he'd left the ship to see that everything was readied for Tori and Miss Jones's arrival. Two female servants now waited expectantly at the entrance to the harem as Mallah delivered them there.

"Serad has insisted that I remain on guard here until he returns," Mallah told the women. "If there is any trouble, you have only to let me know."

"We will," Oma, the elder of the two women servants, replied. Then, turning her full attention to Serad's newly acquired women, she greeted them. "Welcome. I am Oma, and this is Zena. We are here to serve you. Come in and we will show you to your rooms. We have already prepared baths for you, and there are clothes laid out for you to wear."

Tori and Jonesey exchanged wondering glances as they followed the servants farther into the harem. They had never been inside one before, and they were surprised at the beauty of it all. Everything was white, from the marble floors to tile walls. Large arched doorways gave an open, airy feeling to the harem while they allowed cooling breezes to circulate through the interior. There was a private courtyard that was only for the use of the women and Serad, should he choose to join them there, and walkways bordered with flowers, shrubs, and trees wound through it, leading to its center fountain and pool.

"Well, Miss Victoria, if we must be prisoners somewhere, I suppose this is a good place to be. Certainly it's a vast improvement over the ship," Jonesey remarked.

Oma heard her remark and spoke up, protesting,

"But you are not prisoners here in Serad's home. You are part of his harem now, and that is a great honor. Many women have longed for the places you hold. You should be proud and pleased that he has chosen you."

Jonesey sniffed indignantly at her words. "If what you say is true and we are not prisoners, how soon can we leave?"

"Leave? Why would you want to?" Zena was shocked that they would even consider it.

"We want to go home to England. We don't want to be here. Serad kidnapped us from our ship and has brought us to Algiers against our will," Tori explained.

"We know nothing about what you say. We only know that you have been given the honor and privilege of being in Serad's harem and it is our duty to make sure that you are comfortable and happy," Oma stated firmly, refusing to listen to anything disparaging about Serad. Though she was old, she wasn't blind. Serad was a magnificent young man, and she thought he was wonderful. "These are the baths. Come, we will help you undress and bathe. Perhaps after you've rested a while and have dined on a warm meal, you will feel differently about being here."

"I shan't count on it," Miss Jones said tartly, but she did enjoy a very leisurely bath.

Chapter Twenty-Two

Rabi was sitting on a stone bench near the fountain in the center of the harem's garden, meditating on the news that had just come to her through Almira, her chief conveyor of palace gossip. Her mood was troubled, and she was hoping the rumor concerning Serad was false. She was waiting anxiously for him to come to her, as she knew he would, so they could speak privately about what she'd heard.

"Aunt Rabi?" Serad called out her name as he entered the flowering paradise. Malik had told him she would be waiting for him there.

She came to her feet to greet her beloved nephew.

Serad hurried her way. She looked as lovely as ever, and he hadn't realized until then just how much he'd missed her during the long months at sea. They came together, and he enfolded her in a big hug. She was the only mother he'd ever known, and he loved her dearly.

"I've missed you, and I'm so glad you're back," Rabi told him with feeling. "Life is far too lonely when you're away." She gazed up at him with open adoration. In her heart, she still thought of him as Alex, no matter what names they'd been forced to use here in Algiers. He'd grown into a fine man, as handsome as Avery had been, but with a strength of character and will that made him a thousand times the man his father had been.

"Surely Malik keeps you so busy with his requests for chess games that you have little time to be bored or to worry about me," he teased. "As I recall, the night before I sailed you had soundly defeated him and he was demanding a rematch."

The chess games between his aunt and Malik were legendary around the palace, for there weren't many people who could challenge Malik the way she did and get away with it unscathed.

"Don't let Malik know that I've told you, but he's only managed to beat me a handful of times during your absence," Rabi laughed.

"I'll keep your confidence," he returned with a grin, proud of her abilities.

"Good. Now, tell me about you. How was the voyage, and what is this rumor I've heard?" She took his hand and drew him down with her onto the bench.

"What rumor?" Serad asked a little cautiously, not quite sure what she'd heard.

"Word has come to me that you've taken several women from the ship you captured to your harem. Is this true?" Rabi was praying with all her might that it was not. Though they had been forbidden to speak of England and his real heritage, she had tried in many different, quiet ways to instill the correct beliefs in him. She did not want him to turn into a barbarous savage, and she desperately hoped that her efforts had not been wasted.

Serad never ceased to be amazed at how quickly news traveled to the palace harem. He knew he had to tell his aunt the truth, but he wasn't sure how she was going to react to it. "Yes. It's true."

Rabi went a little pale at his reply. "Why?" she asked

in a pained voice, her heart aching. "Did you take them there for safekeeping until their ransom is paid?"

Serad's expression turned serious. "I mean to keep Tori for myself. The other is her companion, an older woman. I didn't want to separate them, so I took them both."

Rabi's heart constricted at his declaration. It seemed everything she'd tried to teach Serad had been for naught and that he had turned out more Barbary corsair than duke. A wave of nausea rushed through her as she remembered her own fear and heartbreak when Muhammed had taken them into slavery, but it was immediately replaced by anger. She could not, would not, let this happen. She had to do something to help the two women. "What about this 'Tori', as you called her? Have you considered what she wants?"

"What does it matter? She's my captive," he answered in all seriousness.

Rabi stiffened at his arrogant words, her anger heating to the boiling point. She knew she had to convince Serad that he was wrong, and to do that she would have to appeal to the nobility she knew was still beating in his heart somewhere. "Do you care for her?"

He shrugged, admitting only to his attraction to her.

"I see," she replied quietly, staying in tight control. "Then I want you to think very carefully about what you're doing."

"I know what I'm doing," Serad stated firmly, not wanting to hear her objections.

"If you take this English girl to be yours without allowing her any part in the decision, how will you ever know what she's really feeling?"

A part of him understood exactly what his aunt was getting at, and her words stung him. "Does it matter?"

"How can you think for one moment that her feelings don't matter?" Rabi demanded of him sharply.

She stood and took several agitated steps away from him, then rounded on him, her hands on her hips to make her painful point. "I thought I'd raised you to be a better man than this. It's a simple thing for a strong man to take what he wants from a woman by brutal force, but the man who does is among the lowest of the low. Physical strength is not the true measure of a man. It takes far more courage and power to be aware of others and put their needs willingly before your own. You have the blood of the Wakefields of Huntington in your veins . . . noble blood. Generations of Wakefield men have served their kings with pride and honor. I had cherished a vision of your becoming a man of honor and dignity . . . a man like your grandfather. I hope and pray that I will not be disappointed."

Serad could see that her eyes had misted with tears, and her words fell upon him like biting lashes from a whip. He couldn't remember a time she'd ever berated him this way. He came to his feet to stand straight before her, looking very much the Barbary pirate but feeling very much the chastised boy. His feelings were in turmoil and he could think of nothing to say. How could he explain to his aunt that he desired this woman more than he'd ever desired another? How could he explain to her that he couldn't bear to let Tori go?

"Well?" Rabi asked. "What are you going to do?"

"She is my captive."

"She is a woman, a flesh-and-blood woman, whose whole life has been torn asunder because you raided the ship she had the misfortune to be sailing on. Will you do worse to her than that?"

"I haven't harmed her in any way," he replied defensively.

"You have taken her from her loved ones, and you have given her no choice in the matter."

"I have treated her fairly."

"Then you will continue to do so and ransom her back home as quickly as you possibly can," Rabi told him bluntly, wanting him to do the right thing. The thought of saving another young English girl from suffering the same loss she had drove Rabi on in this confrontation. Love Serad as she did, she couldn't allow him to do this without him understanding fully the results of his actions. She had to help the woman called Tori so she could resume her life without too great an interruption. A few months wouldn't matter, but years . . . Oh, the years were a different matter altogether.

Rabi's demands left Serad confused and more than a little angry. He wanted Tori and he would not give her up, no matter what his aunt said. But guilt attacked him, too, feeding on the truth of her words. At his aunt's mention of his grandfather and their noble past, he grew even more troubled. Distant, vague memories of an old gentleman, a big house, and the green countryside stirred within him. He frowned, unable to think of anything to say that would soothe her. When he heard a soft, feminine voice speak his name from the far side of the garden, interrupting them, he was relieved.

"Serad! Welcome back." Talitha, Malik's daughter, greeted him happily as she hurried forth to join them.

"Talitha . . . I'd been wondering where you were." He turned to face her with a big smile.

"I've been right here with Rabi, waiting for you." Talitha knew it wasn't quite proper for her to visit so familiarly with him this way, but she'd been unable to resist when she'd heard the sound of his voice.

A small, dark-eyed, pretty young woman, she was adored by all who knew her for her gentle spirit and sweet ways. She had always worshipped Serad, and her feelings for him were definitely not those of a sibling.

He, however, thought of her only as a little sister, and despite all Talitha's dreams and hopes to the contrary, she was slowly coming to accept that that would never change.

"I'm sure you're just flattering me. How many men offered for you while I was away?" He asked the same question of her every time he returned, and it had become a regular part of their banter.

"Only two this time," she confessed.

"And you convinced your father you wanted no part of either of them?" he ventured.

"Of course. How could I care for them, when they have to compete with you for my heart?"

"If only that were true."

Talitha heard the brotherly tone to his words and fought down the sadness that threatened over recognizing that he would never be hers. "Oh, it is, but you don't believe me, so I suppose I'll just have to wait until someone comes along who is as wonderful as you are."

"There are very few men around of Serad's caliber. He's an exceptional man, in all ways." Rabi had been momentarily silenced by the young woman's appearance, but she entered the conversation now, keeping her gaze trained on her nephew. She wanted him to understand that she expected only the most noble behavior from him.

"I know," Talitha agreed.

"It's good to know you both have such a high opinion of me," he spoke up, "and as much as I would like to stay longer, I must go. Hasim mentioned that he was planning a hunting trip for us, and there's much I must do before we go." Hasim *had* mentioned the possibility of a trip, but at the time he'd refused to give him an answer one way or the other. Now, after listening to his aunt, he was more confused than ever about Tori, and he knew he needed some time away.

303

Both women wished him success on the hunt. They knew how much Hasim and Serad enjoyed their outings together. They had gone regularly as youths, and they were renowned for both the accuracy of their marksmanship and the excellence of their riding abilities.

Serad kissed Rabi on the cheek and bid them both good-bye, then made his escape from the harem. He sought out Hasim in the palace to tell him that he was agreeable to the trip.

"Hasim, my brother, I've made my decision. Let's go on the hunt."

"You surprise me, Serad. I had assumed your beautiful woman would hold you close to home."

"You were wrong," he countered, keeping his manner light so as to dismiss any further discussion about Tori. "How soon do you want to leave?"

"How soon can you be ready to go?"

"I have left Tariq in charge of the *Scimitar*. I need only send word to him that I will be gone for a few days and then get my things together."

"I will meet you here at the stables in an hour."

They parted, and Serad went to his own home for the first time since arriving in Algiers. Mallah was waiting there for him. After telling his crewman of his plans, he instructed him to return to the ship and notify Tariq. Serad then ordered his personal servants to tend to his needs. Though he really wanted to go to Tori and find out how she was adjusting to the harem, he did not. He made only a passing inquiry as to the state of the women's comfort along with directions for the servants to buy whatever clothing they needed.

Hasim was ready when Serad met him at Malik's stables. He had chosen to ride his favorite mare on their excursion. Well trained though the horse was, she had not been ridden by her master for many months and was a bit wild. Serad understood her excitement at being freed from the confinement of the stables, but he controlled her with a steady hand and knowing pressure from his guiding knees.

As Serad waited for his brother to mount up, he couldn't help but wonder if the comparison he and Tariq had made between the mare and Tori was really true. Had Tori accepted him as her master more easily than the horse or was she merely playing at the part, biding her time until she could make a break for freedom? The mare could be controlled, but she still had a streak of independence in her. He frowned at the possibility that Tori might be exactly the same way.

The mare, as if sensing the agitation in his mood, moved a little restlessly beneath Serad, and he brought her back under control, giving her his full attention. Determinedly pushing Tori out of his mind, he set about to enjoy his time with his brother.

The sun was low in the west as they left Algiers and rode out into the desert. Both men enjoyed the feeling of freedom that came during these times, and they left their attendants with the pack animals carrying the necessary items for their camp far behind as they gave their horses full rein. The desert landscape swept by in a blur as they charged across the sand. They did not stop until they reached the rock formation that had always been the designated winning marker for their races. It was tight, but Serad's mare proved the quickest this day.

Reining in, Serad turned to his brother and laughed at his frustrated expression. "You're slowing down, Hasim."

Hasim ignored his comment as he drew up beside him and complained, "Not only do you have the prettiest woman, you also have the fleetest mount."

"It's a good thing your wives aren't around to hear

you say that," Serad countered. "It seems that not so long ago you were bragging that your newest wife, Alima, was the most beautiful woman in Algiers."

"Alima is lovely, and she dances like a goddess," Hasim agreed, thinking of her, "but this English-woman of yours is special. I was surprised when you agreed to come along with me. If she were mine, I wouldn't have been so quick to leave her."

"What makes you so sure she is mine?"

"You own her. She's your captive," he said carelessly.

"I don't think any man will ever 'own' Tori. She's as elusive as the wind. Try as you might to capture her completely, she always eludes you."

"But you *have* captured her," Hasim insisted, frowning as he tried to understand what his brother was saying.

"Physically, yes, but there's so much more to her. Haven't you learned that with any of your wives yet?"

Hasim looked troubled. "My wives are warm and willing. What more do I need from them?"

"My brother, you may own their bodies, but what of their minds? Tori challenges me in every way. She is as maddening as she is desirable. There is never a moment when I am completely sure of her. It is a challenge that is as invigorating as any contest of wills I have ever engaged in."

"You say women are interesting?" Hasim had never considered this. He'd always thought of his wives as necessities to satisfy his desires and bear his children. Otherwise, he'd never given them much thought. They were there when he needed them, and gone when he didn't want to be bothered.

"Very," Serad affirmed.

"Then why are you here with me?"

"There is a time to be with women and a time to be with men. Tonight, I feel the need to ride the wind,

306

sleep under the desert stars, and in the morning, I want to see if my brother's aim is still good." Serad deliberately changed the subject.

"You think the quality of my marksmanship has suffered?"

Serad flashed him a confident grin. He remembered vividly the teasings he had suffered because of his young age when they'd first come to Algiers, and he took great pleasure in turning the tables now on Hasim. "They say the eyes lose their strength first. Since you are so much older than I am, it will be interesting to see if that is true. Until now, we have been evenly matched, but I've been at sea for quite a while. Perhaps you've aged more than you know."

"Your confidence in yourself is remarkable for one so callow and untried," Hasim returned good-naturedly, his dark eyes sparkling at the challenge. "At dawn we will find out who has the finest aim and who is the truest shot."

The challenge set, they rode on slowly to the prearranged campsite and settled in to wait the arival of their attendants.

It was much later, long after the sun had set and darkness had claimed the desert, that Serad lay in his tent alone, trying to sleep. Finally, after what seemed like hours, he got up and went outside. The sky was black velvet, spangled with a dusting of stars, and on the horizon hung just a sliver of a pale moon. A coolness at vast odds with the daytime temperatures pervaded the land, and Serad found solace in the sweet whisper of a night breeze.

Serad had thought getting away from Algiers would clear his mind; and it had, to some extent. He could see now that Hasim was right. He had been a fool to go off

307

and leave Tori. She was everything he desired, and she belonged to him—by Barbary standards.

The trouble and confusion came when he held those standards up to the ones Aunt Rabi insisted he follow. How could he be something he was not? He was a corsair in service to the dey of Algiers. He was no English nobleman, no matter what she said . . . Or was he? The memories still hovered dimly in the back of his mind . . . of love and safety spent with that older man whose face he could no longer envision and of a small boat named the *Scimitar*. Was that the heritage his aunt insisted was truly his? Was he pirate or nobleman?

Scowling into the blackness of the night, Serad cast an agonized glance up at the heavens and then strode back toward his tent. One of the attendants stirred and became aware of his movements around the camp. He quickly arose.

"Serad . . . Do you need something?"

"No. Go back to sleep," he answered, and then disappeared into his tent once more. He was relieved when sleep finally came, but it was not to be a restful one. He was up and waiting for Hasim when his brother awoke just before dawn.

Tori and Jonesey sat in Tori's bedchamber, staring about themselves at its opulence.

"This is certainly as elegant as anything I've seen in England, but I wonder . . . if Serad's harem is like this, what does the dey's harem look like?" Jonesey asked conversationally. They had bathed in luxury and dined in splendor and were now relaxing together as the evening grew old.

Tori could not believe her companion's flights of fancy. "I certainly hope I never find out."

"Aren't you the least bit curious? Even after the

stories I'd heard, I'd never dreamed that living in a harem would be like this. Why, our every wish is fulfilled. We have only to ask for it and those two servants rush off to get whatever it is we want."

"What I want is my freedom!" Tori said in agitation as she got up from the bed and stalked out onto the balcony, leaving Jonesey behind.

The night was beautiful, and the breeze was cool and fresh. The glory of the evening was lost on Tori, however. Serad had never returned as far as she knew, and she'd wanted to speak with him. She wondered where he was. Had he sent word back to England yet that they were here? Had he made the ransom demand? Tori leaned on the stone railing and stared with sightless eyes across the lovely courtyard below.

"You know, things could be much worse for us." Jonesey's voice came from right behind her as she came outside to be with her ward.

"I know," Tori agreed slowly, "but it doesn't make it any easier for me to accept that we are now considered to be Serad's property, just because he says it's so." *And here Serad didn't even care enough about his possessions to inquire about them or come to see them.* Tori wasn't quite sure why that bothered her, only that it did.

"What does it matter as long as we're safe? Word will be sent soon, if it hasn't been already. Our ransom will be paid by your grandfather, and soon we'll be on our way to London and your fiancé."

"If he'll still have me . . ."

"Of course he will!" Jonesey defended her honor. "Why, if anyone even suggests anything less than honorable about you, I'll . . ."

"You'll what?" Tori gave her a tender smile as she turned to face her.

Jonesey returned her smile. "I suppose I'm not quite

so fearsome without my umbrella, but I'll make sure there are no doubts in their minds."

"Did I ever tell you that I love you, Jonesey?" the younger woman asked.

"Often, but I'd like to hear it again."

They hugged each other and then went back inside to find the two servants waiting for them.

"Is there anything else you would like before you retire for the night?"

"No. Nothing," Tori answered, then added on sudden impulse to cure her curiosity, "Where is Serad? Will he be coming to speak with us this evening? I have a few things I'd like to ask him."

"Serad?" Oma's eyes opened wide. It was not the custom of the women to ask about the men. The men saw the women only at their convenience. It was the woman's duty to wait quietly and happily to be summoned. "Why, Serad's left Algiers, and we do not expect him to be back for days."

"He's left? Just like that?" Tori was upset. She'd at least hoped to speak to him and ask him if he'd sent the ransom demand. Finding out that he was gone and without a word, infuriated her.

"Yes. It is not our place to question the movements of our master. He tells us only what he wants us to know. Nothing more. It is the way here."

"Well, your ways are wrong," Tori declared in annoyance.

Oma and Zena quietly left the room rather than get caught up in an argument that served no purpose. These Englishwomen would learn the ways of the Barbary States, but it appeared because of their stubbornness that they would learn slowly.

Later that night, when she lay alone courting sleep, Tori wondered why she'd reacted so angrily to the news that Serad had gone. Simple logic told her that she

310

should have been happy to know he was not around. She didn't have to worry about him walking in on her in a state of undress or concern herself with any advances he might make on her. She was here, safe in the harem with Jonesey. She should be content for the time being. At least, that's what she tried to tell herself, but it didn't work. When at last Tori fell asleep, her dreams were a jumbled mixture of Serad and Alexander and her locket. In her mind's eye, they entwined together in a spinning vortex of confusion, and she could make no sense of the images that tormented her. A deep, abiding rest was not hers that night.

Chapter Twenty-Three

"It can't be true!" Edward exclaimed in heartfelt misery as he shared a terrible, pained look with his friend, Alfred Lawrence. "When did you receive word?"

"They came to me late the night before last. I waited until I'd made sure everything he told me was the truth before coming to see you," the marquess explained morosely. "Edward, I don't know what to do. There's been no word . . . no ransom demand made . . . How am I ever going to tell my son and his wife that their precious child has been taken captive by those terrible Barbary pirates?"

The duke went to his friend and put a supportive arm around his shoulders. Alfred was a big, healthy man, but right now he seemed very old and frail. Edward could feel the defeat in him.

"I understand, Alfred," he sympathized completely, remembering clearly the time when he, too, had suffered such a horrible sense of loss. Even now, after the wonder and thrill of Alexander's return, there were still days when he longed for Catherine—longed to see her beautiful face . . . ached to hold her in a fatherly embrace and tell her that he loved her and that he'd tried everything to find her. He barely controlled the shudder that threatened to escape him.

"I know you do," the marquess replied raggedly. Edward was the only one who could truly understand the depth of his loss. "I love Victoria so deeply . . . She's my only grandchild and she means the world to me . . ."

"I felt the same way when Alexander and Catherine disappeared all those years ago, but there is one spot of good news in the situation. You can take heart in the fact that the sailor saw them alive and well when they were taken aboard the pirate's vessel. I'm sure you'll receive a demand for money soon. Those pirates are bloodthirsty, but they're not stupid. Once they find out how much money she's worth, they'll hurry to sell her back."

"I hope you're right, Edward."

So do I, Edward thought to himself.

"What about young Alexander?" He raised an agonized gaze to his friend's.

"We'll have to tell him the truth," the duke said slowly. "There's no point in trying to hide any of this from him. Alexander needs to know. They may not be acquainted yet, but they *are* betrothed."

"And as far as the engagement goes . . .? Are you concerned about . . .?" Alfred feared that terrible rumors might start that would ruin Victoria's reputation and ultimately her future.

Edward held up a hand to silence him. "Say no more. We'll leave things the way they are. I feel certain that Victoria will return, and that she'll be fine. After all, Alfred, if Alexander could disappear for all those years and find his way back to be with me, your Victoria can do it, too. Besides, you know where she's been taken.

Inquiries can be made, and . . ."

"I've already started checking to find the best way to send the payment, if and when the demand comes."

"Good. For right now that's all you can do. That and wait, but know that if you need anything, Alfred, anything at all, you only have to ask."

Alfred thanked his friend from the bottom of his soul. He paused as if gathering his thoughts, and then asked, "Shall we call Alexander in now? I think it's important he learns what's happening from me."

A short time later, David stood before the two men, his expression grave as he listened to their words.

"What can I do to help?" he offered the minute Alfred finished telling him what had happened.

"Right now, Alexander, there's not much any of us can do. I'll let you know the moment I hear anything new. Until then, we'll just have to pray, my boy, just pray."

"I will, sir," David promised. He shook hands solemnly with the marquess.

When they bid him to leave, David quit the room and wandered aimlessly through the mansion. His thoughts were with the woman who was his fiancée yet whom he'd never met. He wondered if Victoria was safe from harm or if some terrible fate, as yet unknown to them, had befallen her. Entering his own bedroom, he sought out the small portrait he had of her and studied her smiling countenance. He hoped with all his heart that she was all right. His conscience had rebelled at their betrothal because he'd believed he was betraying her, and now he worried about her as if they'd known each other for years.

It seemed to David as if his bedroom were closing in around him, so he escaped from the house to walk in the gardens to try to gather his thoughts. Guilt attacked him, no matter how he tried to avoid it. If Victoria hadn't been sailing to England to marry him, none of this would have happened. She would have been safe in India with her parents. The tangled web of deceit that held him grew more strangling every day. As always when he sought peace, he followed the path to the reflecting pool.

Tess had finished her duties and left the house slightly earlier than usual this day. She doubted seriously that she would ever run into Lord Alex again, but she held on to the fragile hope. The one evening they'd spent in conversation had been the highlight of her life, and though she told herself it was crazy, she prayed constantly that they would meet again.

Night after night, Tess dreamed of Lord Alex, and day after day she saw him about the house and grounds but couldn't speak to him. She loved him with every fiber of her being, and she knew that if she had to, she could be satisfied just being near him.

As Tess nearly ran down the walk toward the pool, she let herself imagine that Lord Alex was there, waiting eagerly for her, like a lover long denied. The fantasy was one of her favorites. In her daydream, she would run straight into his arms and they would kiss. Oh, it was a wonderful dream and . . .

"Oh!" Tess exclaimed as she stopped deadstill at the sight of Lord Alex sitting on the bank, his head resting in his hands, a strained expression on his handsome face. "I'm sorry," she gasped as she took a step backward.

David looked up, startled by the unexpected intrusion.

"I'll just go."

"No, don't leave!" he blurted out, almost too quickly. He knew Vivienne would be furious if she found out he was becoming friendly with the servants, but he had to admit to himself that he was glad to see Tess. "There's no reason for you to go."

"You're sure?" She stood wavering between her need to stay and fulfill her dreams and her very real fear of being caught with him.

"I'm sure," David replied, managing a smile in spite of his mood. "Join me."

The smile melted her resistance, and she dropped down on the bank near his side without another word of protest.

"Are you all right?" Tess ventured, her hazel eyes dark with concern for him. He'd looked so forlorn that she'd wanted to throw her arms around him and reassure him that everything would be all right even though she had no idea what it was that was wrong.

David sighed. He longed for a friend, someone he could confide in. They had talked before and she hadn't said a word to anyone . . . Gazing into her beautiful hazel eyes, David believed he could see into her very soul, and he understood in that moment that he could trust her. "Ah, Tess," he half groaned, "things have gotten so complicated . . ."

She encouraged him without seeming nosy or anxious. "Can I help you in any way?"

"It's kind of you to offer, but I'm afraid not. There's been news, and I don't think there's really anyone who can help . . ."

"Do you want to talk about it?"

"I'm sure you'll hear it soon enough from the other servants, but Victoria's ship was attacked by Barbary pirates and she's been taken captive."

"No!" Jealous though Tess had been of his fiancée, she had never wished her any harm.

"Yes. The marquess just found out himself and let us know this afternoon."

"What are you going to do?"

"That's what's so terrible," David said with very real misery. "There's nothing I can do, absolutely nothing."

On impulse, her heart bleeding for him, Tess reached out and put a comforting hand on his arm. "I'm sorry, Lord Alex. I really am."

David stared at her small hand on his arm and then lifted his eyes to hers. Gray eyes locked with hazel ones that now seemed a deep forest green with the empathy she was feeling for him. Suddenly, he saw her not as a servant or as a possible friend, but as a woman, full grown . . . a very pretty woman.

Time hung suspended as David gazed at her sweet face. It had been so long since he'd been allowed to be himself . . . to be David Markham. The veneer of Lord Alex was slipping away, and there was nothing he could do to stop it. He was alone in the romantic twilight with the prettiest, most gentle woman he'd ever met. Tess would never deliberately hurt anyone. She was nothing like Vivienne. David knew she would always be kind and would give far more than she would ever demand. She represented all the good things in the simpler life that he missed. He found he wanted to become a part of Tess's world, to come to know her better . . . to maybe even love her.

David couldn't help himself. Oh, there had been trips to houses of ill repute in London with some of the other young bucks from town, but the quick encounters had left him cold. He had never been one for simply proving himself as a man. He'd always thought there should be more to it than just a physical release. He needed the pure sweetness that Tess's kiss would bring. He needed to taste of that innocence. As the first stars of dusk appeared in the rapidly darkening sky, David bent slowly toward her, seeking her lips with his.

Tess couldn't believe it. Lord Alex was actually going to kiss her! Her eyes fluttered shut as he shifted toward her. She was afraid it was a dream, but if it was, she didn't want to wake up ever! She was with Lord Alex and he wanted her as much as she wanted him! Her heart cried out in ecstasy as she reached for what she'd thought all along was unattainable. It might be hers for only a fleeting moment in time, for he was not of her world and she was not of his, but it didn't matter. She loved him as much as life itself.

A soft whimper escaped Tess just as his lips touched hers for the first time. It was all that she'd ever expected it to be. Lord Alex, here with her in the garden . . . the stars . . . the low rising moon . . . the song of the birds welcoming the arrival of night . . .

When it suddenly seemed that Lord Alex was starting to draw away from her, she opened her eyes in fear that it was going to end far too soon, but her fear was unfounded. She found him only gazing down at her, a tender expression on his face.

"Tess, you are so incredibly lovely . . ." David murmured. He lifted one hand to touch the burnished glory of her hair. It was silken fire beneath his touch, and he kissed her again.

This time, his kiss wasn't just a simple exploration. This time, his mouth moved hungrily over hers.

Tess had been kissed before by several of the boys in the stables, but their bumbling attempts had annoyed her. Lord Alex, however, was altogether different. As his lips claimed hers with demanding insistence, she was more than willing to meet him in that passionate exchange.

David had needed this badly. It was a sharing of spirits and a sharing of souls. He'd felt isolated and alone for so long. Without thought, he crushed Tess to him, enjoying the feel of her full breasts against his chest and her slender arms around his neck as she returned his kisses with equal fervor. His hand sought out the curve of her bosom.

"Oh, Lord Alex," she moaned softly beneath his mouth as a rapture unlike anything she'd ever known rushed through her. He was here! He wanted her! Her dream was actually coming true! Oh, she loved him! How she loved him!

It was her saying the name "Lord Alex" out loud that stopped David. For just a few minutes, he'd allowed himself to be fooled, to believe that things could be different in his life, but with the mention of the name that was not his, a sensation not unlike a bucket of icy water being thrown on him froze his hopes and his heart. It could never be. Nothing could be different. He was a hostage of fate, a captive of his terrible fortune. He could never be David Markham again. He was Alexander Wakefield now, and there was no way out.

Pulling away from Tess, David stared at her flushed, lovely features and pain filled him. He cared about Tess, and it was for that very reason that he could not, would not, use her. He had to stop this now before it went any further.

"What . . . Lord Alex, did I do something wrong?" she asked, blinking in bewilderment as he let her go.

"Wrong? No, Tess. You couldn't do anything wrong, ever," he reassured her.

"Then why . . .?" Her eyes were soft, and they implored him not to let her go, but to kiss her again.

319

"I'm sorry, Tess." David drew away from her completely.

"Sorry? Sorry for what?" She was bewildered. She couldn't believe that he was ending this moment that had been so perfect between them. It was a night made for love, and yet he was withdrawing from her and apologizing for it. It didn't make sense to her.

"For taking advantage of you."

"But you haven't," she protested. "I wanted . . ."

David only shook his head in denial of her words. There was so much she didn't know. "Yes, I have. You're a wonderful girl, Tess, but what might have happened here between us if I hadn't put an end to it would have been wrong. I apologize, and I promise you it won't happen again."

"But what if I want it to?"

"It *can't* happen again. I won't let it. It's not fair to you. There can be no future for us," David admitted miserably. The pleading look she was giving him was nearly driving him out of his mind. He wanted to take her in his arms once more and love her, but he wouldn't no matter how heady her kisses had been.

"I don't care about any of that, Lord Alex. I know you could never love me, and it doesn't matter. I love *you,* and I want to please you."

"Don't say that!" he bit out tersely.

"You're asking me to deny what I feel, and that's not fair. I've loved you since you first came to Huntington House."

"It's useless, Tess." He got to his feet, needing to put a physical distance between them before he weakened in his resolve. Had he been David Markham, he would have swept her up in his embrace, but he was no longer David Markham. He was Alexander Wakefield and he had to act like Alexander Wakefield. "Good-bye."

David gave her a last look, and the tears that brimmed in her pain-filled eyes sent a shaft of agony through his heart. He turned on his heel and strode from the pool, up the path.

Behind him, Tess watched him in forlorn silence until he had gone from sight. Her heart felt as if it were breaking into a thousand pieces in her breast. She tried to think things through, to understand what had happened. It was hard for her to be logical when her emotions were so deeply involved, but she fought to make sense out of everything he'd said.

Only one thing stood out with exquisite clarity in her mind. He had apologized to her for almost taking advantage of her. As she realized that, Tess felt the warm glow of her love for him fill her. He cared about her! He had to! If he hadn't cared, he would have taken what she was offering without a thought. Tales of how the lords of the manors had their ways with the female servants were bandied about the countryside and were common knowledge among the working folks. It wasn't unusual at all for a nobleman to exert his dominance over his maids. But Lord Alex was different, and his words and actions just served to reinforce her high opinion of him. He was a gentleman of the first order. He was the finest of men. He was her true love.

Tess knew they had no future. Tess also knew in a woman's instinctive way that Lord Alex had wanted her, and there was no doubt that she still wanted him. She made up her mind then and there what she was going to do. She was going to go to him and offer herself to him once more. She could accept that they could never be more than lovers. All she had to do was convince him that he wasn't taking advantage of her, that giving her love to him was something she wanted to do, no matter what the future might bring. Tess went back to her own rooms. Before the night was over, she hoped to have given him all of her love.

Vivienne lay sated on silken sheets amidst rumpled covers that gave testimony to her previous activities. She fixed a heated gaze on the man beside her, mentally comparing his fleshy body to the harder, firmer one he'd had all those years ago. They had been apart for a long time but were reunited now, and she was happy about it. Though he might be older and less fit than he had been, he still had the power to excite her.

He leaned over her and kissed her passionately. "Have I told you how glad I am that you're back in England?"

"About a thousand times, but I do love hearing it again and again," she answered as she accepted his kiss. "It pleases me to know that I can steal you away from your wife anytime I want."

"There's no question about that, Vivienne. Compared to you, she's a shadow of a woman."

Vivienne gave a deep, throaty gurgle of pleasure at his words. "You do say the nicest things. It's just a shame that things didn't turn out the way we'd originally planned, but I think everything's going to be all right now, don't you?"

"Your plan is ingenious." He had a great appreciation for intrigue and conniving. She had confided in him all that she'd done in installing David as the future heir to the dukedom, and he thought her most clever.

"I rather thought so, too," she preened. "Soon, we will both have just what we've always wanted . . . each other and the Wakefield money."

He growled in anticipation as he moved over her lush body.

"I still wonder, though, how magnificent a scene it would have been all those years ago if Avery and your precious Catherine had ever found out about us."

"It would have been quite amusing, I think. She was quite the innocent and would have been terribly shocked," he mused as he pressed hot, wet kisses down Vivienne's throat and then lower . . .

"Avery was very jealous of me, but he might have come to enjoy it after a time . . ." she said vaguely as she felt the heat of desire start to pound through her again.

"Catherine never would have, but what did it matter? She would have been my wife by then, and I could have done whatever I wanted without any fear of reprisal."

"Like you do to me?"

"Like I do to you . . ." he said huskily, raising his head up to look at her, his eyes feverishly bright.

"Oh, Gerald," she sighed as she spread her legs to accept him back deep within her. "I did miss you . . ."

"Well, we're together now, and I see no reason why we should ever be separated again . . . In any way . . ."

It was very late, and David was exhausted. He sat alone in the library in a high-backed wing chair, a single lamp glowing nearby, a leather-bound volume of Shakespeare on his lap, a nearly empty snifter of brandy in hand. He'd been trying to read all evening since he'd left Tess, but found it impossible to concentrate. All he could think about was Tess and how very beautiful she was.

With a curse, David slammed the book shut and tossed it carelessly on the table beside him. He drained the remnants of his brandy, set the glass aside, and then ran a weary hand over his eyes. He kept trying to clear his thoughts, but it was no use. As troubled as he was, it was going to be a very long night.

David got up and refilled his snifter with another healthy portion from the crystal decanter of aged brandy one of the servants had left for him earlier. He downed it in a single, fiery swallow. Liquor of that quality was meant to be savored, but right now all David cared about was easing the torment that filled him. The potent brandy burned all the way down to his stomach, and he was glad. He poured himself another to take with him to bed and then extinguished the lamp he'd been trying to read by. That done, he made his way slowly from the library and started upstairs to retire for the night.

Tess had crept up the back stairway what seemed like hours before, and she'd been waiting in Lord Alex's room ever since. Having never done anything so brazen before, she wasn't quite sure what was the proper way to seduce the man you loved, but she thought undressing and waiting in the middle of his bed sounded like a good way to start. She lay there nervously now, waiting, as she had been for the better part of two hours.

Lord Alex usually went to bed at a reasonable hour, so Tess had made sure to sneak up there just before eleven. Since then she'd heard the mantel clock chime midnight and then one in the morning. As jittery as she was, she was also tired, for she had been up since dawn taking care of her duties. As the minutes passed into hours, Tess was beginning to fear that she might accidentally fall asleep in Lord Alex's bed while waiting for him to appear. The terrible thought struck her that he might not come to bed at all and that she might be discovered by one of the other servants sleeping there in the morning. That reason alone was enough to keep her from getting too comfortable, though there were moments when her eyes felt too heavy to keep open.

David made his way slowly down the hall toward his room, his mood tense. He didn't relish lying awake all night, but at least if he stretched out on his bed, he thought he might eventually get a little rest. He opened the door and went inside the dark room without thought. The moment he closed the door behind him, though, he knew he was not alone.

"Who's there?" he asked quietly, not wanting to raise any alarm as he reached out to light the lamp on his dresser.

"No . . . Lord Alex, please don't light the lamp," Tess pleaded nervously.

"Tess?" He said her name softly, shocked to find her there.

"Please don't say anything more. Just come to me . . ."

As David's eyes adjusted to the complete darkness that surrounded him, he could see her in the paleness of the moonlight, kneeling in supplication in the middle of his wide bed.

"Tess . . . You shouldn't be here. I told you . . ."

"I know what you said in the garden, Lord Alex, but I don't care about any of that. I just want to be with you . . ." She spoke in a throaty, husky whisper that sent shivers of excitement through David. "Nothing else matters to me, but pleasing you . . ."

Tess knew that it was now or never. She moved gracefully from the bed to cross the room and stand before him. She linked her arms around his neck and pressed herself fully against him in an offering as old as time. She was naked before him with no defense. She was giving herself to him out of love and no other reason.

David could not resist her. He had wanted her. There could be no denying that, and now he would have her. "I can't promise you anything, Tess," he told her.

"I don't want anything from you," she replied, relieving him of the guilt that threatened. Raising up on her toes, she took the initiative and kissed him.

It was that action that broke the dam of his restraint. With a grunt of primal need, he picked her up in his arms in one easy motion and strode toward the bed as if she weighed no more than a feather. Their lips didn't part until he lowered her to the softness of the welcoming mattress.

"I want you, too, Tess."

"Then I wasn't wrong . . ." she breathed in wonder.

"No. You weren't wrong." His hand swept over her in a bold caress, and he could feel her trembling beneath his touch. He moved away only long enough to shed his clothes, then joined her there, bare flesh to bare flesh.

Their kisses became wild as his caresses became even more intimate. She moved against him as her body urged her to, yet in her untouched state, she was not quite sure what was going to happen between them. She'd seen animals mating and had listened to the other servants teasing and gossiping about the physical side of love, but her own experience was greatly limited. She decided to imitate his caresses in trying to please him, and she was thrilled when he gasped out loud as her hands explored him.

"Tess . . ." he groaned, thinking her learned in the ways of love.

David's need for her was great and he mounted her

without pause. He discovered that she was not experienced only as he entered her. Gritting his teeth, he slowed his demanding, passionate pace to make it special for her.

"You should have told me this was your first time," he managed as he kissed her tenderly.

"Would it have made a difference?" Tess asked, afraid that he might leave her.

"Yes."

"Then I'm glad I didn't tell you," she smiled at him. "I love you, and I wanted to give myself to you. I'm glad you were the one."

"Oh, Tess. You are so special . . . " he groaned, beginning to move with just the right rhythm to take them both to ecstasy's pleasure.

Tess could feel her body expand to hold him more comfortably as he moved within her. As he continued to kiss her and caress her, a delightful blossoming of desire began deep within the womanly heart of her. As they kissed and then kissed again, she began to match his movements. His hands and lips on her breasts thrilled her, and she wrapped her legs around him, arching to bring them closer together. His driving hips brought passion's fulfillment to her just as he reached his own peak, and they crested the glory of love together.

Clasped in each other's arms, they rested. Tess had never known the complete beauty of a woman's love for a man before, but now she knew for certain that Lord Alex was perfect. She had loved him before she'd come to him, and now she adored him.

Tess stayed with him until an hour before dawn, then left him reluctantly with a last kiss. No one saw her slip from his room and return to her own lonely bed. No one saw her lying there smiling into the predawn darkness as she recalled every kiss and every touch they'd shared.

No one saw David, either, as he stood at the window, watching the sky brighten. His expression was haunted and filled with misery as he faced the fact that he could never marry the woman he loved, that they could never have a family, and that he could never tell her that he loved her.

As David stared out at the rich lands of the Huntington estate, only a small part of the duchy that would one day be his, a religious quote echoed through his thoughts: *"What had a man if he gained the world but lost his soul?"*

Chapter Twenty-Four

It was late on their second and last full day in the desert. Serad and Hasim were riding slowly back toward their camp when Hasim noticed how quiet his brother's mare had become.

"I see you've finally gotten your mount under control," he chuckled.

"She was frisky earlier, but I've got her well in hand now," Serad agreed, realizing, strangely, that he'd enjoyed riding her more when there had been a contest of wills between them.

"That seems to be the way with most females," Hasim pointed out. "They're exciting for a time, but after a while they become quite tame."

"Not Tori. Your wives are submissive because they were taught to be. They are your wives and they live to please you."

"I know." Hasim smiled widely as he thought of just how much he'd been pleased.

"Wouldn't you enjoy spending time with a woman who was intelligent and says what she thinks, instead of what she knows you want to hear."

Hasim was stunned. The prospect of one of his wives voicing an opinion contrary to his went against everything they'd ever been taught.

"I find it intriguing. Tori is outspoken, and she doesn't hesitate to tell me her opinions on things. I find I admire her for her daring. She's quite courageous."

"How will you ever keep her in line?" Hasim was puzzled, and wondered why any man in his right mind would knowingly ask for such trouble.

"I don't want to control Tori. I want her to come to me because she wants to, not because I've forced her."

"And does she?"

"Soon I hope she will," he admitted ruefully.

"So, that is why you wouldn't part with her," Hasim said thoughtfully. "You are challenged by her."

"With the exception of my aunt, Tori is unlike any woman I've ever known," he confessed.

"Rabi *is* special," Hasim agreed, thinking of the woman who'd come into his father's life and wrought so many changes. "I care for her deeply, but I still do not fully understand why after my father had put all his other wives aside just for her, she still refused to marry him."

It was something Serad had often wondered about, too. They had lived in Algiers for nearly twenty years, and Rabi had never even considered marrying Malik. She had remained in his harem only as his concubine much to Malik's frustration, and to his own wonder.

Serad had been about to comment when he caught sight of a gazelle in the distance. Putting his heels to the horse's sides, he quickly dismissed any thoughts of women as he raced off after the graceful animal. Until now, he and Hasim had been tied in the taking game during this hunt, but he meant to break that tie right now with his next shot.

Hasim, however, was just as eager as Serad to take the lead in their competition. He charged after him, close on the heels of his fleet-footed mount.

330

Each man thought he had the best chance to bring down the prey. Each man rode at top speed, fully intent on proving his prowess with a gun. To their humiliation, both men missed their shots, and the gazelle raced at lightning speed far out of their range.

"You were quite wrong about my failing eyesight and decrepit old age," Hasim laughed as Serad reined in beside him. "It seems we're both losing our touch."

Serad laughed along with him. "I find my mind is on other things. I think I'll settle for the other kind of challenge I've discovered. The rewards there are far more to my liking."

Later, after darkness had fallen and both men had retired for the night to rest up for the trip back to Algiers the following morning, each lay awake in his own tent thinking of their earlier discussion. Hasim mulled over Serad's words and wondered what it would be like to have a woman who did not immediately rush to satisfy your every whim. The idea was foreign to him. He'd been taught that women were merely possessions, having no will of their own, simple vessels for his satisfaction. The perfect woman, he'd been told, would be there to soothe him when he was weary, she would see to any and all of his needs, she would . . .

Hasim stopped in his thoughts. If all that were true, then he already had the ideal woman in his harem. All of his wives were obedient, eager to please, and silent unless spoken to. If they were the epitome of womanhood, then why was he not satisfied? Why, after a short period of time, was he always looking for another wife?

Hasim thought of his father and Rabi again. As he came to understand their love in this new light, it dawned on him that there really might be more to a woman than he'd thought. It was an illuminating idea and one he meant to explore further. Satisfied with it, he slept.

Serad did not even bother to lie down in his tent. Tori was so heavily on his mind that he knew he wouldn't rest. He sat alone in the quiet of the desert night, remembering the softness of her flesh and the heat of her kisses. He remembered, too, the small portrait of the fiancé she loved. His aunt's words still could not be stricken from his mind. She had insisted he let Tori go, nothing less. Yet Serad wondered how he could ever let her go, when he wanted her so badly.

Serad was annoyed by the doubts that were continually assailing him. He was a decisive man. He did what needed to be done and lived with the results of his actions. It was that part of his personality driving him now as he made his decision.

The solution he'd struggled with suddenly seemed very simple. He would not ransom Tori back, for he wanted her. He would keep her, but he would not force her or coerce her in any way. He would wait until she came to him. Until then, he would remain in mastery of himself. He had managed during the voyage, and he could manage now. He was sure of it.

Serad lay back, and for the first time in many days, he managed to fall asleep and rest peacefully.

In the morning, he rose feeling fit and in complete control. He was glad he'd come on the hunt and straightened out his thoughts. When they mounted up, he was more than ready to return to Algiers.

"Serad is back?" Tori repeated, wondering why her heart leapt at the news just delivered by Oma. In the days since they'd arrived in Algiers and Serad had promptly disappeared, she'd alternated between enjoying her escape from his enforced companionship in the stateroom and agitation over the fact that he'd been so disinterested in their fate as to leave without a word. He was the one who had taken them captive to demand a ransom, and yet she had no reason to believe that he'd done anything about it. As she considered his return, her annoyance with him won out over the budding gladness in her heart.

"Yes, Serad has returned and he wishes for you to join him in his quarters."

"I see." At news of his invitation, Tori fought down a surge of excitement. She told herself that the only reason she cared he was back was because she and Jonesey would be able to find out more about their future. Certainly, she didn't care anything about him personally. She knew who and what he was.

"He has asked that you wear this when you come to him." Oma held up a robelike garment made from emerald silk.

It was an exquisite dress that would cling to her every curve and reveal far more than it would hide. It was a creation made for a man's enjoyment.

"Tell Serad that I will be glad to come and visit him but that I will wear my own clothes, thank you," Tori dictated sternly, wanting the servant to know that she was serious. Having nearly succumbed to the power of his passion once, she had no intention of allowing herself to be put in that kind of situation again. For her own peace of mind, she would remain dressed in her own things—her high-necked, long-sleeved gown.

Oma looked stricken. "But, you cannot do that . . ."

"I most certainly can," she replied with dignity. "Take that garment away. I won't be needing it."

"I can't go to Serad and tell him you refuse. He would be furious."

"Then don't tell him. I'll tell him myself when I go to him," she announced with confidence.

Oma thought her a very foolish woman, and she quickly tried to come up with a way to force her to wear the silk garment. An idea glimmered, and she answered pleasantly, "As you wish. Shall we go to the baths then? Serad is not expecting you for another hour."

Tori agreed and followed the servant from the bedchamber. Oma drew a warm bath and smiled approvingly as Tori sank down in the marble tub and rested her head back against the side. She waited patiently for her to close her eyes as she usually did when she soaked in the tub. She felt victorious the moment Tori seemed to completely relax, and she quietly gathered up her English clothes and hurried from the room to dispose of them. She came back to find that Tori had not missed her at all, and she offered up a prayer of thanks to Allah for his help in her deception. Feeling her master would be pleased with her accomplishment, Oma resumed helping to prepare Tori for going to him.

Her bath finished, Tori rose from the tub and looked around. "Where are my things?" she asked Oma. She'd expected her clothes to be right where she'd left them and was dismayed to find they were gone . . . all of them. Her eyes narrowed suspiciously as they rested on the servant whose expression was unusually passive as she stood holding a bath towel for her. "Oma?"

"Serad wants you to wear the other. It would not do to displease him," the servant answered firmly, letting her know just whose wishes she obeyed.

Tori felt her temper rise as she snatched the towel out of Oma's hands and wrapped it securely around herself. "I don't care about pleasing Serad. Why should I? I absolutely will not wear that . . . that thing!"

"Miss Tori?" Jonesey had heard the ruckus, and she rushed into the baths. "What's wrong?"

"Serad's back," she replied hotly.

"Why are you angry? It's good that he's back. Now we can find out about going home. . . ."

"No, it's *not* good. Serad expects me to wear *that* when I go to see him," she explained, pointing to the beautiful garment Oma was holding.

"Oh." Jonesey was silenced by the sight of the seductive dress.

"I told Oma that I wouldn't wear it. So she took my clothes to try to force me to, but I won't go to Serad at all if he expects me to wear it."

An intriguing smile lit up Jonesey's face as a thought occurred to her. "Of course you'll go to see him. It's the only way we'll be able to find out anything," she told her. "I have an idea. Come with me . . ."

"What have you got in mind, Jonesey?"

"Oma may have taken your clothes, but she didn't take mine," the old woman answered, her eyes twinkling at the thought. Tori was much taller than she was, but at least her spare dress would cover more of her ward than that silken wrap would. As they entered her bedroom, she dug her one other, rumpled, well-worn dress out of the trunk. "Here, wear this with my blessing and whole-hearted approval. I think you'll look quite the English lady in it, don't you?"

Tori couldn't help but laugh at her idea. She held the tattered gown to her breast. "Thank you, Jonesey. I don't think I've ever appreciated borrowing someone's dress more."

Oma watched from the doorway, her expression one of open distress. Serad had been quite pleased to send the lovely emerald silk for Tori to wear. She was sure he would not be happy about this, but she didn't know what she could do about it. These two stubborn women were unlike any females she'd ever known. Women of her acquaintance had always wanted to please the men in their lives, but these Englishwomen were independent

335

and outspoken and totally unconcerned with Serad's happiness. She wasn't sure how her master was going to react to Tori's direct disobedience of his instructions.

Jonesey looked up to see Oma watching them, a severe look of disapproval on her face. "You may go. We'll call you when Miss Victoria is finished dressing."

Oma quietly backed out of the room.

When she'd gone, Jonesey turned back to Tori. "Are you ready?"

"More than ready," she agreed.

It wasn't a simple matter to fit someone as tall as Tori into a gown that was fashioned for a woman as small as Jonesey, but somehow they managed. The sleeves were short, the cuffs reaching high above Tori's wrists. The neck was too tight and had to be left unbuttoned. The bodice was strained and the waist was so pinched that Tori had to breathe in shallow little breaths. The skirts were a good five inches off the floor revealing her trim ankles and a bit of slender calf.

Jonesey stood back to study her. "Well, I would have been happier if I had weighed thirty pounds more when this dress was sewn, but I'm afraid it's the best we can do for now."

"As long as I don't make any sudden moves, I'll be fine," Tori tried to reassure her. "I may be miserable, but I still feel more capable of dealing well with Serad in this gown than I would in the silk one."

"Be careful, Miss Victoria," Jonesey warned her. She was worried about Serad's intentions and her young ward's ability to handle him. He was a very handsome, powerful man, and Tori hadn't encountered anyone like him before. If there had been anything more Jonesey could have done to protect her, she would have. As it was, she put her faith in Tori's quick wit and her own fervent prayers.

"I will, Jonesey."

They shared a knowing look, and then called for the servant to return. Oma appeared in the doorway ready to take Tori to Serad, and her eyes widened in shock at the sight of her wearing the older woman's gown.

"Let's go," Tori spoke up before the disapproving servant could say anything.

Oma simply nodded, knowing to argue was useless. Serad would handle it. She led the way from the bedroom without a word.

Serad was waiting for Tori in a small chamber adjacent to his bedroom that served as a sitting room. He had bathed and donned a vest and pants for the evening, and he was now anxious to see her. It was impossible for him to sit and be patient, so he paced the room, finally going to stand by a window that offered a view of the center garden below.

Serad tried to appreciate the beauty of the trees and blossoms, but his mind was focused completely on Tori, as it had been almost every moment since he'd left her. He wanted to see her, to speak to her, to hold her and kiss her once more. The memory of those few burning moments when he'd held her in his arms in his cabin would not fade, and . . .

"Serad?" Musa, one of Serad's male servants, spoke from the doorway.

"Yes?" He turned, surprised by the interruption.

"The woman is here."

"Bring her to me," he replied, wondering at the odd tone in his voice, but dismissing it in his excitement.

Serad watched the doorway expectantly for Tori to appear. The moment he'd been looking forward to was finally here. Tonight, he was certain he would make her his. What had begun in his cabin would be taken to its rightful conclusion.

Serad thought of the emerald silk wrap he'd chosen
for her. He'd selected the silk knowing how perfect it
would be on her, and he hoped she liked it. He had even
purchased a gold-and-emerald necklace to replace the
locket and chain he'd taken from her. He'd searched
hard to find a flawless stone, and the moment he'd set
eyes on this particular jewel, he'd known it was the one.
He was eager to fasten the clasp at her throat and even
more anxious to see his sparkling gem resting between
her breasts.

A sound clued Serad that she was near, and his
anticipation grew even more intense. His mind filled
with visions of Tori wearing the emerald wrap! He was
expecting her to appear in the emerald wrap! He was
excited about seeing her in the emerald wrap! When
she appeared there before him, he blinked in shock. It
was Tori all right, but she was definitely not wearing
the emerald wrap. Tori was wearing a very plain, very
short, very tight, very *ugly* English daygown.

"You wanted to see me?" Tori spoke her words in all
innocence as she moved to stand in the doorway of
Serad's chambers. She was prepared for an eruption of
fury from him, and she believed she was angry enough
to sustain herself through whatever confrontation
followed. What she hadn't expected was to come face-
to-face with her captor and be jolted by a surge of
longing unlike anything she'd ever known. He was so tall
and so wonderfully handsome. Her gaze was hungry
upon him, though she tried everything she knew to
deny the very sudden realization that she had missed
him and that she was thrilled that he was back.

Struck speechless by her blatant disregard for his
commands, Serad could only stare at her in the ill-
fitting outfit. For a few seconds all manner of thought
left him as disappointment ravaged him. Then,

suddenly realizing that this was Tori he was dealing with, he burst out laughing. Serad didn't know why he had been foolish enough to expect Tori to do anything he wanted her to do. In their constant battle of wits, she had always managed to surprise him, and he realized now that it had been silly of him to have forgotten that.

Tori had been anticipating an angry reaction from him, and his amusement caught her completely off guard. Her first surprising reaction to his laughter was hurt. As annoyed as she'd been at him, she knew she should have remained angry, but then she looked down at herself and realized just how very comical the clothing really looked on her. Unable to prevent it, she began laughing, too.

Her laughter sounded musical to Serad, and suddenly he wasn't laughing anymore. His gaze focused on her lovely, animated features. His regard dropped lower, tracing the slender column of her throat down to the straining buttons at the bodice of the clinging gown. The memories of the kisses he'd bestowed there returned with heated power and sent desire flashing through him. He wanted her . . .

Tori quickly noticed that Serad was no longer laughing, and she glanced up to find his gray eyes upon her. His expression was serious. She went still.

You missed him . . . He's back!, a small voice revealed to Tori, in the back of her mind, but a last logical fragment of her consciousness vehemently denied the allegations of her heart. This was Serad, she tried to remind herself, the man who had taken her captive and who stood before her now looking every bit the powerful Barbary prince. Surrounded by the luxury of his abode, dressed in an open, embroidered vest and loose-fitting pants, he was the confident conqueror, the man who held her against her will. There was primitive passion in him, and even as she feared it she was drawn to it and to him by forces she didn't understand.

"Why didn't you wear what I sent you, Tori?" Serad finally asked, his tone deep and slightly ominous as he took a step toward her.

The part of Tori that was struggling to retain her sanity instinctively urged her to back away and retreat to safety. She, however, refused to give him quarter as she met his gaze squarely and answered, "I prefer to wear my own clothes."

"I find it difficult to believe that that dress is yours," he remarked as he let his gaze slide over her once more. "Somehow it looks like it might belong to someone else . . . your shorter companion, possibly?"

"You're right, it *is* Jonesey's," she replied with dignified calm. "I was forced to borrow it when Oma stole my things."

"Oma 'stole' your clothing?" Serad was incredulous. His servants were all impeccably honest.

"Yes, she did. When I refused to wear the garment you sent, she took mine. I guess she thought I would be forced to wear yours if I had nothing else."

"But you proved too clever for her," Serad finished the thought for her. "I should have warned the unsuspecting Oma about you."

He moved steadily toward her. This fiery spirit of hers drew him to her as readily as any aphrodisiac and his control began to fail. He suddenly wanted—no *needed*—to strip the offending garment from her lovely body. "It seems during my absence many of the lessons I taught you were forgotten."

"I've forgotten nothing," she asserted, still holding her ground.

"Oh? I thought you'd learned that I was the victor and the master."

"You may have the superior force for now, but you

will never truly conquer me," Tori continued to defy him and her own private yearnings. The flare of anger that shone momentarily in his eyes warned her that she traveled on dangerous ground, but she was too caught up in the moment to take heed.

"That is where you're wrong," Serad responded slowly, his gaze darkening. "I have no need to conquer."

"I will never be yours."

"You already are." He gave a soft laugh as he reached out to toy with the top, straining button on the bodice. With little effort, he managed to loosen it, and the material parted by itself revealing an enticing bit of cleavage.

"Don't . . ." She maneuvered slightly out of his reach.

"It was a mistake to try to hide your charms from me, Tori, for you see, even though you attempt to disguise yourself, I know what you look like without the clothing." The memory of seeing her in the bathtub aboard ship returned with a vengeance, and heavy, hot desire burst into full flame within him, burning through the reins he'd placed on himself.

"That was precisely why I borrowed this dress." In a woman's way, Tori sensed the change in Serad. She backed away from him until she found herself flush against a cool stone wall with nowhere left to run or hide.

"You didn't enjoy our kisses, Tori?" he asked softly as he continued his pursuit. When he saw a flicker of uncertainty in her eyes, his mastery of himself completely disappeared. "The jest was well played, but it is finished. Since you chose not to wear my gift to you, then I prefer that you wear nothing. Take the dress off."

His order was dictated with such arrogance that he

aroused Tori's anger.

"I will not," she adamantly refused, and her green eyes flashed dangerously at his imperious command.

"There is no point in denying me, Tori. You already know the outcome of any confrontation we might have." He closed to within touching distance of her again. The desire he felt for her could not be contained, and he lifted one hand to release another button.

Tori gasped and clutched at the cloth to hold it modestly together. She realized the danger she faced and sought a weapon to defend herself. In a last effort to stop him, she put one hand on his chest to hold him away from her as she lifted her eyes to his. She meant to deny him, but it never happened. She meant to use Alex to protect herself, to claim her love for him and try to dissuade this pirate. But when she gazed into the smoldering depths of his gray gaze an answering response to his passionate need was born within her.

Suddenly, Tori, too, was remembering the ecstasy that had been theirs when for the shortest of times the barriers between them had been gone and they had been only man and woman, flame and desire. She was confused. She was on fire. She wanted him . . .

"Serad, I . . ."

"Tori . . ." Her name was a groan as he kissed her.

Chapter Twenty-Five

Tori knew she should stop Serad. She tried to push him away and even turned her head a bit to avoid him, but it was no use. His mouth found hers with unerring accuracy, and from the first breathless touch of his lips on hers, Tori's world was turned upside down. Suddenly, the desire to escape Serad was gone. She didn't want the kiss to end . . . She didn't want to leave him . . .

No longer were they master and slave, captor and captive. They were only male and female, perfect together, meant to be as one. Logic meant nothing before the wonder of their need for each other. The universe narrowed to the two of them.

Tori surrendered to Serad's enthralling kiss, confessing eagerly to herself that this was what she wanted. She had missed Serad while he'd been gone. She had thought only of him during the past few days, never of Alex. This was Serad . . . and he was here . . . with her . . . wanting her as much as she wanted him.

Any last thread of control Serad might have had over himself snapped the instant his mouth moved possessively over Tori's. He wanted her. He had waited for this moment for what seemed an eternity. He had ached for this kiss and this embrace. Nothing was going to stop him. By the dawn's first light, he would have made her his in all ways.

Serad pressed Tori back against the wall and then moved his body intimately against hers. He let her feel and know the strength of his desire for her. His lips finally left hers to explore the delicate shell of her ear and then to trail heated kisses down the side of her neck.

"I want you, Tori. I've waited as long as I can . . ." he growled as he lifted his head to gaze down at her.

Tori said nothing, for, in truth, she didn't know what to say. Her flushed cheeks and passion-glazed eyes, however, testified that she was feeling the same desire that he was. She lifted her face to him, and he kissed her again. Serad's lips moved with persuasive arousal over hers, parting them, tasting of the sweetness of her mouth. His tongue dueled with hers, and she answered that exciting mating call with abandon.

Tori's hand on his chest was trapped between them now, and beneath her palm she could feel the power of his heartbeat. The hair-roughened skin of his chest was hot to her touch. In an innocently sensuous move, she slipped the hand around to his back and caressed the thick, corded muscles there. That small movement on her part brought her fully against his chest, and they both were jarred by the electricity of the contact.

Aroused by her play, Serad deepened his kisses, and Tori met him in kiss after torrid kiss. She could feel the hardness of the wall against her back, and yet it didn't matter. All that was important was Serad and being close to him.

"Serad . . ." she whispered his name as his lips left hers to seek out the hollows of her throat. Chills of excitement shivered through her as he nuzzled there, and she could feel her breasts swell and the peaks tauten with the beginnings of passion.

Serad brought his hand up to caress her, and he could feel the hardened crests even through her layers of clothing. It was then that he knew he could bear it no more. He had to strip away that hated gown and hold her naked against him. He had to caress her and kiss her and make love to her.

His kiss turned wildly passionate as he bent and picked her up in his arms. He cradled her to his chest and did not end the kiss as he strode from the antechamber straight into his bedroom.

Tori was lost in a haze of sensuality. She linked her arms about Serad's strong neck and returned his embrace with equal fervor. The fact that he was carrying her into his bedroom didn't matter. She wanted was to be in his arms, to share his kisses and to know his love. When Serad knelt upon his bed to lay her down, she kept her arms around him and drew him down with her . . . and then it was heaven as he covered her slender body with his.

Serad's breathing grew strained as he braced himself on his elbows above her and fitted his hips to hers in that most intimate of embraces. They were perfect together as he had known they would be. His need to have her became urgent now as his blood heated, and he knew he had to get even closer. He was desperate to have her naked, silken softness beneath him.

"Kiss me . . ." Tori whispered as she looked up at him. He seemed magnificently handsome as she studied him in her passion, and she wondered how she'd managed to hold herself from him for so long. There was no resistance in her, only acceptance of what she realized she should have known from the beginning. What was happening between them was meant to be. It was wonderful . . . it was perfect.

At her words, Serad paused and time seemed to

stop. His gray eyes locked with hers for what seemed forever, and then he obeyed her command and claimed her lips in a flaming exchange that pushed them both to the brink of bliss.

Serad could wait to be with her no longer. He began to unfasten the rest of the buttons from her gown with feverish ease. When he'd finished, Tori willingly helped him strip the miserably tight garment from her, and she was glad to be rid of it.

"You're beautiful, Tori," Serad told her, his voice hoarse in his desire. "You're the most beautiful woman I've ever known . . ."

Tori realized vaguely that she should have been embarrassed by her nearly unclad state, but she wasn't. Serad's words reassured her, and she took a deep feminine pride and pleasure in knowing that he found her pretty. Only when he loosened her chemise and slipped it down from her shoulders completely baring her breasts, did she grow self-conscious and try to cover herself.

"No, don't . . ." Serad coaxed gently to discourage her attempt. "I want to see you. All of you . . ."

He eased the tension of the moment by kissing her with great tenderness. When she seemed to relax, Serad drew back to gaze down at her lithe body. The glory of her slender shoulders and rounded breasts enthralled him, and he caressed her with great care, cupping and molding the soft flesh. His lips traced patterns of fire upon her bared bosom giving Tori a taste of the rapture to come.

Tori could not believe the sensations that were rocketing through her. Unable to help herself, she began to move restlessly beneath him, seeking that which she could not find—that elusive release that seemed just beyond her grasp.

Serad's caresses grew more demanding as his own

passion raged to new heights. No other woman had ever set his senses on fire this way, and he was desperate to join with her, to unite their bodies, but he knew he couldn't rush her. He had to teach her of desire's ecstasy. He had to initiate her into the rites of love.

Serad continued to kiss and caress her until she was moaning with the aching emptiness of her passion. Only then did he seek out her most private place to assure himself of her readiness for him. When he was certain that her desire matched his, he discarded his own clothing and positioned himself above her.

Braced on his forearms over her, his eyes now dark with passion as they locked with hers in unspoken communication, he let his hips tease hers in the rhythmic motion that hinted at what was to come. Ecstasy quivered through Tori, and she let her eyes close. Her breathing became rapid and shallow and her lips parted as if waiting for his kiss.

As his mouth covered hers with commanding force, he grasped her hips and lifted them to his. Slowly, he moved into her hot, satiny depths. It was agony and yet it was ecstasy for him as he drove deeper into the very heart of her. He met and conquered her innocence with a heated thrust and then laid claim to the destiny that he'd long known was his.

Tori went completely still for a moment as she adjusted to the wonder and newness of Serad's complete possession. The whispered descriptions she'd heard from gossipy girlfriends of this ultimate act of love were a mere shadow of the truth. To be so completely linked to Serad was more spellbinding than anything she could ever have imagined.

"Tori . . ." Serad said her name in a rasp as he fought not to lose himself in her velvet hold and end the beauty of their joining too quickly.

She lifted her gaze to his and nearly drowned in the stormy gray depths of his eyes. She did not speak, but let her actions speak for her as she lifted one hand to caress his cheek. He lowered his head to kiss her and she met him fully in that flaming embrace.

The fear that he'd hurt her overcome, Serad held her close and began to move. Tori innately recognized the sensuality of his rhythm, and she started to arch her hips in time to his motions in order to accept him more fully. She could feel the tension building . . . a thrilling, aching knot of excitement that clamored for release. With each powerful thrust, she gloried in his branding. She matched his movements instinctively as his hands skimmed over her with learned caresses.

Serad was trying to pace himself for her enjoyment, but the rapture of finally having her was too much to be long denied. He clasped her to his heart as he sought the crest with hard-driving motions that sent her senses reeling. They peaked, celebrating the bliss of their oneness, mindless in their pleasure.

One in body, their hearts gave birth to a joy neither could recognize yet. They clung together, savoring what had just transpired, knowing that one taste would never be enough. They lay together, their bodies still fused in love's embrace, not talking, not thinking, just being . . .

Serad's thoughts had been blissfully peaceful until the rapture faded, and he'd slowly become aware of what he'd done. A pall fell over his mood as his aunt Rabi's words resounded through his conscience: *"Only the lowest of the low would take a woman against her will."*

A coldness settled heavily in Serad's soul. He was a man who kept his word, but he'd broken every vow he'd made to himself not to force Tori. She had not come to him freely.

Serad tried to justify it all by telling himself that she'd been responsive enough once he'd touched her, but the truth remained, taunting him with its ugliness. He had pushed her against a wall and had practically torn the clothes off her.

Serad always prided himself on his steely nerve and self-restraint. Never before had he completely lost control this way. The force of his attraction to Tori almost unnerved him. Why was it that this particular woman had the power to drive him to mindlessness? Serad had no answer. He knew only that he was filled with deep-seated feelings of guilt and disgust over his own behavior.

Tori stirred as the night air slowly cooled her love-heated body. Disbelief filled her as she gradually became aware of what she'd done, and that was followed immediately by a terrible sense of anger with herself. She wondered how in the world she could have given in to Serad so easily? He was a barbarian, a savage, a pirate! He was a wild man, a man of no breeding or culture . . . and yet, she'd responded to him as she'd never thought possible to respond to a man. He had kissed her once and all had been lost! She hadn't even fought him! If anything, she believed she'd encouraged him!

It was that thought that sobered Tori. She couldn't deny to herself that she had loved every minute in his embrace. Serad's lovemaking had been so special that she could hardly bear to think about it. Their coming together had been exciting beyond measure. It had been a wondrous thing. Any thoughts of Alex and home had vanished when she'd surrendered to Serad's embrace, and just thinking of it now left her heart and body glowing in remembered warmth.

An image of the dashing corsair played in Tori's mind as she lay quietly in his arms, her eyes still closed.

He was the most handsome man she'd ever known, and yet he was also the most maddeningly arrogant. He was totally wrong for her. There was no way she could even think about a life with him. If she were to stay there in Algiers, she would have to forfeit everything—her family, her home, the future she'd planned so happily as the wife of the next Duke of Huntington—and become completely subservient to Serad's wishes.

Still, even as Tori realized the painful truth of her situation, a troubling thought crept into her mind and heart. Though it could never be between them, she had to admit to herself with painful candor that she had wanted Serad just as much as he'd wanted her. Suddenly very much physically aware of him, Tori shifted slightly in his embrace. Little did she know that her simple movement stirred Serad's desire for her again.

Serad had been lying there in silence, miserably contemplating the consequences of what he'd done. When the fire of his passion for her threatened to ignite once more, he berated himself for this weakness he had for her. His lack of restraint concerned, confused and angered him, and he knew he had to get away from her intoxicating nearness before he lost all of his self-respect and took her again right then and there.

Without saying a word to her, Serad withdrew from her and quickly got up. He did not even look at her as he wrapped one of the discarded sheets around his waist and started from the room.

"Serad?" Tori couldn't believe he'd gotten up and left her so easily.

He faced her, his expression unreadable. "I will send a servant to you to take you back to the harem. Dress yourself." He spoke coolly with little emotion. His gaze raked over her naked body impassively, then he turned and left the room.

That Serad had displayed no emotion at all told Tori everything she needed to know. Her own expression hardened before the indifference in his. She had known that this was the way it would be. He would call her to him at his convenience when he wanted to and then discard her just as easily. She lifted her chin in mute testimony to her battered, but still standing, pride.

Fighting down the despair that threatened, Tori dressed in Jonesey's ugly dress and started to rush from the room. Just as she reached the door, one of the houseservants appeared to accompany her back to the harem. She followed the man there in total silence, then retreated to her room quietly so she wouldn't have to face anyone. She needed quiet now. She needed time to think.

Serad had gone out on the balcony overlooking the courtyard to wait until Tori had gone from his bedchamber. He gave himself a mental pat on the back for having passed the test he'd set for himself. He'd had the strength of will to leave when he had to. If he'd remained with Tori one minute longer, there was no doubt in his mind that he would have made love to her again. Ordering her to the harem had been the most difficult thing he'd ever done, but having accomplished that, hope grew within him that he could regain his self-control and with it his self-respect. He'd managed to deny himself her love once, and having mastered his desire for her then, he felt confident that he could do it again.

Serad gazed up at the star-studded night sky, and thoughts of Tori, naked and writhing in her passion beneath him, slipped into his thoughts. Loving her had been wonderful. She was everything he wanted in a woman. She was spirited and exciting. She was intelligent and witty, not to mention absolutely beautiful. Memories of her response to his caresses after he'd broken down her initial reluctance thrilled him, but as quickly as he began to dwell on her sensuality, the heavy weight of his guilt descended again.

Serad realized that he was going to have to work to win Tori over so she would come to him because she wanted him and for no other reason. The idea was very English in concept and very foreign to his adopted culture. He was torn between his aunt's ways and the Barbary ways. It was deeply troubling for him, but the abiding truth was that he wanted her and would do whatever he had to win her. His decision made, Serad planned to start the very next morning. It would be difficult for him to keep his own needs in check while he wooed her, but he would do it because she was worth the sacrifice.

Feeling a little bit better, Serad returned to his own bed and as he rested he found himself longing for Tori and wishing she was lying beside him, sharing his bed, his love, and his life.

"You look troubled, Rabi. Is there anything I can help you with?" Almira asked as she found her mistress sitting near the window in her bedroom in Malik's harem.

Rabi looked up and smiled slightly, glad to see her. "I think so, Almira, my dear friend. I think so."

"What is it you want me to do? Does it have anything to do with Serad?"

"You know me far too well, and, as usual, you're right. Have you heard anything about him or his women captives?" Rabi knew Almira was a veritable font of information of the goings-on in Algiers.

"Very little," she confessed, "but it's not from a lack of trying. All that I've managed to learn coincides with what you already know—that Serad left on the hunt with Hasim the day he returned to Algiers and that they got back earlier today."

"There's been no news about the women?"

"No, nothing."

Rabi looked very thoughtful, then asked. "Do you think you could get a message to them without anyone finding out?"

"I could try."

"I can't risk putting anything in writing, so my message will have to be relayed by word of mouth. Can we trust anyone to do this for us?"

"I have many friends who will help if we need it," Almira assured her. "What is it you want to tell them?"

"It isn't so much what I want to tell them, as it is what I want to *do* for them."

Almira gave her a puzzled look.

"I want to help them escape," Rabi concluded.

"You *what?*" Almira was truly shocked, for it was a very drastic thing for Rabi to suggest.

Rabi looked up at her servant, her eyes haunted with the memories of her own past. "I cannot allow my nephew to take these women captive against their will. They are English citizens. They have families who love them. They do not deserve to have all their dreams snatched away from this way. It's cruel . . . heartless . . ."

She could hear the bitter sorrow in Rabi's voice, and she knew in that moment that her mistress was reliving her own fate.

"Almira, I have to help them," she went on earnestly, "It's too late for me, but I can help these women. I can't just stand by and not try to go to their aid. I can't!"

"I understand," the servant replied, "and I'll help all I can."

"Thank you."

As Almira left her mistress, her thoughts were tinged with sadness. Almira had tried to keep Rabi happy through these long years they'd been together, but she had never been able to completely convince her that her life there with Malik was an idyllic one. A part of her mistress had always clung to the past, longing for what might have been, aching for the man she'd loved and had lost.

Though Rabi didn't know it, Almira had heard her cry herself to sleep several times. She had never approached her at those private moments or mentioned them afterward, for she was certain Rabi didn't want anyone to know just how much she still missed her old life. But Almira knew, and in that knowledge came complete understanding of her mistress's motivation in wanting to help the Englishwomen, and she decided she would do everything she could to help carry out her wishes.

When Almira had gone, Rabi let her gaze drift out over the gardens again. Her thoughts were still lingering on the past. How could it be that nearly twenty years had passed, when it seemed like only yesterday that she'd been brought before Malik and he'd claimed her as part of his bounty? Now, here she was, older and wiser and still missing her father, her home, her fiancé, and the life she'd left behind.

She had come to care for Malik during their years together. He had always been kind and attentive. He had lavished her with presents and made her the sole resident of his harem. But in spite of all his efforts, she had never given up her love for Gerald, and in clinging to that part of her past, she had never given Malik her heart.

Rabi sighed. It was almost time to go to Malik now. She thought of the handsome dey and knew he was a good man. She did enjoy his company, and the evening would be an exciting one as always, but there was still a part of her that ached for her freedom and the life in London that had once been hers.

Chapter Twenty-Six

By first light, Serad knew exactly what he was going to do. He summoned his servant to him and gave the orders he wanted executed that very morning. Confidence filled him as he ate his breakfast. This plan of his to win Tori was going to work. He was sure of it. His aunt would be proud of him.

It was nearly noon when everything had been taken care of and he had finally sent for Tori. In preparation for the trip he'd planned for them, he had donned a loose-fitting white cotton garment called a *kibr* that fit much like a tunic over his shirt and pants. He had even put on the traditional white headdress to protect against the hot desert sun. Dressed much as a desert sheik, looking quite foreign and very imposing, he waited expectantly for her to come to him in his chambers.

"Serad?"

He looked up to see the male servant he'd sent after Tori standing alone in the doorway looking rather embarrassed. "Yes?" he asked cautiously.

"The woman would not come, Serad. Short of using physical violence on her there was no way I could bring her to you."

"She wouldn't come?" He gave an exasperated shake of his head, for he should have known what her reaction would be to one of his commands.

"She said if you wanted to see her, you could come to her there in the harem," the servant finished.

Serad scowled. Her stubborness was a match for his, but he knew who would win this battle of wills. He had made his plans for them and she was going to go along with them—no matter what. "I will see to it myself," he told the man, dismissing him.

Serad strode from his chambers intent on retrieving Tori and following through with his plans.

"Tori!" He called her name as he stood in the middle of the garden.

Tori had been busying herself in her own chambers when she heard Serad's call. She'd been expecting an angry reaction from him and she was prepared. After she'd left him, the night had proven long, empty, and hot, and it had given her plenty of time to think. She had come to the conclusion that giving in to Serad had been a foolish, tragic thing and that she could never allow it to happen again. Refusing his earlier summons to come to him had only been the first step in her efforts to stay as far away from him as she could.

"Serad has come himself this time, and he wants to see you now," Oma related nervously as she came rushing into the room. She had known there would be trouble when she'd been forced to send Serad's man back to him with the news that Tori would not budge from her room. Now, Serad had come himself. She knew he was not happy.

"He does, does he?"

"He's in the garden."

Tori felt a little sense of victory as she nodded and started from the room. It annoyed her that she had to wear a native dress. Sometime early that morning,

Oma had taken all of Jonesey's things, too, undoubtedly on Serad's order, and both women had been forced to don the other clothing. Still, there was a small triumph for her. Serad had come to her. He had not had her dragged to his quarters, and that was something.

Tori made her way out to where Serad waited. Her first sight of him clad in the desert clothing shocked her. For an instant she almost thought it was a stranger who stood with his back to her, and then, instinctively, she knew it was him. She studied Serad unobserved. She was coming to understand that he was a very complex man and wondering how many different facets there were to him. First he had been the fierce pirate captain with turban and scimitar, then the royal prince, and now the sheik in headdress and robes. Though she told herself it was wrong, she was attracted to him in all guises. No matter what he wore, no matter what he did, she found she desired him.

"You wanted me?" Tori finally spoke.

Serad glanced up at Tori, and his heart constricted in his chest. *Did he want her?* She looked breathtakingly lovely in the Algerian dress, just as he'd known she would. He could only stare at her. *Did he want her?* The question was absolutely ludicrous. *Want* wasn't the word for it.

"It is customary that when one is summoned to one's master, one goes," he dictated tersely.

"I have no master," she answered simply.

"We have had this conversation before." He was trying to be cool and composed as he dealt with her defiance.

"Yes, we have."

"I see you've adopted our style of dress. I approve."

"I had only the choice of coming to you naked or wearing this. Wearing this was the better decision."

"You look beautiful."

"I would prefer my own clothing."

"Your things will not be returned to you. I prefer you in that. Oma!"

"Yes, Serad?" The servant appeared in the archway.

"Bring a haik to me now." Serad knew the sun would be punishing and cruel to Tori if she did not have on the proper dress for their trip. He wanted to make sure she was protected. "Do you ride?" he asked, changing the subject.

"Yes," she answered distrustfully, her chin set stubbornly when she noticed the doubt of her riding abilities in his expression.

"Good . . . good." He smiled. "Ah, here's Oma now . . ." He took the haik from the servant and then sent her on her way. When they were alone again, he held out his hand to her. "Now, Tori come with me," he invited.

"I'm not going anywhere with you," she declared firmly, standing her ground. She knew she couldn't be alone with him. It was far too dangerous to her peace of mind.

"I *said,* come with me," Serad repeated tersely as he kept himself rigidly in control. The invitation had gone out of his tone, and his eyes had turned steely.

"I choose not to." She flaunted his authority once again.

Serad told himself that he'd tried to be kindly. He'd tried to make her see reason, but her comment hit him where he was most vulnerable. In the way of men when hurt, he struck back the only way he could—with physical action.

Serad didn't consider what he was about to do. He wanted to win Tori, but how could he unless she cooperated? Frustrated, he closed the distance between them in four determined strides and without another word picked her up and threw her over his shoulder.

"What do you think you're doing?!" Tori shouted in outrage as she pummeled his broad back with ineffectual blows. "Put me down."

"Be quiet," he commanded, tightening his grip on her with ominous intent. "I am very close to showing you the way we discipline unruly female captives." Serad's choice of wording was bad, but he was so annoyed he didn't care. He had made plans for them, and he intended to carry them out. She was going to enjoy herself, whether she knew it or not!

Tori could feel the explosive anger in him and wisely said nothing.

Jonesey, however, had heard Tori's shriek of outrage, and she came running to help. She cut off Serad's retreat, confronting him with her hands on her hips.

"Just what do you think you're doing with Miss Victoria?" she demanded, her manner as threatening as it could be for a five-foot-tall woman.

"Do not challenge my authority, woman!" he thundered. *Was there no end to his aggravation?*

Jonesey had never been talked to in that forceful a manner before, and had she been made of lesser stuff she might have shown her fear before him. But she did not give up. "You can't carry her off this way. I forbid it!"

Serad stopped, and, still holding onto the squirming, miserable Tori, he glowered down at Jonesey. When he spoke his voice was coldly imperial. "If you plan to see the sun rise tomorrow, then I suggest you remove yourself from my presence."

Jonesey opened her mouth to respond, thought the better of it after seeing the look in his eyes, and backed out of his way. As Serad once more started from the women's quarters, she gathered enough courage to yell after him, "If any harm comes to her . . ."

"Jonesey . . . hush . . . don't . . ." Tori gasped as Serad picked up his pace and she was jounced around a bit, knocking the breath from her. She knew he was furious and she didn't want him riled any more than he already was. She didn't want Jonesey hurt, and she knew she could take care of herself.

"But Miss Victoria . . ." the older woman protested in horror, for she understood Serad's intentions and was certain of what her fate would be.

The rest of her words were lost to both Serad and Tori as he finally made his escape from the harem. Jonesey stood there, staring helplessly after them. After a moment of desperation, she turned and went back inside. As she did, the worried look slipped away and a small smile lit her features. She couldn't help but admire how strikingly handsome Serad had looked and how marvelously romantic it would be to be carried off that way. She put a hand over her breast to try to stop the fluttering of her heart and told herself she was too old for such fantasies.

Serad's stride was purposeful as he walked straight for the stables. He wasn't at all pleased with the way things had gone so far, but he told himself it could only get better.

Serad was pleased to see that the two horses were tied up side by side as he'd instructed. He'd meant for this outing to be a pleasant diversion for Tori and for himself. He'd thought if they spent some time together alone, away from the harem and life in Algiers, she would become more amenable. Now he wondered.

Moving forward, Serad could have easily deposited Tori directly on her own horse, but after the way she'd fought him so far, he was not about to trust her riding alone. Instead, he set her on her feet and, ignoring the icy glare she shot him, he adjusted the haik on her head and about her shoulders. When he was done, the long, flowing cape-like garment covered her from the top of her head to her knees.

"I don't want to wear this," she snapped.

"Right now I don't care what you want." He took a critical look at her and decided it would provide enough cover for the short trip. Swinging up onto his mare's back, he unceremoniously reached down and snared her around the waist to draw her up and across his lap.

"What are you doing?" Tori asked, shocked by his actions and the feelings that were surging through her as he held her tightly against his broad, powerful chest.

"We're going for a ride," he informed her as he wrapped the haik around her more protectively.

"Just where do you think you're taking me and why do I need to wear this thing?" Tori asked. She hoped wherever it was that he was taking her, it wasn't far. She didn't want to be this close to him. Being held on his lap, pressed against his chest like this, definitely was a sensual experience. Thoughts of the previous night rushed heatedly through her mind.

"You'll see," he answered evasively. The feel of her soft against him was filling him with memories of their joining the night before and he longed to make her his again. "It's not a long ride, but you have to be covered and you'll need to hold on to me."

"Surely this can't be comfortable for you. Why don't you let me ride the other horse?" Tori suggested, wanting to put as much physical distance between them as she could. It was disconcerting to find she could be this angry with him and yet desire him at the same time.

"No. I'll keep you here with me. That way I'll know exactly where you are and what you're doing."

"You think I could get away from you on horseback?" Tori ventured in a deliberate taunt.

"You could not escape me, but I want to save myself

the chase," he answered with arrogant self-assurance as he retrieved the other mount's reins and put his heels to his own horse's sides to start them on their way.

"If you think women can't ride as well as men, then you haven't seen any Englishwomen ride. I've been riding to hounds since I was old enough to keep my seat."

"Riding to hounds?"

"Fox hunting," she explained.

"You enjoy such sport?"

"Very much."

He nodded thoughtfully, and recalling his determination to win her over, he said, "Later we will ride together, and you can show me your skill. For now, though, we will stay as we are."

They made the ride from Algiers amidst stares from many who were in the streets at that time. Tori knew she was the object of much interest and yet she held her head high as they made their way through the narrow passages. Though she would never admit it to Serad, she was glad that she had the bothersome haik around her while making the trek through the city, for it afforded her some protection from the Algerians' prying eyes. When at last they left the city, Tori couldn't help but wonder where he was taking her, but he offered no information and the trip was made in silence.

The two-hour ride to Serad's secret oasis was usually an enjoyable one for him, but this time, he found himself in a state of agonized torture. Having Tori so close to him, he was completely aware of her as a woman. He could feel the softness of her. He could smell the scent of her. The heat of her seemed to burn him wherever they touched. Every time she shifted positions, her bottom came in near-painful contact with his loins, and he had to grit his teeth to keep from pressing his more ardent attentions upon her right there on horseback.

Tori attempted to hold herself erect and away from any contact with Serad. She didn't want to be close to him, for to touch him reminded her vividly of the night before, and she wanted to forget that that had ever happened. She told herself she wanted to go back to England and go on with her life just as she'd planned— or at least that was what she was trying to convince herself of as they made the ride out into the wilds of the desert.

It was very difficult for Tori to maintain her rigid posture, and after the first hour, she got tired of holding herself so stiffly. Every inch of her body started to ache from trying to avoid the enforced intimacy of their positions, and she almost wished that she could allow herself to lean back against Serad's chest and relax. She was just about ready to give in to that temptation, when they topped a low-rising hill and he reined in the horse.

"There . . ." Serad spoke, pointing in the distance. "That's where we're going."

Tori's first view of Serad's secret destination was breathtaking. After endless miles of hot, dry, lifeless desert sand, the palm-bordered oasis with its sparkling blue-green pool looked wonderfully refreshing and inviting. A large, airy-looking tent was standing not far from the water's edge, and several camels were tied up nearby. As she looked on, she could see servants hurrying about to prepare the site. "Is it a mirage?"

"Hasim and I thought so, too, when we first found it many years ago. Very few people know about this place, and we like it that way." Serad felt his excitement grow at the prospect of having Tori there, all alone, all to himself with no chance of interruptions. It would give them time to get to know each other and perhaps give her time to come to terms with staying with him. He wanted her desperately, and the last hour and a half with her sitting there before him had only served to emphasize that need.

Serad nudged the mare forward, eager to cross the last mile. When he drew to a stop before the tent, several attendants rushed forth to meet them.

"Serad, it's good that you are here. All is in readiness for you."

"Good. You may go as soon as we have settled in."

The man nodded his understanding. "We will return late tomorrow as you've instructed."

"That will be fine."

One man helped Serad as he handed Tori down and then dismounted himself. The other took the reins to both his mare and Tori's unridden horse and led them away to be rubbed down and fed.

"Come, Tori. I will show you our humble abode for the night." He took her hand and urged her along with him into the tent that had been set up just for them.

Tori had never seen anything like it, and she stopped just inside the door flap to stare around in surprise. The ceiling was high, allowing for whatever cooling breezes there might be. The hot sand of the desert floor was covered with rich, plush carpets. Piles of brightly colored, satin-covered pillows served as the only furniture, but they looked very inviting after the time spent on horseback. A vast array of foods had already been prepared for them and were being set out now.

"How did they know when to have the food ready?" she asked.

"I had told them this morning what our time of arrival would be."

"You were very sure of yourself," Tori remarked, put off by his confidence in himself.

"I *am* very sure of myself," he stated calmly as he moved behind her to remove the haik. "My judgment is sound. Had I not insisted upon the haik to cover you, you would have suffered much from the sun."

It was hard for her to admit it, but she had known after the first hour in the saddle that he'd been right about their apparel. His sheik's clothing may have looked foreign to her, but it was very practical in this climate.

"With time I think you will come to see that I am not given to rash decisions or undisciplined actions." His gaze met and held hers.

"So you deliberately attacked our ship . . ."

He smiled slightly, a silver flame glowing in the depths of his eyes. "Of course. I knew the prize on board was of great worth."

Tori was unable to say a word in response. Though she knew she should hold herself in icy reserve, she felt herself begin to warm to him.

After a long, quiet pause, he touched her cheek with a gentle hand and said, "Come, let's enjoy ourselves. Welcome to my humble abode. Make yourself comfortable. I'm sure you must be tired and in need of refreshments."

His touch sent sensual awareness through Tori and her defenses began to crumble.

"I am," she agreed cautiously, moving farther inside to sit upon some pillows. She wasn't quite sure what to make of this change in Serad. He had dragged her out of the harem like she was his personal possession, yet now he was being very solicitous of her. Tori knew if she wasn't careful, she might come to care for him, and that was something she couldn't allow to happen.

There was no future for her with Serad. Her future was with her fiancé, Alexander Wakefield, in London. She had reminded herself of that continually since

366

they'd ridden out of Algiers so she wouldn't surrender to Serad's overwhelming attractiveness again. He might have her there alone in the middle of the desert, but she still had some control over what happened to her.

Serad dropped down easily on the cushions beside her, and after they'd washed their hands in the bowls provided by the servants, they dined on the delicacies provided. The servants returned some time later to tell Serad that they were departing, and he waved them off with little interest. Finally, the sun began to lower in the western sky, and they were alone.

"Would you care to bathe?" Serad asked. "The ride was a hot one, and the water of the pool is delightfully cool."

"I will bathe, if I may do so privately." She didn't trust herself with him in such an intimate setting.

"There is no one else about, Tori. We are alone."

"You're the one I was talking about."

"What is it you fear?"

"I'm not afraid of anything . . ." Tori argued too quickly, averting her gaze.

He gave a soft, meaningful laugh. He'd seen the spark in her eyes and felt a small thrill of triumph. "Could it be that you are afraid of what I make you feel? I've seen you without your clothing. I know how lovely your body is, and I know how responsive you are when I touch you . . ." He ran a caressing hand down her arm, going slow, being gentle with her.

She flushed with heat at his words. It was true, and he knew it. It was frightening to think he had such power over her, but it was also exciting. Grasping for a last way to defend herself, she said, "I had meant to save myself for my betrothed. I was to come to him untouched."

Her words pained his conscience. He stiffened and

367

dropped his hand away from her. When he spoke, his tone was reserved, "Come. I'll take you only as far as the water's edge."

Without speaking she got to her feet and Serad stood, too. He led her out of the tent and down to the water, but did not touch her again.

As they walked side by side in the moonlight, Tori wanted to tell Serad that she didn't want to bathe, that all she wanted to do was to go back to the harem with Jonesey. She stopped herself, though, for she realized it would be a lie. As irritating a man as Serad was, she found him irresistible. As arrogant as he was, she needed to taste of his love another time.

Tori had wondered if the ecstasy they'd shared had been a dream. She had wondered if his lovemaking had really been that perfect, that arousing, that exciting. She had wondered, and now as he walked slowly by her side, she knew. It had all been true. She couldn't stop her body from responding to him, even without any physical contact. This attraction she felt for him had grown more powerful with each passing minute. His nearness was exhilarating. She wanted him . . . in all ways, at all times.

Only a last thread of sanity remained, and it cautioned Tori to fight him. It reminded her of what he was and that she would find no lasting happiness with him. Tori ignored the warnings.

Chapter Twenty-Seven

Tori's words had cooled Serad's ardor and reaffirmed his determination to play the gentleman. He was resolved to prove to himself that he could be the kind of man his aunt wanted him to be. It wasn't that he particularly relished the idea, but it was somehow strangely important to him that he do so.

Serad was very conscious of Tori beside him. He knew the next few minutes were going to be the true test of his will. He wanted her desperately, yet if he could deny himself and not touch her, it would be a great victory for him. He would prove the kind of man he really was. It was not going to be easy, for at that very moment there was nothing he wanted to do more than strip the ugly, borrowed dress from her slender body and lay her down upon the warm desert sands.

With every step Tori took on her way to the water's edge, she was overwhelmingly aware of Serad's powerful male presence. Her need to be in his arms sharing his kiss was driving her to distraction. Having resisted him for so long, it troubled her that she now wanted that which she'd fought against. She didn't fully understand what it meant. She didn't recognize the longing for what it truly was.

"Enjoy your bath," Serad said abruptly as they reached the bank.

Tori was surprised by his words that sounded very much like a cool dismissal. She glanced up at him expectantly, and she was puzzled when he merely smiled at her, his expression curiously benign. She was astounded by the courtesy he was displaying.

Tori stared up at him in the dimness of the rapidly fading light, expecting to see . . . She wasn't sure just what, but *something*. Serad's handsome features proved unreadable, confusing her even more.

Serad assumed that she was standing there regarding him so silently and so seriously because she was waiting for him to give her the privacy she'd requested. It took a major effort of will on his part, but he finally turned around.

Tori was honestly shocked by his gentlemanly action. She frowned, then wondered why she had done so. Had she expected him to sweep her up in his arms and have his way with her? Had she expected him to take the decision from her? The thought was troubling. She wanted him badly, yet it seemed that he was not going to press his attentions on her at all. Perplexed, Tori realized that she did have all the privacy she needed for her bath and she went on with that, quickly shedding the gown and letting it drop to the sand. Completely naked, Tori moved into the welcoming water. It felt like liquid velvet on her skin, and she sighed in appreciation. As it washed over her in a gentle caress, she moved out to a deeper area and slipped beneath the surface to wet her hair.

Serad was doing battle with himself. He'd known it wasn't going to be easy to ignore her while she bathed in the pool behind him, but he'd never thought it would be this hard. Vision after vision of her slim, naked form slipped into his thoughts, and his body heated in remembrance. He remembered, too, the time on board the *Scimitar* when he'd considered sharing her bath with her. That memory alone left him heavy with passion and almost ready to throw his resolve to the wind and go after her. Instead, he stared up at the sky and began to count the multitudes of twinkling stars.

It was then that Serad heard Tori's sigh. It sounded so sensual that a muscle worked in his jaw as he fought to maintain restraint. In a gesture of defense, he crossed his arms across his chest.

Tori stood up in the water, and her long hair sleeked back from her face in dripping splendor. She seemed a water nymph, the innocent seductive beauty of the deep. She glanced up toward Serad and found she was unable to tear her eyes away. In the fading light, he appeared a tall, proud silhouette against the cloudless evening sky. Tori's pulses quickened as she gazed at his broad-shouldered form and her heart began to beat a thundering rhythm. He looked the majestic warrior, the brave, indomitable male. In that moment, she realized that she loved Serad beyond all reason and all logic.

His name escaped her lips in a whisper.

Serad was confident he was going to do this. He was not going to turn around and look at Tori, even though he wanted to so very much. He was not going to charge out into the middle of the pool like a wild man and take her in his arms and make passionate love to her. He wasn't. No, he wasn't. He was going to stand there and continue to stare up at the heavens, asking God why he was doing this to himself. He remembered hearing once that harsh self-discipline was good for the soul, and he knew by the time Tori's bath was over, his soul was going to be in very good condition. But then, he heard her sigh his name.

Like a sailor of old mesmerized by a siren's song,

Serad turned. Tori stood in waist-deep water, a slender, pale enchantress risen from the deep. He started to go to her, then in a last desperate attempt to control himself, he clenched his jaw and stopped right where he was.

"What is it, Tori? Do you need something?" He barely recognized his own voice, so harsh with desire was it.

Tori had hoped he would understand her unspoken invitation and just come to her. When he didn't, she wasn't quite sure what to do, and she felt embarrassed at his question. How could she tell him she wanted him to make love to her? She was afraid to say the words out loud, so in the language of lovers through the ages, she simply lifted her hand to him in a silent gesture of invitation.

Serad stared at her in shock. He wasn't going to do this. He had to stop himself. He had to . . .

The hell he did! This was what he'd wanted. This was what he'd been prepared to wait for. He'd wanted Tori to come to him, and she was—now, here, tonight.

Mindless to the fact that he was still dressed, Serad walked straight out into the water. With great care, he picked her up in his arms and kissed her. His mouth slanted across hers with arousing force as he crushed her wet body to him. Holding her tightly against him, he carried her from the pool.

Serad took no notice of his drenched clothing. He was focused solely on Tori and the hours to come and he strode without pause to the tent. She had come to him of her own free will! His heart sang. Kicking aside the tent's doorflap, he strode inside and knelt to lay her upon the rich, plush rugs. Her arms clung to his neck as he would have moved away to shed his clothes, and so encouraged, he kissed her again like a starving man at feast.

Tori thrilled to his exciting embrace. She was filled with longings as old as the sun, and she knew Serad was the only man who could make her feel this way. She loved him . . . As terrible a truth as it was to her, she finally admitted it to herself. This pirate . . . this desert prince . . . this mysterious sheik had stolen her heart, and she would be his forever in all ways.

The moon had risen and was lighting the night with its soft, mellow glow. Inside the tent, in the sanctity of their love retreat, there was just enough illumination for Serad to see the beads of water that still glistened tantalizingly on Tori's skin. In arousing, erotic play, he began to kiss and lick each tiny droplet from her body. His lips forged paths of feverish excitement upon her willing flesh until she was moaning aloud in frenzy of need.

"Oh, Serad . . . Please . . ."

"Please what, Tori?" He rose up above her to gaze down at her. He could see the need in her eyes, but he had to hear her say it. He had to know that this was what she wanted.

His demand was torture for her. She didn't understand why she had to say it out loud. "Please . . ." she whispered raggedly.

"No, love, I have to hear the words from you. Tell me, Tori. What is it you want from me?" he urged in a deep voice that was gruff with sensuality as his hand sought the soft, round fullness of one breast. He teased the hard peak with knowing caresses.

"Make love to me, Serad. I need to . . ." She didn't finish her thought as he pressed a heated kiss to the taut crest.

"You need to *what,* Tori?" Serad asked as he nuzzled at her breast and then at the throbbing pulse at her throat.

She arched as he continued to work his magic with

373

his hands. He stoked the fire of her desire until she was nearly mindless, and it didn't matter what was said, it only mattered that he filled her with his strength and made her his once more. "I need to have you inside me . . ." she finally blurted out in her weakness.

Her words sent a lightning shaft of desire through him, and he could wait no longer.

Serad undressed and then returned to her. He sought her lips with his as he slipped his hands beneath her hips. He lifted her to him and drove home the proof of his claim upon her. Tori was his, and he would never let her go.

Any logical thinking was wiped from his mind as he thrust deep inside her. When her arms encircled him, encouraging him on, he obliged. His kiss was a blazing imitation of his body's actions and she reveled in it. She lifted her legs to wrap them about his waist and when she did, Serad gave a groan of ecstasy as he rolled sideways, bringing her with him. He continued to move within her, celebrating their coming together. His hands sought her breasts as his hips ground against hers. They were one in body, and it was perfect.

The fierceness of his loving possession took Tori over the precipice. The heat within her erupted in a glorious explosion of ecstasy. All thought was lost. She could only *feel* as surges of pure rapture vibrated through her.

"Serad!" She cried out his name as she clung to his broad shoulders.

Knowing that he'd brought her pleasure completed the perfection of the moment for Serad. He sought his own release then, plunging deeper into her hungry body. He matched her in that wonderful joy, attaining the heights of love as his body pulsed within her.

Serad kept his arms wrapped around her as they soared to oblivion together. Complete in each other, they tasted of love's delight and then drifted to the peace just beyond.

The night hours passed in rapturous bliss as they sought and found ecstasy again and again. Sometime after midnight, Serad rose and drew Tori up with him.

"Where are we going?" she asked, clinging to his side, never wanting to be apart from him again.

"Since you didn't get to bathe earlier, I thought we could do it now . . . together."

His idea left Tori feeling decidedly wicked, but tonight there would be no modest protests or fears. Tonight she was on a sensual exploration with the man she wanted and she would not resist him in any way.

The water felt chilly against their love-heated flesh. Tori shivered, but she wasn't sure if it was from the water or from the excitement that urged her onward.

"Put your arms around my neck," he told her, suddenly deciding that bathing was the last thing he wanted to do with her.

Tori went to him and eagerly did as she was told. The almost fiery heat of his chest against her cool breasts aroused her and she moved against him, enjoying the water swirling about her.

Serad surprised her when he took her by the waist and lifted her, guiding her legs to link them about his hips. She stared at him in wide-eyed wonder over the intimacy of that contact. Her soft vulnerability was open to him without barrier, without defense, and his masculine pride was ready and waiting to enter her feminine enclave.

They said no more as he braced himself and then slipped easily within her. The contrast between her hot, tight body surrounding and holding him and the cold water left him nearly ready to explode. He began to move, unable to help himself.

The motion of the water about them added to the

sensuality of their mating, and Tori had never imagined anything could feel so wonderful. Between his kisses and caresses and the water's silken touch, her senses were crying out for satisfaction. Serad thrust hungrily into her waiting womanhood, giving her all of himself.

Caught up in the power of their joining, they reached the pinnacle together, each wanting to give the other equal joy. Tori collapsed against his chest, sobbing in the aftermath of ecstasy.

No more thought was given to bathing as Serad shifted her to his arms and carried her back to the warm seclusion of the tent. He had always known that this place was special and now he knew why. Forever, he would remember this night and the wonder of Tori. She had come to him and given herself freely. It had been heaven for him.

Tori could not believe the breathless beauty of what had just transpired between them. When he lay her down upon the rugs again and moved away from her, she uttered her protest at this separation from him.

"Serad . . ." She called his name, wondering why he was moving away from her.

"I have a gift for you . . ." he said in a husky voice as he retrieved the emerald necklace he'd meant to give her the day before. Tonight, now, was the perfect time to replace the necklace he'd taken from her and thrown to the bottom of the sea. Tonight was the time to replace that Englishman in her heart. She was his now. There was no way she could claim to love another and respond to him as she did.

"A gift?"

He returned to her with the treasure in his hand. "I bought this for you. It reminded me of you." He held it up so she could see it, and she gasped at the beauty of the precious gem.

"It's lovely," she exclaimed in awe, touching it gently as he placed it around her neck.

Serad fastened the chain and then bent in a deliciously sensual move to kiss the stone where it lay nestled between her breasts. It was a simple matter to continue his caresses, and Tori arched in ecstasy as he kissed her breasts, too. They came together once again in a flawless blending of hard and soft. The victor became the vanquished as he claimed her and she took all he could give. Sated, they slept.

Dawn came and Serad roused to find Tori still slumbering by his side. The new day called to him, and taking great care not to rouse her, he slipped from the bed, dressed, and went outside to enjoy the freshness of the morning. He thought of the night just past and smiled. It had been a pure paradise to love her. He knew in that moment that no matter what, he could never let her go.

He tended to their horses and then retrieved his rifle and set about cleaning it. It was some time later when he looked up to find Tori standing in the door of the tent, holding the flap before her to shield her lovely body from his view.

He chuckled at this renewed sense of modesty on her part as he went to greet her. "You've slept well this morning," he said as he came to stand before her. He lifted one hand to caress her cheek.

"I had reason to," she replied with a soft smile. "I was up very late last night."

"Perhaps we should make a practice of sleeping away the morning?"

Serad's smile was gentle and loving, and Tori felt her heartbeat quicken. She had no regrets about what had passed between them last night. She loved him.

"Or perhaps," he continued, "we should never leave our bed at all?" His gaze darkened as it dropped to the glittering jewel that named her as his. He brushed the tent flap away from the front of her so she stood in all her naked splendor before him in the daylight. His eyes caressed her, traveling from the beauty of her bosom to the curve of her waist and her trim thighs. Her legs were long and shapely, and the memory of them locked about his waist stirred his passions again.

As he realized the direction of his thoughts, Serad gave himself a fierce mental shake. Want her though he did, there were other things he'd planned for them to do today. A wry smile curved his lips as he realized how very easy it would be to take her back to his bed and never get up again.

"Come, let's ride this morning," he invited as he moved inside the tent.

"Ride?" Her eyes rounded at his invitation. She had thought from the intensity of his regard that he'd wanted to make love again.

"I am eager to see if your boast is true. I only need to saddle the horses and we can go. I await your pleasure," Serad told her.

Tori gave a small laugh. "There are few things I enjoy more than riding, but I fear I have not suitable clothing."

"What do you normally wear to ride?"

"I have riding habits at home . . . skirts that are split so I can ride astride," she explained.

He looked thoughtful, then went to his small trunk of clothing and handed her a pair of his trousers and one of his tunics. "I'm sure they're far too big for you, but if you roll up the bottoms they will do for today."

Tori pulled on Serad's clothes and couldn't help but laugh as she practically drowned in them. She rolled long cuffs on the pants and sleeves, and when he gave her a belt it helped make the tunic look more like a dress. She knew she looked silly, but it was worth it if she got to ride. It had been months since she'd last ridden, and she could hardly wait to sit a horse again.

Serad's eyes went over her with amusement, noting the way she practically wallowed in his clothing. "I'll always prefer you in silk, but it will pass for today."

Tori longed the entire time for her riding boots, but made do with her own low-heeled shoes. Serad had gone out ahead of her to saddle the horses, and when she joined him they were tied up and ready to be ridden. He helped her mount and was surprised when she chose to ride astraddle. Swinging up on his own mare, Serad led the way from the oasis. He kept the pace slow at first to make sure she was a good rider, and then with that proven, he put his heels to the mare's side and they rode to the wind.

Tori was in heaven. She was dressed like a boy and riding astride. It was her favorite way to ride, though it had always drawn disfavor from her father and from Jonesey. She enjoyed the feeling of freedom that was hers as she pursued him across the desert sands. The ride was invigorating and stimulating as he challenged her on horseback and she matched him stride for stride. Only the proof of Serad's superior mount spelled the difference, and by the time they returned to their camp, she had earned his respect for her riding ability.

"You never cease to surprise me, Tori," Serad told her as they reined in at the oasis. "You were very honest in your estimation of your skill."

She smiled, pleased by his comment. "Someday, I will have a horse the equal of yours, and then we will see who the real horseman is."

"I'll look forward to the challenge."

*   *   *

379

They shared a light midday meal and then he decided to see if she was as good with a gun as she had been on a horse.

"I recall you bragged also of your talent with a gun," Serad commented as he came to her side holding two rifles. "Are you willing to take this dare?"

The fact that he trusted her enough to give her a gun made her feel good, and she grinned at him proudly. "Of course, just set your target. It's been a few months since I last hunted tiger in India, but I don't think I've forgotten how to shoot."

The news that she had hunted tiger impressed him, and Tori again won further respect from him with her marksmanship. He realized with some chagrin that he'd been very lucky she hadn't wanted to shoot him first and talk later that day in the cabin on the *Scimitar!*

Tori knew she couldn't wear Serad's clothing on the return trip to Algiers. Going to his trunk, she found that he'd brought the emerald garment along and she put it on. When Serad entered the tent moments later, he went completely still.

She was mesmerizing in the emerald silk, and the necklace he'd given her sparkled in the light. She looked as he'd thought she would look that first night she had come to him, and he went to her without pause.

There could be no denying his desire for her. Every minute he was with her, he wanted her. She was unlike any woman he'd ever known, and the thought that she'd put on the silk garment to please him stirred him to take her in his arms. They came together in ecstasy, knowing this was their last chance to enjoy the privacy of their desert paradise before it was time to leave for Algiers . . .

As the sun had begun its westerly descent, the servants arrived to dismantle their camp, and Serad and Tori rode for the city. She was wearing Jonesey's dress again. As he watched her riding her own mount proudly beside him, Serad vowed to find her some practical clothing for accompanying him in the desert. Certainly, this would not be their one and only trip to the oasis, and though Algierian women did not ride with their husbands, Tori was different. He wanted her with him and he intended that they would ride together often in the future.

Malik shot Hasim a strange look as he digested what he'd just been told. "You're certain about this?"

"I know it's hard to believe, but it's true," Hasim reaffirmed. "I went to speak with Serad about the trouble you've been having with Muhammed Ibn Abbas, and that's when I found out from his servants that he'd taken the Englishwoman and gone into the desert."

"He took the woman into the desert . . ." The dey gave a disbelieving shake of his head before remarking thoughtfully, "I believe my other son has fallen in love."

"I believe you're right." Hasim smiled knowingly.

"It is about time. Do you know when he'll return?"

"Tonight," Hasim answered.

"Then we will delay your departure until then, but no later." His expression turned serious as he thought of his old enemy Muhammed and the threatening news they'd just heard concerning his activities.

Almira sought out her mistress with the gossip she'd heard about Serad just as soon as she could, for she knew how concerned Rabi was about her nephew and his captives.

"You're certain about this?" Rabi asked, her expression bleak after listening to the tale of her nephew's activities.

"Yes, Rabi."

"I see." She realized sadly that her words of warning to Serad had not touched him as she'd hoped, and it filled her with despair.

"They are supposed to be returning from the desert tonight."

"Thank you, Almira."

"There is something else, Rabi . . ."

"Yes?"

"I have also heard that Malik is planning to send Serad on a trip with Hasim this very day and that they should be away for almost a week."

Rabi's eyes narrowed thoughtfully as she came to understand what the servant was telling her and what she had to do. "Almira . . . is it possible?" There was no need for her to say more, for she knew what her mistress wanted.

"I have made all the contacts that are necessary."

"Then we must act. The sooner the better."

Chapter Twenty-Eight

Serad and Tori returned to the city at dark, and she went willingly to the harem to bathe and change clothes while Serad retired to his own chambers. There he found his servant waiting for him with the news that his aunt needed him. His first fearful thought was that she was ill, and he left to see her immediately.

Rabi was upset. During her previous talk with Serad when she'd scolded him about his behavior, she'd hedged on telling him the complete truth behind their remaining in Algiers all these years. After hearing of his activities with his young captive, though, she'd known it was now time to have it out with him. She'd sent Almira to his home with the message for him to come to her as soon as he returned, and she waited for him now.

As disturbed as Rabi was with Serad's failure to heed her words, she was also nervous about what she was going to say to him when he finally did come to see her. Malik's threat to separate them, along with her fear of Avery and what he might do if he found out they were alive, had kept her silent for all these years. She had never forgotten her brother's vicious betrayal. She realized Avery could be in London right now, living the high life, and if so, she and Serad might face grave danger if they ever managed to return.

But returning to England and their family was not something Rabi thought would ever happen. Serad was very happy with his life in Algiers. As the son of the dey and very successful corsair *reis,* Serad had just about everything a man could want and seemed truly a North African now, but even so in her heart and soul, she still thought of him as Alexander and always would. Though it hurt her to admit it to herself, she doubted his title and inheritance in England would hold any great attraction for him. Still, Rabi knew the time had come when she had to be completely truthful with him, if not for his own sake, then for the sake of the girl he held hostage.

"Aunt Rabi?" Serad was relieved when he found her at her favorite place in the garden. "Are you well?"

Rabi didn't say a word at first, but just turned to look at him. He was used to finding love, approval, and affection in her regard, and the sadness he saw mirrored there in her gaze unsettled him.

"I'm, fine," she answered slowly. "I sent for you because it's time we had a talk . . . a very serious talk."

Serad stiffened; he could never remember her acting this way. "What do you mean, Aunt Rabi?"

"I want you to know that you are Alexander Wakefield, the future duke of Huntington," Rabi said quickly, sorrowfully, "and I cannot tell you just how disappointed I am over what you've done."

Alexander . . . The name touched a chord in his heart. He remembered bits and pieces, but he knew there was a lot he'd forgotten. Still, he was a full-grown man now, a captain of a ship. He had a life he enjoyed in Algiers. Why should he care about the past? His life was here and now. His aunt's criticism hurt, though, and he had to defend himself. "What I have or have not

384

done does not concern you."

"But it surely does!" Rabi returned. He was still her nephew, and she had raised him. "I never thought that you would do to someone else exactly what had been done to me . . ."

Serad looked confused. "I don't understand."

"Twenty years ago, I was young and so very innocent. At the time, I lived at Huntington House with you and my father. It was a safe and wonderful existence. I was engaged to be married to Lord Gerald Ratcliff, the man of my dreams, the man I loved."

"Why are you telling me this?" he ventured cautiously.

"Because it's time you heard the complete truth."

"The complete truth? I don't understand."

Rabi told him everything, beginning with Avery's betrayal and how they'd ended up on the ship bound for France and then on to how Muhammed had captured them and taken them as prisoners to Algiers . . . and to Malik. When she mentioned their escape attempt from the palace after they'd been given to Malik as payment of tribute, she saw a flicker of remembrance in his eyes.

"From that night on, after Malik found us and brought us back here, he forbid me to use our real names or speak of our past. He said that if I did, he would separate us and I would never see you again. It was a threat I took very seriously, and I'm taking a great chance even now by revealing all of this to you, but I feel the time has come when I must speak out. I cannot allow you to destroy the life of the young woman you are now keeping in your harem, and you will do that if you do not let her go home to her family. You must release her, Alexander. You *must*," Rabi deliberately used his English name to jar him.

"Have you been that miserable here with Malik? Are

you truly that unhappy?" he asked, his eyes dark as he reflected on her words. He had always thought Malik to be a fair and honest man, and this tale of behavior that was almost ruthless on his part was troubling.

"No . . . no. Malik has always treated me with the utmost of respect and kindness. But what I want you to understand is that I had no choice in any of this. I was forced to give up *my life* . . ."

"Then you are unhappy," he concluded.

"No. I am not unhappy, but who knows what kind of a life I might have led if I'd been allowed to go home. Don't you understand? My life, my family, and the freedom to choose my own future were all brutally taken from me. My happiness was stolen, and I was never given the chance to get it back." Her eyes reflected the longings of her soul, and the secret heartache she'd lived with all these years. She'd remained there in the harem as Malik's lover, but had always refused his offers of marriage, for she believed in her heart that she still belonged to Gerald.

Serad was filled with conflicting emotions as he met her eyes. He wanted Tori. He didn't want to free her. Yet, his aunt's story had shown him another side of the situation, and the pain and suffering his actions could ultimately cause. He grew deeply troubled. When he'd returned from the oasis, he'd thought his life was near to perfect. Tori had come to him willingly, and they had made passionate love without restraint. Now, all that was changed.

"Then you've never really loved Malik?" he challenged.

"Don't you understand? Someone else planned my life for me. I was never given the chance to choose for myself," she answered slowly.

"Is it really so terrible for you here?"

"A cage, gilded or not, is still a cage. But it's not me

we're talking about now, it's too late for me. But there's still Tori. Give her her freedom. Allow her to return to her family and her future. What you've done is wrong . . . so terribly wrong!"

"But I want her, and she wants me," Serad defended himself.

"And I'm sure you gave her a choice between sharing your bed and going home, didn't you?" she demanded of him fiercely, forcing him to see things from a different perspective. "What right do you have to take from her all she holds precious?"

"Malik did that to you?"

"He wanted me as you want Tori."

Her statement was simple, but it filled him with turmoil. He had thought by making Tori want him that he had won a great victory, but his prize now seemed meaningless. Given the choice, would Tori stay or go? And, more importantly, was he man enough to give her the choice?

Serad abruptly excused himself and left her. Rabi watched him go. Her heart was aching for him, but she knew she'd done the right thing.

Hasim called out to Serad as he saw him making his way from the palace. He was startled when his brother gave him a surly look.

"What is it?" he asked harshly. He had hoped to find someplace where he could think in solitude.

"Father wants to see you. In fact, we've both been looking for you for a day and a half now."

"Is there trouble?"

"Yes. Our informants have told us that Muhammed has plans to assassinate Father. He's refused to pay tribute and has begun to attack our ships in the waters to the west," Hasim explained quickly as they headed for Malik's chambers.

"Why now after all these years?"

"No one knows for sure."

"Does Malik have a plan of what he wants us to do?"

"Yes, that's what he's been waiting to talk with you about."

Serad nodded in understanding.

Malik was pleased when the servant announced that his two sons had come to him. He met them in a small audience chamber and quickly filled Serad in on the details of Muhammed's treacherous villainy.

"I've always known the man hated me and was my undeclared enemy, so his actions do not altogether surprise me. What does surprise me is that he waited so long."

"What do you want us to do?"

Malik outlined his plan. He knew Muhammed was operating out of a certain area off the coast, and he wanted the *Scimitar* to go after him.

"Hasim will sail with you and take whatever else you think you'll need. How soon can you be ready to leave?"

"I'll contact Tariq right away, and then once the crew is on board, we can sail immediately."

"Fine. I will be looking forward to hearing of your success."

"So will I," Serad agreed. As he spoke, a memory flashed in his mind of Muhammed looming over him and his aunt all those years ago. When he left Malik and Hasim to prepare for the voyage, Serad couldn't help but think that in bringing Muhammed to his just end, he would also, in a way, be seeking some revenge of his own.

*   *   *

Tori was in the harem waiting eagerly for Serad to send for her. She had bathed and perfumed herself, and, with Oma's help, she'd donned a native dress just to please him. She wanted to look her best. Her spirits had been bright since they'd returned from the oasis, and any time a less than pleasant thought appeared on the horizon of her mind to mar her happiness, she pushed it aside. She loved Serad. He had been kind and attentive and wonderful, and she had thrown all caution to the wind and allowed herself to care for him. She could hardly wait to be in his arms again.

Jonesey had been very worried about her while she'd been gone, but Tori had convinced her that everything was fine. Though the older woman had remained concerned, she'd held her tongue and decided to wait and see what would happen.

Tori was sitting in her bedchamber, biding her time, when Oma appeared, carrying a dinner tray.

"Where is Serad? Am I not going to dine with him tonight?" she asked in confusion, a little hurt by what she perceived as a rejection. She had imagined they would share a quiet meal and then spend another heavenly night in each other's arms.

"No. He is leaving within the next hour and will be gone for some time," Oma replied.

"What?" Tori was shocked. *How could he be leaving?* "Doesn't he want to see me?"

"No. He did not request you."

Her answer outraged Tori. How could Serad not want to see her after what they'd just shared? How could Oma stand there and tell her so calmly that he was leaving? For a moment, Tori knew a terrible sense of forboding, but she shoved it away. She was confident that there had to be some mistake, so she boldly announced, "Then I will go to him."

"I do not think that would be wise . . ." Oma began,

but she was too late, Tori was already out of the room and heading for Serad's bedchamber.

"Serad?" Tori said his name as she came through the door without preamble. "Oma said that you were leaving and . . ." She stopped as she found him in conversation with the man she knew as Tariq from the ship. His servant was also there, packing a trunk for him.

Serad, Tariq, and the servant all looked up in shock. It was unheard of for a woman to venture from the harem to seek out a man.

"What are you doing here?" Serad demanded. Even though he was irritated by the intrusion, for it distracted him from concentrating on the deadliness of his upcoming mission, he couldn't help but think of how absolutely gorgeous Tori looked in the Algierian gown. He was sure she'd worn it just for him, and he suffered an immediate and potent jolt of desire. With an effort, he fought it down.

"Serad . . . I . . ." Tori swallowed nervously. The cold-eyed man she faced was not the same man she'd spent several days making love with.

"I did not send for you." He was worried about Malik and still feeling the pain from his aunt's story. The last thing he'd needed right then was to see Tori and be reminded of just how much he wanted her.

"I know, but . . ."

"I will take her back to the harem," the servant offered.

"Fine, do that. Then return and finish what you were doing," Serad dictated.

So abruptly and arrogantly dismissed, Tori suddenly felt violently ill. Her love for him had been a folly. He hadn't really changed. Serad was just what she'd always thought he was—a barbaric pirate and nothing more. She had romanticized him into someone who didn't exist. She was his possession to be used and discarded at his whim. He had told her that often enough. How could she have forgotten?

Straightening her shoulders, Tori turned without another word and left Serad's chambers. She had come to tell him that she missed him. Now, she was leaving heartbroken in the knowledge that she'd never meant anything more to him than any one of his other servants. Biting her lip to quell her tears, she didn't wait for the servant to lead her, but returned to the harem ahead of him.

Serad had seen her expression change from one of happiness to hurt, and though he longed to take her in his arms and tell her everything would be all right, he couldn't right then. Vowing to talk to her later, he turned his attention back to Tariq and went on with their planning.

Rabi passed a troubled evening. She had no idea what effect her talk with Serad had on him, and while she hoped it would make a difference, she feared deep down inside that it wouldn't, for he had been under the male-dominated Algerian influence for far too long.

When Almira confirmed for her later that night that Serad had left his home and was readying the *Scimitar* to sail on orders from Malik, she put her plan to free Tori and her companion into action. Knowing that it was essential her efforts be kept in strictest secret, she had Almira make all the necessary contacts to smooth the escape of the two Englishwomen to freedom. Fearful of putting anything into writing lest Malik discover her intrigue, Rabi sent her messages strictly by word of mouth.

First, Rabi notified the Redemptorist Fathers, who worked in the city arranging for the ransom and return of Christian captives, that there would be two women coming to them soon and that they should be prepared to rush them out of Algiers as quickly as possible. When word came back from the priests late that very night that a ship would be leaving for London the very next afternoon, Rabi knew she had to press onward. She waited until after midnight and then sent Almira to Serad's home.

Tori was lying on her bed, unable to sleep, staring off into the darkness with sightless eyes. She felt trapped and miserable. She had not spoken to Jonesey since returning from her ill-fated attempt to see Serad, and she was glad. She didn't think she would have been able to bear it if the other woman had witnessed her pain. A sound just outside her window drew her attention, and Tori rose from her bed to see what or who was there.

"Are you Tori?" a woman's hushed voice called.

"Yes . . ." Tori could make out the image of a woman dressed in the traditional Algerian garb, her face and head covered with her haik so that only her eyes showed.

"I must speak with you. It is urgent."

Tori was at a loss to imagine just who this could be or what she wanted. "Why?"

"I've been sent here to help you escape from Algiers," the voice responded softly. "We must talk privately. We can't let anyone know . . ."

Tori left the window and rushed outside to meet with the woman. She was careful to make sure she wasn't observed. She didn't know who this woman was, but she felt certain she was a godsend.

"I know that you and your companion are here against your will, and I've come to tell you that arrangements have been made to help you leave here tonight and sail for home tomorrow."

"Who would do this for me? And why?"

"That is not for you to know. Only know that it is someone who understands your situation and wants to offer you comfort. Will you go?"

"Yes." Tori needed no time to think about that decision.

"What of your companion?"

"She'll go, too. There's no need to even ask."

"Good. Be quiet then, for we can't risk rousing any of Serad's servants. Dress as I am dressed so you won't draw any attention to yourself while we make the journey through the streets. I'll wait here for you, but we must leave quickly."

"I understand, and I thank you."

Tori went back inside, making sure that her movements were furtive and silent. She sought out the sleeping Jonesey and woke the older woman with care.

"Miss Victoria! What is it?"

"Shhh . . ." Tori held a finger up to her lips to silence her. "Keep your voice down. There's someone here who says they can help us escape."

"What?"

"She's waiting for us in the court, but we have to hurry and dress."

"We're going home?"

"That's what she said. Come on, we must go while we have the chance."

Jonesey threw on her clothes and then followed Tori to her bedchamber, where she donned one of the robelike garments, too. That done, they crept from the harem and out into the court where the mysterious woman waited.

Almira had secluded herself behind some foliage and when she saw the two women appear, she went out to get them. "Stay close behind me and look neither left nor right. Keep your eyes down as much as possible. You didn't forget anything, did you?" she asked as they

393

moved quietly from the house.

Tori cast one last glance back at the house. She thought of how happy she'd been when she'd returned from the desert, and she thought of the heartbreak that had been hers for daring to dream.

"No. I haven't forgotten a thing," Tori answered flatly.

But as she disappeared into the night, she couldn't help but question the empty feeling inside her and wonder if she'd left her heart behind.

It had been four days since the *Scimitar* had sailed from Algiers, and Serad and Hasim felt certain that they were closing in on Muhammed and his band of traitorous cutthroats. The crew of the *Scimitar* was ready and willing to fight, for they loved Malik *Dey* and gave him their full allegiance. With speed and intent, they scoured the seas where Malik had told them Muhammed had been plying his devilry, and they were rewarded for their search late that afternoon when the lookout spotted the other ship.

Serad's orders were fast and succinct as he prepared to attack. Sails were set and the course laid out. Fleet as they were, they intercepted the evil pirate's ship and the fighting began. The struggle that ensued was a fierce and ugly one. When the smoke had cleared, Muhammed's vessel was mortally wounded and sinking fast. Darkness fell across the waters and hampered their efforts to find survivors from the other ship. By the time dawn came, there was nothing left to mark Muhammed's grave.

The *Scimitar* had sustained some damage in the battle. Though she would be sailing home far more slowly than she'd sailed out, the general mood on board was good. Hasim was well satisfied with the outcome of the battle, and he knew his father would also be pleased that his arch enemy had been killed.

Serad's mood, however, did not match that of the other men, and he had retired to his cabin for much-needed solitude. Now that the challenge of Muhammed had been met and dealt with, he had time to think. It was not a pleasant thing for him to have to face, this forfeiting of a treasure so valued. The more he considered the decision he had to make the more torn he became.

Serad tried to tell himself that all women were alike, that Tori was no more special than the next, but he knew that was not true. She *was* special. She was wonderful. As he looked around the cabin he was inundated with memories of the days and nights they'd spent here . . . of her sleeping on the floor in defiance of him, of her bathing in his tub, and finally, annoyingly, of the moment when he'd torn the proof of the other man's claim upon her from around her neck. Even now he felt the pang of resentment for the unknown man, and he acknowledged that he had come to care deeply for her . . . that he had come to *love* her.

That thought, so unbidden, struck Serad suddenly and forcefully. He was jarred to the very depths of his soul by the revelation and could only stare about himself in bewilderment. *Love? He loved her?*

Serad felt as if a great weight had been lifted from his shoulders as he accepted the truth of his feelings for Tori. But at the very same time he felt even more confused, for his aunt's chastisements were still battering his conscience. If he loved Tori, and he knew now that he did, how could he not want what was best for her? If he loved her, wouldn't he have to be honorable enough to allow her to make her own decisions about her life?

Facing up to the facts, Serad made his decision. In

loving Tori, he would have to put her needs ahead of his. He would have to care for her before himself. He would have to give her what she most wanted—her freedom, and then when she had it, he would ask her to stay with him and be his wife. Serad knew he would eventually have to tell her the rest of his life's story, but he would do that later after everything had been settled between them.

His outlook much improved, Serad left his cabin to seek out Hasim and Tariq. He found his second-in-command first.

"Tariq! Is there any way to hurry the repairs on the *Scimitar* so we can put into Algiers more quickly?" Serad asked, a fire burning hotly within him now that he had made up his mind what to do. He felt he couldn't possibly get home to Tori fast enough. He was sorry now that he had been so terse with her before he'd left, and he knew he would have to apologize for that before he did anything else. But that didn't matter, all that mattered was seeing her again, holding her close and telling her of his love.

"We're doing all we can, Serad," his friend responded. "Why the sudden urgency to return home?"

"Yes, my brother, could it be that there is a special reason why you are in such a hurry to get back?" Hasim asked as he joined them where they stood by the rail near the helm.

"You could say that," Serad answered with an easy smile.

Both Tariq and Hasim were surprised by his complete change in attitude. An hour or so before, Serad had been surly. Now, he seemed almost mild-mannered.

"What's happened since you went belowdecks to improve your mood so much?"

"What happened is that I made a decision, and now I

have only to follow through on it."

"A decision about Tori?" Hasim inquired.

He nodded. "I love her and I have made up my mind to ask her to be my wife."

"She is a beautiful woman," Tariq said agreeably, thinking of just how lovely she'd looked that evening when she'd come rushing uninvited into Serad's quarters. "A trifle headstrong, but I think you're man enough for the challenge."

"I'm sure he is," Hasim agreed.

Serad was pleased by their confidence in him. Yet, despite the passionate time he and Tori had spent at the oasis, he couldn't help but worry that when he offered her her freedom she would eagerly leave him and flee Algiers to return to the fiancé she claimed to love. The prospect haunted him, but he held firm in his resolve. Serad just wished his ship were undamaged so they could make the trip in more haste.

Chapter Twenty-Nine

When Oma and Zena had discovered Tori and Jonesey's disappearance the morning after Almira secreted them out of the harem, they'd been frantic to find them. They had enlisted the help of Serad's other servants in the search, but all to no avail. The two women had disappeared into the city without a trace, and Oma and Zena knew there would be trouble when Serad returned home and found out about it. They were not wrong.

Serad and Hasim met with Malik as soon as they reached Algiers to report on Muhammed's death. Though he hid it well before Malik and Hasim, Serad was uneasy during the entire audience. He was glad when it ended, and he could rush home to talk to Tori.

Serad knew what had to be done, and he wanted to be finished with it. His servants seemed unusually nervous when he first arrived home, and it puzzled him. It didn't for long, though, for he soon found out the cause when he requested Tori to be brought to him.

"I cannot bring her to you, Serad," his servant told him.

"Why not? Is she refusing to come to me again?" he asked with a light-hearted chuckle. He was certain that she was probably annoyed with him for the way he'd treated her before he left, but he was ready to make amends. "Carry her here, if need be."

"No, Serad. I cannot. It is not that she is refusing. It is that she's gone."

"What?!"

"Both women disappeared the day after you set sail."

Serad stared at the man in shock. "They're gone?" he repeated to make sure he'd heard him correctly.

"Yes. We searched the house and the city, but could find no trace of them."

Serad's eyes narrowed to dangerous slits as he regarded him. "How did this happen?"

"No one knows, Serad. Oma and Zena slept, as they always do. Sometime during that first night you were gone, the Englishwomen slipped from the house unobserved, and vanished. We tried everything to find them, but it was almost as if they had been wiped from the face of the earth."

A muscle in Serad's jaw worked as he fought to control the emotions that swept through him. After the time he and Tori had spent at the oasis, he'd thought things were different between them, but obviously, he'd been wrong. Still, he couldn't imagine where Tori could have gone. She had to be close by somewhere, and if she was hidden someplace in the heart of Algiers, she could be in real danger. The idea haunted him, and he rushed from his quarters to find the two female servants and question them further. He got little satisfaction from the interview, though, for they had seen nothing and heard nothing and knew nothing.

Stymied, Serad finally realized who he needed to talk to next. His Aunt Rabi might be able to help him. She might have an idea where Tori and Jonesey could have gone. He made his way to Malik's harem to find her.

Since she'd heard of the *Scimitar's* return, Rabi had been expecting Serad to come to her. Her manner was proudly regal as she came forth from her chambers to meet with him in the gardens.

"I see you have returned from your trip," she said almost too casually as she welcomed him back. "I've heard that your victory over Muhammed was complete."

"His ship was destroyed," Serad confirmed.

"That's good. I'm sure Malik is most pleased."

"I didn't come to talk about the trip or Malik," he finally admitted. "I've come because I need to talk to you about Tori."

"What about her?" Rabi deliberately turned her back on him and wandered over to stand by the fountain.

Serad followed her. "Aunt Rabi, she's disappeared, and I don't know where she's gone. I thought you might be the one person in all of Algiers who might be able to help me."

Rabi faced him, and her expression was serious as she answered him with complete honesty. "At this very moment, I would imagine she and her companion are nearly halfway home."

"She's really gone?" Serad stared at her in shock. He didn't know what he'd expected her to say, possibly that they were hidden somewhere in the city and that he would be able to find her and get her back that very day. It took him completely by surprise to find that his aunt knew about her disappearance and that Tori was actually gone from his life.

Rabi gave a proud lift of her chin as she met his regard. "She left Algiers shortly after you sailed."

Serad couldn't believe it. Tori was gone. He'd never gotten the chance to offer her her freedom or to tell her of his love. His anger flared and then died as he realized

400

quickly what he had to do. He couldn't let her go without telling her of his feelings. He had to go after her. "What ship did she sail on and when?"

"I can't tell you that. Just let her go, Serad. Please, let her go home." She softened her plea to him.

"I can't," he agonized, feeling desperate. How could he let Tori go when he needed her so badly?

"But you can. There are other women who would love to be in your harem and your life . . ."

"Aunt Rabi . . . you don't understand," he admitted painfully. "It's no longer a matter of *owning* Tori."

"Then what is it a matter of, if not to bring her back by force again and keep her in your harem?" she prodded, needing to know what was truly in his heart.

"I want her to be my wife."

"Oh? You plan to bestow upon her the *honor* of being your *first* wife—your first wife, no doubt, of many? I remind you, my nephew, that she is not a native woman of Algiers who will meekly accept such a fate. She is English, and, as such, the concept of sharing a husband with other females is ugly and humiliating. When we marry, it is one man and one woman, and it is forever."

"I know that, and I can accept that, but I can't let her leave. I have to go after her, Aunt Rabi. I have to tell her how I feel."

"And how *do* you feel?"

Serad lifted troubled eyes to hers. "I love her," he confessed.

"You love her?" Rabi was thrilled that he'd finally recognized and put the name to what he was feeling for Tori. Her eyes warmed as she gazed up at her nephew adoringly.

"Very much, but I never had the chance to tell her. I didn't even realize it until I had time to think about everything while we were at sea this past week. That's why I have to find her. I can't let her leave without telling her how I feel about her."

Rabi reached out to put a gentle, restraining hand on his arm. She was glad that he'd come to grips with his own emotions, but there was still Tori to consider. "But Serad . . . what if you find her and tell her of your love, and it makes no difference? What if she still wants to return to her home? Would you be able to let her go? Would you love her enough to put her happiness before your own?"

His eyes met hers and there was no evasion when he answered, "Yes. I would. I couldn't do anything else."

Rabi stood on tiptoes to press a loving kiss to his cheek, her heart swelling with love for him. "I do not know the name of the ship on which she sailed, but it left Algiers the day after you departed."

Serad left his aunt and began the painstaking task of discovering which vessel Tori and Jonesey had taken from Algiers. His frustration grew as each lead turned up nothing, and he was close to fury when late in the day he finally discovered the name of the slow-moving trading vessel they'd sailed on.

Once Serad knew the ship and its destination, he was like a man possessed, and there was no stopping him. Though the repairs to the *Scimitar* had been started, there was not enough time to fully restore her for the voyage. Serad didn't care. He calculated that the other ship's speed would still be far slower than theirs even with the damage and that they should be able to catch up to them long before they made landfall in England. He sent a brief message to Malik and Hasim explaining his plan of action and without bothering to wait for a reply sailed from the harbor that very night.

*   *   *

Captain Demorest of the British navy's frigate, *Bellwether,* heeded his lookout's call that a ship had been spotted on the horizon. Ever on the alert for raiders plying the heavily trafficked trading routes, they plotted an intercept course.

As the Englishmen prepared to intercept and identify them, Serad was watching them with a sense of great unease. The *Scimitar* had been at sea for almost two weeks now and had not met any other vessels. Serad had been pleased and had hoped it would stay that way until they found Tori. This appearance of the British navy ship worried him. His ship was still not at full speed or maneuverability. He did not want a fight that would end in a sure loss. He valued his men and his ship far too much to put them at such risk. He only wanted to find the merchantman and get his woman back, but it looked like fate had taken that simple course of action from him and replaced it with a far more dangerous one.

"Shall we change course to avoid them?" Tariq asked as he came to his *reis's* side.

Serad grew angry and frustrated as he considered his few alternatives. "Yes, but don't do anything that would draw their suspicion."

Tariq hurried to do as he'd directed, leaving Serad alone. Serad wanted to avoid a confrontation at all costs. They would continue on as quietly as possible and hope the other vessel made no attempt to stop them.

Serad's hope to slip peacefully away was dashed when Captain Demorest finally realized just who he had in his sights and went after them with a fire in his blood. Knowing they could not risk a fight, Serad raced to the helm to join Tariq.

"Shall we ready the guns, Serad *Reis?*" one of his men asked, ready to fight the English with all their might.

"No!" he ordered curtly, a heavy mantle of guilt settling on him. Had he given more thought to his men's safety he would not have rushed off after Tori as he had in a damaged ship. It was too late to deal with that, though. He could only try to escape the British frigate.

"No?" His crew was shocked.

"It would be suicide. We'll try to outrun and outmaneuver them. It's our one chance."

He and Tariq shared a worried look and then concentrated on matters at hand, pushing thoughts of Tori from his mind.

The moment Captain Demorest had identified the *Scimitar,* there had been no turning back. They'd heard of the ship and its master, and they were determined to see it off the high seas once and for all.

"Bring our guns to bear, men!" Demorest ordered as the *Bellwether* steadily gained on their prey.

The *Scimitar's* slowness puzzled him. Every rumor he'd heard about the vessel had mentioned its speed. This sluggishness made him cautious and all the more ready to use force. Serad was known for his remarkable seamanship, and Demorest didn't want to find out the hard way that the slow speed was just a ruse and all the tales of his sailing prowess had been true.

"Fire when ready!" Demorest followed up, wondering, too, why the corsairs were trying to get away. Everything he'd ever heard about them had led him to believe that they would turn and fight.

The *Bellwether's* guns roared into action. On board the *Scimitar,* Tariq looked to Serad for orders.

"Shall we return their fire?"

"No. Hard astarboard. Let's see if there's not *still* another way we can get out of this."

His men rushed to do as they were told. All knew the *Scimitar* was still not capable of her normal full speed or of her usual quick maneuverability and that they would have to rely on Serad *Reis's* abilities and a lot of luck to get them through this.

With Serad at the helm shouting out orders, they eluded the British barrages time after time. It was only through his superb ability to predict the English captain's moves that they managed to stay untouched by the vicious and continual attacks. But it was their lack of manageability that finally doomed them, for the *Bellwether* unleashed a broadside that tore through their riggings and left them completely dead in the water.

Serad was sickened by their defeat and by the knowledge that his own impulsive decision to leave port before the repairs had been completed had led them to this end.

"Shall we fight them, Serad *Reis?*" his men wanted to know.

Serad and Tariq watched the frigate draw near and saw them preparing their grappling hooks. They knew they were capable of killing more than their share of the British sailors if a fracas would erupt, but in the end there was still no way they could win.

"No. Don't offer any resistance," Serad called out. "There has been no bloodshed so far. Let's keep it that way."

Captain Demorest couldn't believe that he was actually about to board the infamous *Scimitar*. His ship and crew were the best, and he was proud of their effort. Even as he admired his own men's work in defeating the other vessel, he couldn't help but admire the actions of the other captain. He had never seen such a display of excellent seamanship. It was obvious the ship had sustained some kind of damage and was not capable of normal sailing, and he knew it was for that reason and that reason alone that he had won the victory that day.

When Demorest reached the deck of the *Scimitar,* he looked for the man who was the captain. He spied Serad standing regally near the helm and knew just by his bearing that he was the one. He noticed that each crew memeber was heavily armed with a scimitar and a pistol, but none of the weapons were raised in attack.

"Are you captain of this ship?"

"I am Serad, *reis* of the *Scimitar,"* he answered proudly.

"I am Captain Demorest, and I am placing you under arrest," he announced. He studied the man who stood before him, wondering at his nationality, for though he bore an Algerian name, he certainly didn't look North African. "Mr. Fox . . ."

At his command, one of his men came forth with irons and fastened them on Serad's wrists and ankles.

"What of my men and my ship?"

"Your men will be taken before the magistrate and he will decide their fate. Your ship is now the property of the Crown."

Serad nodded tersely. He was relieved that his men didn't face immediate death, but his relief did little to ease the pain of his failure. He knew he would not fare as well as his men, and the thought of losing the *Scimitar* was second only to the realization that he would never see Tori again.

Demorest studied the man standing before him. It seemed a terrible waste to put such an excellent strategist and sailor in chains and take him back to what he was sure would eventually be his execution, but he knew Serad was no ordinary sailor. He was a famous corsair who had wreaked havoc on the seas for many years. There would be many back in London who would celebrate his capture and his death.

Giving orders for the men of the *Scimitar* to be similarly bound, he set up one of his own officers with a skeleton crew to sail the wounded captive ship behind the *Bellwether* on the trek back to London. Their going would be slow on this their return trip, but the end acclaim would be worth it.

It was two days later when a merchant ship that traded regularly with Algiers passed the slow-moving *Bellwether* on its way to England with the captured *Scimitar* sailing behind it. Knowing Malik *Dey* would want to know of it, they increased their speed for that Barbary State.

Tori and Jonesey could hardly believe it as the shores of England came into view. They had made it back home safely! Their relief was tremendous, and they weren't sure whether to laugh or cry at this first sight of their homeland.

"What do we do once we reach port, Miss Victoria?" Jonesey asked.

"The good Fathers gave us enough money to hire a conveyance, Jonesey, so I think we should leave the ship immediately and go to my grandfather's town-house in the city."

"But what if he isn't there?"

"It won't matter. There's always a staff in residence, and if he's not in London, I'm sure they'll know where he can be reached."

Excitement shivered through both women as they waited for the ship to be tied up and the gangplank lowered. They hired a carriage without difficulty and were whisked away from the ugliness of the dockside life.

As they traversed the city on their way to the marquess's stately townhouse, their fears seemed to melt away. They were home. They were safe.

"Jonesey, I can hardly believe we're here. Everything almost seems unreal now. Like it happened to someone else . . ." Tori turned tear-filled eyes to her companion.

Jonesey could see how their captivity had worn on her young charge, and she reached out to take her hand reassuringly. "My darling, you handled yourself beautifully. I'm proud of you . . . very proud of you."

Tori drew a ragged breath as Serad entered her thoughts. She'd tried not to think about him, to keep from remembering their idyllic days in the desert together, and she'd managed fairly well until now. She stared out the window of the carriage, taking in all that was familiar to her, feeling herself return to being Lady Victoria Lawrence. Yet, even as she felt her true self return, there was a part of her that would always be Tori.

It seemed an eternity before the conveyance rumbled to a stop before the marquess's imposing three-story brick home. As soon as the carriage door had been opened by the driver, Tori descended and ran for the steps. Jonesey remained to thank and pay the man, then followed hurriedly in her ward's wake.

"Miss Victoria! You're behaving like a hoyden! A lady never runs and never . . ." she scolded as she mounted the steps.

"Grandfather!!" Tori was crying as she knocked on the door. She flew through the portal the moment it was opened by an unsuspecting servant.

Alfred had been in the parlor visiting with a group of old friends when he heard all the commotion in the front hall. He had just risen from his chair to see to the cause when he heard his beloved granddaughter calling his name. He stood still as disbelief and shock rocked through him, but those two terrible emotions soon gave way to joy when Tori appeared in the parlor doorway.

"Victoria!? My God, child, is it really you?"

"Oh, Grandfather!! We're home! We're home at last!" she cried, feeling much as she had as a little girl when she was forever swept into his warm, loving embrace. It seemed nothing had changed in that moment, but in her heart she knew everything had.

Malik received the message from the merchant ship's captain and immediately called for him to come to the palace for an audience. He truly believed that the man must have made a mistake. After talking with him, though, he realized the truth. Serad and his ship and crew had been taken by the English and were on their way there now to prison and possibly to death. Anguished, Malik knew he had to tell Rabi the news right away before she heard it through the palace gossip, and it was not something he looked forward to. He sent for her and received her in his private chambers.

Rabi was surprised by the unusual summons from Malik, for she rarely saw him during the day. She went to him as requested without delay.

She had been curious when she'd entered his rooms, but that curiosity turned to worry when she saw his expression.

"Yes, Rabi. I have news . . ."

"What is it? Is something wrong?"

"It's Serad . . ."

She gasped. "Serad?"

"I have witnesses who saw the *Scimitar* under British control being sailed for England behind an armed frigate. Evidently there was substantial damage to the ship. I have every reason to believe that he and his men are now in the hands of the English government . . ."

"Oh, my God!" She raised tormented eyes to him as her mind raced, seeking ways she could help. There was only one way, and she knew she had to do it. "Malik," she said in his name in a heartfelt plea, "I can save Serad."

"How?"

"You must allow me to return to England. If I get there in time, I can help him."

Malik stared at her, his eyes cold at first, wondering why she would dare bring up the subject he had ordered her never to speak of again. "No."

"Malik! Serad will die if I do not go to them and tell them his true identity! You must let me save him! You must!" Her tears were real as she stood up to him as she hadn't done in twenty years.

He didn't know what to say or do. Rabi had asked nothing of him in all these years. She had obeyed his every wish. Now, Serad's life depended on his decision. Did he dare allow Rabi to go and risk losing her? Did he dare to set her free or did he keep her with him and condemn his adopted son to almost certain death?

"What is it you can do?" he asked hesitantly.

"My father is very powerful and very rich. He has influence at court, and I'm sure he would save him. Serad is his grandson . . ." As she explained, she prayed that her father was still alive and that Avery was not now the Duke of Huntington. "Please, Malik, if you allow me to go, I know my father will see to it that Serad and his men are freed. I know it!"

"I will give you my decision tonight," he replied, still unable to face the thought of letting her go. He loved her, and he feared she would never return to him.

"Malik, it can't wait until tonight. If there's a fast ship in port, I could be ready to sail this afternoon . . ."

She grabbed his arm in a desperate gesture to convince him of her true fear for Serad.

Malik gazed down into the aquamarine beauty of her eyes and knew he had no real choice. He loved her and he loved Serad. If he allowed Serad to die because of his own selfishness, he would never be able to forgive himself . . . and she would never forgive him.

"Please . . ." Rabi whispered in a choked voice, meeting his gaze fully.

Love her as he did, he could not deny her. In this, she was right. There was no other way. "Of course you must go. I will see that the fleetest ship in the harbor is readied for you."

Rabi threw her arms about his neck and kissed him. "Thank you. Serad's life depends on it." She wanted to say much more to him. She wanted to tell him that she knew what he was worried about, but she could bring no promises to her lips.

Malik wanted to clasp his love to him and never let her go. He wanted to demand that she return to him quickly, but he feared to even broach the subject. He feared that once she was away from him, she would eagerly return to her old life and never come back. In all the years Rabi had been with him, she had never told him that she loved him and she had always declined to become his wife. Even now after all this time, it still pained Malik to realize that he had failed to win her love.

It was with a heavy spirit that Malik held Rabi close to his heart for a moment and then released her. If he kissed her again or touched her any longer, he would never be able to let her go. His face was set when he stepped away from her, but his eyes mirrored the pain and agony of his soul.

"I will send one of the servants for you when the ship is ready to sail."

411

"Thank you." She tried to meet his gaze again, but he turned away from her. Though she could feel his desperation, she had to go!

With that she turned and left him, saving Serad's life foremost on her mind. She knew the voyage to London would be the longest trip of her life.

Chapter Thirty

David held Tess close and kissed her tenderly. They had just passed another blissful night in each other's arms, and he was trying to ignore the fact that the morning sun was casting its first blush across the horizon.

"I have to go," Tess whispered regretfully. As she spoke, though, her arms were still looped around David's neck and her lips were still softly seeking his.

"I know," he answered with a sigh. In the months since their first passionate encounter, the feelings he had for Tess had blossomed. Though he'd known in the beginning that there could be no real future for them, he hadn't been able to resist her, and now he found that he loved her with a fierceness that surprised him.

Guilt ravaged David. Care for her as he did, it hurt him deeply that he was using her. Still, he couldn't deny himself. Tess was the most important thing in his life right now. Where all else was falsehood and lies, his feelings for Tess were real and good and very, very special.

Tess hated leaving him, but she knew she had to. Slipping from the bed, she began to dress silently while he lay quietly watching her. She glanced up to find his gaze upon her, and she gave him a warm smile.

"Don't tempt me, Tess," David told her in a soft voice, imagining how wonderful it would be to take her in his arms and make love to her for the rest of the morning. He loved the way she cried his name when they came together, and he loved the way their bodies melded. It was almost as if they'd been made especially for each other, and it grieved him to think that he could never take her as his wife.

"I would love to tempt you, but imagine what Dalton would say if I was found out," she replied in a hushed voice as she finished pulling on her clothes. Returning to the bed, she kissed him once more, then started from the room.

"Tess . . ."

She turned to look back at him and was surprised to find that he followed her across the room. There was no chance to speak as he swept her into his arms and kissed her passionately and with desperation.

"Oh, Lord Alex . . ." His kiss left her breathless, and her eyes had an almost starry quality as she stared up at him in wonder.

Her use of his false name ruined the moment for him, and he stepped away from her. "Take care of yourself, Tess."

She thought she heard a touch of sadness in his voice and she didn't understand it. "I'll be thinking about you all day," she promised.

"I'll be thinking about you, too," he told her gruffly.

Tess left the room, moving cautiously so as not to be discovered as she moved through the mansion to return to her own quarters.

David watched the door close and then went to stare out the window at the rising sun. He didn't know why he suddenly had such a feeling of unease and discontent. Things were the same as they had been for months, and there was no reason for him to be this unsettled. He loved Tess, and though they would never be able to marry, they could at least share this much. Telling himself that was going to have to be enough, David turned away from the view of the bright new day and back to the dark shadows of his room and his life.

Tess was as happy as she could be given the circumstances. She loved Lord Alex and would have done anything for him. It thrilled her that he wanted her, too. She knew they could never be married, but she intended to love him forever. A small, satisfied smile curved her lovely lips as she thought of the night just past, and she prayed that he would not grow weary of her.

David was in the study with his "grandfather" going over some important papers regarding one of their estates when a messenger arrived from London late that afternoon. Edward had not been expecting anything, and he was curious to see what the urgent news was.

"You say he's from Alfred?" the duke asked.

"Yes, Your Grace," Dalton answered.

"Bring the man in."

"Right away." The elderly servant stepped out into the hall again to usher the messenger into the study.

Edward was seated at the desk with David standing just beside him, and they both looked up expectantly when the man entered the room.

"Your Grace, the Marquess of Ravensley sent me to deliver this to you," he said, handing the sealed missive to Dalton to give to the duke.

"Thank you. You may remain while I read it and see if there's any need for a reply."

The messenger nodded and remained respectfully silent.

David had tensed when he'd heard the letter was from the marquess, and he looked on expectantly as Edward opened the note and scanned it quickly.

> *"Edward—*
> *God was with me and has answered my prayers.*
> *Victoria and her companion returned to London*
> *just this week in excellent health. All is well*
> *Look forward to hearing from you and Alexander.*
> > *I remain—*
> > *Alfred*

Edward reread it again just to make sure he hadn't misunderstood anything, then handed it to David with a wide, happy smile.

"Thank God!" Edward said with emotion.

"What is it?" David asked.

"The girl's back. Victoria's home."

"She is?" he repeated, stunned.

"Alfred didn't say much, but it looks as if everything will go as planned after all," he announced, his pleasure obvious as he handed him the letter to read.

David read through it, and as he did his feelings became turbulent. While he wished only good things for his unseen fiancé, he now knew his time with Tess would be ending and the realization tore at him like a vicious, clawed beast.

"There will be no return message." Edward dismissed the messenger, then he announced to Dalton, "This is the best news we've had since Alexander returned, Dalton."

"Indeed, Your Grace."

Both men were beaming with pleasure. Neither was aware that David was struggling with his reaction to the return of the missing girl.

"Have the staff prepare our things. We will be traveling to London at once. Lady Victoria Lawrence, the future duchess, has returned home. I think it's time she met her duke, don't you, Dalton?"

"Yes, Your Grace."

"Alexander?"

"Yes, Grandfather?"

"What do you have to say?"

"I'm glad Victoria's back and I'm very glad she's safe. I'm looking forward to finally meeting her," he replied tactfully.

"The introductions may be a few months late, but I have no doubt Victoria was well worth the wait."

"I'm sure you're right, Grandfather," David tried to sound enthusiastic, but all he could think about was having to leave Tess. He had never wished anything bad for Victoria, but everything had been very simple when she'd been missing. He knew it was going to be a real test of his abilities to court Victoria and be convincing, while Tess held his heart.

Edward was eager to be on his way to London so he could congratulate his old friend on his good fortune and welcome his future granddaughter-in-law properly.

David was caught up in the flurry of activity involved in getting ready to make the trip and had no time to say good-bye to Tess. As the Wakefield carriage pulled away and moved down the drive, he did not know that Tess had heard the news of Victoria's return and was standing at the window of the now-deserted parlor watching him go and fearing that he was riding out of her life forever.

Wearing one of the new fashionable gowns her grandfather had ordered for her, Tori was waiting in her room with Jonesey for her fiancé to arrive.

"Miss Victoria, you look lovely. I think your hair done up that way is very attractive," Jonesey complimented her.

"Thank you," she replied mechanically as she continued to stare out the window of her second-floor bedroom at the busy street below to see if there was any sign of the Wakefields.

"I can tell you're excited about meeting your Alexander."

Tori wanted to tell her that he wasn't "her" Alexander, but she didn't. "I'm nervous, that's for sure."

"Well, there's no need to be. You look positively radiant. You'll do beautifully. I'm sure he'll be impressed."

"Oh, Jonesey, you are so wonderful!" Tori turned and embraced her companion with true affection.

"Of course I am," Jonesey replied, a little flustered by the unexpected hug. "But you are, too."

"Isn't it strange, though, how completely everything has changed?"

Jonesey saw the shadows lurking in Tori's eyes. "You mean life today as opposed to a month ago?"

Tori nodded. "The time with Serad almost seems unreal . . ."

"Eventually I hope you'll be able to look at it as if it were nothing more than a bad dream. You haven't changed. You're still the same sweet, loving child you always were."

Tori wanted to tell Jonesey that she was wrong, that she *had* changed. Being with Serad and knowing him for just that short period of time had changed her in ways she couldn't begin to describe.

It had been particularly ironic, too, that Jonesey had mentioned dreams. Though Tori had not told anyone, since they'd arrived in London and their lives had settled into a routine of sorts, she had yet to get a full night's rest. Every night she would fall asleep easily, but then in the dark hours just past midnight she would come awake, haunted by dreams of Serad. Some nights she would never get back to sleep as visions of him loomed in her thoughts. Others she would doze fitfully until dawn and then give up the effort and rise for the day. Tori was beginning to wonder if he was going to haunt her for the rest of her life.

"I'm glad Grandfather waited a week before contacting the duke," Tori remarked.

"So am I. It gave us the time we needed to get you a suitable wardrobe made up, and it also gave you some time to rest."

"I needed that," Tori agreed, just wishing that she'd managed to get some. "But our reprieve is over. This is it, Jonesey. Tonight, I get to meet Alexander face-to-face for the first time."

"I'm so happy for you, dear," Jonesey told her with deep emotion. "I wish you only happiness."

They shared a tender smile, but Tori quickly looked away when she heard a carriage stop out in front. A glance out the window revealed the Wakefield carriage and two men climbing out of it.

"They're here . . ." she breathed.

"And everything is going to be wonderful."

"I hope so, Jonesey. I truly do."

A few minutes passed before the butler came for Tori, and she followed him from her room with all the grace and presence of a future duchess. As she descended the staircase, Tori said a small, fervent prayer that Alexander Wakefield would be man enough to wipe Serad out of her mind once and for all.

*   *   *

It was just a short time later that Alfred was proudly finishing off the very proper introductions.

"Victoria, this is Alexander . . ." he announced, beaming with pride at what a marvelous match this looked to be. "And Alexander, this is my Victoria."

Tori had only managed a quick glance at Alexander when she'd first entered the room, but she lifted her emerald gaze to regard him forthrightly now. While she had seen his likeness in the locket that Serad had taken from her and had known he had dark hair and gray eyes, she was still startled by the uncanny resemblance he bore the pirate. Tall, dark, and handsome with arresting gray eyes, Tori almost groaned out loud. How in the world was she ever going to be able to forget Serad when Alexander looked so much like him? She hid her distress well, though, and managed to greet him with equanimity.

"Hello, Victoria . . ." David bent over her hand with practiced ease, ever the gentleman. He thought her far more attractive than her small portrait had revealed, and he was pleasantly surprised.

"Hello, Alexander, and please . . . call me Tori," she returned with a smile that didn't reach her heart. She wondered why, even in this first innocuous meeting she was mentally comparing him to Serad. There could be no comparison. There was no one who could compare with Serad. He was strong . . . and handsome . . . and powerful and . . . Tori suddenly realized the direction of her thoughts and grew even more determined to make a success of this engagement. With a concerted effort, she turned on her charm.

When the duke and the marquess retired to the study some time later to give the two young people a chance to get acquainted, Tori and David were already en-

420

joying a lively conversation as he brought her up to date on the goings-on in London during the season and told her about his interests and she told him about her life in India and her activities there.

Tori had not known what to expect from Alexander, and she was happy to find that he was interesting and well read, too. When her grandfather asked her what she thought of him later that night after they'd gone, she had to admit that she thought he was a very nice man and :hat she'd liked him very much. Encouraged by this news, Alfred knew that he and Edward had done the right thing in keeping to the marriage contract.

"Well, Alexander, what did you think of Victoria?" Edward asked when they were in the carriage on their way back to their London home.

"You were right, Grandfather. She's a beauty." In the elegant, understated, turquoise gown she'd been wearing, Tori had looked lovely. Even as he acknowledged her stunning looks though, Tess was in his heart, her hold on his love unshakable.

"I think so. And her background is impeccable. Her family's holding, while not as vast as ours, will do nicely. Yes, I think she's quite a good match for you."

David nodded solemnly, wondering what Edward would think if he knew who he really was.

"There's no need to rush into anything, of course," Edward was saying. "Take all the time you need and get to know each other. It's important that you like each other. Love can come later."

The next two weeks passed in a blur of activity for the betrothed couple. At Edward's urging, David escorted Tori to every important social event in town. Others from their social set gathered around them and they became a most sought-after couple.

As the days passed and they grew more familiar and comfortable with each other, a bond of sorts formed between them and they became friends. One evening at a ball during an unusually romantic moment on a deserted balcony, David did kiss Tori, but the embrace aroused no burning desire within him. It was pleasant, sweet almost, but held none of the wild emotion he experienced with Tess. He did not at any time press his affections upon her.

Tori found her fiancé to be genuinely interesting. When he kissed her, she thought his embrace nice, but nothing at all like the explosive ecstasy she'd shared with Serad. It infuriated her that she kept comparing the two of them. Try as she might, she had not been able to wipe the maddening pirate from her memory. He was constantly haunting her, ruining this, her one chance for happiness. Wasn't this what she'd fought with him about? Hadn't she told Serad over and over again that she loved Alexander and wanted to come home and marry him? Yet, now that she was here, she couldn't forget the fierce corsair who had swept her off her feet and into his arms.

To all the world, the engaged couple gave the appearance of being thrilled with their arrangement. Little did anyone suspect that both Tori and David were existing in their own private hells, and David became even more morose when Edward suggested they all travel to Huntington House for a stay and his invitation was immediately accepted by the marquess.

David's life suddenly threatened to become one long, endless stretch of misery and tension-filled days. He knew he would have to devote all his attention to Tori, and the thought that Tess would be there, watching him do it and suffering because of it, hurt him.

His conscience began to badger him again. He liked Tori, and the more he considered the sham he was foisting upon her and the pain he was causing Tess, the more agonized he became. They both believed he was Alexander, and the deception was getting to be more than he could stand. David was beginning to wonder if he could live with the future he'd created for himself.

"Alexander? What are you thinking about?" Tori asked as she slowed her horse's pace so she could ride abreast of him.

Tori's question cut through the haze of unhappiness that surrounded David, forcing his attention back to the present, back to their ride across the open green fields of Huntington. "Nothing in particular, why?"

"Oh, I don't know. Sometimes you have the most thoughtful expression on your face. It's almost as if you're pondering the world's problems and trying to find solutions for them all."

"You give me far too much credit, Tori." He managed a derisive laugh. If he couldn't solve his own problems, how in heaven's name could he manage to help the world?

"Oh, I don't think so. I think you're a very intelligent man."

"Thank you, but there are moments when I have my doubts."

"Well, don't. Come on! I'll race you to that copse of trees!" She pointed to the small grove a mile or so away, and then put her heels to her horse and was off.

Left in her dust, David could only follow. His steed was quick, but her head start was too large. She beat him by half a length and was laughing in delight when he reined in beside her.

"You certainly are an excellent horsewoman."

"Thanks. I love to ride. Tiger hunting was exciting,

but I really enjoyed riding in the desert. I . . ." She suddenly realized she was thinking of Serad again, and she could have sworn out loud. Was she never to have any peace?

"You went riding in the desert?" he asked with interest. They had spoken very little about the time she'd spent in the hands of the pirates, and he wanted her to feel free to discuss it if she wanted to.

"Yes, it was quite different from anything I'd ever done before. While the desert seems quite barren, it can be beautiful."

"Was it a difficult time for you?"

"It was hard . . ." She paused, trying to think of the best way to phrase it. "But Jonesey and I kept our spirits up. After all, I had my family and you to come home to. I'm glad things worked out as they did. Jonesey said I did well. She said I conducted myself in a manner suitable for a future duchess." As she said the words, though, an image of Serad appeared in her mind, bending over her, kissing her. Suddenly, Tori found herself wondering what his reaction had been when he'd returned to find her gone, and she wondered, too, where he was and what he was doing at that very moment.

Chapter Thirty-One

"Take a look, George," the filthy, toothless guard chuckled as he threw open the door to the dark, dank, windowless cell. Stepping just inside, he held the torch he was carrying up high so his companion could see the savagely beaten man who was chained to the far side of the cell. The prisoner was sitting listlessly on the floor, his back braced against the wall for support, his head down, his eyes closed. "What did I tell you? He don't look much like a cutthroat pirate now, does he?"

"Hell, no, Sam. He looks like some slovenly drunk off a back alley," George commented, staring at the man they'd been told was a dangerous Barbary corsair.

"He ain't drunk, he's near dead. Why, Fred and me, we took turns on him last night when they first brought him in. He ain't near so proud any more now that we straightened him out."

"I can tell," George remarked. He knew how much Sam enjoyed beating the prisoners.

"You know what he claimed last night?"

"What?"

"It was the damnedest thing. He tried to tell us that he was related to a duke!"

"A duke?!" George bellowed with laughter.

"That's what he said. That's when Fred and me really got mad and gave it to him. He ain't going to be claiming to be related to nobody anymore. Imagine . . . him related to royalty!" He guffawed at the thought as he turned and led George out of the room, then slammed the door shut and locked it securely.

Serad didn't bother to look up until the sound of their voices had faded away. Not that it mattered much, for there was no light in his cell and only the faintest of glows shining through the tiny barred window in the door from the passageway beyond. He stared up through blackened, swollen eyes at the one small fragment of light in his life, wondering if he would ever see the sun and the sea again.

Serad had known returning to England in chains would be bad, but he had never thought his life would end like this—alone in a pitch-black hole in the ground. He tilted his head back against the cold, unforgiving stone of the wall and let out a deep, ragged sigh.

Tori slipped into his thoughts like a warm spring breeze, and in spite of his pain and degradation, Serad smiled. He loved her, and what pained him the most was the fact that he had never gotten to tell her. His thoughts drifted to his aunt, Malik, and Hasim, and he wondered if they'd heard of his capture yet. It had been weeks now since he'd had the misfortune of crossing paths with Captain Demorest, and he had no idea how long it would take for the news to spread. Worry for his men returned to plague him, and he could only hope that they were faring better than he was. He stared off into the darkness, wondering if a death fighting at sea wouldn't have been preferable to being left in a hellhole to rot.

Letting his eyes drift shut, Serad rested. He didn't know if the guards would come back, but he knew he would have to conserve his strength just in case they did.

Malik stood alone in his bedchamber. His mood was dark and surly as he stared out the window to the gardens below. It had been over three weeks since Serad had sailed and two weeks since Rabi had gone after him—two miserable weeks that had been the longest, loneliest ones of his life. Malik was worried about Serad, and he hoped Rabi could save him as she'd promised she would. But even though he knew it had been necessary for her to go, he missed her. He felt lost without her, and he ached to hold her in his arms again, to kiss her and to take her to his bed.

As he thought about the beauty of their lovemaking, the doubts he'd held at bay so long returned. With a muttered curse, Malik strode from the room to escape the memories of their nights together. He told himself that Rabi would come back to him, that he just had to be patient. But even as he tried to convince himself, the uncertainties remained to haunt him. He'd always known Rabi wanted to return to her home and family. He'd always known she'd loved another. Stubborn woman that she was, she had held her heart away from him all these years, and no matter how hard he'd tried, she had never fully surrendered that part of her. A heaviness settled in his soul.

Malik reached the gardens and moved onward into his harem. Only his daughter, Talitha lived there now, and it was strangely silent and deserted as he moved through the wide halls to enter Rabi's rooms. He could have filled all the rooms with many willing women, but he had no interest in others. He wanted only Rabi. He needed only her.

"Father? Did you want to see me?" Talitha heard his footsteps and came forth to greet him. The moment she saw his forbidding expression she knew he was worrying about Serad and Rabi. "Would you like to talk?"

Malik took a quick look around Rabi's empty bedroom and then turned to gaze upon his only daughter with affection. She was a sweet, sensitive young woman, and he loved her very much. "I don't know that I would be very good company."

"You are always good company, Father." Talitha came forward, smiling gently as she took his arm and drew him outside into the garden away from Rabi's rooms.

"It's good you think so. There are not many who would agree with you right now."

"You're worried about Serad, that's all."

"You're very observant, much like your mother was."

They began to walk together through the flowering foliage to the center of the garden where only the fountain's soft, melodic splashing disturbed the peace of the night.

"Are you concerned about Rabi, too?"

"Very much. I love her as I loved your mother," he answered simply.

"I know. She'll come back with Serad just as soon as she can, Father. I'm sure of it," Talitha said with assurance.

Malik wondered how it was that she could be so certain, but then he considered her youth, and understood. His daughter was still too innocent in the ways of the world to understand the cruelties of life. First, he had lost Lila, and now he had lost Serad and his beloved Rabi . . . perhaps forever.

"I hope you're right, sweet one."

"You'll see. Nothing's going to happen to either of them. They're going to be fine."

When Malik left her a short time later, he found his mood a little improved. Talitha's gentle innocence and unwavering faith made everything seem clearer. He loved Rabi. He had to believe she would return to him and he had to believe that Serad would be all right.

Up the coast from Algiers, a dark-clad, solitary figure moved silently through the night heading for the city with murder on his mind.

Tori and her grandfather returned to London, refreshed from their week's stay at Huntington House. The last day there the subject of the wedding had come up and they had agreed on a date in five months. Alfred had calculated they would need that long for her parents in India to be notified and make the trip home, not to mention the ordering of the gowns and all the other things that had to be taken care of.

Tori had been swept along in the happy tide of their planning. She told herself that her future was going to be perfect and that she would be content with Alexander. He was a good companion and an interesting conversationalist. They shared many similar interests, and while his kisses did not excite her the way Serad's had, she didn't worry. She had tasted passion once and it had made her the fool. She would settle for gentle caring this time, and be satisfied.

No one had sensed the edge of unhappiness in Tori's agreement to all the plans—no one, that is, except Jonesey. The older woman was far too knowing, and though she didn't get the opportunity to speak with her about it right away, the moment they were alone in her room in London, she spoke her mind.

"Miss Victoria, I think we need to talk."

"About what?" Tori hedged, always cautious when she used that tone of voice.

"You know about what. I've been watching you with Alexander, and I get the feeling that you're not really happy."

"I'm very happy," she denied far too quickly. "I'm engaged to a very handsome, intelligent man, and I'm going to be a duchess."

"And I'll venture to say you're going to be downright miserable in a few years, if you're not careful," she said pointedly.

"Why do you say that?"

"You don't love him."

"Does it matter? I *like* him. Alexander's everything a man should be. He's kind and considerate and handsome . . ."

"He may be all those things, not to mention rich and titled, but Victoria, he's not Serad," Jonesey finished.

"I know that." There was just the slightest edge of sadness to her words.

"How do you feel about Serad, Victoria?"

"Serad means nothing to me. He was a brute, and I'm glad I got away from him when I did."

"I never noticed he was such a brute," Jonesey said thoughtfully.

"Jonesey, what is your point?" Tori demanded. "We're back home, my life is going the way it's supposed to be going, and now you're bringing up a past I want forgotten."

"I just wanted to make sure that the past was forgotten for you, Miss Victoria. Sometimes we get so caught up doing what we're supposed to do that we lose sight of what we want to do."

"If you think for one moment that I want to go back

430

to Algiers and be with . . ." Tori snapped, but the older woman held up a hand to silence her tirade.

"*I* don't think anything. I just want *you* to think, that's all."

Tori stared at her, perplexed.

"If you need anything I'll be in my room," Jonesey told her as she left her alone.

Tori had meant to go to bed, but Jonesey's incisive remarks had stirred all the feelings she'd been trying to hide and trying to deny. Serad . . . She allowed herself the freedom to think about him now, and she remembered everything. He had not been a brute; in fact, if she faced it, she realized that he had been very careful not to hurt her in any way. The only time he'd been too forceful with her had been the day he'd carried her from the harem. Tori smiled at the memory in spite of herself. Deny it though she might, the time she'd spent with him in the desert had been beautiful. She had fallen completely in love with him then . . . and, she confessed to herself reluctantly and painfully, she was *still* in love with him. True, he was arrogant, but he had also been kind. True, he had been demanding, but he had also been gentle. Tori's heart ached, and she wondered how she could ever go through the rest of her life married to a man she "liked," when she'd tasted of Serad's passionate love.

Unable to even think about resting, Tori left her bedroom and went downstairs to the study in hopes of finding something to read. Her grandfather had already retired and so she was alone as she studied the endless shelves of leather-bound books. Tori wanted to find a book that would take her mind off her situation, but no particular title drew her attention. It was then that she happened to see a newspaper lying on the desk.

Tori wasn't usually given to keeping up on the news

of the world, but for some reason tonight, she decided to read it. The first page offered little in the way of enlightenment, but on the second page, what she read shocked her so deeply that she could only stand there and stare at it in complete disbelief.

"Captain Demorest of the frigate Bellwether *reports that he and his men took the pirate ship* Scimitar *captive on the high seas several weeks ago. The ship was brought into port today, and its captain and crew were taken to Newgate."*

All the color drained from her face as she stared in horror at the article. The *Scimitar* . . . its captain . . . The paper slipped from her numb fingers and she ran from the room and up the stairs. She didn't bother to knock, but opened Jonesey's door and barged in without pause.

"Get dressed!" she told her companion frantically.

Jonesey had just settled into the comfort of her bed in her cap and long-sleeved, floor-length, high-necked nightgown when Tori came bursting through the door. She stared at her in surprise, wondering at her look of shock and terror. "What's happened?"

"It's Serad . . ."

"Serad?" She had no idea what she was talking about. "What about him? Is he here?" Jonesey was thinking it would be perfectly romantic if the handsome devil had come all the way to London to claim Tori for his own. Tori's next words wiped all romantic thoughts from her mind.

"No . . . I mean, yes. Jonesey, they've captured him and taken him to prison. I have to go to him. I can't just let him die."

"Dear God, you do love him!"

"Oh, yes. I love him with all my heart, and I have to help him."

The elderly woman was up and out of bed before Tori could say another word. "Where is he?"

"Newgate." She spat the name of the terrible prison.

"We'll tell your grandfather, and he'll . . ."

"No! We can't do that. He'd be glad Serad has been caught and taken there. Didn't you hear him talking to the duke about it? He was saying all the pirates should be drawn and quartered and all kinds of awful things. I'm sure he'd want Serad dead, and I'm positive he'd never allow me to go to him. I've got to save him myself."

Jonesey felt herself being caught up by Tori's desperation. While she wanted to argue the point, she realized Tori was right. The marquess would never approve of going to the pirate's aid and would probably think that Serad was getting exactly what he deserved. Against her better judgment, Jonesey began to dress. She was determined to stay by Tori's side and try to keep her out of harm's way, even if it killed her.

"I will get ready. But you're going to need money, you realize. In order to get in to visit Serad you'll have to bribe the guards and I'm sure they're going to want a goodly amount. Wear a dark cloak with a hood. I wouldn't want any of those nasty men being able to see you too clearly."

"I'll be right back." Tori hurried off to get the money she'd need and her largest, most concealing cloak.

When she returned, Jonesey had dressed and also donned a disguising cloak. They crept from the house as quietly as possible, not wanting to alert the servants to their departure. They hired a conveyance near the house and ignored the surprised look of the driver when they asked to be taken to the prison as quickly as possible. When the carriage drew to a stop, Tori saw the ugly building looming before them and knew stark terror. Only her love for Serad and her determination to help him gave her the strength to go on. With Jonesey staying staunchly by her side, they approached the prison's main door.

Tori was amazed at the influence money could have. For nominal amounts, she was certain a person could do anything they wanted to inside this horrible place. The gruff, ugly guard who met them at the door leered at her while she paid him what he asked.

"You look to be a pretty thing. My name's George. If you . . ." he began suggestively, lifting a hand to try to push her hood back away from her face.

Jonesey was on guard. She had defended Tori from worse than him and she stepped boldly forward to confront the gross man. "You keep your filthy mitts off her and just do what you're just paid to do. We're here to see the pirate captain. Now take us to him!"

George eyed the little woman with irritation, but knew better than to try anything stupid. He liked the money more than he wanted the woman. "Come on," he growled resentfully.

It was a nightmare for Tori and Jonesey to be led through the hellish place. They continued on undaunted, though, for their goal of saving Serad wouldn't allow them to quit.

When at last the guard stopped before a locked door in a barely lighted corridor, deep in the bowels of the prison, both women girded themselves.

"He's in there," George said sharply.

"Open the door," Tori demanded, sickened by all that she'd seen.

The guard unlocked the door and opened it wide for her to enter. "Be careful. He's a dangerous one." He gave a demonic laugh at his own jest.

Jonesey stepped in front of the man to block his access to the room. She knew Tori needed privacy and she meant to see that she got it. Her tone was sharp and furious as she addressed him. "You get back and mind your own business. We paid you well for this time."

George gave a shrug and moved off. He waited just a short distance away.

Tori moved inside the dark, dank room the moment the guard left. It was difficult to see, but the light from the corridor allowed just enough illumination so she could make Serad out sitting on the floor across the cell. He looked terrible, and when she said his name it was a hoarse emotional whisper.

Serad had been half asleep, but at the sound of her voice, his head jerked up and he peered into the darkness. When he saw her standing there silhouetted against the doorway, he honestly believed he was losing his mind. She looked the angel, and he wondered how cruel his mind could be to conjure up such a lifelike image of her to taunt him with there in his purgatory. "Be gone. Why do you torture me so?" he said in misery.

"Oh, God . . . Serad," Tori cried. She had seen the look of pained disbelief on his battered features and could stay apart from him no longer. She rushed to him and dropped to her knees at his side. Tears were already trailing down her cheeks at the sight of him so beaten and chained.

Tori brushed back her hood and framed his face with her hands to gaze at him. He was her proud pirate, her arrogant corsair. What was he doing shackled here in this dungeon?

Only when Tori actually touched him did Serad actually believe that she was real, that she was actually there. He could see her lovely features and smell the

435

sweet scent of her perfume. "Tori? What are you doing here?"

His pain was her pain, and she ached for him. Without waiting another moment, she kissed him. It was a kiss of desperation, a kiss of love nearly lost and now found.

When the kiss ended, Serad lifted one hand to touch her cheek and trace the path of the crystalline tears she'd shed for him. He drew a ragged breath as he was filled with tenderness and love for her. "Why did you come?"

"I had to. I couldn't let anything happen to you," Tori confessed. Her eyes were sparkling with tears and her heart was pounding in her breast.

"You must go. There's no telling what might happen to you here," he insisted. She looked so beautiful that he wanted only to hold her close and never let her go, but he couldn't. It had been foolhardy for her to come there. She was placing herself in danger, and, love her as he did, he wouldn't be able to stand it if anything happened to her.

"Don't worry about me. We bribed the guards. We're safe," she told him.

"We?" He had no idea who she could have brought with her.

"Jonesey and I . . ."

Despite everything, Serad managed a chuckle. He should have known.

"What have they done to you?" she asked in a choked voice as she lifted a hand to touch his injured cheek.

"It doesn't matter, Tori. You shouldn't have come," Serad dodged away from her hand, embarrassed at her seeing him this way. There had been nothing he'd wanted more than to see her again and tell her he loved her, but now that she had come, he couldn't bring himself to do it. He had nothing to offer her. He was

436

going to be executed soon . . . and then there was still her fiancé, the man she'd wanted from the beginning . . . the man she really loved.

"How could I not come . . . when I love you?" She whispered the truth and waited breathlessly for his response to her declaration.

"Tori . . ." He stared at her, feeling as if his heart had just been ripped from his chest. *She loved him!* But what did it matter now? Though he wanted to tell her that he loved her, too, he didn't. He loved Tori more than life itself, and it was for that very reason that he wouldn't tell her of his own feelings for her. He remembered what his aunt had told him about have her life stolen from her, and he wouldn't do that to Tori. He loved her so much that he would make certain she stayed with the rich Englishman who could give her what he believed she needed and wanted.

"I can help you, I know I can. My fiancé is Alexander Wakefield, and his grandfather is the Duke of Huntington. I'm sure he has enough influence and wields enough power at court to get you out of here . . ."

"No . . ." The word escaped Serad when he heard Tori say the name of her fiancé. He stared at her in shock, trying to make sense out of what she'd just said. *She was engaged to Alexander Wakefield?* The absurdity of it was almost too much for him, but then the reality set in as he recalled everything his aunt had told him about their past. There was some kind of dangerous intrigue in progress, and Serad knew now that his grandfather was a victim of it.

Tori thought he was protesting her idea, and she went on. "Serad . . . I must," she insisted. "Don't you understand? I love you, and I won't let this happen . . ." Her gaze met and locked with his.

Serad saw for the first time the depth of her love for

him, and it hurt him as it enthralled him. Though he was troubled by what he'd just learned, he couldn't resist taking Tori in his arms and kissing her again. Neither of them noticed his bonds as he held her close and told her with his kiss just how much she meant to him. Tori clung to Serad, wishing she could free him this very moment, but knowing that it was going to take some planning on her part.

George appeared in the doorway, ignoring Jonesey's protests that he should let them have a few more minutes alone.

"Your time is up," he interrupted brazenly.

Tori and Serad broke apart.

"I'll be back," she promised before he could speak, and she pressed one last desperate kiss on his lips. Drawing her hood up to camouflage her identity, she fled the prison cell. In her heart, she was crying, but to the guard and Jonesey she showed only a proud demeanor. Serad needed her and she would not fail him. As difficult as it would be for her, she would seek out Alexander and ask for his help.

Chapter Thirty-Two

While their guests had departed early in the day, David and Edward had stayed on at Huntington House until much later in the afternoon. They did not arrive back in London until dark.

David had made the entire journey in virtual silence. Staring out the carriage windows, he'd been lost deep in thought, and his somber mood had worsened with each passing mile that took him farther and farther away from the woman he loved. He'd thought his life had been difficult before, but now he truly knew the meaning of pain.

Tess had come to his bed that last night. She'd heard that the wedding date had been set, and her heart had been broken. Her unhappiness had left him anguished, and parting from her in the predawn hours had been almost unbearable. David felt torn between confessing all, marrying Tess and possibly going to the gallows for a crime he didn't commit or going through with the marriage and living in lonely luxury for the rest of his life.

With each mile that had passed, the right thing to do

had become more and more clear to David. He'd known he could no longer go on deceiving Tori and living a life that wasn't his. He cared about her, and she deserved better. She thought she was marrying Alexander Wakefield, not an impostor, and he wondered how she would feel about their match if she knew the truth.

By the time they finally reached their London townhouse, David had made up his mind to seek out Tori the following day and tell her the complete truth. She deserved that much from him. Then after they'd talked, he would decide what to do next.

David was feeling a little better that night, but not much. He was glad when morning came. Confessing his deception and lies to Tori was not going to be easy, but he wanted, no, *had* to be forthright with her.

David was just preparing to leave for the Lawrence home a little after nine when a messenger arrived with a note for him from Tori. He'd thought he was being a bit forward by seeking her out so early, and her unexpected missive surprised him. He opened it a bit cautiously, wondering at its contents, and he was intrigued and puzzled by what he read.

> *Dear Alexander,*
> *It's essential that I speak with you right away. Please come at once. I am in dire need of your help.*
>
> > *As always,*
> > *Tori*

David couldn't imagine why she would need his help, but he was more than willing to do whatever he could for her. Calling for his carriage to be brought around, he set off right away.

*   *   *

Tori hadn't slept all night, for her worries about Serad had consumed her. Time seemed to be passing far too slowly, and she was immensely relieved when a decent morning hour finally arrived so she could send the message to Alexander.

As she waited for him to arrive, Tori wasn't quite sure how to handle the situation. She liked Alexander and trusted him implicitly, but she couldn't imagine how he was going to react when she told him that she loved another man and needed his help to get that man out of prison.

A shudder wracked Tori as she thought of Serad locked in that dungeon in chains. Just the memory of his torture kept her determined to do whatever was necessary to rescue him.

A knock sounded at her bedroom door and drew her thoughts back to the present. When the maid announced to her that Lord Alexander had arrived and was waiting below to see her, she rushed from the room.

Tori's face was a mask of control, and her trembling hands grasped her skirts so Alexander wouldn't know just how nervous she really was. She descended the staircase with apparent ease, looking every inch the lovely young lady. Only Jonesey knew of her inner turmoil, and she was safely upstairs in her room where she'd agreed to stay until after Tori had spoken with Alexander. Tori had made sure that her grandfather would be out that morning before she'd sent the note, for she needed time alone with Alexander.

"Alexander, I'm so glad you came . . ." she said softly as she came into the parlor to greet him.

"Tori, you look lovely this morning," David said as he rose from the sofa to take her hands in his and kiss her cheek. "I got your note and came right away."

His offer of help was so open and so warm that for just a moment Tori's carefully erected defenses faltered.

David caught a glimpse of the misery that she was trying to control, and it startled him. "Tori . . . what is it? How can I help?"

"Oh, Alexander, you're such a good man, but there's so much I have to tell you . . . so much you don't know . . ."

"I'll do whatever I can. You know how much I care about you."

Tori swallowed tightly. She didn't want to hurt Alexander, but she had to save Serad. Her life would have no meaning if anything happened to him.

"Alexander, I do need your help . . . desperately. But after I tell you what I need, you may not want to be a part of it."

David couldn't imagine what was bothering her, but he knew he would do no less than his best for her.

Tori mentally squared her shoulders as she faced him. "I need your help in getting a man out of prison."

"You *what?*" David was stunned.

"Serad has been captured. They brought him back here and have put him in prison. I have to rescue him. I won't let him die. I can't . . ." Her eyes were feverish with her intent as she looked at him.

"Serad is the pirate who captured your ship?"

Tori nodded tightly. "Yes . . . and Alexander, I love him."

Time stood still as they stared at each other. In none of David's wildest dreams would he have imagined anything like this happening to him. He'd thought he would be breaking Tori's heart when he told her of his love for Tess. He'd thought he would be ruining her

442

life. He'd been afraid to tell her the truth, but now he knew he could.

"Tori, I will do whatever you want me to do to help you rescue him." He opened his arms and she came into them, a deep sob tearing from her.

"Oh, thank you, Alexander. I knew I could count on you," she said as she hugged him back.

"There's something else we have to discuss," he told her very seriously.

Tori stepped back, not quite sure what he was leading up to.

"When I received your note this morning, I was already on my way here to speak to you."

"You were? Why?"

"I, too, have something very important that I have to tell you about. You're the only one I can confide in about this because you're the only one I trust."

"I don't understand? What could possibly be wrong outside of the fact that your betrothed just declared her love for another man?" She smiled slightly.

They sat down on the sofa and David reached out to take her hand.

"What I am about to tell you is not a pretty story, Tori, but it's one I think you should know."

Tori listened attentively as David began to tell her the truth of his life. He told her everything from the sordid details of his arrest, to Vivienne's blackmailing of him to take Alexander's place, to how he'd fallen in love with Tess. He explained how he'd agonized over the decision to tell her everything, and how he couldn't live with his part of the deception any longer.

"My real name is David . . . David Markham," he concluded, pausing in his confession to give her an opportunity to speak.

Tori was bewildered by all that she'd learned, but

there was no condemnation in her eyes as she gazed at him. "But the duke . . . ?"

"That's why I needed to talk to you. I don't know what to do. I've come to love the duke. He means as much to me as my own grandparents did. I don't want to hurt him, but I can't go on living this terrible lie any longer. I've deceived everyone I care about, and yet Vivienne controls my very life."

"Alex—I mean, David . . ." Tori was still reeling from learning he wasn't Alexander Wakefield. "I think I know you well enough to know that you would never harm anyone. I'm certain you didn't kill that girl."

"Thank you," he said with heartfelt emotion. "But the authorities didn't believe me. Since Vivienne got me out of prison, she's threatened to see me hang if I dare upset her plans to get her the Wakefield money."

"And Tess?"

"As you love Serad, I love Tess," he answered simply. "She means the world to me."

"I understand."

"What are we going to do?"

"Right now, we're going to plan how to get Serad out of that prison. Once he's safe, we'll solve your dilemma, and when we do it, we'll make certain that as few people as possible are hurt."

David gave her hand a squeeze and managed a smile. "I believe you, Tori."

"What can we do about Serad?"

"I've heard that money is the key to opening the doors of that prison," David offered.

"That's true, Jonesey and I managed to see him last night."

"You *what?*"

Tori gave him a proud look. "I found out late last night that he was there, and I had to make sure he

444

was all right."

"The two of you went to the prison unescorted?"

"Tess would do it for you if it meant saving your life, wouldn't she?"

"Yes, she would." He paused, considering that Tess very well might have to do just that when the truth of his real identity came out. "How much did you pay for the visit?"

Tori told him, and he nodded thoughtfully.

"I know how much I'd better get then. When do you want to go?"

"I wish we could go this minute, but we'll have to wait until tonight. We are supposed to be going to a ball tonight, aren't we?"

"Yes."

"Then come for me as you normally would, and then we'll go on to the prison instead."

"I'll be here."

"Thank you. He'll need a change of clothing, too. Do you have something he could use?"

"How tall is he?"

"He's about your size really."

"I'll bring something. Where do you want to take him once he's free?"

"There's an empty room over our carriage house that no one ever uses. He would be safe there for at least one night," Tori replied. "Then I'll have to find a way to get him out of the country. First I just want to get him out of that prison."

David admired her courage. "You're a very brave woman."

She kissed him lightly on the cheek again. "And you're a wonderful man, David. You'll never know how much your help means to me."

"I know, Tori. Believe me, I know. I just confided my

445

most terrible secret in you and you didn't judge me."

"We all do things we regret. You and I are both getting the chance to make things right. Everything will work out for us, you'll see."

"I hope you're right, Tori."

"I am." Even as she said the words, though, Tori was praying fervently for them to be true.

Tori thought evening would never come, but at long last, darkness claimed the land and Alexander, now David, arrived to claim her for their outing. She had told Jonesey what they were planning, and the older woman was nervous about it, but agreed to say nothing and pray that all went well. Tori bid her grandfather a fond good night where he sat in his study, then grabbed up her cloak and left the house with only one thing on her mind—saving Serad.

David helped her into the carriage, then gave the driver orders where to take them. If the driver was shocked, he showed no sign of it. He drove straight for the prison and stopped by the main entrance.

"Pull down to the shadows and stay there until you see us come out," David directed.

"Yes, sir."

David waited until he'd driven away, and then took Tori's arm. She had taken care to put the hood up to disguise herself.

George stared at the couple coming toward him and immediately recognized the woman as the one who'd been there the night before. He smiled. The purse she'd given him last night had been a rich one, and he was looking forward to getting more money from her now.

"Evenin', guvnor', ma'am," he said, smiling at them both.

David nodded in response. "I've come to see about the pirate captain."

"What about him?"

"I want him out."

George gave him a measured look. He looked to be a very rich bloke, and George intended to get every farthing out of him that he could. "It'll cost you."

"How much?" David hated dealing with this despicable man, but he knew it was the only way.

George named an outrageous sum, and David immediately put that amount of money before him.

"I want Serad out now."

"Don't worry, you'll get your man," George replied, pocketing the huge sum. He called out to another guard. When Sam appeared, he directed him to get the pirate captain from his cell.

Sam nodded and hurried off. He knew something was afoot, and if he cooperated, he'd be handsomely paid by George for his effort.

"I'm going with you," Tori spoke up.

"Now, wait—" George started to protest.

David cut him off. "The woman goes or there is no deal."

He waved Sam and the mysterious female on to get the prisoner.

"There's one other thing . . ." David said when they had disappeared down the corridor.

"What's that?" the guard asked suspiciously.

"I want to make sure that no one knows Serad is gone. It wouldn't do for the authorities to come after us in a few hours, now would it?"

George nodded at the other man's shrewdness. "I think I know just how to do that, but it'll cost you extra."

The man's greed was undeniable, but David knew

there was no other way. If the authorities found out that Serad had gotten out of prison, there would be a hunt for him, and God knew what would happen to Tori if they were found. He had to make sure they were safe. "How much extra?"

While David finished up the dealings with George, Tori was following the other man through the maze of filthy halls and down the cold stone steps to the corridor that led to Serad's cell. Tori was so nervous and excited that she was shaking. She was terrified that something was going to go wrong and their plan to get him out would fail. The next few minutes were the most critical, she knew. They stopped before the locked door, and she stood by as the guard opened it.

"Serad!" She hurried inside to find him much as he had been the night before.

"Tori?" After she'd left him the night before, Serad hadn't known what to expect—freedom or death. It had been a miserable twenty-four hours, and he was hard put to control the excitement he was feeling over her return. He got to his feet as quickly as he could.

"I've come to get you out. Guard! Hurry up! Get those manacles off him now!" she ordered angrily, standing aside so he could free him.

When Sam unfastened the chains, Tori rushed into his arms.

"Ah . . . Tori . . ." He kissed her again, not caring that the guard was standing there. All that mattered was that she was there with him and he was free.

"Come. We have to get you out of here now!" Tori said huskily when they broke apart, very aware of the guard's avid gaze on them.

Serad and Tori followed Sam from the damp dungeon. Tori kept glancing up at him to make sure he was actually there and safe. Serad was completely aware of Tori at his side, but he kept his attention on the guard. He didn't trust anyone in the prison and he knew he wouldn't relax again until they were far away.

When Tori saw that David wasn't waiting for her at the main entrance, she hurried Serad on outside to find him already there with the carriage waiting for them.

"Get in, Tori," David directed from where he was sitting with the driver.

"You don't want to sit here with us?"

"I think you could use some privacy," he told her with an understanding smile. His gaze moved to the tall, dark-haired man standing by her side, and he studied him for a moment in the dark shadows of the night.

"Thank you, Alexander," she said using that name for authenticity in the presence of the driver. Then, she and Serad climbed into the carriage, and when the order was given, it moved off quickly.

As the three of them made their escape from the prison, George looked over at Sam and smiled widely. "We've made a fine living for ourselves tonight."

"We did?"

"That we did. We've only got one thing left to do, and then I'll pay you your share."

"What's that?"

George went on to explain how they would place the body of the prisoner who had 'accidentally' died earlier that day in the cell that had been the pirate's. He instructed Sam that if anyone else were to ask about the pirate, they were to say he'd tried to escape and had been killed. Sam agreed to his plan without a thought, and when the work was done, he collected a goodly sum from his cohort.

Inside the warm haven of the Wakefield carriage as it rumbled off down the street away from the prison, Serad donned the change of clothing Tori gave him, then sat back rigid and silent in the seat. *He was free . . . he was free . . . he was free . . .* The words rang through him like a litany. Only when the vehicle made a turn and entered a busier thoroughfare to blend with the traffic did he breathe a sigh of relief and turn to Tori.

Tori was still nervous, too, as they made their escape, and she found she was holding her breath as the carriage moved away from the prison. When Serad looked at her, she managed her first real smile.

"You're safe . . ." she breathed, and she went into his arms without another word.

Serad clasped her to him as his mouth met hers in a flaming exchange. Wrapped in each other's arms, they shared the embrace both had dreamed of for weeks. When the kiss ended, they drew apart to gaze at each other.

"I love you, Serad," Tori said softly.

"Tori . . . are you sure?"

"Oh, yes."

"But what about your life here?" he asked, needing to know the truth of her feelings for him while she still believed him to be a pirate.

"It isn't important. Nothing is, except the fact that I love you and you're free." She lifted starry eyes to his, her expression revealing without further words the depth of her devotion.

"Tori . . ." He bent and kissed her softly. "I love you, too," he admitted.

"You do?" Her heart swelled near to bursting with happiness.

"I was on my way to find you and tell you when the *Scimitar* was taken."

"How could anyone have caught you?"

"We'd sustained some damage fighting my father's enemy, and I foolishly sailed to find you before the repairs were made." He paused thinking of how his impetuous actions had caused so much horror. "It was the one decision I'd ever made without fully thinking through my actions. I may have lost my ship, but I haven't lost you." He paused to look at her, knowing the price had been worth it, but also knowing that he wouldn't rest until he'd found a way to save his crew . . . and until he put an end to the impostor masquerading in his place.

"I'm so glad you're safe," she was saying as she clung to him. "I love you so much. I should never have left . . ."

Serad wanted to relish the moment, but the memory of her fiancé and his deception wouldn't let him. He had to expose him for the liar that he was, and he had to do it now.

"What about your fiancé?" he asked with more than a little wariness.

"Alexander's been wonderful. We owe all this to him. He helped me with . . ."

Serad glanced out the window and saw that they were now on a quieter, nearly deserted street. He knew it was time for some questions to be answered.

"Tell the driver to pull the carriage in over there, where it's dark."

There was a fierceness in his tone that she had never

451

heard before, and it puzzled her. "But . . ."

"I want to talk to your fiancé."

Tori rapped on the roof and asked the driver to stop where Serad had indicated.

"I don't understand. Can't this wait?"

Serad ignored her protest. The moment the carriage stopped, he alighted from it.

"What's wrong?" David asked as he started to jump down to see if he could help.

"That's what I'd like to know," he seethed, grabbing him by the shirtfront and dragging him the rest of the way down and slamming him up against the side of the carriage.

David had no idea why Serad was acting this way. He was tempted to fight back over his rough handling, but for Tori's sake he remained calm in spite of the pirate's threatening gestures.

"Don't! Serad, stop! What are you doing?" Tori demanded as she jumped down from the carriage and raced to where the men stood.

"Just who are you and why are you masquerading as Alexander Wakefield?" Serad snarled as he held David pinioned before him.

"What?" Tori and David both were shocked by Serad's outburst. They couldn't imagine how he'd learned about the deception.

"I said, who are you?" he asked, giving David a violent shake.

"Serad, what are you doing?" Tori grabbed his arm in an attempt to make him stop.

"This man is not Alexander Wakefield," he announced angrily.

"What are you talking about? How could you know that?" Tori begged him to tell her.

"He's not, because I am."

"You're Alexander?" Tori stared at him in bewilderment.

"Dear God!" David muttered in a shaken voice as he stared up at the dark-haired, gray-eyed man who loomed over him. He looked at Tori standing there in shock by Serad's side and suddenly realized the truth.

"My Aunt Catherine . . ." Serad, now Alex, said Catherine's English name slowly, testing it upon his lips, "and I were kidnapped by my father, Avery Wakefield, in order to get money out of my grandfather. He was going to sell me and my aunt into slavery in France. Our ship was taken by Barbary pirates, and I was raised in Algiers as the son of the *dey*."

Tori listened in horror to his tale. "Your father's dead . . . missing for over twenty years now," she offered softly.

"Good. I hope the swine died a miserable death," Alex said with murderous intent.

"Oh, Serad . . . I mean Alexander," Tori knelt beside him to look him in the eyes. "Let David up."

"David?" He frowned as he looked at her, wondering suddenly if she'd played a part in the betrayal.

"Tori, tell him everything . . ." David spoke up.

Alex released him and stood up, still ready for an attack if one should come. There was none, though. There was only pain and sorrow as Tori revealed to him his mother's vicious blackmailing of David and her plan to control his grandfather's money.

"Then I think it's time I paid my *mother* a visit." He spat her name. "Where is she?" He glanced from David to Tori.

David told him the address, then said, "We'll go with you. I think it's time all the truth came out."

David and Alex shared a long, measuring look. Then

Alex nodded his agreement.

"Let's go."

Tori had been watching both men and waiting to see what would happen. The peace they declared filled her with joy, and without the slightest hesitation, she went to Alex. Their eyes met and locked.

"I love you, Tori," Alex said gently.

"And I love you . . ."

"Alex," he supplied with a heartrending smile.

"Alex," she repeated.

Chapter Thirty-Three

The carriage had stopped and the driver was waiting to help her descend, but Catherine could not bring herself to climb down just yet.

"Catherine . . . what is it?" Almira asked as she sat close beside her within the dark interior of the vehicle. At Catherine's insistence, she had begun calling her by her English name during their voyage, and it now came easily to her.

"Oh, Almira . . ." she said in a voice choked with emotion. "I'm home. I'm actually home."

Catherine stared up at the Wakefield townhouse, its windows alight in seeming welcome even at this late gloomy hour. She was overwhelmed with memories. Her father was here . . . Tears fell, but she hardly noticed. She was torn between the ache of having missed her home and family and the thrill of being back. The house looked the same. It was almost as if nothing had changed. But Catherine knew that was a fantasy. Though in the night things might appear as they had twenty years ago; in truth, everything had changed, herself included.

Thoughts of Alex's peril drove her on, and she took the driver's hand to allow him to assist her. Wrapped in the folds of the dark, voluminous cloak the ship's captain had given her, she stood there on the walk for a moment longer, gazing at the front door and preparing herself for what the next few minutes would bring.

"Are you ready?" Almira asked, as she joined her. She, too, had been given a cloak by the captain, for their mode of dress had not been suitable for this damp, chilly London night.

"Yes . . . yes, oh, yes."

Dalton heard the knock at the door and was puzzled by who it could be. It was rather late for social callers. He hoped there wasn't any kind of trouble about tonight.

"Yes?" Dalton said with regal dignity as he opened the portal to find two women standing on the doorstep. "May I help you?"

Catherine gazed up at the family butler with open adoration. He had changed so much . . . and yet so little. When she spoke, his name was a tearful cry, "Hello, Dalton . . ."

"Lady Catherine?"

When Catherine saw the light of recognition in his eyes, she could not restrain herself. She threw her arms around him and hugged him as great sobs wracked her. She had never forgotten all his tender caring and gentle kindness, and she had missed him terribly!

For a second, Dalton *hadn't* recognized her, but her voice . . . oh, her voice hadn't changed. "Good heavens! It is you!" He returned her embrace with open enthusiasm, a rare thing, indeed, for a man so proper. Then realizing he had yet to inform her father of her return, he called excitedly, "Your Grace!"

The old servant didn't bother to try to control the happiness surging through him even as the duke came rushing into the hallway. He hugged her tightly just as if she were his own daughter come home. He had adored her, and losing her had been almost as hard on him as it had on Edward.

Edward had been upstairs preparing to retire for the night when he'd heard the servant's call. He came to the top of the steps and was slightly irritated at having been called back. At the scene below, though, he went completely still. "Catherine . . ." He said her name in a whisper of disbelief. *Catherine . . . could it really be his Catherine come home?*

Catherine pushed slightly away from Dalton to gaze up at her father. "Oh, Father . . ." she was crying in earnest now as she ran toward him, her arms outstretched.

Edward started down the stairs as Catherine started up them. They met halfway, enfolding each other in a welcoming embrace. Edward's reunion with Alexander had been tempered with caution because of the doubts about his identity, but there could be no doubts about this. This was his Catherine. This was his precious daughter. His love. His life. By the grace of God, she'd come home to him.

"Catherine! Dear God, I can't believe it." He smothered her with kisses, holding her to his heart, never wanting to let her go. He was barely able to release her long enough to look at her.

"Oh, Father. I'm home . . . I'm really home!" she cried.

It was an emotional moment for all of them. Almira stood quietly aside, watching with tears in her eyes.

Edward kept an arm around his daughter as they descended the stairs. He was gazing at her, unable to believe his eyes.

"Come . . . come into the parlor. We must talk. Who is this you've brought with you? Where have you been? How did you manage to get here?" The questions seemed to have no end.

"This is Almira, my maid and companion. She made the trip from Algiers with me."

"Algiers?" Edward stared at her aghast. "Is that where you've been all these years?"

"Yes . . . since the beginning. But I can tell you about that later. There's something more important that you have to know."

"What is it?" he asked as they moved into the parlor.

Catherine grasped her father's hand as she told him with great urgency, "It's Alex, Father. He's in desperate trouble, and you're the only one who can help him."

"Alexander is in trouble? But he only left here a few hours ago and . . ."

"What? You mean you've seen him? You know about the *Scimitar* and . . ."

"The *Scimitar?*" Edward frowned as he immediately recognized the name of Alexander's toy boat and suddenly realizing that they were not talking about the same thing.

"The *Scimitar* is Alex's ship. He's been taken captive by the navy and is being held in prison here."

"Catherine, you're not making sense. What do you mean Alexander was taken captive by the navy? He's been living here with me for months, ever since Vivienne brought him back from . . ."

"Vivienne?!" Catherine's eyes shot sparks at the mention of the woman. "Vivienne is here? What of Avery?"

"Avery disappeared when you did, and we never heard from him again. But Vivienne finally located Alexander in America and she brought him back to me . . ."

"Oh, no she didn't!" Catherine exclaimed in outrage. "Alexander had been with *me* ever since the beginning."

"What?" Edward was staggered by the news. If Alexander had been with Catherine, then who was the young man he'd come to love and care for? Had Vivienne . . . ?

"If Vivienne brought someone here and has been passing him off as Alex, I can tell you he's an impostor. Alexander and I were kidnapped by Avery. He was going to sell us into slavery in France, but luckily a Barbary pirate took our ship instead. I guess Avery must have been killed during the attack, I don't know. But we were taken in captivity to Algiers and given in tribute to the dey there. His name is Malik. Malik raised Alex as his own son, and now he's known as Serad. He's made his living on the sea as a corsair and his ship is named the *Scimitar* . . ."

"Dear God . . ." Edward lifted his shocked and troubled gaze to look at Dalton who was hovering near the door. "Alexander isn't Alexander."

"It would seem so, Your Grace," Dalton responded worriedly.

"But what of Alexander? Where is he? You say he was taken prisoner?"

Catherine told him all she knew, then Dalton spoke up.

"Only yesterday, Your Grace, there was an article in the paper about a pirate being taken to Newgate."

"Father, we have to hurry. I'm sure they want him dead. We have to save him."

Dalton ordered the carriage brought around and directed one of the other servants to see to it that Almira was given a room in the maids' quarters. Edward and Catherine were ready and waiting when the vehicle pulled around, and they climbed in and were off to Newgate.

"I hope we're not too late . . ." Catherine worried.

"I would think there's still time if he was only taken

459

there yesterday." Edward took her hand in his to reassure her.

They regarded each other lovingly, and he put an arm around her to draw her near. Catherine rested her head on his shoulder and allowed herself the heavenly delight of being a young girl again for just that brief period of time. It felt so good to be cherished and protected this way. Only a father could impart that kind of love, and she had missed it desperately.

"My darling, I have missed you so," Edward said sadly. "We have so much to talk about . . . So much has happened."

"Father . . ." She sat up straight to look at him as she asked the question that had been haunting her for years. "I have to know . . . what happened to Gerald?"

Edward blanched and went still at her inquiry. Catherine was puzzled by his hesitation.

"Father? What is it? He's not dead, is he?"

"Sometimes I think I would have preferred that," Edward growled. He would have understood if the young man had slowly lost interest in Catherine as the months had passed and she hadn't returned, but Gerald Ratcliff's hasty taking of another fiancée just a few months after Catherine's disappearance had been a terrible and ugly betrayal to Edward. He had despised the man ever since, for he'd realized that Gerald had only been after the Wakefield dowry and couldn't possibly have loved Catherine for herself.

"What do you mean?" Catherine's hands were clenched in her lap as she prepared herself for what she anticipated had to be awful news.

"Ratcliff waited only a few months before claiming another fiancée," Edward said bluntly. "He was married within the first year after you disappeared."

Catherine swallowed with some difficulty. "He married . . . so soon?" All her dreams about Gerald

460

and what their future would have been like together were destroyed in that moment, and she realized what a fool she'd been to mourn the loss of the man for all these years.

"Catherine, I'm sorry . . ." Edward touched her cheek. "I know how much you loved him."

"I loved who I thought he was, Father," she admitted slowly, finding it painful to give up a dream she'd harbored so long.

"I thought he was a better man, too," Edward agreed unhappily. He went on to tell her of the pain of losing her and Alex and the misery of the separation. She told him of her years with Malik, of how she'd tried to escape and then had been forbidden to speak of home and family, and of how Malik had agreed to let her go when Alex's life had been at stake.

"How do you feel about this man Malik?"

"He is a good man. I care for him a great deal. He was never harsh or cruel to me, and he came to love Alex as his own son." An image of Malik seared her mind. Malik asking her to be his wife, Malik sending all of his other women away, Malik loving her totally and without reservation, and in all that time she had never once ever told him that she loved him. Malik . . . Her heart constricted in her breast.

Their discussion was interrupted as the carriage stopped before the prison.

"What do we do now?" Catherine asked nervously. The building was very forbidding looking, and it filled her with fear.

"First, we'll arrange to see Alexander and make sure he's all right. Then we'll make inquiries and see what must be done to free him."

"Do you think that will be difficult?"

"It's my understanding that money and influence can accomplish anything, and we have both, my dear child.

We have both."

"Thank heaven. If anything happens to Alex . . ."

"We won't let it. We'll save him, and after we do, I think it's time we all paid Vivienne a visit."

Newgate was as horrible as Edward had imagined it would be. He detested the thought of dealing with the guards, but if it meant saving his grandson from the gates of hell, he would do anything.

George was there, and he watched Edward's approach with interest, trying to imagine what this dignified-looking old man wanted.

"I am the Duke of Huntington," Edward announced. "I understand you have a prisoner here by the name of Serad?"

George was astounded that there was someone of this importance interested in the pirate, but he kept to the original story. "We did have till a while ago."

"What do you mean?" Catherine gasped, fearing he'd already been executed.

"The fool tried to escape, and he was shot dead, he was."

"You're wrong, he can't be dead!" Catherine insisted desperately. She had traveled all this way to rescue him. He couldn't be dead! He couldn't!

"How? I want the details, and I want to see the body!" Edward demanded as he put a supportive arm about Catherine's shoulders.

George hurried to tell him the lies he'd created for just such a moment. "They already took the body away, but I can tell you true, it was him, the pirate Serad, who was shot and killed. Deader than a doornail he was . . ."

Catherine and Edward were heartbroken as they turned and left the prison. Their steps were slow, their spirits crushed.

Catherine's tears fell unheeded, and she moaned over and over again, "He's dead . . . he's dead . . . I didn't get here in time."

Edward was as grief-stricken as Catherine, but he was also furious. Someone was going to pay for this, and he knew just who that someone was. Vivienne. . . .

They climbed in the carriage and he directed the driver to take them to Vivienne's home.

A low-burning lamp cast Vivienne's bedroom in a soft glow. On the bed, Vivienne gave a throaty laugh as she clung to Gerald. They had just enjoyed a delicious evening together, having decided to go to bed instead of dinner, and she was looking forward to his remaining there with her until the early hours of the morning. His wife be damned!

An abrupt knock at her bedroom door startled her and she gave a muffled curse. "What is it? I told you we didn't want to be interrupted!"

"Lady Vivienne . . . You must come downstairs. Your son and his fiancée are here, and they've brought a visitor with them."

"Tell Alexander that I'm indisposed and that I will see him tomorrow," she snapped, wondering at his audacity in coming to her home at that hour.

"Yes, ma'am."

Confident that David would obey her command, Vivienne turned back to Gerald and kissed him fully on the mouth. It was a hot, passionate exchange as he was caught up once more in her driving, insatiable lust. They were locked in that heated embrace, when suddenly the bedroom door was kicked open and slammed back against the wall with a loud crash!

Vivienne gave a shriek of outrage as she twisted

violently to glare at whomever had dared intrude. She saw a shadow of a man appear in the doorway, and her eyes widened in fright as he stepped forward into the light. She recognized him instantly and was so shocked that she did not even hear the words he uttered so tightly.

"Good evening, Mother." Alex came farther into the room followed by David and Tori.

"Alexander . . ." His name was strangled from her as she clutched the sheets to her to hide her nakedness.

"Yes, Mother. Your long-lost son has returned." Alex took a menacing step toward the bed. Any tenderness he might ever have felt for his own flesh-and-blood mother had died long ago. He saw her now only as a conniving shrew who'd tried to kill him and Catherine.

"Now, see here!" Gerald blustered, feeling the threat in his movements and growing afraid for his own life.

"Shut up, Ratcliff!" Alex snarled, recovering quickly from the shock of seeing him in bed with her. "I wonder what Aunt Catherine would think to see the two of you together. Maybe you two were in conspiracy with Father from the beginning."

"Alexander . . . let me explain . . ." Vivienne began to plead, wanting to win him over, hoping he still had some feelings for her since she was after all his mother.

"There's nothing left to explain, David's told me everything. Now, it's just a matter of informing Grandfather and seeing everything set to rights."

"David? You fool! You absolute fool!" Vivienne turned a vicious glare on him. She had never been so frantic in her life. Desperation seized her. All of her carefully made plans were being shattered. The real Alex had returned and now Edward would find out everything. Her life was over. "Alexander . . . I'm your mother. I love you." she pleaded in one last panicked

464

attempt to save herself. Tears of very real humiliation and fear poured down her cheeks.

"You're not my mother. A mother loves her children, she doesn't try to have them destroyed!" he told her savagely. He stared down at her tear-ravaged face, but didn't feel anything but contempt.

Vivienne turned to David. "Do something! You didn't kill that woman in America, but you could kill *him!* We can go on with the charade and no one will know! Your future is at stake! Think of the money! Think of the power!"

David stared at her in complete astonishment. "I didn't kill the girl?"

"No, I set that up so I could convince you to help me. But now that you have everything you've ever dreamed of, are you willing to give it all up? You may really go to jail for masquerading as Alexander! Do something! Save us all!"

"You're mad!" David said in complete disgust. "Alex, what do you want to do?"

"I want to see my grandfather. I . . ."

The sound of angry voices in the foyer below came to Alex as he was speaking, and he turned in their direction.

Edward and Catherine had stormed into Vivienne's house right past the protesting servant who'd opened the door. They demanded to know where she was and upon being told headed straight up the stairs.

"Vivienne! I want to speak with you!" Edward was nearly shouting as he reached the top of the steps with Catherine close behind him. They started down the hall toward the open doorway. As Edward neared it, a tall, dark-haired young man stepped out to face him.

"Grandfather?" Alex stood perfectly still, gazing at him with open love. It was as if no time had passed, as if it had only been yesterday that they had talked of

465

painting the name on his toy boat. Alex couldn't prevent the surge of tears that filled his eyes, and he didn't even try. He swallowed, his throat working in agony as he tried to speak, to say more, to tell him that he loved him and had missed him.

"Alexander!" Catherine's cry tore through the momentary silence and she ran past her father to throw herself into his arms. "You're not dead!" She turned back toward her father, opening one arm to him. "It's Alexander . . ."

"Alexander . . ." Edward had instinctively known, but he'd been unable to move or speak until Catherine's excitement broke through the numbness. He moved forward to embrace the both of them. Tears fell unheeded.

When they moved apart to look at each other again. "Aunt Catherine," Alex asked. "Why are you here and why did you think I was dead?"

"Once word reached us that you'd been taken prisoner, I had to come after you. I knew Father could save you, so I returned to England and went to the prison to get you out. The guard told us you were dead, though . . . but it doesn't matter why, as long as you're alive!"

Edward gave him another hug, then asked in a deadly voice, "Where's Vivienne?"

Alex nodded toward the bedroom door just as David and Tori stepped out.

"You!" Edward said as he started to enter the bedroom. He fixed a serious regard upon the young man he'd believed to be Alex for so many months. "I'll deal with you next!"

David nodded and stepped aside respectfully to allow him to enter the bedroom. Tori stayed with David and took his hand in a gesture of support as they waited with Alex to see what would happen.

Catherine followed her father inside, and was jarred when she found herself facing Vivienne clad in a long, sleek dressing gown and Gerald rapidly throwing on the last of his clothes.

"Gerald?" She said his name in bewilderment as she glanced back and forth between the two.

"Catherine . . ." He looked up and stared at her in complete shock. "I didn't have anything to do with it! She planned it all with Avery! They were the ones!" he blustered, ever the coward as he tried to get himself off the hook.

Edward glared at them both in fury. "Ratcliff, you may be assured that the truth of your actions will be made known to your wife and her family, and you will be ruined in society. Your wife's family is quite powerful, and I'm sure they will not take kindly to the news. Especially since you live entirely on her funds."

"But . . ." Gerald could see his whole life falling into ruin. He slunk from the room, a defeated man, the glorious dreams he'd shared with Vivienne gone forever.

"And now you, Vivienne!" Edward turned the full wrath of his anger on the woman he'd supported all these years. "Your deceptions and lies are nothing short of vicious. You are no longer a part of my family. You will leave this home and with it all funds I have provided."

Vivienne knew it was over. She had been so close and now it was finished. His sentencing her to poverty was far more cruel a fate than death, and she could only stand there and stare at him with hate-filled eyes. "I despise you!" she seethed.

"I can only take solace in the fact that your treachery has been found out," Edward returned with equal malice. "Be gone by morning!"

He turned his back on the both of them in disgust

and left the bedroom with Catherine. Confronting the others in the hall, he looked at David. "And you . . ." he demanded. "Just who are you?"

"My name's David Markham, and I . . ."

"Grandfather," Alex interceded to help, "he was blackmailed by my mother into playing the role."

"Is that true?" he demanded of David.

"Yes, sir, but I know what I did was wrong, and I'm sorry. I'm more than willing to pay whatever price you deem necessary for my part in the deception." David met Edward's assessing regard squarely.

"He just saved my life, Grandfather."

"You did?" Edward asked, surprised.

"He did." Tori defended David, too, even as she put her arm around Alex's waist.

The duke looked perplexed for a moment, then smiled. "I'm sure there's a good explanation for all of this, and I'm more than willing to listen. But let's go home and talk there."

Chapter Thirty-Four

Edward stood at the window of his study gazing out across the small garden at the back of his townhouse. He smiled contentedly to himself. He'd known many dark moments in his life, but they had all faded into oblivion now. At last, everything was as it should be. His family was back together again, and that was all he'd ever wanted.

Edward thought of Alexander and Tori's wedding and his eyes lit up with the glow of inner happiness. It had been a quiet, private ceremony, but that was the way they'd wanted it. Tori had been a beautiful bride, and Alexander the perfect groom. Tori's beloved parents had arrived just in time for the wedding, and they, too, could see the depth of the couple's love for each other shining in their eyes. Her family hoped the good Lord would bless them and keep them happy.

Alexander had told Edward before they'd left on their short honeymoon that he planned to remain in England and resume his rightful place as his heir. The news had thrilled him, and Edward had been hard pressed to maintain his composure. He was looking forward to spending time with him. They'd both agreed that the first thing they were going to do as soon as

Alex returned was to paint the name *Scimitar* on the toy boat. It was something that had been too long delayed as it was.

David came into his thoughts, then, and Edward felt good about the way things had worked out with him. Once he'd learned the whole truth of Vivienne's perfidy, he'd understood the difficult situation David had been forced into. Edward had been especially appreciative of his quick thinking in arranging the "death" of Serad after his escape. Alexander had been able to assume his rightful place as the future duke, and no one had ever found out about his pirate past.

There had been a few questions about David's identity, but Edward had turned them away, telling those who asked about Vivienne's treachery. Having come to care for David as he had, Edward had been determined to see his future made easier. He'd learned of his love for the maid Tess and had sent him on his way to Huntington House with his blessing. He knew David planned to propose, and he hoped they would be as happy as Alex and Tori promised to be.

And then there was Catherine. At the thought of his beloved daughter, Edward's smile became tinged with a faint touch of melancholy. Though they had just been reunited, he now had to give her up again. Catherine had come to him the morning after Alexander's rescue with the news that she loved Malik and intended to return to Algiers to marry him.

Alexander had been thrilled by her decision. She'd remained in London long enough to celebrate the wedding with them, but was scheduled to leave for Algiers today. A sound at the doorway drew him from his thoughts and he turned to find Catherine standing there watching him.

"Good morning, Father."

"Good morning, darling. You look lovely this

morning," he complimented her as she stood before him wearing a new daygown they'd had made up for her on a rush order from the seamstress. It was the same color as her eyes and made her look particularly pretty.

She thanked him, smiling at him softly. She had been so happy to return home, and their reunion had been everything she'd hoped it would be. But now, it was time for her future. She was a woman, a woman in love, and she had put aside her childish dreams. She loved Malik, and she wanted to tell him so. "I believe it's time for us to leave for the docks."

"Are you packed?"

"Yes, Almira has everything ready."

"I don't want to lose you again," Edward admitted as he came to give her a fatherly kiss.

"You're not losing me, Father," Catherine told him with a teary smile. "I want you to keep the promise you made to me that you'll come visit us in Algiers with Alex and Tori."

"We'll come. I want to meet the man who's won your heart."

"Malik's wonderful. You'll like him, I'm sure," she confided. Her heartbeat quickened as she thought of Malik and how torn he'd been when she'd left him. She missed him, ached for him really, and she couldn't wait to tell him of her love.

"If you and Alex both like him, then I can do no less."

"Your Grace, the carriage is waiting," Dalton announced.

"Oh, Dalton, I'm going to miss you. Will you travel with Father when he comes to visit me?"

"I'd be honored," he answered, feeling proud that she wanted him, too.

Catherine embraced him and gave him a kiss on the

cheek. "Take care of my father," she whispered in his ear.

"I will."

Dalton watched as Edward escorted her from the house and they entered the carriage. After they'd driven off, he turned back inside and wiped the tears from his eyes.

Malik was restless. He hadn't slept the night through since Rabi had left, and lately he'd found it difficult to get even those few hours of sleep. Leaving his bedchamber, he moved into the sitting room and lit a lamp. His gaze fell upon the chess set that he and Rabi had used so often, and he felt a pang of loss. Wandering to the arched windows that overlooked the garden, he stared out across it, seeking some peace and contentment, but none would come. He owned the world, but without the woman he loved by his side, it mattered little.

Malik was gazing out at the black velvet night, deep in thought, when he heard the sound of hushed voices below. He frowned, wondering who besides himself would be up at this time of night. Caution always edged his decisions, and he got his knife from his bedtable before leaving his rooms to see who was about.

Muhammed had been waiting for this moment for years. He'd finally managed to sneak inside the palace, and now all he had to do was catch Malik alone and put him to death. He was sure that the dey's guards would be relaxed since Serad had sunk his ship and his own death had been reported. That gave him the advantage of surprise, and he intended to make full use of it.

Muhammed was just starting inside the palace from the garden when he heard footsteps coming his way. He

472

expected it to be one of the guards and it surprised him when he saw Malik. He attacked immediately, firing his pistol with deadly intent.

Malik managed only one cry of warning to alert the palace guards before his knees gave way beneath him. He managed to glance down and was stunned to see blood staining his white tunic. Thoughts of Rabi entered his mind as he fell to the marble floor, and darkness claimed him, sweeping him away from the pain and heartache and loneliness.

Catherine could hardly believe that they had finally made port. The voyage back to Algiers had seemed endless, and she couldn't wait to be with Malik again. To honor him, she had gone below and donned an Algerian gown. Dressed now as his woman, she stood on deck, watching the city that would truly be her home in her heart and her life come into full view.

Almira stood with Rabi on deck, glad to be back where they belonged. One thing was puzzling her, though. "Catherine?" she asked. "What shall I call you now that we are back in Algiers?"

Catherine's expression turned tender as she smiled at her maid. "Call me Rabi. It is the name Malik chose for me, and I will use it with pride from now on."

Almira returned her smile, and they waited eagerly for the gangplank to be lowered. Together, they made their way directly to the palace.

Rabi's heart was pounding as she approached the entrance. She hadn't realized how much she'd loved Malik when she'd left, but she knew now and she would never leave him again.

"I need to see Malik right away," Rabi announced to the guard. She knew she was being exceedingly bold, but she didn't care. This was desperately important. "Please tell him that I will be waiting for him in the harem."

The guard gave her a strange look, but she thought nothing of it. She assumed he was just surprised that she'd returned to Algiers so quickly. She and Almira continued on to the harem, and she went out to the garden to await Malik.

Rabi was surprised when a few minutes later, Hasim appeared.

"Rabi . . . thank Allah, you've come."

He sounded so desperate and looked so haggard that she came immediately to her feet. "What is it?"

"It's my father . . ."

"He's hurt?"

Hasim nodded as his eyes met hers. "We thought we'd killed Muhammed when we sank his ship, but he managed to escape. He gained access to the palace and shot my father four days ago. The guards killed Muhammed afterward, but by then the damage had been done."

Rabi could see the deep sorrow and concern in his haunted gaze. "Take me to him," she demanded. "I must see him. I must speak with him."

Hasim led her from the harem. "He's been unconscious for some time now. He lost a lot of blood."

Rabi nodded as she listened, for she didn't trust herself to speak. Malik had almost been killed. She could only thank God that she'd returned when she had. Her resolve became unshakable. She was going to save Malik. She felt she had wasted their previous years together by not recognizing her love for him, but she meant to make all that up to him, starting today. He would survive. She would not allow him to die.

Hasim brought her to Malik's bedchamber, and she entered only to pause just inside the door. Malik, her love, lay motionless on the bed, his chest swathed in white bandages, his coloring pale. A sob escaped her as she rushed to his side. The physician who'd been tending him was startled by the interruption, but seeing that it was Rabi, he quietly left the room to give her time alone with him.

"Malik . . ." Rabi whispered as she sat beside him and took his hand. "Malik, my love. I've come back to you . . ."

There was no response from Malik. He lay unmoving, only the slight rise and fall of his chest proving he was still alive.

"Malik . . . !" she began again, talking to him in a low voice, demanding he return to her.

Time began to slip by, but she did not stop talking to him. Over and over, she said his name. She told him of her love and of how she wanted to marry him just as soon as he opened his eyes. She told him of Serad's safety and his reunion with his grandfather, and she told him of his marriage to Tori.

Through the rest of the day and all of the night, Rabi remained, never moving from his bedside. Dawn found her still beside Malik, her head resting on the bed as she finally gave in to her exhaustion.

Malik wasn't sure what pulled him back from the brink. He had faced death and had no fear of it, but the soft call of a distant voice refused to let him pass. Over and over the voice insisted he return. Over and over he heard it plead with him to come back.

Malik felt as if he were swimming upward from the bottom of a deep body of water. Blackness surrounded him. Before he had welcomed it, but now he fought against it as he searched for the source of the voice. He needed to hear it again.

Malik opened his eyes. He blinked. It was daylight. Hadn't it been night? He was confused, and then he looked down and saw her.

"Rabi?"

It was a harsh whisper, but it was all that was needed to rouse her from her light, fitful rest. Rabi sat up, and the weariness was instantly gone from her as she found herself gazing into Malik's golden eyes.

"Thank God!" she cried. "Oh, Malik . . ."

"You have returned to me?" he managed with difficulty.

"I love you. How could I have stayed away?" Rabi asked, crying as she took his hand and pressed it to her lips. "I thought I was losing you. I thought you were going to die and leave me."

A fierce, possessive light shone in his eyes. He had waited years to hear her say those words. His soul felt invigorated. He loved Rabi . . . and she loved him. She had returned to him.

"What of Serad?"

"Serad is fine. He will return soon too." Rabi knew there would be plenty of time later to tell him all of what had happened.

"And what of your home?"

"My home is with you, my love. If you still want me, I will be your wife."

It took most of his strength but Malik managed to lift a hand and touch her hair. "I have never stopped wanting you, Rabi."

"Nor I you, Malik. It took almost losing you to find out, but I love you." Rabi bent over him and pressed a soft kiss to his lips. "And I will stay with you forever."

"That is all I ever wanted, my love . . ."

Epilogue

"It's beautiful . . ." Tori breathed as she stood beside Alex on the bank of the reflecting pool. The water was a smooth mirror reflecting the green leafy canopy of the arching tree limbs overhead and the lush, flowering shrubs that surrounded it. It was as much a paradise as their oasis had been.

"Almost as beautiful as you," Alex responded as he gazed down at her. He had been eager to see his favorite childhood place again and had brought Tori here the moment they'd settled in at Huntington House. As he looked around, Alex discovered that he had not exaggerated the pond's beauty in his mind, for he found it was much like he'd remembered it.

Tori was thrilled that he'd wanted to share the spot with her, and she went to him and looped her arms around his neck. "I can see why you loved it here. It's very peaceful . . . and so secluded." She stood on tiptoes to press a kiss to his lips.

"It was my hideaway as a boy. I used to come here with Grandfather and sail my boat. I had dreams of being a sea captain, even then . . ." For a moment, there was a faraway look in his eyes.

"I'm glad things worked out for Tariq and the others."

Alex smiled. "Grandfather really does have influence, and he certainly knows how to use it. I was relieved to hear that he'd gotten them all released and that they are on their way back to Algiers."

"I'm sorry you lost the *Scimitar,* though," Tori told him. "I know how much your ship meant to you."

Alex looked sad for a moment, but then he managed a lopsided grin. "Well, at least I still have the original *Scimitar . . .*"

He moved away from her to pick up the toy boat he'd brought with them, and he proudly showed her the newly painted name on the side. "Grandfather painted it for me."

Tori's happiness was so great, she felt tears well up in her eyes. "I love you, Alex, and I hope you're happy."

He heard the catch in her voice and walked back to her. "Of course I'm happy. We're together, I'm back with my grandfather again, and I've made peace with Jonesey . . ." Alex couldn't help but chuckle as he remembered the look on Jonesey's face when he'd handed her the brand new umbrella when they had returned from their honeymoon.

"I think if I hadn't married you, *she* might have."

"Oh, I don't know . . ." Alex grinned. "I always thought she had a soft spot for Tariq."

"Never! It was you she liked, but she had to protect me from you, you know."

"And she did an admirable job . . . for a while. I'm glad she eventually failed, though."

"So am I." She kissed him softly. "But are you going to miss your home in Algiers? I feel like you've given up so much for me."

"No, Tori. I've given up nothing. I've gained my

whole life. And it's not like I'll never see Malik, Aunt Catherine, and Hasim again. We'll be traveling back to Algiers in a few months with Grandfather. What more could I possibly want? *My* life is as close to perfect as it could be, but what about you?"

"Oh, Alex, you know I'm happy. I still find it difficult to believe that everything worked out the way it did, but I'm not foolish enough to question my good fortune."

"So you really were in love with your fiancé?"

"Of course," she said with mock indignation. "I just didn't know it was you at the time, that's all."

Alex set the *Scimitar* to sail on the pool, and then stood back to watch it skim smoothly across the water. His mind was filled with memories of the adventures he'd dreamed of as a child, and he marveled at the many turns his life had taken.

Tori remained where she was watching Alex, and the love she felt for him filled her with a deep, abiding warmth. As he stood on the bank, he looked every inch the cultured gentleman in his dress pants and white shirt, and she couldn't help but smile. He had been her pirate captain and her sheik, and now he was her English nobleman, and she had loved them all.

Tori's pulse quickened and she moved to join him. He sensed her presence and gazed down at her. Without speaking, she slid her arms around his waist and pulled him to her for a kiss.

"I love you, Alexander . . ."

He smiled as he took her up on her unspoken invitation. "I love you, too."

With ease, Alex lifted her up in his arms and lay her upon the soft grass nearby. He moved over her, covering her body with his as he kissed her again.

"Just how private is this place?" Tori asked.

"Very," he murmured.

"I think this might become my favorite place, too."

As the *Scimitar* sailed a straight course on the glassy waters of the reflecting pool, Alex and Tori came together. In the privacy of their Eden, they rejoiced in their love and knew that their life together would be as perfect as the *Scimitar's* voyage.